CRIMSON THAW

BRUCE ROBERT COFFIN

Severn River Publishing
SevernRiverBooks.com

ISBN: 978-1-64875-658-0 (Paperback)

ALSO BY THE AUTHOR

The Detective Justice Series

Crimson Thaw

Bitter Fall

Dark Harbor

The Turner and Mosley Files

The General's Gold

The Cardinal's Curse

The Pirate's Secret

The Pharaoh's Tomb

The Emperor's Palace

Never miss a new release!

To find out more about Bruce Robert Coffin and his books, visit

severnriverbooks.com

For Paula. Thank you for believing.

“Believe nothing you hear, and only one half that you see.”

—Edgar Allan Poe

1

October 8, 2024

Maine State Police Detective Brock Justice struggled to keep his unmarked SUV directly behind the dark sky-blue Interceptor of fellow trooper Evan Mathers as both vehicles sped along Route 35 amid a flurry of falling autumn leaves. Adrenaline surged through Brock as he felt the pull of four hundred horses beneath the hood and the promise of closure. The man they were on the way to arrest was one of the most despicable creatures Brock had ever encountered. Terrance "Terry" Kirke would finally stand trial for one of the most heinous killings Brock had ever investigated.

Kirke had been on the radar of the State Police Major Crimes Unit South for some time. His name had come up in multiple investigations, but somehow or another Terry had always managed to wriggle off the hook. Each time it was the same old story. A convenient alibi provided by a friend or family member of Terry's not worth the paper it was written on would suddenly rear its head. Multiple witnesses recanted their statements, claiming they'd made a mistake after wrongly identifying either Terry or his brother, Darrell, as the perpetrator of one violent crime or another. Terry had always been too slick and far too mean for the police to make a case against him stick. Until now.

This time Terry had gone too far, beating a local man to death with a framing hammer. And there wasn't a single nervous witness or bogus alibi in sight. This time they had Terry firmly by the short hairs. He'd left his DNA at the scene. Only a trace amount, but combined with the surveillance video obtained from a nearby business, Brock was confident Terry would spend his remaining days in maximum security incarceration at the prison in Warren, Maine.

As Brock and Evan headed toward Kirke's compound just outside the sleepy Maine town of Bar Mills, several members of the York County Sheriff's Department were en route to convene with them as backup. The emergency strobes and flashing headlights of the state vehicles were activated, but not the sirens. The procedure, known in police jargon as a code two response, was intentional. While Brock and Evan were in a hurry to take Terry into custody, the last thing either trooper wanted was to give him a heads-up they were coming. The element of surprise was always the cop's best weapon.

"Twelve one three." The voice of the state police dispatcher emanated from the base radio speaker.

Brock turned up the volume on the radio, then keyed the dash-mounted microphone. "Twelve one three, go."

"Twelve one three, be advised we just received a 10-21 from York SO. Your backup has been involved in a 10-55 with serious PI. They will be indefinitely delayed."

"A traffic accident," Brock said aloud to an empty car. "That's just great."

"Twelve one three, did you copy?" the dispatcher said.

"Ten four," Brock growled.

Sighing in frustration, he adjusted his grip on the wheel. Given Kirke's violent nature, common sense dictated that he and Evan wait until they had additional backup units to assist. As if reading his mind, Mathers radioed.

"One thirteen to twelve one three, thoughts?"

We're this close, Brock thought. *No way I'm gonna let someone else make this collar.*

"Switch over to tactical," Brock said.

"Copy," Mathers said.

Both troopers switched their base radios to the MSP tactical channel.

"Your call, brother," Mathers said. "What do you want to do?"

"Stick with the plan," Brock said. "We can handle this guy, Evan."

"Roger that."

They traversed the remaining ten miles to Bar Mills in less than eight minutes. In synchronized fashion, both men extinguished the blue lights on their vehicles as they rounded the last corner. Mathers pulled to the right shoulder, allowing Brock to enter the property first, then parked his marked SUV perpendicularly across the end of the driveway, negating the possibility Kirke could escape by vehicle.

"Twelve one three, show us out at that location," Brock said.

"Ten four, twelve one three," the dispatcher said.

Brock waited for Mathers to remove the rifle from its mount behind the passenger seat of the SUV. Both men made the final approach to the house on foot.

Scattered around the Kirke dooryard were several dilapidated cars in various stages of disassembly. Only Terry's late-model candy-apple-red Camaro looked operational. Brock reached out and placed his palm flat atop the hood as he passed. The metal was cool to the touch, indicating the car hadn't been driven recently.

The peeling two-story gray saltbox with newspapers covering the upstairs windows wasn't in much better shape than the vehicles occupying its front yard. Brock and Mathers split up as they approached the front door to the residence. Brock waited off to one side of the entrance, giving Mathers a chance to get into position at the left rear corner of the house. The last thing they wanted was to give Terry an opportunity to flee out the rear of the home or allow him to circle around and ambush them.

Brock waited until he heard the single carrier click from Mathers's portable radio, the signal that he was in position, before he knocked on the storm door.

Brock slid his suit coat to one side, exposing his badge and gun. He rested his sweaty palm on the butt of his semiautomatic Heckler & Koch handgun as the adrenaline coursed through his veins. The H&K .45 was still holstered, but Brock knew that might change in an instant depending upon how things went.

He banged his fist against the rusted doorframe again.

"Terrance Kirke, I know you're in there. State police, we need to speak with you."

Brock heard a deadbolt slide in its track, but there was no way to know if the lock was being engaged or opened. A moment later, the interior door to the home swung open several feet and Terry's smug face appeared in the opening.

"Morning, officer," he said wryly. "What can I do you for?"

"We need you to come with us," Brock said.

A quizzical expression crossed Terry's face as he stood up on tiptoe to look past Brock. "Who's we? Did you bring extra help? 'Cause all I see is you standing there."

Unable to see either of Terry's hands, Brock tightened the grip on his sidearm. "Step outside, Terry."

"Okay, okay," he said, lifting both hands in front of his waist in a gesture of surrender before reaching toward the latch on the storm door.

Mathers's voice erupted in an excited burst of static. "Got a runner!"

Before Brock could react, Terry slammed the inside door, locked it.

Brock keyed the mic on his own radio. "I'm going in." He slid his gun from the holster and opened the storm door. Brock drove the sole of his shoe into the wooden door just below the tarnished brass handle. The frame splintered with a loud crack and the door flew inward, banging into the wall.

Brock moved quickly into the entryway, his gun pointed forward. Directly in front of him was a long, darkened hallway flanked on the right by a flight of stairs leading to the home's second-floor landing. To his immediate left was a cluttered space that looked like it might have once served as a small living room, though a ratty couch and a large flat-screen were the only clues. The remainder of the room was packed floor to ceiling with cardboard boxes.

"Terry, we have a warrant for your arrest," Brock said. "Show yourself."

The response came in the form of a deafening gunshot from the second-floor landing. The bullet knocked loose a spray of plaster from the wall directly above Brock's head.

Instinctively, Brock ducked and returned fire as he dove for cover behind the couch in the room to the left of the entryway.

"Twelve one three, shots fired, shots fired," Brock shouted into the radio. "Ten seventy-four."

Heart hammering inside his chest and ears ringing, Brock regrouped and moved back toward the entryway. He listened for anything that might give away Terry's position. After a moment, he heard the floor squeak directly overhead. Kirke was moving toward the front of the house. Brock had visions of the man escaping through a second-story window and trying to reach the Camaro. If Brock hoped to trap him on the second floor, now was the time. He stepped back into the entryway, keeping his gun trained toward the top of the stairwell. Brock reached the base of the steps, then began a long, slow ascent. Placing one foot in front of the other, he scanned the railing and balusters running the length of the second-floor hall, careful to be sure of his footing before continuing on to the next step. The last thing Brock needed was to lose his balance and tumble to the bottom of the stairwell, likely breaking his neck, only to lie there in the entryway like a sitting duck.

Brock rose until he could see the landing was clear, alternating his aim between the closed door at the top of the stairs and the blind spot to his left behind the broken balusters supporting the second-floor railing. He paused following each step, listening for Terry to give away his position again, but the house was silent. Brock fought to stay focused, but his mind kept wandering back to Mathers and whatever he might be dealing with outside. Brock's portable radio had gone quiet, a good indication that Mathers might well be doing exactly what he was, trying to stay alive.

Brock took another measured step; this one elevated his sightline enough to allow him a view of the entire hallway floor. The immediate threats were the closed door directly across from him and whatever lay in wait at the far end of the hall toward the front of the house. As Brock reached the landing, he paused again. Wherever Terry had gone to ground, he wasn't giving himself away.

As Brock took another step toward the closed door, the landing betrayed his position with a loud crack. He froze, waiting to see whether the noise would prompt a response from Terry, but nothing happened.

After what seemed like an eternity, Brock continued toward the door. He half expected it to be locked as he reached out and twisted the knob, but it turned freely. Keeping his .45 trained on the threat in front of him, Brock shoved the door open. Unlike the home's front door, this one did not bang into the wall. Something was impeding its movement. He made a quick visual sweep of the room, then stepped back behind the doorframe, giving himself a glimpse through the crack between the door hinges. He imagined Terry hiding there, but it was merely another stack of boxes. Confident the space was safe, Brock stepped over the threshold, then turned to peek past the doorframe toward the far end of the hall. Wherever Terry was hiding, Brock would need to navigate the narrow and cluttered passageway to find him.

The far end of the hall formed a T-intersection. At either end were open doors, both rooms darkened by the window coverings he'd seen from the outside. Not even Terry's shadow would give him away. It was a fifty-fifty proposition. Brock knew Terry had to be hiding in one of the remaining rooms, but which one, the left or the right? And was he hiding, or waiting?

Brock wiped the sweat from his eyes with the sleeve of his suit jacket. His heart raced as he tried to recall every officer survival class he had ever taken. Every simunition training course. Hallways were the worst. Nowhere to hide. No place to find cover. And unlike simunition rounds, where the bad guy could pepper an unsuspecting officer with plastic paint-filled pellets, Terry was using lead. Playing for keeps.

Brock lowered himself into a crouch, attempting to minimize the target he presented should Terry pop out of his hiding place with guns blazing. Making doubly sure of his footing as he had on the stairs, Brock moved slowly along the hall, left hand wrapped tightly beneath his gun hand to steady his aim, right index finger snugged against the trigger; Brock kept the barrel pointed forward, alternating between each of the doorways at the end of the hall. There would be no time for sight alignment. If Terry forced his hand, it would be close-quarters combat. Front sight only. Exactly as he had been taught on the range. The gun was nothing more than an extension of his hand. Acquire the target, point, and shoot.

He was halfway down the hallway when it happened. Time seemed to slow to a crawl as Terry's gun, and the hand holding it, materialized in the left-hand doorway. Brock saw the muzzle flashes as Terry fired blindly and wildly down the hall. The bullets split the air as they whizzed past, missing him by inches. Brock felt one of the rounds graze the right side of his face, searing the skin of his cheek before punching through the wall directly behind him. Brock dropped to one knee and returned fire, striking the doorjamb and splintering the wood where he had seen Terry's gun only a split second before. The hall smelled of spent gunpowder, and a cloud of bluish smoke hung in the air. The ringing in Brock's ears had become even more pronounced. He kept his front sight trained on the doorway as he struggled to regain his feet. Warm blood trickled down his neck, soaking his collar, as he slid along the right wall of the hallway, attempting to get a better angle on the doorway should Terry reappear. A maneuver referred to in cop parlance as "slicing the pie," and Brock had a big old piece of pie to share with Terry. He inched forward, gun trained on the open door.

As Brock neared the end of the hall, his finger tightened against the trigger instinctively. His heart was pounding so hard it felt as if it might thump right out of his chest. He crouched even lower, hoping to make it more difficult for Terry to shoot him. Brock rolled his upper torso around the jamb, gun at the ready, but the doorway and the area immediately beyond it were empty. Brock's arms and legs were growing weary. He knew this was a symptom of the adrenaline dump his body was experiencing. Under stress, he was expending his allotment faster than his body could replace it. He paused for a moment to compose himself and prepare for the final push. He took several deep breaths, exhaling slowly after each one, then took a quick peek into the room, darting part of his head through the doorway and immediately withdrawing it. In that moment, Brock captured a mental snapshot of the room. An unmade double bed to the right, a cluttered bureau to the left, a window at the center of the far wall, more cardboard boxes stacked upon the floor, and no sign of Terry Kirke.

As he opened his mouth to call out to his adversary, Brock caught sight of a fresh blood trail on the floor just beyond the doorway. Terry's blood. One of the bullets from Brock's sidearm must have found its mark. How badly Terry was injured was anybody's guess. But Brock knew he would have to be a fool to assume his adversary was incapacitated in any way.

"Terry," Brock said. "I know you're in here, and I know you're wounded.

There's nowhere to go. Why don't you just give yourself up and we can walk out of here together?"

"How do I know you won't just shoot me anyway?" Terry said. "You know how you cops are."

Brock could hear the pain in Terry's voice. "Because that's not how this works. You shot at me first, or have you forgotten?"

Terry's laugh was cut short by a raspy cough.

"That doesn't sound good, Terry. Throw your gun down, and I'll make sure you get an ambulance."

A symphony of approaching sirens filled the brief silence that followed.

"Hear that, Terry? Backup is coming. Better to just give yourself up while it's just you and me."

"What difference does that make?" Terry said.

"Once the others arrive and find out you shot me, I won't be able to make any guarantees about your safety. Better to give up now and take your chances in court."

Brock felt the blood flowing from his cheek as he waited for Terry's decision. The burning sensation was agonizing and constant, like someone holding a lit match to his skin.

"All right, cop, you win. I surrender."

"Toss the gun toward me and show yourself, hands in the air."

Brock heard a heavy thud as the gun landed on the floor and slid to a stop just inside the doorway. Knowing Terry might possess others, Brock proceeded accordingly.

"Now walk toward me. Hands in the air."

"Okay," Terry said through clenched teeth.

Brock swung around the doorframe and extended his arms, acquiring the target. Terry sat slumped forward on the hardwood floor directly in front of the window. His right arm was elevated while the left hung limply at his side. Both hands appeared empty.

"Get both hands up, Terry," Brock shouted.

"I can't lift my left arm, man. You shot me."

Brock stepped over Terry's gun and moved farther into the room. He saw the blood flowing freely from a bloody hole in Terry's bare left shoulder.

Brock quickly closed the distance between them, the front sight of his H&K trained on the center of Terry's chest. "Roll over on your stomach. Face down."

Terry groaned and awkwardly complied.

"Now cross your legs, lift your feet toward your butt, and bring your arms straight out to the sides."

Again, Terry obeyed.

In one smooth motion, Brock moved in, straddling Terry's calves, putting his full weight on top of the prone man's ankles. Brock holstered his sidearm, then pulled one arm at a time behind Terry's back, handcuffing him tightly. As Brock brought the left arm up, Terry cried out.

"Take it easy, will ya? Dammit, that hurts."

"So does getting shot in the face," Brock countered.

The sound of the approaching sirens grew louder still. Backup was nearly there. As Brock stood and reached for his portable radio, the sound of hollering came from behind the house. Mathers and another man were shouting at each other. As Brock moved back toward the window, struggling to see through the grungy panes, the blast of a rifle ripped through the air.

2

April 7, 2025

Brock sat in his newly assigned unmarked staring across the paved lot at the Bangor barracks of the Maine State Police. Home to Troop E, the Major Crimes Unit North, and the Computer Crimes Unit, the barracks would be his duty station for the foreseeable future.

The industrial-looking single-story structure was bookended by the outer perimeter fence of the Bangor International Airport. The eight-foot-high cyclone barrier prevented access to the tarmac as well as every other secure area of the facility. The barrack's grim exterior wasn't alleviating Brock's trepidation. The battleship-gray corrugated steel façade appeared every bit as inviting as a root canal.

Much had changed over the previous six months. Brock's career had skidded off the fast-track right into Siberia, or at least the Maine equivalent. His marriage, already on shaky ground before the shooting, was now officially over. It had ended without a fight with the stroke of a pen in a quiet civil proceeding at the Cumberland County Courthouse. Everything Brock possessed had been boxed up and moved by way of a rented U-Haul and now sat stacked on the living room rug of his new apartment like a monument to failure.

Ironically, his career felt like it had ended in a courtroom as well. The York County Superior Court, where, during a weeklong manslaughter trial, Brock had testified against a fellow trooper about what had been deemed a bad shooting. Ultimately, Evan Mathers was found not guilty in the death of Darrell Kirke, but the outcome changed nothing. None of Brock's former coworkers wanted anything to do with him. Even dear old dad, who had sat stoically at the rear of the courtroom throughout the entire trial, had turned his back on him for having the audacity to cross the thinnest of blue lines. Brock was an outcast. A pariah among his fellow troopers. As he sat there staring at the front door to the barracks, he couldn't help wondering if northern Maine was far enough away.

A moss-green police Interceptor turned into the parking lot and slid into an empty space two down from where he sat. The dark-haired middle-aged female seated behind the wheel gave him the once-over before stepping out and approaching him on foot. *Time to go to work*, he thought.

"You must be Detective Justice," the woman said. "I'm Lieutenant Penelope Cumberland."

"Pleased to meet you, ma'am," Brock said as he presented his hand in greeting.

Cumberland ignored his gesture and continued, "Come inside, Detective. I'll give you the five-cent tour. Oh, and knock off the ma'am stuff. It's either Lieutenant or Penny. Got it?"

"Yes, Lieutenant."

Brock had heard all about Cumberland. She was known to be a no-nonsense commander who was afraid of no one. She had worked her way up through the ranks at a time when women were still relatively scarce in the field of law enforcement. She wasn't the first female to smash the glass ceiling of the good old boys' club, but if the rumors were true, she might well be the toughest. Cumberland had unofficially been dubbed Penny Dreadful by the rank and file. Brock had been warned anyone foolhardy enough to utter that nickname in her presence might find themselves rewarded by a swift and lengthy stretch of unpaid leave for insubordination.

They entered through the front door to the barracks with Brock following several steps behind the lieutenant. The reception desk was unmanned, and Cumberland used her key to gain entrance to the inner sanctum.

The interior decor of Troop E was slightly more familiar to Brock than the building's exterior had been. Typical in most law enforcement circles was the distinct and intentional line of demarcation between the uniformed side of the house and the one belonging to the detectives. A dividing line as sharply contrasted as the Mason–Dixon, and a clear imparting of the us-and-them message. Brock wondered if this division was part of the problem in nearly every law enforcement institution.

"You can drop your bag and coat there," Cumberland said, pointing out a vacant, cramped cubicle in the least desirable corner of the space designated for the detectives.

"Thanks," Brock said as he placed his cloth briefcase on top of the desk and draped his overcoat over the well-worn swivel chair. A quick look around the room at the other cubicles only confirmed what Brock already suspected: his new workspace had been cannibalized of anything worth possessing by the other detectives in the unit, swapped out with their worn and broken castoffs. The unspoken message was he was the new guy. After a dozen years on the job, it was a role Brock was unaccustomed to playing. He glanced back at his space and wondered which detective had recently departed from the bureau? And why?

As if reading his very thoughts, Cumberland said, "Used to be Jim Larsen's desk. He retired."

Familiar with the name, Brock nodded. Larsen had been something of a legend long before Brock joined the state police.

"Jim was beloved around here," Cumberland said, hesitating a moment as if reminiscing.

"So were his things, apparently," Brock said before he could stop himself.

Cumberland gave him a look he couldn't quite read. She ignored the comment and led him to her private office.

"Take a seat," she said, closing the door behind him.

Brock sat, then waited as she went through her routine.

Cumberland's corner office was everything he had come to expect. A fishbowl of sorts, composed of two glass walls that looked out over the major crimes bureau, and two solid walls that would normally be full of commendations and certificates of achievement. At least they were in the offices of most SP commanders. The only thing gracing Cumberland's painted walls was a framed portrait of her accompanied by two good-looking twenty-somethings. A man and a woman. Brock assumed they were Cumberland's grown children. The only other wall hanging was a framed Master of Public Administration diploma from Boston University. Brock guessed Cumberland considered her degree and her children to be her greatest accomplishments. It was admirable and a refreshing change after his last commander. The lieutenant of MCU South had been vertically challenged with a severe case of little man syndrome and a bad comb-over. Brock was pretty sure every commendation, certificate of achievement, and celebrity selfie Lt. Harold Long possessed were displayed on his walls at the Troop A barracks. At least Cumberland put her family and education before pictures of past presidents and A-list celebrities.

Brock watched in amusement as Cumberland sat down behind her desk and punched up her voicemail as if he weren't there, jotting notes on the pad of paper beside her phone. She continued through the messages, listening to each before deleting or saving them and moving on.

After she had finished, Cumberland cradled the handset and placed her pen beside the notepad, then looked across the desk at Brock.

"I didn't want you here," she said after a moment. "I think it's important you know that up front."

Brock, having already assumed this wasn't a conversation, said nothing.

"I campaigned hard against your transfer to Major Crimes North, but I was overruled. Surprised?"

He wasn't.

"My stock has fallen a bit as of late," Brock said after realizing she was waiting for him to respond.

"You might think the reason I didn't want you was because you testified in open court against one of your own."

"The thought had crossed my mind," Brock said.

"I couldn't care less about that, Detective. If Trooper Mathers did what you said he did, then he got exactly what he deserved, and you should be commended for your honesty."

Cumberland reached over to the faux wood credenza flanking her desk and grabbed a thick folder from the top of one of the stacks. She placed the folder on the desk between them and flipped it open.

The folder contained photocopies and clippings of newspaper coverage of his homicide cases. He recognized many of the stories, even those covered by the *Bangor Daily News*, though coming from southern Maine where the *Portland Press Herald* still lorded over what passed for news, Brock didn't normally read the Bangor publication.

"The contents of this folder are why I didn't want you here," Cumberland continued. "You were a rising star in MCU South. A legacy hire, second-generation trooper, glory boy. Did things your way and got results."

"You say it like it's a bad thing," Brock said, grinning and hoping to lighten the mood.

"It is," she said, staring through him until his grin withered. "Perhaps if you and the former Trooper Mathers had waited for proper backup, you wouldn't have found yourselves in the position you were in."

Brock opened his mouth to respond but then thought better of it. Cumberland hadn't asked him into her office for his opinion.

"MCU North is a small unit, Detective Justice, only five detectives and an evidence tech to cover the counties of Aroostook, Washington, Piscataquis, Penobscot, and Hancock. Basically, half of the state. We maintain a good working relationship with all the county sheriff departments, a relationship that benefits our agencies equally by combining resources. We operate as a team here, and we are nothing if not efficient."

Brock was doing his best to maintain a stoic, attentive expression, but Cumberland's canned speech was unnecessary. They both knew why he'd been transferred here, and it had nothing to do with mutual aid agreements. Brock was quite familiar with the practice, having come from Troop A in York County. While there were frequent dustups between the rank and file of neighboring agencies, Brock had found when it came to "playing nice," it was often the upper echelon of those agencies who were the least benevolent.

"I have zero patience for hotdogging detectives who make waves," Cumberland continued. "We can't afford it. I can't afford it. Do I make myself clear?"

"Yes, ma'—Yes, Lieutenant," Brock said, giving her a nod.

A sharp knock came from outside the door.

"Come," Cumberland said, her eyes never leaving Brock's.

The door opened a crack, and a pale young man with strawberry-blond hair and a bad complexion stuck his head inside. "I'm sorry to bother you, Lieutenant, but there's an urgent call for you from Hancock SO."

"Thank you, Andrew," Cumberland said as she glanced down at the flashing light on her desk phone.

Before departing, Andrew acknowledged Brock with a slight nod.

"That is Andrew Webber," Cumberland said. "He is our office assistant and the person who truly keeps this place running. Be good to him."

"Got it," Brock said.

"Excuse me a moment," she said as she punched the flashing line on her phone and picked up the receiver.

"MCU North, Lieutenant Cumberland speaking."

Cumberland's phone call with the Hancock County Sheriff's Department lasted several minutes. Brock waited in awkward silence, still feeling like he'd been called into the principal's office for a dressing down. He supposed that was precisely what Cumberland was doing. Establishing her ground rules while showing him exactly who was in charge. Though Brock was confident her reputation had negated the need for any such display.

Despite hearing only Cumberland's half of the conversation and watching as she scribbled notes onto a clean sheet of paper, Brock managed to glean that game wardens had found a body somewhere in the area.

"I'll send someone right over," Cumberland said, looking directly at Brock as she said it. "Thanks for the heads-up, Pete."

She ended the call, then handed the sheet of paper she'd been scribbling on to Brock.

"Here you go."

"What is this?" Brock said as he glanced at the notes.

"Your first case. Let's think of this as a trial run. I still don't know what

I'm going to do with you, but for now, I'm pairing you up with a brand-new detective."

Brock struggled to keep from rolling his eyes. "Gee, thanks."

"Her name is Chloe Wright, and she is a lateral from the uniformed side of the house. Chloe is a talented investigator, as you will see, but she has no hands-on homicide experience. That's where you come in. I want you to teach her everything you know."

Brock's mind raced through the reasons he would have normally fought against such an assignment, but he knew Cumberland wasn't making a request.

"It's in the town of Blue Hill," Cumberland said. "I've written the address down. Call me as soon as you have an update."

With that, Cumberland picked up her phone and punched an outside line, effectively dismissing Brock from any further conversation.

Brock sat there for a moment before standing and crossing the room. He opened the door, then stopped and turned back to her. "What about my new partner?" Brock said.

Cumberland managed a smirk. "She'll meet you there."

3

Blue Hill, Maine

It took the better part of an hour for Brock to drive from Bangor to Blue Hill and another fifteen minutes to locate Second Pond. He wondered how many bodies of water the small Maine town had to necessitate numbering them.

During the trip, he replayed the conversation with his new boss. Although it hadn't been much of a dialogue, mostly just Cumberland laying down the law. Brock was mildly annoyed she hadn't paired him with a seasoned detective. He had more than paid his dues, and babysitting Chloe Wright hadn't been part of the plan. In fact, nothing about his current situation was part of the plan. When he had seen the name of the town scribbled on the note she had handed to him, he thought briefly of telling her to assign the case to someone else, but the resolute look on her face made it clear reassignment wasn't an option.

As he turned off Mines Road onto Douglas Loop, the dirt road skirting Second Pond, his cell phone chimed with an incoming text message. He slid the phone from his inside coat pocket and glanced at the screen.

How is it going so far? Feel like you're back in the saddle?

He immediately recognized the number as belonging to Kimberly Millick.

Millick was the second shrink he had been assigned following the shooting. Initially, Brock had no intention of attending even one more visit than necessary, but as the attorney general's review of the shooting began to go south, along with Brock's marriage, it just seemed easier to continue seeing her.

Brock pocketed the phone without responding to her message and dug out his credentials. A black Hancock County Sheriff's SUV partially blocked the pond access road. Standing beside it, clipboard in hand, was a uniformed deputy wearing dark glasses.

"Help you?" the deputy said as Brock pulled alongside the SUV.

Brock held up his badge and ID. "State police. I've been assigned to—whatever this is."

The deputy accepted the wallet and studied Brock's ID a bit longer than necessary before recording his name in the crime scene log. Brock glanced down at the deputy's name tag. It read *T. Hanscomb.*

"Heard about you," Hanscomb said.

"Good for you," Brock said as he snatched his ID from Hanscomb's outstretched hand.

Hanscomb stepped back, leering at Brock as he drove past. Brock wondered how long it would be before people moved on. Or until he decked someone.

The gravel access road was a mess. Steep and heavily rutted from rainwater runoff and melting snow, the road would have been unnavigable for a passenger vehicle. Brock inched past several SUVs and pickups parked alongside the roadway, each one bearing the reflective logo of the Maine Warden Service or Hancock County Sheriff. At the bottom of the way was a small dirt turnout packed with several additional marked and unmarked law enforcement vehicles and a flatbed wrecker. He wondered how many of these people really needed to be there. Crime scenes, if that was what this turned out to be, were hard enough to manage without having fellow cops and first responders tromping through everything. If he was to take the lead on this, gaining control of the scene would be the first order of business.

The pond itself was now in full view, and Brock could see clear across the water to the woods on far side and the foothills beyond. Typical of Maine's early springs, rime ice still lined the perimeter of the pond while patches of snow shaded from the sun's rays peeked out from beneath the woodland undergrowth. Frozen reminders that they were only several weeks past the winter season.

To Brock's left, the shoreline stretched out onto a wooded peninsula, jutting into the pond like a gnarled finger. Three hundred feet or so off the end of the promontory bobbed a large black-and-white rigid inflatable boat, or RIB as they were generally known. The vessel was equipped with a Bimini top and a large outboard engine. Two figures sat hunched over either side of the RIB as if they might be fishing. Brock was sure that wasn't what they were doing.

He parked beside a brand-new charcoal-colored Interceptor. Despite its civilian registration plates, Brock immediately recognized it as an unmarked detective's vehicle. Chloe's vehicle, he assumed, but the fledgling Detective Wright was nowhere in sight. As he opened the door to step outside, he realized just how unprepared for this little venture he was. Mud season, a running joke in most parts of the country, was an actual thing in Maine, causing many northern businesses to close down for several weeks until the topsoil became firmer and more tourist friendly. As he eyed the wet brown earth, Brock cursed himself for not having switched out his footwear before driving to the scene. His dress shoes would surely be ruined by the time he reached the rear hatch, where his rubber boots were neatly stowed and all but useless.

"Looks like you should have dressed for the outdoors, son," a gravelly voice said from beyond the open door.

Brock looked up to find a white-haired game warden, dressed in khaki pants and matching windbreaker, fixing him with a toothy smile.

"I find these rubber boots from L.L. Bean work better than those Oxfords," the warden continued, his voice deeply tinged with an accent Brock normally associated with Down East fishermen.

"Gee, thanks," Brock said as he stepped out and instantly sank several inches into the muck. "I'll try and remember that."

"Happy to help," the warden said as he drew nearer and extended a hand. "Kenny Doiron. You must be Brock Justice."

"Good to meet you, Kenny," Brock said. "I don't suppose you could tell me what I'm doing out here."

"Sure I can. A handful of staties and warden divers were out here training this morning, and they ran across a snowmobile submerged in about thirty feet of water."

Brock made no attempt to hide his irritation as he popped open the hatch of the SUV and dug out his boots. "They dragged me all the way out here for a damn snowmobile accident?"

"I wouldn't exactly describe this one as an accident," Doiron chuckled. "But you're the homicide investigator. I'll let you make that call yourself."

"Can't wait," Brock said as he sat down on the Ford's rear bumper and peeled off his muddy shoes. "I don't suppose you've seen my new partner anywhere around here. Chloe Wright?"

"Detective Wright? Of course I have."

Brock waited several ticks for Doiron to elaborate. When it became clear he wouldn't without further prompting, Brock followed up.

"Mind telling me *where* I can find her?"

"Now where did she get off to?" Doiron said as he placed his hand over his eyes like a visor and made a show out of searching the area. "I expect she'll turn up any minute now."

4

During the next fifteen minutes, Brock met with two surprises. The first came as a lime-green-and-gray snowmobile bobbed to the surface of the pond. Assisted by underwater inflatable bags and the RIB, the divers slowly guided the snowmobile toward the shore. As they drew nearer, Brock could see what appeared to be a fully clothed corpse seated astride the snowmobile. The second surprise came as one of the divers, clad in a maroon-and-black formfitting wetsuit, broke away from the group. After shedding her air tank harness and fins, the diver waded out of the shallow water directly toward him.

"You must be my new partner," the diver hollered as she hurried up the beach, extending a sodden hand. "Chloe Wright."

Brock had hoped to establish his supervisory role at their first meeting, but his obvious astonishment at learning Chloe was one of the divers had blown the plan entirely out of the water. Brock, realizing his mouth was hanging agape, quickly closed it.

"Brock Justice," he said after clearing his throat.

"I never imagined I'd be the one to discover our first case together, did you?" Chloe said, cocking a thumb in the direction of the snowmobile.

Brock caught a glimpse of a smirking Warden Doiron standing nearby.

"No," Brock said. "I certainly didn't."

Chloe stood beside him dripping onto the sand while they watched the wrecker driver winch their crime scene onto the shore. Lake water poured from every opening in the snowmobile while bottom vegetation clung to the skis and track.

Doiron stepped up beside Brock and offered some insight. "You're probably not familiar with this kind of thing, Detective, being from the southern part of the state and all, but we make a routine out of springtime recoveries from lakes and ponds. All winter long, folks get liquored up and head out onto the ice whether it's safe or not. A little something I like to call A-L-L-E-N-S."

Brock turned to face him. "A-L-L-E-N-S? What's that?"

"You know, the coffee brandy. I always say you can't spell stupid without those letters. Some folks just can't hold their liquor. Add a little brandy and you get instant asshole. Cars, trucks, ATVs, and snowmobiles, it don't seem to make a lick of difference. I've found all of them at the bottom of one body of water or other come springtime. Even had a submerged Farmall tractor once. Guess Darwin's law applies double when it comes to thin ice."

"But how many of your springtime recoveries were handcuffed to a corpse?" Chloe said.

"The body is handcuffed to that thing?" Brock said, unable to hide his disbelief and understanding for the first time exactly why he had been called to the scene.

"Yup," Doiron said with a chuckle. "And to answer your question, young lady, this is definitely a first for me."

The wrecker driver disabled the winch as soon as the snowmobile and its gruesome cargo were completely clear of the water.

Brock checked the time on his watch as he removed the notebook from his jacket pocket and made several entries.

Chloe leaned in for a peek. "What are you writing?"

Brock retreated slightly to avoid having her drip lake water onto the pages.

"I recorded the date and time the snowmobile was removed from the water, the name of the wrecker service, and NCIC," Brock said, referring to the National Crime Information Center, a national law enforcement database maintained by the Federal Bureau of Investigation.

"Why NCIC?"

"I want to check missing persons from the area."

"Why?" Chloe said. "The victim may well have identification. We haven't checked yet."

"They might," Brock said. "But someone still should have reported them missing. If there is a report, then there will be a date and time, a reporter, and likely an assigned detective."

"Guess you're right," Chloe said. "It's as good a place to start as any."

Brock paused for a moment to look her up and down. "Any chance you brought a change of clothes with you?"

"You don't approve of my diving suit?" Chloe said, proudly holding up her fins and turning slightly as if posing for a camera.

"I'm just not so sure the people we're going to interview will."

Chloe gave him a hard look. "My civvies are in the back of my vehicle. I'll change after we take a closer look at the body."

Brock, Chloe, and Doiron stood out of the way observing as state police evidence technician Mike Fuente went about photographing the body in situ. Brock had heard of Fuente, though the two men had never formally met. Fuente was known for being overly thorough, exactly the type of evidence technician every homicide investigator wanted. Brock made notations of everything he observed while fielding nonstop questions from Chloe.

The body, slumped forward over the instrument cluster, was dressed in an insulated plaid chamois shirt, blue jeans, and insulated boots. Curiously absent from the clothing was a helmet, hat, or even gloves. Brock made a note of this, as it was unusual to see someone out on a snowmobile without proper winter attire. The victim appeared to be a Caucasian male of above average size and weight with dark hair plastered to his sodden scalp. Apart from a mustache, the man was clean-shaven and had a cleft chin. The right arm was stretched taut, handcuffed at the wrist to the lower right side of the sled through the upper control arm of the right ski assembly. The head was turned slightly to the left, revealing one wide-open eye. Overall, the body was in remarkably good condition with only minor evidence of decomposition. Brock chalked it up to having been submerged in icy water.

"How long do you figure he's been under?" Brock asked Fuente.

"Tough to tell. Best guess, and that's all it would be, early January to sometime in early March."

"The ponds froze over late this year," Doiron said. "You might remember we had a really mild December. More rain than anything. Probably couldn't have driven a sled out onto the ice much before mid-January."

Fuente nodded. "Let's go with late January to early March, then. I'll check to see when ice-out happened, but I'll know better after the ME gets a look."

"Thanks," Brock said as he made another notation.

"You gonna try and put everything in that notebook?" Chloe said, jokingly.

Brock stopped writing and gave her an annoyed look. Cumberland hadn't been kidding when she said Chloe was new to this. "Yup," he said. "And when this notebook is full, I'll start another, and another, and I'll keep going until the case is solved. You've never worked a homicide, have you?"

Chloe's face reddened as she glanced over at Doiron. "No. Not as a primary."

"And not as a secondary either," Brock said. "You may think this note-taking thing is a bit obsessive, but trust me, if I miss something later on when I'm writing my reports because I failed to note something of importance to this case, any defense attorney worth a damn will skewer me in the courtroom. And that is unacceptable. Got it?"

"Got it," Chloe snapped.

Brock knew she was pissed at him for outing her in front of the warden, but he also knew she would remember both the lesson and the reason for it. And in remembering, perhaps Chloe would avoid making the same dumb mistakes Brock had made early on.

"That's a pretty expensive sled," Doiron said as he studied the snowmobile.

"How can you tell?" Brock said.

"'Cause I know snowmobiles."

"It's an Arctic Cat ZR 9000 Thundercat," Chloe said, jumping in again, in a likely attempt to recover her footing with Brock. "It's a few years old now, but they still go for about seventeen grand."

"For a snowmobile?" Brock said, making no attempt to hide his surprise. "You're kidding."

"Nope," Doiron said. "Chloe's right. And the price goes up from there depending upon the options. 'Course the dead body is always extra, unless you can get the dealer to throw it in for free."

Brock ignored the lame joke, figuring any acknowledgment on his part would only encourage the warden to continue. They all turned to the sound of an approaching vehicle.

A gray SUV bearing the State of Maine seal on the door rolled slowly down the dirt road toward the pond. Brock immediately recognized the sharp features and short graying hair of the driver as belonging to the state's chief medical examiner, Dr. Pamela Isleborn.

"Wow, she got here fast," Fuente said.

Brock wasn't surprised. It was the same in every line of work. The more mundane and tedious the job, the more excited people got whenever something unusual presented itself. And there weren't too many things more unusual than a corpse handcuffed to a snowmobile.

5

Dr. Isleborn wasn't known for being much of a conversationalist, so the introductions were terse as she got right down to work.

Despite having worked with her on at least a dozen murder cases, Brock couldn't recall having had one meaningful conversation with the woman. She was professional to the point of being robotic.

Isleborn's features were as abrupt as her no-nonsense personality. Unlike her predecessor, Dr. Ellis, Dr. Isleborn had not been born with a funny bone. Short in stature with salt-and-pepper hair and hazel eyes, she had the sinewy physique of a long-distance runner. One more thing that differentiated the two doctors.

"How was the body located?" Isleborn said without looking up to address anyone in particular.

"We were conducting a training dive with members of the warden service," Chloe said. "I literally swam up on him. Pretty spooky."

"And was the body astride the snowmobile as he is now?" Isleborn said.

"That's exactly the way I found him," Chloe said.

The doctor nodded and resumed her inspection. Placing her gloved hands on either side of the victim's head, she lifted it like a ten-pin bowling ball to examine the entire face.

Brock couldn't help but notice the eye he'd previously believed to be wide open was in fact missing its upper and lower lids. The right eye, previously hidden from view, was in a similar condition, giving the corpse a ghastly surprised appearance. Brock imagined the victim projecting a similar expression upon realizing the fate that awaited him. Though Brock had observed similar recoveries over the years, the altered expression of the dead in underwater recoveries never failed to disturb him.

Isleborn spoke into a handheld digital recorder. "There is surprisingly little evidence of predatory activity due to the remains being encased in clothing. The most notable damage inflicted appears at the tips of the fingers and the missing flesh around the eyes."

"They actually ate his eyelids?" Chloe said in disgust. "Gross."

"Fish gotta eat, too," Doiron quipped.

"Any chance I could get some assistance with the restraints?" Isleborn said.

"Mike, would you grab a quick shot of the serial number before you take those," Brock said to Fuente.

"Sure thing," Fuente said as he leaned in and snapped a close-up. The evidence tech then spun the camera around, allowing Brock to view the display screen.

Brock noted the handcuffs were manufactured by Smith & Wesson and that they appeared unremarkable. After recording the serial number in his notebook, Brock handed his handcuff key to Fuente. The evidence tech used the key to remove the metal restraints before bagging and tagging them. The handcuffs, along with everything else taken from the scene, would be documented and placed into evidence for later processing.

Brock, Fuente, and Doiron assisted Isleborn in lifting the body and placing it on a clean plastic tarp that had been laid out on the ground beside the snowmobile.

The doctor's examination was painfully slow, something greatly appreciated by Brock and any homicide investigator worth their salt. After a time, Isleborn stood erect and slowly stretched her back in a well-practiced yoga-like maneuver that Brock figured she had probably fine-tuned over the years.

"Looks like his ride's here," Doiron said.

They all turned to look as a black funeral livery arrived on scene and began its slow descent down the steep gravel slope.

"No way they make it down and back without getting stuck in that thing," Doiron said.

Brock agreed and waved them off.

The livery stopped in the middle of the access road near the top of the rise. Two attendants exited and began to unload the collapsible stretcher.

As soon as Isleborn gave the okay, the body would be bagged, strapped down onto the stretcher, carried to the SUV, then transported to the ME's office for a full postmortem examination.

Brock's attention returned to Isleborn, his pen at the ready. "What do you think, Doc?"

She regarded him for a long moment before speaking. Brock almost repeated the question, thinking perhaps she was caught up in her own thoughts and hadn't heard him.

"My preliminary examination has revealed no obvious trauma, beyond the expected predatory damage to his digits and eyelids. There are no outward signs of contusion or injuries to the face. Nothing on the neck to indicate strangulation. There are, however, signs of trauma to the parietal bone near the base of the skull."

"Do you think he drowned?" Chloe said, earning a raised brow and look of annoyance from Isleborn.

Brock gave her a nearly imperceptible headshake, having learned that Isleborn was not predisposed to guessing. She wasn't known for suffering fools either. Brock had seen other overzealous investigators chastised by the doctor as she made clear the only results that mattered were the ones revealed following a complete autopsy. Anything prior to that was nothing but imprudent supposition, and she had said as much on more than one occasion.

"Are you new, Detective?" Isleborn said.

"Brand new to homicide," Chloe said proudly.

"It shows."

Chloe's face reddened again.

"Okay to check for ID, Doc?" Fuente said, failing to suppress a grin.

"By all means," Isleborn said. She pocketed her recorder as her attention returned to Brock. "I have an opening tomorrow at eleven."

"We'll be there," Brock said. "Thanks, Doc."

6

Fuente located a waterlogged cell phone in the victim's jacket and a leather billfold inside the back pocket of his blue jeans. Inside the wallet was a Maine driver's license identifying him as Lee Owen. Owen's address was a post office box in Portland, Maine.

"What did you say his name is?" Doiron said, kneeling for a closer look at the man's face.

"Lee Owen," Brock said. "Why? Do you know him?"

"I did. Although, Spike looked a tad better the last time we crossed paths."

"Spike?" Brock said.

"His nickname," Doiron said. "After Red Sox shortstop Spike Owen. I'm guessing that would have been before your time."

Brock made a notation about the name and connection with Doiron in his notebook.

"By the way, that Portland address is an old one," Doiron continued.

"How do you know?" Chloe said.

"Because Spike is a local. I've had numerous run-ins with him in the past."

"You happen to know where he lives?" Brock said.

"Nope. But I know where he worked. Blue Hill Marine."

Brock stepped away from the scene, dug out his cell phone, and placed a call to the state police dispatcher.

Brock's hunch turned out to be spot-on. Lee "Spike" Owen had been reported missing to the Hancock County Sheriff's Office in January. After a short runaround with the record clerk, Brock was switched to the assigned detective's extension. He left a voicemail message as he followed Chloe in her vehicle to the local fire station so she could shower and change into her regular street attire. They left Chloe's unmarked parked at the fire station lot and drove straight to the marina.

Blue Hill Marine, located at 13 East Blue Hill Road, was one of two marinas located in town. The gravel lot appeared to have been carved out of a heavily wooded area off Route 176, providing access to Mill Stream at the upper end of the Blue Hill Peninsula. Surrounded by dormant grass and skeletal deciduous trees, the marina was a bevy of activity as many of the locals were anxious to get their lobster and fishing boats back into the water.

Brock drove beyond the main building, which housed the marina offices, and continued past long rows of dry-docked fishing and pleasure boats, many still entombed in their white winter shrink-wrap. He parked the unmarked in front of a large Quonset-style building. The structure, open on one end, was clad in weathered shingle siding with a badly rusted roof. A sign attached to the end of the building read "Boatyard Repairs."

"Why are we stopping here?" Chloe said. "The offices are back there."

"I want to get their attention," Brock said. "If we stopped back there, we probably would have found the owner or general manager, and they would have undoubtedly given us the company line."

"And now?"

"Now, all the employees have made us as cops," Brock said as they climbed out of the SUV. "These unmarked Interceptors stick out like a sore thumb. And for those a little slower on the uptake, my necktie will undoubtedly clinch it."

"You think any of the employees will talk to us if they know we're cops?" Chloe said.

"Probably not. But I guarantee we won't get the company line. If we're lucky, one of these guys will panic and say or do something stupid."

"Probable cause?"

"We build a case one block at a time," Brock said as he nodded toward the burly middle-aged man approaching them on foot. The clean-shaven man wore gray Carhartt pants, a plaid chamois shirt, and a Blue Hill Marine ball cap. His eyes were hidden by a pair of mirrored sunglasses.

"Get your notebook out," Brock said.

"Owners aren't supposed to park down here," the man said as he cocked a thumb over his shoulder toward the office building. "Good way to get that shiny ride of yours all dinged up."

"Luckily I don't own it," Brock said with a grin. "It's a state vehicle."

"You cops?"

"Detectives Justice and Wright," Brock said as he displayed his credentials, waiting while Chloe fumbled with hers.

"And you are?" Brock continued.

"Ralph Dixon," he said after a cursory glance at their IDs. "I'm the marina foreman."

"Just the man we're looking for," Brock said louder than he needed to, for the benefit of those who had stopped to watch the interaction. "Someplace we can talk, Mr. Dixon?"

"Yeah, my office. Follow me."

They followed him inside the Quonset hut to a small enclosure at the right front corner of the building. A small electric space heater performed double duty, both warming the space and acting as a drier for the wet gloves and socks hung directly above it.

Dixon removed a stack of ledgers from one of the guest chairs, then gestured for Chloe to sit.

"I'm fine, thank you," Chloe said as she remained standing.

"Suit yourself," Dixon said as he plopped down in a rusting swivel chair that groaned each time he moved.

"Wondering why there are two boatyards in Blue Hill?" Brock said, attempting to slow-walk their reason for being there with a bit of conversation. "I would think in a town this small, one would be plenty."

Dixon grinned. "You'd think so, wouldn't ya? Truth is, the family I work for opened this boatyard in the 1930s. The man who started it noticed that people were beginning to get into pleasure boating. Guess he figured between the fishermen and the pleasure boaters, he could make a pretty penny. Turns out he was right. The family now owns both boatyards. This one, the one we call Marine West, is sort of a do-it-yourself facility primarily for the lobstermen and the local sailboat crowd."

"And the other?" Brock said.

"The east boatyard is mostly used to service people from away. They come up for a few months in the summer and need a way to get their yachts in the water. Some even store them there during the winter months. It works well for everyone to keep the fishermen and the vacationers separate."

"I would imagine," Brock said.

"So, what can I do for the state police?" Dixon said as he fished a foil pack of America's Best Chew from his pocket. "I'm assuming one of my boys got into trouble again, right?"

"We're here about Lee Owen," Brock said.

"I wondered when he'd turn up," Dixon said with a frown before inserting a pinch of tobacco between his cheek and jawbone.

Chloe opened her mouth to respond, but a look from Brock stopped her in her tracks.

"We call him Spike around here," Dixon added.

"When was the last time you saw or spoke with Lee, Mr. Dixon?" Brock said.

Dixon leaned back in his chair to look at one of the stained pinup calendars hanging from a plywood wall. "Guess it would have been the 17th of November."

"How can you be so sure about the date?" Chloe said.

"Because it was the last day the marina was officially open. Guys like Spike either go on unemployment during the winter or do odd jobs. A few of them plow snow, sand lots, stuff like that. What's he done, anyway?"

"Were you aware he had been reported missing?" Brock said.

"I guess I had caught wind of it. Didn't take it too seriously, though."

"Mind if I ask why?" Brock said.

"Most of my workers are good dependable family folk, just trying to keep food on the table and a roof over their heads. Then there are the other kind, like Spike Owen, who like to drink, gamble, get into the occasional bar fight, and always seem to be in trouble with the law. Guess maybe I figured he had gone back to where he's from, Portland."

"Why hire him, then?" Chloe said.

Dixon fixed her with a knowing smirk. "Ever work at a boatyard, Detective?"

"No, sir."

"Went to college, right?"

"Majored in criminal justice," Chloe said proudly.

Dixon nodded. "I figured as much. This might come as a surprise to you, but I don't get a lot of criminal justice majors applying to work here, Detective Wright."

Brock watched the color flood into Chloe's cheeks.

"Spike is a good worker. Why I keep him around."

"Any idea who Lee's friends were?" Brock said. "Who he hung out with at the boatyard?"

"He's pretty tight with Frankie Desmond. Maybe Frankie knows something."

"Is Desmond working today?" Chloe said.

Dixon nodded as he spit into an empty mug. "You drove past him when you came in. He's unwrapping one of the lobster boats. So, you're here working on a missing person case, then?"

"Owen isn't missing," Brock said.

Lines creased Dixon's forehead. "But you said—"

"We found him this morning," Chloe said.

"Great," Dixon said. "We need all the help we can get this time of year. Tell him to get his butt back here."

"I'm afraid he won't be helping you, Mr. Dixon," Brock said.

"Why not? She just said you found him."

"We did," Brock said. "At the bottom of Second Pond."

7

Dixon led them back outside to find Frankie Desmond.

"There's the boat he's supposed to be prepping," Dixon said, pointing in the direction of the launch. "He can't be far."

Brock and Chloe followed Dixon down toward the shoreline where several men were unwrapping one of the larger fishing boats.

"You guys know where Frankie is?" Dixon asked the workers.

"Went home sick," one of the men said, smirking at Chloe as he did. "Said he wasn't feeling well."

"I wonder if his sudden illness had anything to do with our arrival," Chloe said.

Dixon shrugged. "You should ask him yourself."

"You have an address?" Brock said.

"Back in my office. I'll get it for you."

As they departed from the marina, Brock's cell rang with an incoming call from the Hancock County Sheriff's Department. He placed his phone in the dash-mounted cradle and punched the speaker button.

"Detective Justice," he said.

"This is Detective Brady from Hancock SO, returning your call. I understand you cleared one of my file sixes for me. Lee Owen, right?"

File 6 is the NCIC designation for a missing person. After a missing report is filed with a law enforcement agency, the department of record is required to enter the pertinent details into the national database. The information can then be shared with every department in the United States. Any law enforcement officer encountering the missing person can quickly ascertain their status with a couple of keystrokes.

"That we did," Brock said. "He's on his way to the medical examiner's office as we speak."

"Heard he was cuffed to a snowmobile. That true?"

"It is," Brock said, dismayed but not altogether surprised that the information had already leaked. "Any mention of Owen receiving threats in your report?" Brock said.

"Um, hang on a sec."

As he listened to Brady shuffling papers in the background, Brock couldn't help but wonder how much effort, if any, Brady had put into locating Owen.

"Got it right here. Nope. No mention of anything like that."

"Who filed the report?" Brock said.

"Girlfriend. Name's Melinda Hamilton. Said Owen never came home after a night out."

"You have an address for her?" Brock said.

"Yup. She lives in Blue Hill."

Brady provided Hamilton's address and telephone number along with a promise to email a copy of the complete report to Brock. Brock envisioned a small attachment.

Melinda Hamilton lived on Beech Hill Road in a second-floor rear apartment about a mile from the center of town. The building was a three-story with a flat roof. Brock parked on the opposite side of the street.

As they approached the building on foot, Brock could see that the bright white paint covering the clapboard siding was at least several layers thick. *Lipstick on a pig*, he thought. Typical of many low-end rental properties. After finding the main entry doors to the building unsecured, Brock and Chloe headed inside, mounting the steps to the second floor.

Neither one of them was looking forward to breaking the news of Lee Owen's demise to his girlfriend. Death notifications were one of the grimmest aspects of police work, and Brock knew Chloe had likely made her fair share as a road trooper. Death simply came with the territory.

The two of them exchanged a glance upon hearing a baby screaming through the door to Hamilton's apartment.

"This is gonna be fun," Chloe said, her sarcasm on full display.

Brock crossed to the far side of the door while Chloe stood just short of it. The reason for their visit didn't trump officer safety.

Chloe reached out and rapped on the wood door. After several moments, a shrill voice called out from inside the apartment. "Yeah? Who is it?"

"State police," Brock said.

There was a slight pause before the woman inside responded. "What do you want?"

"We're looking for Melinda Hamilton," Brock said.

"You found her," Hamilton said. "What can I do for you?"

Brock gave Chloe a nod.

"Ms. Hamilton, we need to speak with you about Lee Owen, and we'd rather not do it through a door."

Another pause preceded the sound of a safety chain being pulled back. The door opened, revealing a young blond woman holding an infant who couldn't have been more than six months old. The baby, whose mouth was smeared with a greenish paste-like substance, stopped screaming long enough to regard the newcomers with big blue eyes.

"You have news about Lee?" Hamilton said, her eyes shifting between the detectives.

"We do," Chloe said, maintaining an appropriately stoic expression.

"Then I guess you'd better come in."

After letting them inside, Hamilton shuffled over to the dining room table and sat down.

"Close the door, and say whatever it is you've come to tell me,"

Hamilton said as she went back to trying to feed the screaming baby while *The Price Is Right* blared from the television in the next room.

Brock moved into the dining room and gestured to a chair to Hamilton's right. "May I?"

"Of course," Hamilton said.

Chloe followed suit on the opposite side of the table.

Brock made the introductions, then set about delivering the unwelcome news as calmly and sympathetically as he knew how.

"We are very sorry for your loss," Brock said when he had finished.

"Don't be," Hamilton said, catching both detectives by surprise. "Spike wasn't much of a boyfriend anyway. Come on, Zoe. You gotta eat. Just a spoonful, okay?"

Brock and Chloe exchanged a knowing glance as Zoe accepted the unappetizing spoonful of what looked to Brock like pea soup, sans ham.

"There's a good girl," Hamilton said, a split second before Zoe sneezed, spraying the greenish substance all over the high-chair tray and beyond. Instinctively, Brock leaned as far back as his chair would allow. Destroying a suit coat and tie was the last thing he needed after already ruining a pair of dress shoes at the scene of the body recovery.

"Is Zoe Lee's baby?" Chloe said. Brock could see she was attempting to change the topic of discussion while projecting just the right measure of sympathy.

"Yeah, but he wasn't much of a father either. Asshole's involvement pretty much ended at conception."

Brock had experienced every conceivable reaction from the loved ones of homicide victims. Family, friends, and lovers of those whose lives had been snuffed out at the hands of another were wholly unpredictable. Some wept, some screamed themselves into a rage over the loss, sometimes becoming combative, while others simply folded in on themselves like origami people, refusing to show any emotion at all. But in every death notification Brock had been part of, he couldn't remember anyone having used the word "asshole" as a term of endearment when referring to the deceased.

"When was the last time you saw or spoke with Lee?" Brock said.

"I can't remember the exact date. It would be in the report I filed a couple of days later. But I know it was a Saturday in January. He got a phone call late afternoon, then headed out."

"Did he say where he was going?" Chloe said.

"Where did he always go?"

Unsure what Hamilton meant by the comment, Brock paused a beat to make a mental note.

"I don't know," Chloe said.

"Then I guess that makes two of us," Hamilton said.

"Can you tell us if Lee had any enemies?" Brock said. "Or if he might have received any threats in the weeks before he went missing?"

"I threatened to change the locks if he stayed out all night again," Hamilton said as she made another valiant attempt to get Zoe to ingest some soup. "Does that count?"

"I was thinking more about someone who might have wanted to do him harm," Brock said.

"Nah, not really. I mean, Spike was always in trouble. That's what they called him, Spike. People gave him too many second chances, if you ask me. Me included. He was too good-looking, if you know what I mean. He could be a real charmer when he wanted to be. When he was sober and when he wasn't banging somebody's wife or girlfriend."

"Did he make a habit of staying out all night?" Chloe said.

"What do you think?" Hamilton said, pinching her face as if she'd tasted something sour.

Brock knew in a small town like Blue Hill, if Owen had been having multiple affairs with women already spoken for, his infidelity presented a motive. It also meant if Owen was as promiscuous as Hamilton seemed to think, the number of suspects had just increased exponentially.

"I don't suppose you'd be able to provide us with any names," Brock said.

"I'll get you a list," Hamilton said sarcastically.

The television crowd erupted from the next room, causing Hamilton's head to swivel in that direction. "Man, I hate it when that happens," she said.

"When what happens, Ms. Hamilton?" Chloe said.

"When someone wins a new car. You can always tell by how loud the audience gets. It's like they turn into an NFL crowd after a touchdown. I could win one of those, you know. If I could just get on the damn show."

Brock remembered having the exact same thought as he sat in front of his television during the first depressing week of what ended up being a six-month paid suspension following the botched arrest and shooting of Terry Kirke.

"Do you know if Lee had any other employment, aside from working at the marina?" Brock said, attempting to refocus Hamilton.

"He was doing some odd jobs for Doc Phinney."

"Doc Phinney?" Brock said.

"Yeah, Keith Phinney. He's the town GP. Nice man. Everybody goes to him."

"Do you know specifically what he did for Phinney?" Chloe said.

"Nope. All I know is it was part of his probation or something. You'd have to ask Phinney."

"Lee was on probation?" Chloe said. "Do you know what for?"

Hamilton shot her a look that was easy enough for Brock to read.

"Because he was a friggin' thief. Why else?"

"Do you happen to know who his PO was?" Brock asked, knowing he could get the information from state records easily enough. "His probation officer?"

Hamilton ran a hand through her unkempt hair in frustration. "Um, I don't know. Al or Albert something. I can't remember. I only met the guy once."

"Would you mind if we had a look through Lee's belongings?" Brock said.

"His belongings?" Hamilton said with a wry laugh. "See those cardboard boxes over there in the corner? That's everything he owned. I packed it all up when I knew he wasn't coming back. I'd planned to throw it all out, just haven't gotten around to it yet. You want it? Take it."

8

They departed from Melinda Hamilton's apartment along with a half dozen boxes of Lee Owen's belongings. Brock made sure Chloe wrote out a receipt for Hamilton with a promise of an itemized list once they'd had a chance to examine the contents. Hamilton said she didn't care about any of that, but experience had taught Brock the importance of covering your butt in these situations for two reasons. The first being that some of the contents might end up being relevant to the murder case, and the second was to prevent Ms. Hamilton from later accusing them of absconding with something valuable. It was a lesson he hoped to spare Chloe from learning the hard way.

"Where to now, boss?" Chloe said after securing the boxes in the back of Brock's SUV.

Brock studied Chloe's expression for a moment, trying to gauge whether she was being sarcastic or simply respectful. Seeing nothing that would indicate either, he let the comment slide.

"I thought we'd take a swing by Franklin Desmond's place," Brock said. "See if he's feeling any better."

"I know where he could get some pea soup," Chloe said.

Brock allowed himself a slight smirk at her comment. He had no idea what kind of homicide detective Chloe would make, but the gallows humor was a necessary self-preservation skill that would serve her well.

The address Dixon provided for Franklin Desmond turned out to be a 1970s vintage double-wide trailer that someone had plopped down at the center of a wood clearing a quarter mile down a dirt fire road in the neighboring town of Surry. The muddy area surrounding the mobile home was spotted with small patches of dormant grass and soiled remnants of melting snow and ice. Scattered throughout the yard was all manner of detritus consisting of lawn furniture with tattered webbing flapping in the breeze, a Craftsman push mower with a busted push bar half-buried in a snow pile, a large yellow-and-white plastic playhouse caved in on one side, and a pink tricycle. A silver Toyota Corolla sat unoccupied in the driveway facing a dilapidated garage, and parked beside it was a black GMC half ton. Brock remembered seeing the rusty pickup parked at the marina.

"This should be interesting," Chloe said as she reached for the door handle.

Brock reached out a hand to stop her.

"How fast can you run?" he said.

"What?" Chloe said, clearly annoyed.

He pointed through the windshield at a bare circular patch on the side lawn. "What do you see over there?"

"I don't know, Brock, crop circles?"

"Funny. I was thinking more about the steel post at the center of that crop circle and the dog chain attached to it."

"I didn't catch that. Thanks."

They stepped from the SUV and walked across the mud-covered expanse toward the wooden steps that led to the trailer's side door. As they crossed the yard, Brock kept his eyes peeled for the beast responsible for the brownish landmines scattered atop the snowbanks. As he reached the steps, Brock held a hand up, signaling Chloe to stay back. He wanted her to have a fighting chance in case they had to make a hasty retreat. As with angry black bears, the key to surviving an attack was never about outrunning the animal so much as outrunning the person you were with.

Chloe nodded and took a position on the lawn just off the steps.

Brock ascended the first two steps, then rapped on the storm door. He caught a flash of movement through a nearby window as sheer curtains were pushed aside. This was immediately followed by a deep, prolonged growl as the blocky face and droopy jowls of a large canine appeared in the window. The growl quickly became a series of loud barks.

"Knock it off, Max," a shrill voice commanded from inside. Only partially deterred, Max returned to growling.

The inside door opened about a foot, and a woman's face appeared in the gap. "Yeah, what do you want?"

"Sorry to bother you, ma'am. We're with the state police. My name is Detective Justice, and this is Detective Wright. We're looking for Franklin Desmond."

"Frankie isn't here right now."

Brock did his best to hide his disbelief. "Oh, that's too bad. We just missed him at work. We were told he wasn't feeling well. Are you Mrs. Desmond?"

"Rachel," she said. "What's this about, anyway?"

"Well, Rachel, we just need to ask your husband a few questions about one of his coworkers."

Rachel said nothing.

"Isn't that his truck?" Brock said, nodding toward the GMC.

"Yeah, but he ain't here. Came home early. Took off again on his four-wheeler."

"Sounds like he's feeling better," Brock said as he followed her gaze toward a well-worn dirt track leading from the garage into the adjacent woods. Brock removed a business card from his coat pocket and scribbled his cell number on the back before handing it to her. "Would you have him call me when he gets back, Mrs. Desmond?"

"I don't know how late he might be."

"Whenever he gets in is fine. I'll be working anyway."

"I'll pass it along."

"Much appreciated," Brock said as she closed the door in his face.

Brock and Chloe retreated to the SUV, careful to avoid stepping on one of Max's many lawn decorations. The last thing either of them wanted inside the SUV was the pungent odor of dog doo.

"You think he's hiding inside?" Chloe said as they reached Brock's Interceptor.

"I'd say it's fifty-fifty on that front. But between Rachel and Max, we aren't getting inside to find out."

"There are ATV tracks all over the backyard and a trail right there," Chloe said. "I wonder if he keeps a snowmobile in the garage too."

Brock wondered the very same thing.

As Brock fired up the ignition, his cell phone rang with a call from Lt. Cumberland. He knew she was looking for an update. Brock let it go to voicemail. If there was one thing he'd learned while working as a detective in MCU South, it was to control the information flow. While he might be training Chloe to become a homicide detective, it didn't mean he couldn't train the lieutenant too.

"That's interesting," Chloe said as she checked her own phone.

"What is?" Brock said.

"I had the dispatcher run the registration tags on the Arctic Cat. It was reported stolen back in January."

"Not surprising," Brock said.

"Maybe not," Chloe said. "But you might be surprised who the owner is."

"Who?"

"Keith Phinney."

"As in Doc Phinney?" Brock said.

"The very same."

9

Chloe ran Keith Phinney's name through several databases looking for the address of his practice and his home. The medical office was located in downtown Blue Hill while the home address was listed in the town of Sargentville. Brock checked the time. It was nearly five thirty. Brock knew if Phinney was like every other general practitioner he had ever met, the doctor would be booked with patients right up until the end of office hours. At this time of day, they'd have a much better chance of speaking with him at his residence.

"You hungry?" Brock said, realizing they'd both skipped lunch.

"Ravenous," Chloe said. "What did you have in mind?"

"I noticed a tavern near the center of town. Figure it's as good a place as any to grab something while we wait for Phinney's office to close for the day. We can kill two birds at once."

"Two birds?"

"Yeah, we gotta eat. And there's no better place for small-town gossip than the local watering hole."

"What about Phinney?" Chloe said.

"We'll phone his residence on the way to dinner."

Marlintini's Bar & Grill was housed in a sprawling single-story building a half mile from the center of Blue Hill on Route 176, not far from Second Pond. A large blue-and-gold sign stood sentry in front of the business, advertising specialties of "meatloaf, pot roast or turkey dinner, every day, curbside or takeout." It was exactly the kind of place Brock had pictured when he said local watering hole. A workingman's place built for the weekends and the hard drinking that accompanied them. He could imagine a live band, jukebox, and dance floor even before they stepped inside.

Marlintini's parking lot sat adjacent to a large tan two-story building, which housed a barber shop, massage parlor, and Mike's Market II, which Brock took to be a grocer.

Due to the early hour, fewer than a dozen vehicles were parked in the lot. Even so, the pickups outnumbered the passenger cars two to one. Brock parked the Ford beside a black oversized four-by-four with a lift kit a couple of rows back from the main entry doors.

"What do you figure he's compensating for?" Chloe said as she hooked a thumb in the direction of the truck.

Brock glanced at the registration as they walked past. "Jacked," read the vanity plate.

"Figures," Chloe said, confirming she too had seen it.

Brock didn't see a jukebox, but the sound system was cranking out a country tune as they entered the tavern. The restaurant was divided into two separate spaces: one side was dominated by a glossy horseshoe-shaped bar while the other was filled with tables and booths for those seeking a more family-friendly dining experience.

"Where do you want to sit?" Chloe said, raising her voice to be heard above the music.

Brock caught the eye of a waitress, who gestured for them to sit anywhere they liked.

"Come on," he said as he headed toward the bar side of the house.

They commandeered an empty four-top near the front windows directly across from the bar, allowing Brock to keep an eye on the unmarked and the comings and goings of patrons.

After several minutes, the same waitress appeared with two dinner menus and an order pad. She wore a name tag that read *Judy*. "What can I getcha to drink?"

"Diet Pepsi for me," Chloe said.

"Same," Brock said.

"Be right back," Judy said.

"My kind of place," Chloe said as she drummed her fingers on the table to the rhythm of the music playing.

Brock nodded but said nothing.

"You aren't into country music, are you?" Chloe said.

"Not really my thing."

"What do you like?"

"I'm more of a seventies guy. Steely Dan, Doobie Brothers, Pink Floyd, like that."

"Ah, oldies."

"Not that old."

They perused the menu in silence as they waited for their drinks. Brock scanned the items listed, but he had already made up his mind to try the meatloaf. Judy returned several minutes later.

"You ready to order? No rush, but the place will start to fill up, and we're short-staffed in the kitchen tonight. You don't get your order in now, you might be waiting awhile."

Chloe ordered the Blue Hill Bacon Burger special, aptly named due to the addition of crumbled blue cheese and bacon. Brock changed his mind and went with the open-faced turkey sandwich with stuffing, cranberry sauce, and fries.

"Why do you think he was cuffed?" Chloe said as she removed the paper covering the business end of her straw. "I mean, I get the stolen snowmobile thing. And given Owen's rap sheet, it does sound like something he would do. But how does he come to be handcuffed?"

"I don't know," Brock said. "Hamilton said he had been doing some work for Phinney. Maybe he saw the sled while he was at Phinney's house and decided he just had to have it."

"I can't imagine the town doctor hooking him up and sending him across the thin ice, can you?" Chloe said. "I mean, by all accounts, Phinney's a good guy. And he did take the Hippocratic Oath."

"So did Jack Kevorkian," Brock said.

"Who?"

"Doesn't matter," Brock said with a shake of his head as a refrain from Steely Dan's "Hey Nineteen" played in his head.

"Whoever cuffed him probably wasn't planning on the body being recovered so soon," Brock said absently. "How deep was the water where you guys found him?"

"About twenty-five feet. Deepest part of the pond."

"Exactly my point," Brock said.

"But why use cuffs? They all have serial numbers. Why not use something like zip ties or something that couldn't be traced?"

Brock had no idea. "It may have been the only thing the killer had available at the time. Speaking of which, any luck running the serial number I gave you?"

"I had the dispatcher enter it into NCIC. Nothing back yet."

"If we don't get a hit, we can try contacting the manufacturer. Smith & Wesson should have a record of where those were sold."

"You don't think Owen was killed by a cop, do you?"

It was exactly what Brock had been wondering. "Let's hope not," he said with a sigh.

"Here you go," Judy said as she set their orders down in front of them. "One Blue Hill Bacon Burger special with fries, and a turkey sandwich."

"It looks almost as good as it smells," Chloe said, inhaling deeply.

"The burger is my fave," Judy said. "Refill your drinks?"

"Please," Brock said as he handed her the nearly empty tumbler.

"Back in a sec," Judy said as she scurried off toward the bar.

They ate in silence as the tavern gradually began to fill. The music volume made it difficult for Brock to organize his thoughts. As they ate and made small talk, Brock kept one eye peeled for familiar faces.

"You expecting someone?" Chloe said as she caught him scanning the room again.

"Actually, I am," Brock said. "Franklin Desmond."

10

The Phinney home was located on the Gulf of Maine coast in the town of Sargentville, near Little Deer Isle. As Brock and Chloe traversed the long and winding paved drive through a grove of evergreens toward the seaside estate, it became obvious the small-town doctor was living an opulent lifestyle.

"Um, this is a little nicer than I imagined," Chloe said. "This guy's only a general practitioner, right?"

"The estate would seem in keeping with the price of the snowmobile you quoted," Brock said.

"You think he married into money?" Chloe said.

"Or was born into it," Brock replied.

The driveway looped, forming a small cul de sac as it passed in front of a set of granite steps that led to the home's entryway. At the center of the circle stood a large topiary trimmed to look like a lighthouse, complete with a lighted beacon. Brock parked the SUV to the right of the entrance.

As Brock and Chloe exited the vehicle, a tall, slender woman with short dark hair descended the steps to greet them.

"You must be the state police officers," she said.

"Detectives Justice and Wright," Brock said by way of introduction.

"Emily Phinney," the woman said. "My husband is just changing out of his work attire. He won't be long, if you'd care to follow me inside."

They followed her up the steps and into the house.

"Your home is beautiful," Chloe said as they passed through the foyer, earning a polite smile from Emily.

"Thank you. Keith designed the house himself, even overseeing construction. He has such great attention to detail."

"Wonder he didn't become an architect instead of a physician," Brock said.

"I thought about it," a voice said from above them.

Brock looked up to see Keith Phinney trotting down the hardwood steps from the second floor.

"Dr. Phinney," Brock said. "Thank you for seeing us on such short notice."

"No problem at all," Phinney said. "I'm always happy to assist law enforcement whenever I can. You folks have a thankless job."

"Detective Justice," Brock said as he shook Phinney's hand, then turned to introduce Chloe. "And this is Detective Wright."

"Pleased to meet you both. Can we get you anything? Coffee, maybe?"

"I'm fine," Chloe said.

"Coffee would be great," Brock said.

"Honey, would you mind?" Phinney said to his wife.

"Of course," Emily said before turning to Chloe. "You sure I can't get you a cup?"

Chloe exchanged a glance with Brock before answering. "If it's not too much trouble."

"No trouble at all. Back in a flash."

"Come on in," Phinney said. "We'll be more comfortable in the great room."

The great room was an impressive space featuring a cathedral ceiling with exposed wooden beams and a prow window wall overlooking the ocean. Dominating the center of the space was a massive floor-to-ceiling fieldstone fireplace. Surrounding the room's upper level were at least two dozen mounted wild game heads, consisting of several deer, a moose, a mountain lion, a ram, two bears, even an elk head.

"Hunter, are you?" Brock said as he and Chloe sat down across from the doctor.

Phinney smiled. "These are my pride and joy. I hope neither of you are put off by them. Some folks might find hunting a strange pastime for a doctor, I suppose."

"Not at all," Chloe said. "I've been hunting since I was twelve."

"There's nothing like the thrill of the hunt," Phinney said. "It's the circle of life."

Emily returned with mugs of coffee for each of them, then sat down in an overstuffed chair near her husband.

"Emily tells me you're here about a police matter," Phinney said.

"That's correct, Dr. Phinney," Brock said.

"You're a guest in my home. Please call me Keith."

"Well, Keith, we are investigating a suspicious death," Brock said.

Phinney's brow furrowed. "Not one of my patients, I hope."

"I'm not sure," Brock said. "But we have been told he worked for you. Lee Owen."

"Lee?" Emily said. "Oh my."

"Yes, he was working for us part-time," Phinney said. "May I ask how he died?"

"We have reason to believe he was murdered," Brock said matter-of-factly, hoping to elicit a telling response, but Phinney only shook his head.

"His death may have been by drowning," Brock added.

"That's horrible," Emily said.

"When was the last time either of you saw him?" Brock said.

Phinney exchanged a look with his wife before responding. "I guess the last time we saw Lee would have been sometime in January. He just stopped showing up. As a matter of fact, I still owe him money for some work he'd done."

"Do you mind me asking what it was he did for you?" Brock said.

"Not at all. Odd jobs. Exterior maintenance. Snow removal. That sort of thing."

"Owning a home on the ocean might sound like a romantic notion, but it also requires a great deal of upkeep," Emily said. "The salt air wreaks havoc on everything."

"Lee was a pretty handy carpenter and groundskeeper," Phinney added.

"Do you have any records we might be able to look at?" Brock said. "Cancelled checks, time sheets, anything like that?"

Phinney's face reddened slightly. "I'm embarrassed to admit this, but my arrangement with Lee was under the table. I paid him in cash so he wouldn't have to pay taxes on the money."

"I hope you aren't planning to report us to the IRS," Emily said.

"Don't worry," Chloe said. "Tax law isn't our area of expertise."

"Can I ask what Lee's death has to do with us?" Phinney said. "You said he drowned."

"May have drowned," Brock corrected. "We don't know for sure. Not yet. But we did recover Mr. Owen's body earlier today from the bottom of Second Pond. He was found with your snowmobile."

"With my snowmobile?" Phinney said, furrowing his brow. "I'm afraid I don't understand."

"He was with the snowmobile you reported stolen in January," Brock said.

Brock watched as something unsaid passed between Phinney and his wife. Concern? Confusion? It was impossible to tell.

"I don't understand," Phinney said. "I did report one of our snowmobiles stolen back at the end of January."

"Someone broke into our carriage house and stole it," Emily said.

"We know," Brock said. "We have the report. Do either of you remember having any contact with Lee following the theft?"

"Now that you mention it," Phinney said. "No."

"Are you telling us Lee stole our snowmobile?" Emily said.

"He was handcuffed to it," Chloe said.

Brock winced at her ill-timed comment.

Phinney opened his mouth to speak, then closed it. His eyes wandered between both detectives. "What exactly are you implying here? It was my understanding the two of you had come here seeking our help on a case. Now you're telling us someone may have murdered our handyman. It doesn't sound like you want our help at all. It sounds like we're suspects. Do we need an attorney?"

"No one suspects you or your wife had anything to do with the death of

Lee Owen, Keith," Brock said, attempting to repair the faux pas made by Chloe. "But we follow all leads, wherever they go."

"And our home was one of the first stops you made, was it?" Phinney said.

"We were hoping you might be able to provide some answers about what Owen might have been involved in that got him killed. And why he might have stolen your property."

"I honestly wouldn't know," Phinney said. "Like I said, he just did some occasional work for us." Phinney stared at Brock for a long moment without speaking. Finally, he set his mug on the coffee table and rose from the couch. "You know, I don't think I'm comfortable continuing this conversation until we've had an opportunity to speak with our attorney."

"That's certainly up to you," Brock said.

"Yes, it is, Detective. Emily will show you out."

It was clear the goodwill had dissipated as Emily led them to the front door without further fanfare or discussion.

As they reached the front steps, Brock turned and handed Emily a business card. "I apologize if we offended either of you, Mrs. Phinney. It certainly wasn't our intention. My number is on the back, if you change your mind about talking with us."

"Good night, Detectives," Emily said before retreating inside and closing the door.

11

Brock was pissed at himself. He should have seen it coming. The misstep wasn't Chloe's fault. It was a rookie mistake. He should have made a point of telling her to go easy and let him run the interview. He wasn't used to working with an inexperienced detective.

"That was my fault, wasn't it?" Chloe said as they exited the driveway.

Brock took a moment to consider his response. "No. It was mine. I should have done a better job prepping you before we got in there."

"Prepping me?" Chloe said, coming to her own defense. "I didn't say anything that wasn't true."

"The point is, I was intentionally holding back that piece of information until it became necessary to share it. Questioning people as part of a murder investigation is a bit different than working the street."

"How so?" Chloe said as the anger grew in her tone.

"It's more of a soft sell. Our job was to give the Phinneys the bare minimum and play nice. Watch how they reacted to things we told them. Look for tells or slip-ups. Lock them into statements. But most of all it was to make them feel comfortable around us. Keep the door open for questioning as we get further into the case."

"Weren't you planning to tell them about the handcuffs?" Chloe said.

"Eventually. Not necessarily tonight."

"But what if one or both of the Phinneys are responsible for killing Lee Owen?"

"Well, if they are, it's going to be a lot harder to prove it now without their cooperation."

The rain had started up again as Brock dropped Chloe off at the Blue Hill fire station to retrieve her SUV. He'd been hoping to end their first day working together on a high note. The botched interview with the Phinneys wasn't part of the plan. He wondered how long it would be before their attorney complained to someone. Someone like Lt. Cumberland.

"Where to next?" Chloe said as she gathered her belongings and stepped from the car.

"I think we'll call it a night. It's been a long day, and we'll have a longer one tomorrow. I'll meet you at the barracks in the morning, then we'll drive down to Augusta for the post. Let's say eight thirty."

"Okay. See you tomorrow morning." Chloe hesitated for a moment before closing the door.

"What's up?" Brock said.

"Nothing. Good night, Brock."

Brock's new apartment, which he desperately needed to spend some time unpacking and organizing, was in the town of Ellsworth, located north of Blue Hill and east of Bangor. Though he was mentally exhausted from what had been an eventful first day back on the job, he knew there were still a few things he could do without Chloe. Things like picking up a copy of the burglary/motor vehicle theft report filed by Keith Phinney from the Hancock County Sheriff's Department. As it happened, the sheriff's office was located right in Ellsworth. *So much for settling in slowly*, he thought.

Halfway to Ellsworth, he stopped at a Dunkin' for a large coffee. As he pulled away from the drive-through window, his cell phone rang. He slid the phone from his pocket half expecting it to be Cumberland ready to deliver her first ass chewing, but it wasn't. It was Kimberly Millick, his therapist. He thought about ignoring the call, as he had her earlier text, letting it go to voicemail, but she had caught him in a weak moment.

"Hey, Kimber," Brock said.

"Hey, yourself," Millick said. "Is this a good time to call? You never responded to my text."

"Yeah, sorry about that. Busy day."

"How so?"

He hated it when she did that. He pictured himself sitting across from her in her office, spilling his guts about pretty much everything while she continuously asked how something made him feel.

"Let's see, new detective squad, new apartment, new partner, new boss, and a new homicide case. I think that about covers it."

"So, pretty much routine day in the life of Brock Justice," Millick said.

"Pretty much."

She disarmed him with sarcasm, as she always did. It was the one thing that worked on him, her ability to compartmentalize crazy.

As the miles passed, Brock gave her a slightly less abbreviated version of the day's events, and she let him talk, uninterrupted. He hated to admit it, but it felt good just to get some of it off his chest.

"Tell me about your new partner," Millick said. "Has she been a detective long?"

"Her name is Chloe Wright, and she's hardly my partner, just a trainee my boss stuck me with. She's been a trooper for about seven years."

"Capable?"

"More than capable," Brock said as he thought back to her dive recovery.

"So, the problem is...?"

"She doesn't know the first thing about investigating a murder."

"You mean she's exactly like you were when you first transferred into Major Crimes."

She had him there, and they both knew it.

"Perhaps if you began to think of Chloe as your partner instead of something your new boss saddled you with it might go a little easier, for both of you."

Brock knew she was right. Hell, it was one of the reasons he stayed with her after bailing on the department's shrink after the shooting. He had only been looking for someone who would sign off on his return to duty, but there was something about Kimberly he liked. She didn't put up with his crap. Brock had never been blessed with a sister, but if he had, he would have wanted her to be exactly like Kimberly.

Brock ended the call with a promise to keep her in the loop. Five minutes later, he turned into the lot of the Hancock County Sheriff's Office, parking in the lot adjacent to the concrete stairs leading up to the side entry doors. He grabbed his coffee and headed inside.

Brock displayed his credentials to the bored-looking uniformed deputy sitting at a desk on the other side of the security glass. Brock waited for the man to hoist his substantial girth from the chair and come to the door to speak with him. The deputy pointed to a sign taped to the glass partition. The sign read: FOR ASSISTANCE FROM THE SHERIFFS OFFICE OR HANCOCK RCC PICK UP THE RED PHONE.

Below the note was a large red arrow pointing to the right. Brock followed the arrow to a crimson-colored wall phone. He looked back at the deputy and mouthed the word "Seriously?"

The deputy crossed his arms in defiance and smiled.

Brock moved two steps to his right and snatched up the receiver. As he held the handset to his ear, he heard it ringing in the next room.

"Hancock County Sheriff's Office," the deputy greeted in an overly cheerful tone. "Deputy Swann speaking. May I help you?"

"Detective Justice, Maine State Police. I'm here to pick up a copy of a report."

"Detective Justice, huh?" Swann said with a slight chuckle. "Any relation to Buford T.?"

Having heard the same tired line more times than he could count, as he imagined his father had, Brock had learned the best way to combat the ignorance was to simply pretend he didn't understand the movie reference.

"Who?" Brock said.

"Never mind. What do you need, Detective Justice?"

Brock repeated the purpose of his visit.

"Unfortunately, our records division closes at five," Swann said, clearly pleased with himself.

"I spoke to one of the clerks earlier today," Brock said. "He told me he'd leave a copy of the report here at the front desk."

"Well, why didn't you say," Swann grumbled before setting the phone down.

The deputy stood and crossed the room to a file bin. Brock watched him flip through a stack of manila envelopes, stopping when he found the one he was searching for. He finally opened the security door, but instead of passing the envelope to Brock, he held out a hand.

"That'll be five dollars."

"You're not serious?" Brock said.

"'Fraid so," Swann said with a gleam in his eye.

"You ever hear of professional courtesy?"

"I don't make the policies here, Detective, but I do enforce them. Five dollars, please."

Brock reached into his pocket and removed the state police money clip his father had given him as a wedding present and slid a wrinkled Lincoln from the stack. It took all the restraint he had to not pull Swann through the door into the lobby and wipe the smug look off his face as he handed him the money.

The deputy handed Brock the report before adding a final insult. "Would you like a receipt?"

"No thanks. I'm not sure I could afford the additional fee." Brock started toward the exit, then stopped and pointed at the sign taped to the glass. "It's possessive, by the way."

"What is?" Swann said, still smirking.

"*Sheriffs* should be spelled with an apostrophe. As in *sheriff's* office. You know, as in belonging to the sheriff."

The faux pleasantries departed from Swann's face. "Have a good night, Buford."

12

Chloe hurried across the bar to a booth where Detective Jordan Zimmerman sat waiting for her. He raised a hand in greeting.

"I thought you'd decided to blow me off," Zimmerman said.

"Not at all," Chloe said as she removed her wet coat and draped it over one of the empty chairs at their four-top. "Not after the day I've had."

Zimmerman had been Chloe's training officer when she joined the state police more than seven years ago. The two of them met regularly during the years that followed. He remained her mentor and trusted adviser, but more than that, he had become her friend. And now they were working together again as detectives.

Two pint glasses stood on the table in front of Zimmerman. He slid the untouched one toward Chloe. "I took the liberty of ordering your usual."

"Zim, you are the absolute best," Chloe said as she raised the glass of amber liquid. "What should we drink to?"

"Your first official day as a detective."

"How about the end of my first official day as a detective?"

"Cheers," Zimmerman said as they clinked the glasses together.

Chloe took a long pull from her beer.

"That bad, huh?" Zimmerman said.

"Let's just say Brock Justice hasn't made it easy."

"Runs in the family."

"Really?"

"Yeah. His father, Albert, was known for being a dick too."

"I thought his father was a recipient of the Legendary Trooper Award," Chloe said.

"Oh, don't get me wrong, Albert Justice was an outstanding cop. Doesn't mean he wasn't a dick, though."

Chloe laughed. "I guess so."

"Tell me all about your first case, Detective," Zimmerman said.

Chloe summarized the entire day, starting with locating Lee Owen's corpse underwater. As she relayed the tale, Zimmerman ordered another round.

"No shit?" Zimmerman said. "Handcuffed to a snowmobile, huh? That's something you don't see every day."

"I think the worst part of my day was when I let the cat out of the bag to the Phinneys about Owen being handcuffed to their stolen sled."

"Brock was keeping that from them?"

"Yeah, but I didn't know it was part of the plan because he never told me. Not sure why I blurted it out like I did. Guess I just wanted to be part of the interview instead of sitting there like a dolt. I mean, it isn't like I haven't interviewed suspects before, Zim."

Zimmerman winked. "If I'd been your training officer, we'd have discussed it in advance."

"Oh, what I wouldn't give for that."

"Well, you never know what the future holds," Zimmerman said as the bartender arrived with two more beers. "Tell me more about Brock Justice."

Brock grabbed the envelope and his worn cloth briefcase off the passenger seat before trudging up the outside staircase to his second-floor apartment in the dark. Having forgotten to leave the outside light on, he stood in the rain fumbling with his keys for a moment until finding the correct one and unlocking the door.

He turned on the overhead kitchen light, then tossed the envelope on the table and placed his briefcase on one of the two chairs. He hung his wet overcoat on a peg beside the door, then paused to look around at his new digs. It was hardly homey, but the apartment had come furnished and was reasonably priced, one of the few benefits that came with relocating north. He made the short walk to the refrigerator and peered inside as if groceries might have miraculously arrived during the day. They hadn't. Staring back at him was a cardboard to-go box containing three leftover slices of hamburger, green pepper, and Greek olive from his previous night's visit to Pat's Pizza and a four-pack of Mast Landing IPA. He peeled off a can of beer, grabbed the box, and returned to the table.

Brock's apartment was the converted attic space of a turn-of-the-century Cape Cod. His landlord, Mrs. Jeanne Anderson, a widow, lived alone on the first floor. Brock listened to the sound of her television coming up through the floor. The laugh track sounded like she was watching one of the many network sitcoms. He smiled as he thought of the widow cautioning him about making noise when he came home late or playing loud music. The irony was that due to the elderly woman's diminished hearing, it was she who was more likely to disturb him.

He eyed the envelope as he ate. A single word had been scrawled across the front in black marker: *Justice*. An elusive concept. He wondered if Lee Owen would get justice. Lee of the shady reputation. Lee the philanderer with a criminal history. Yet despite all the man's known faults, and likely a few more they had yet to uncover, Brock knew Lee deserved his best—their best—effort. He and Chloe would work this case as thoroughly as he worked every investigation. Lee may not have been a saint in anyone's eyes, but someone had handcuffed the man to a snowmobile, then watched as it sank like an anchor to the bottom of a frozen lake. It didn't get much more sadistic than that.

He tossed the remaining crust from his slice back into the box, then slid the envelope over and tore it open. The contents consisted of an incident report fact sheet, a narrative precisely four paragraphs long, Detective Brady's sparse handwritten supplemental report, and several images of the crime scene that the reporting deputy likely snapped by way of a cell phone. The photographs depicted damage to one of the carriage house doors—where the Phinneys kept their snowmobiles—an empty bay where the snowmobile had been stolen from, and tracks left in the snow where the sled had departed from the building.

Brock read the deputy's narrative twice. According to Dr. Phinney, both he and his wife were away when the overnight break-in occurred, though not together. Keith had attended an all-night poker game, while Emily, his wife, had gone to visit her sister in Vermont. This raised two possibilities for Brock. The first was that the burglar had known the Phinneys' schedule. The second possibility, though far less likely, was that the perpetrator had been extremely lucky in choosing a night when no one was home. Would the Phinneys have shared their plans with Lee Owen? The report also stated that although the house was equipped with a burglar alarm system, the carriage house was not. Another check in the lucky column?

He turned to the detective's supplement. No known suspects, no physical evidence recovered from the scene, snowmobile vehicle identification number entered into NCIC. In other words, Brock had been correct. Little had been done by way of investigating. Next to nothing, in fact. The report filed by the Phinneys was an insurance report, plain and simple. He wondered what the Phinneys' financial situation was. Based solely on appearances, they were doing quite well, but Brock knew how deceiving appearances could be, especially when it came to money. He had met more than a few people over the years who lived extravagant lifestyles, but it was all bad debt. Loans, second mortgages, and maxed-out credit. A house of cards. Were the Phinneys living in a house of cards? It would be worth checking out, but to get a look, Brock and Chloe would need a lot more than suspicion.

He tossed the sparse report onto the table and grabbed the last slice of pizza from the grease-stained box. As Brock savored the last bites, he could feel exhaustion beginning to creep over him. He wasn't sure if it was the alcohol or the events of his first day back on the job in more than six months, but either way he needed some rest if he was going to face tomorrow head on. As he took a long swig of beer, his cell phone vibrated with an incoming text message. He recognized the number the text had originated from despite his not yet having entered her profile information into the phone. The number belonged to Lt. Cumberland.

So much for keeping a low profile.

Cumberland had attached a jpeg to her text. Brock clicked on the image to open it. It was a screenshot from the *Bangor Daily News*' online page depicting Chloe Wright in her wetsuit standing beside Phinney's partially submerged snowmobile. The picture had been shot at an angle that blocked Lee Owen's face but still managed to reveal one pale hand cuffed to the sled.

The headline read: *Embattled Trooper Catches First Murder of the Year.*

"Goddammit," Brock said to an empty kitchen.

His phone vibrated again, and he toggled back to the text thread. Cumberland sent one additional line.

We'll discuss in the AM.

"I can't wait," Brock said as he tossed the remnants of the pizza back into the box.

Maybe he wouldn't sleep after all.

13

Brock and Chloe made the eighty-mile trek from Bangor to Augusta. The cold driving rain was relentless, and the wipers on Brock's Ford weren't doing much to keep the windshield clear. Making the long drive even more miserable was the fact that it came on the heels of the dressing down he'd received earlier from Cumberland. The lieutenant's office door had been closed, but between her raised voice and the proximity of her throne to MCU's coffee station, Brock was quite sure everyone in the office heard it, including Chloe.

Cumberland had asked Brock how he could let a reporter get so close to a crime scene. Brock explained it wasn't his doing, if in fact that was what had happened, and Brock had his doubts. It would have been just like one of the cops to send the picture to the newspaper, hoping to jam him up. Besides, T. Hanscomb, the smug sheriff's deputy handling the initial scene security, had allowed far too many people inside for Brock's liking.

The lieutenant had gone on to say that the colonel himself had called to chew her a new one for failing to keep a leash on Justice for one single day. Brock briefly considered telling her what the colonel could do with his leash, but given Cumberland's mood, he had decided against it.

Sheets of water from passing tractor trailers blasted the side of the unmarked like jets from a car wash as they traveled along I-95 toward the

Office of Maine's Chief Medical Examiner. Brock shot an occasional glance in Chloe's direction, but she was deeply engrossed in something on her cell phone. The upside was for once she wasn't peppering him with questions.

Being paired with a new partner was a lot like going on a blind date; there was nothing remotely comfortable about it. Brock had wondered whether Chloe might use the long ride to try and get to know each other a little better. Maybe swap some personal information or stories. But she had barely spoken since departing from the barracks. As her training officer, Brock was more than happy to keep things strictly professional if that's what Chloe wanted. Sharing his personal issues with other troopers had never been high on Brock's docket, anyway.

As the miles passed, he busied himself running down a mental checklist of the case. Everything they had done thus far, whom they had spoken to, whom they were looking for, and what still needed doing. As in every homicide investigation, the to-do list remained fluid, growing and shifting with each new piece of information obtained.

"How many have you attended?" Chloe said, dragging Brock from his reverie.

"How many what?"

"Autopsies."

Her uneven tone and the look on her face told Brock this would be Chloe's first postmortem.

"Quite a few," Brock said. "You?"

Chloe shook her head. "Never have had to."

Brock was shocked, and he was sure it showed in his expression. "In seven years, you never attended a post?"

"Nope."

"Well, I'm sure you saw your share of dead bodies when you worked uniform. This isn't all that different."

"Aside from dissecting them, you mean."

Brock didn't respond.

"You ever get used to it?" Chloe said.

"I'm not sure we're supposed to. That's kind of the point. Nothing highlights the reality of what murder *is* like having the doctor point out the damage inflicted on the victim by another human being."

Chloe looked away without responding. Brock couldn't tell if his comments had satisfied her curiosity or not, but she had finally pocketed her phone. It was only a guess on his part, but Brock was fairly sure he now knew what she'd been doing on her phone. Researching autopsies.

"Everyone reacts differently," Brock continued. "The trick is to think of the body as a crime scene. The postmortem is nothing more than an exercise in evidence gathering. We're here to get additional information from the medical examiner, period. Cause and manner of death. The how and the why Owen died are the important first steps in understanding what happened and who may be responsible."

Chloe nodded.

Thirty minutes later, Brock turned from College Avenue into the lot of the old Maine State Police Headquarters. He drove down the hill past the old Troop D barracks to the office of the state's medical examiner. Tucked away at the rear of the lower lot like some dirty little secret, the nondescript brick building abutted the tree line. Brock had always wondered if locating it there had been intentional or simply convenient. He parked the SUV next to the state police evidence response team (ERT) vehicle already in the lot. The white Ford conversion van was outfitted with a squatty-looking cargo box with multiple outside storage access doors along either side. The ERT van had always reminded Brock of an ice cream truck. The only thing missing was the music.

"You ready?" Brock said as he killed the ignition.

Chloe took a deep breath before reaching for the door handle. "Let's do this."

14

The examination room was a large open space as devoid of emotion and warmth as Dr. Isleborn herself. Something akin to a butcher shop combined with a surgical theater. Stainless-steel tables, hoses, floor drains, sinks, digital hanging scales, and harsh overhead lighting all added to the uneasy emotions Brock had always associated with being in the room. It was simultaneously fascinating and disturbing.

Brock and Chloe stood in the observation bay separated from the examination bay by a long glass wall. The see-through barrier was a way of ensuring the safety of those witnessing but not actually conducting the procedure. While the glass partition may have eliminated exposure to bodily fluids or injury from the many surgical instruments, it did nothing to alleviate the sights, smells, and sounds that accompanied every autopsy.

Isleborn, dressed in surgical scrubs, had already commenced the examination. She was clearly put off by the detectives' tardy arrival.

"Nice of you to join us," she said.

"Sorry about that, Doc," Brock said, making an extra effort to sound contrite.

Evidence Technician Mike Fuente stood not far from Isleborn and her assistant, digital camera hanging from one hand. He nodded at Brock and Chloe.

Lee Owen's clothing had been cut and removed from his body and now lay spread out on a nearby examination table. As with every piece of evidence, the clothing would be retrieved, bagged, and tagged by Fuente for further processing and storage.

Lee Owen's nude body lay faceup on the cold steel table. The back of his neck was cradled by a stiff rubber stand, arms by his sides, and legs fully extended. Were it not for the missing eyelids and the blue-gray pallor of his skin, Owen might have looked like he was asleep.

The skin covering Owen's chest cavity had already been incised and peeled back, revealing the pale bones of his rib cage. Isleborn, working alongside an attractive young assistant Brock had never seen, donned the head-mounted splatter shield and picked up the electric bone saw.

Brock caught the barely audible groan from Chloe as the realization of what she was about to witness hit home. At the sound of the saw's high-pitched whine, Chloe reached out a hand to steady herself against the metal frame of the viewing window.

"You okay?" Brock said.

"I'm f-fine," Chloe said in a shaky tone that reflected otherwise.

Standing to her left, Brock did his best to keep one eye on her and the other on the postmortem examination taking place. The last thing he wanted was for her to collapse, possibly injuring herself in the process.

Isleborn worked quickly and efficiently, not wasting a single movement, recording every observation on a pedal-activated audio recorder, the notes from which would later form the basis of her autopsy report. Mike Fuente walked around in the background, immortalizing every significant discovery in high definition from various angles. After cutting, the front of the rib cage was removed, exposing the victim's internal organs, each of which would be surgically removed, examined, weighed, and sampled for any subsequent testing. The doctor's proficiency made Brock wonder how many thousands of times she had performed this ritualistic study of a corpse.

In the world of law enforcement, people loved to wax poetic, especially criminal defense attorneys, about the Fourth Amendment and its importance in protecting one's privacy against unlawful search and seizure. It was one of the pillars of the Bill of Rights, after all. Brock wondered how many of those self-made scholars had ever borne witness to an actual post-mortem. He couldn't think of a single investigative procedure more invasive than having one's insides cut out and examined by a doctor following death. Surely nothing he did as a detective came close. But despite the seemingly unreasonable and graphic nature of autopsies, the examination remained one of the most important steps in building an unassailable murder case. Establishing both the cause and manner by which a wrongful death occurred was paramount to proving the crime of murder. In the law enforcement realm, everyone is familiar with the investigative terms: who, what, when, where, and why. Brock wondered how many of them ever bothered to contemplate the manner in which detectives arrived at the how.

Fifty minutes later, postmortem complete, they watched as Isleborn's assistant replaced the front of the rib cage and began to stitch together the large Y incision in Owen's chest. Despite her obvious discomfort at witnessing the procedure, Chloe had done remarkably well for her first PM.

"Ready to talk with the doc?" Brock said, trying to gauge the condition of his pale-faced trainee.

Chloe began to nod, then abruptly slapped a hand over her mouth and hurried past him toward the hallway.

Dr. Isleborn was grinning as she waved Brock into the examination room. It was the first time he could remember her showing even the slightest bit of emotion. The reactions of first timers always had that effect on medical examiners and seasoned detectives alike.

"Your partner all right?" Isleborn said as she removed her protective gear.

"She's my trainee," Brock corrected. "And she'll be fine. So, what do you think?"

"He was definitely murdered," she said as she glanced back at the body. "Though the handcuffs should have been the first clue."

"Drowning?"

"Yes, in concert with a blow from a blunt impact weapon that cracked the back of his skull, damaging both the lower portion of the parietal bone and the upper occipital bone. The injury caused massive brain swelling."

"Any speculation on the type of weapon?" Brock said.

"Something akin to a steel bar. Based solely on the hexangular injury pattern, I'd say something like a crowbar, perhaps. The victim was still breathing when he entered the water."

"Conscious?"

"Difficult to say. I suppose it is possible, but the brain injury would have killed him if he hadn't drowned first."

Brock had tried to imagine how terrifying being handcuffed to a snowmobile as it slowly sunk to the bottom of a dark frozen lake had to have been. For Owen's sake, Brock hoped he'd been unconscious, sparing him from having that horror burned into his final memory.

"Something else I discovered," Isleborn said as she held up the victim's right hand. "See these callouses at the base of the proximal phalanges?"

Brock nodded.

"They are quite typical in someone who made their living by manual labor. Was the victim in the trades?"

"Yeah. Worked at a boatyard. Moonlighted as a handyman."

"The callouses are more pronounced on this hand, making it his dominant hand."

"Okay," Brock said tentatively, unsure exactly where she was going with this.

"This is the hand we found cuffed to the snowmobile, correct?"

"Correct."

"Which means, even without the head injury, Mr. Owen couldn't have throttled up the snowmobile to get it to go through the thin ice. Snowmobile throttles are located on the right side of the handlebar."

"Meaning someone else had to operate the throttle," Brock said, completing her thought.

"Very good, Detective."

"Did you get BAC results yet?"

"His blood alcohol level was point-oh-seven."

Brock considered this. Owen had been drinking but was under the legal limit for drunk driving by Maine standards, and he was likely still able to function. Was that the reason for the steel bar across the back of his head? Had he fought his attacker when he realized what was about to happen?

"Aside from the head injury, were there any other indications of a struggle?" Brock said.

"No," Isleborn said. "I found no cuts, no contusions, no defensive wounds at all."

Brock wondered if Owen had consumed something other than alcohol. Some other substance that may have rendered him more compliant. And if he had, was it his choice, or had someone else spiked his drink? Assuming for the time being that Owen had been planning to break into the Phinneys' carriage house, wouldn't he have wanted a clear head?

"I know what you're thinking," Isleborn said. "And I'll email the results of the tox screen as soon as I have them."

"Thanks, Doc."

Brock checked in with Fuente before departing. "Any luck processing the cuffs yet?"

"Haven't had time to even look at that stuff, let alone process anything," Fuente said. "And I'm still trying to dry out the phone."

"Understood," Brock said.

"But, barring another body, I'll try and carve out some time this afternoon."

"Thanks, Mike. I appreciate it."

Outside it had stopped raining, and the clouds were breaking up, allowing glimpses of a sapphire sky.

Brock found Chloe leaning against the passenger side of the SUV, head back, eyes closed.

"You okay?" Brock said.

"Just needed some fresh air," Chloe said. "I imagine the doctor and her assistant probably had a good laugh over that, huh?"

"We should head back," Brock said, ignoring the comment.

"Actually, we should head over to Hancock County SO," Chloe said. "I just got a voicemail from Sheriff Parlin himself. Says he has information that might be helpful to our case. A possible suspect."

"How well do you know this guy?" Brock said, thinking back to how he'd been treated by the sheriff's gatekeeper the previous night. Brock had learned from experience to be suspicious of anyone offering up unsolicited information, especially in a homicide case. Even when the unsolicited information came from a fellow law enforcement official.

"Pretty well," Chloe said. "Gene is well liked by just about everyone. I patrolled this area for years, remember? He's always been nice to me."

"Okay," Brock said. "Let's see what Sheriff Parlin knows."

As they turned onto Route 3, Chloe said, "You don't like me much, do you?"

Brock was momentarily taken aback by her comment. "Why would you say that?"

"Oh, let's see, because they stuck you with me and because I have, like, zero homicide experience. Also, I know it wasn't your choice to come to MCU North."

"The last part is true," Brock said, choosing his words carefully. "But I don't have anything against you, Chloe. Hell, I hardly know you."

"Just so you know, I wasn't all that crazy about being partnered with you either."

"No?"

"No."

"Probably heard all kinds of stories about me, huh? How I only got hired onto the state police because of my father. How I crossed the thin blue line and screwed over a fellow trooper unfairly."

"Something like that," Chloe said.

"Well, you shouldn't believe everything you hear. The truth is, you don't know a thing about me either." Brock should have ended there, but he didn't. "And just for the record, you're my trainee. We aren't partners."

Brock watched as Chloe opened her mouth to respond, then closed it. He kept quiet, waiting for her to speak again, but as one minute became five, and five became ten, it was clear she had nothing more to say.

15

Springtime in Maine, especially the early part of the season, is a working conundrum. Typically, there is more rain than sunshine. And when the sun does make an appearance, it hardly warms the air at all. The grass, largely dormant in most yards and fields, looks more like a monochromatic tapestry of straw, nothing remotely resembling the multitude of greens sure to follow. And the branches of oaks, maples, birch, poplars, and every other common variety of deciduous trees, bare save for the buds, always slow to bloom, preferred to sleep in until May or June.

Despite the temporary cessation of rain, the drive to Ellsworth was proving to be longer and more uncomfortable than the trip to Augusta had been. The silence between Brock and Chloe was deafening. The storm clouds outside may have cleared, but the invisible ones hanging over them were still very much present.

As the miles slowly ticked by on the odometer, Brock's thoughts drifted back to the events that led to him being assigned to MCU North. Brock had wanted—no, needed—his father's support, but their history, and perhaps Brock's ego, kept him from reaching out for it. To Albert, a cop's cop, Brock was breaking a long-standing rule by crossing the thin blue line. Breaching a barrier erected by past generations of police officers to protect one another from the influence of a corrupt and often ignorant society. But like all things beneficial, the line itself had eventually become blurred, running like watercolor until the dividing line was indistinguishable as anything more than a way to conceal the corruption that existed within the blue rank and file.

What Albert didn't know was how much Brock had struggled with his decision to come clean about what he had witnessed. Brock and Evan Mathers had become the best of friends during their time together in uniform. They had been inseparable. And the last thing Brock wanted was to drop Chloe in it. Even now the truth wasn't fully known. Mathers had a dirty little secret only Brock knew. A secret that had caused an otherwise squared-away law enforcement officer to act in a manner highly out of character and left their friendship in tatters. And the shooting had cost Mathers everything. His job with the state police, his pension, his marriage, and, most importantly, his reputation.

Brock had done the honorable thing when he recounted the incident to investigators despite the pressure from the higher-ups to alter his account. When charges were eventually filed by the prosecutor, Brock was forced to tell the story repeatedly during countless depositions. The ultimate humiliation had come during the trial when Brock had to sit in the courtroom in front of his peers and listen as his account and career were repeatedly called into question by Evan's defense attorney. The man had shredded Brock on the stand, making him admit he had been seeking treatment for PTSD following the shooting from a department-sanctioned psychiatrist. The fact that the therapy was mandated by the department hadn't factored into it. Brock's account of the events on the day of the shooting were deemed highly suspect by both expert witnesses hired by the defense. They testified that his version of what transpired was likely warped by the stress of having himself been shot. Ultimately, the jury bought the alternate version, spun like a web, finding Trooper Mathers not guilty.

Brock knew he had done the right thing despite the unrelenting pressure to recant his testimony. In the end, it didn't matter. Doing the right thing had come attached to a weighty price tag. For all his losses, Mathers had walked from the courtroom a free man. While Brock, a virtual pariah, had been sent packing to the furthest reaches of the Pine Tree State.

As they neared the town of Belfast, Chloe finally broke the silence.

"Any chance we could stop for coffee? I really need caffeine."

"Sure," Brock said. "What's close?"

"There's a Dunkin' coming right up on Route 1. Take a right at the next intersection."

"Okay."

"Listen, I'm sorry for what I said about working with you. That was a cheap shot, and I shouldn't have said it."

Brock glanced at her but said nothing.

"Truth is, I was embarrassed about how I reacted at the autopsy. I took it out on you, and I'm sorry."

"Don't worry about it," Brock said. "And you have nothing to be embarrassed about."

"Still, I tend to speak my mind about things before thinking them through."

Brock cracked a smile. "Guess maybe we have something in common after all."

It was nearly 2:15 p.m. by the time they arrived at the sheriff's department. As Brock guided the SUV into the same space he had availed himself to the previous night, he wondered if the same charming deputy would be manning the desk. Mercifully, Deputy Swann was nowhere to be seen. Today the desk was manned by a pleasant middle-aged woman who, after learning the reason for their visit, not only was helpful but picked up the phone to notify the sheriff he had visitors, free of charge. After confirming Parlin was available, the woman waved them into the secure area, then led the way to the sheriff's office.

"Come right in, Detectives," Parlin said in a booming voice as he rose from behind his desk and stuck out a meaty hand in greeting. "You must be Al's boy, Brock. Jeepers, you're the spitting image of your old man, son."

Parlin's appearance was exactly what Brock had conjured up during the trip to Ellsworth. He was tall, well over six feet, with rugged good looks and an infectious smile. In every aspect the man was a stereotypical small-town celebrity, Brock thought. Change the uniform for a dress shirt and chinos and the sheriff could have been out in the community, kissing babies and stumping for votes for state representative, or even senator. Parlin was a born politician.

"Nice to meet you, Sheriff," Brock said as he grasped the sweaty offering. "Chloe tells me good things."

Parlin moved on to Chloe. "Look at you, Detective Wright. I know it isn't politically correct of me to say this, but you're even prettier out of uniform."

Chloe laughed.

"That didn't come out at all the way I meant it, but you know what I mean."

"I do," Chloe said, blushing slightly. "And thank you, Sheriff."

"Sit, sit. And enough with the sheriff business. Call me Gene. Can I get either of you something to drink? Coffee? Soda?"

"Nothing for me, thanks," Chloe said.

"I'm fine, Gene," Brock said, trying to bring the conversation back on point. "Chloe mentioned you might be able to assist us with some information on the case we're working."

"Right down to business. I like that. I've asked one of my deputies to join us. He should be right—"

There was a sharp rap on the office door a moment before it swung open, revealing a tall uniformed deputy.

"You wanted to see me, Sheriff?" the deputy said as he eyeballed both visitors. His eyes fixed on Brock.

Brock should have been surprised, but he wasn't. It was Deputy T. Hanscomb, the same uniformed deputy who asked to see Brock's identification before allowing him into the crime scene only the day before.

"Tommy, come in," Parlin said. "I'd like you to meet Detective Brock Justice, and of course you already know Chloe. Brock, this is Tommy Hanscomb, one of my finest road deputies."

"Only one of?" Hanscomb joked.

"We've met already," Brock said as he stood and gripped Hanscomb's outstretched hand, squeezing a little harder and a little longer than necessary. To his credit, Hanscomb didn't flinch, giving as good as he got while maintaining eye contact.

"Nice to see you again, Detective Justice," Hanscomb said.

Brock finally released the deputy's hand, and Hanscomb moved on to Chloe.

"Hey, Tommy," Chloe said.

"Hey, yourself, Detective Wright. And congratulations on the promotion."

Hanscomb dragged another chair into the room and placed it beside Chloe's in a move clearly designed to elicit a response from Brock. It didn't.

As soon as they were all seated, Parlin resumed the conversation. "As you know, Tommy, the detectives are working on that Blue Hill murder."

"Yeah," Hanscomb said. "I heard through the grapevine you identified the victim and the sled's owner."

"We did," Brock said, still trying to understand how Hanscomb might be able to help. "And they were not the same. The snowmobile was reported stolen from a local doctor the very same night Lee Owen went missing."

"You're talking about Keith Phinney," Parlin said.

"I am," Brock said.

"I got a call from Keith at home last night," Parlin said with a chuckle. "He was a little miffed after your visit."

"I think Dr. Phinney may have read too much into our questions," Brock said. "You can understand why we would question Dr. Phinney about the theft of his snowmobile."

"Of course," Parlin said. "You want to know if he has an alibi."

"Not to put too fine a point on it, Gene, but yeah," Brock said, irked at the prospect of justifying anything to Parlin, or one of his finest road deputies.

"I can help you with that," Parlin said as he glanced at Hanscomb. "Keith was at my house that night playing poker with some friends. The reason I remember it so well is because Keith called me right after he arrived home the next morning to find his garage burglarized and his sled missing."

"Mind if I ask who else was present?" Brock said, surprised by the alibi.

"Not at all. One of those unlucky enough to be at the table that night was Tommy here."

Hanscomb smirked at Brock. "Lost my shirt."

"Anyone else?" Brock said.

"Your dad was there too. In fact, Al was the big winner. Damn near cleaned us out."

Brock realized he and Chloe had walked into an ambush. Parlin could have just as easily picked up the phone and called him directly, but he didn't. Instead, Parlin had set this up to look like Brock and Chloe now owed him a favor. The consummate politician.

"We'll need statements from both of you to that effect, Sheriff," Chloe said.

"Of course. Always happy to help."

"Sounds like Dr. Phinney is off the board," Chloe said.

"Your message to Chloe said you had information about a possible suspect in Lee Owen's murder," Brock said.

Hanscomb weighed in again. "You're looking for The Bear."

"The what?" Brock said.

"It's his nickname," Chloe said. "He's an outlaw biker named Harold 'The Bear' Perreault."

"Exactly right," Hanscomb said. "I'm impressed."

"You want to hang on to this one," Parlin said to Brock. "Chloe knows all the players around here."

"I'm beginning to see that," Brock said. "What makes you think this Perreault guy might be responsible?"

Hanscomb spoke up again. "I've got friends in the DEA."

"Who specifically?"

The smirk returned to Hanscomb's face. "Sorry, but *I'm* not gonna put another cop in a jam."

Brock felt his face reddening as he fought the urge to knock the smug deputy out of the chair.

"My information, and where it came from, is totally off the record," Hanscomb said. "Think of this as a proffer. I give you what I got, and you either make a case with it or you don't."

"What *can* you tell us?" Chloe said.

"Word on the street is, The Bear has been smuggling fentanyl across the border from Canada using snowmobile trails and off-road vehicles."

"And?" Brock said, thinking about Frankie Desmond, who fled during their visit to the marina and later by way of an ATV.

"And Lee Owen may have been working for Perreault," Hanscomb said. "At least until he made the fatal mistake of coming up light on a delivery."

16

"What do you think?" Chloe said as soon as they were back inside Brock's SUV.

"I think I don't care too much for Deputy Hanscomb," Brock said. "Guy's a first-class a-hole."

"Tommy's not a bad guy. You just don't know him like I do."

And Brock was hoping to keep it that way.

"Besides, he's given us a lead, right?"

"All he's given us is an inadmissible rumor, Chloe. It's gonna take some serious work to even begin to link Owen's murder to this Perreault guy. Assuming he's even responsible."

"So, what's this about your father and Gene Parlin?" Chloe said, changing the subject. "You didn't tell me your dad lived around here."

Brock realized he hadn't told her much of anything. "After my mom passed, Dad sold the house in southern Maine, then winterized our camp in Blue Hill and moved in. He's into all that outdoorsy stuff."

"You're not?"

"No."

"You spend much time with him?"

Brock shook his head. "We've never been close."

The truth was, despite the larger-than-life image Albert Justice projected, Brock's father wasn't much of a dad. He liked being outdoors, and he liked drinking with his friends, at least the ones he hadn't alienated. Brock was pissed at himself for not having brought up Albert at the first mention of Blue Hill, but Lt. Cumberland hadn't exactly been in a conversational mood at the time. Besides, what were the odds Albert would end up being part of an alibi in Brock's first MCU North murder case? Surprisingly good, as it turned out.

Brock and Chloe returned to the Troop E barracks to regroup and develop a game plan. It had become painfully clear to Brock just how different working with fewer resources would be. No longer did he have the luxury of a large group of detectives at his disposal. What had been routinely farmed out to the MCU South detectives not assigned as primaries would now fall to him and Chloe. *Welcome to modern-day policing in rural America*, he thought.

Brock grabbed a dilapidated cardboard box from the rear compartment of the Ford and lugged it across the parking lot while Chloe held the lobby door open for him. It was a small gesture but clearly a token attempt to make amends.

"What's that?" Chloe said as she followed him into the detective bay. "I thought we had all of Owen's belongings."

"This is stuff from my old office," Brock said, dropping the box atop his desk blotter. "Figured I might as well make my cubicle homey."

"Hey, Chloe," a voice called out from the other side of the room. "Heard you two caught your first cold case."

Brock turned to see one of the detectives he had yet to meet standing in front of the coffee bar with a smug look on his face and a "World's Best Detective" mug in his hand.

"Nice one, Zim," Chloe said. "Brock, this is Jordan Zimmerman, Troop E's resident joker."

The mustachioed detective approached Brock and stuck out a hand. "You must be the infamous Brock Justice."

"I must be," Brock said. As he studied the detective's face, Brock couldn't help but wonder how many hours Zimmerman spent in front of a mirror perfecting his Hercule Poirot appearance. "Nice to meet you, Jordan."

"Likewise. And call me Zim."

Before Brock could respond, another man came around the corner. This one Brock knew. Not personally, only from what he had read in the papers. Arthur Wheeler had been in a horrible rollover motor vehicle accident several years before. The accident happened during a high-speed pursuit. Art, along with several other troopers, had been chasing a pair of armed bank robbers. The injuries he had sustained had left him paralyzed and confined to a wheelchair for the rest of his life.

"Brock, this is Art," Chloe said. "Our resident wizard of all things IT."

"Pleasure to meet you, Art," Brock said.

"The pleasure is all mine," the dark-haired detective said. "And around here they just call me Wheels."

"Wheels it is, then," Brock said with a nod.

"Did I hear right?" Zimmerman said. "Was your stiff really handcuffed to a snowmobile?"

"He was," Brock said.

"Cuffed and sunk. That's a first."

Brock said nothing, hoping a brief uncomfortable silence would untether them from Zimmerman's attention.

"Well, we'll let you get settled in," Wheeler said. "Let me know if I can be of any help."

Zimmerman gestured toward the lieutenant's office. "And let me know if you need any help navigating the Dreadful One's hierarchal waters. They can get a bit choppy."

Brock nodded.

As if in response to Zimmerman's comment, Cumberland's voice sliced through the room. "Justice, Wright, my office."

Brock glanced at Chloe, who simply shrugged.

"Good luck," Wheels said.

Zimmerman raised his mug in salute, then wandered back to his desk on the far side of the detective bay.

Brock removed his overcoat and tossed it over the back of his chair before gesturing to Chloe. "After you."

"What did the ME have to say?" Cumberland said even before they made it all the way into the office. She hadn't offered up the guest chairs, so Brock and Chloe remained standing as Brock filled the lieutenant in on the details of the autopsy.

"Pending tox, then?" Cumberland said before he had finished.

"She's definitely ruling it a homicide," Brock said. "But yes, pending toxicology results."

Cumberland redirected her attention to Chloe. "How did your first autopsy go, Detective?"

"She did great," Brock said before she could respond. "Think she's got a real knack for this, LT."

"Glad to hear it," Cumberland said as her desk phone rang. "Keep me up to speed. No more front-page surprises. We clear?"

"Crystal," Brock said.

"And close the door on your way out."

17

Brock grabbed two boxes of Lee Owen's belongings taken from Melinda Hamilton the day before and carried them into the conference room. Chloe was hot on his heels with two more. Brock set his on the table, then went over to the wall-mounted whiteboard and erased someone's idea of an inappropriate joke. It was a rudimentary drawing of a snowmobiler sinking below cartoonish waves surrounded by fish and yelling for help.

"I'll give you one guess who's responsible," Chloe said as she sat down at the table.

"Not even a contest," Brock said, shaking his head.

"So, where do you want to start?" Chloe said.

"I like to keep a visual reference of all the players and our progress. It helps me to see connections between the people and any gaps in our investigation. You throw the names at me, and I'll add them to the murder board. Good?"

"Works for me."

Brock populated the board with a black erasable marker, beginning with the name of the victim, Lee Owen. Each name was preceded by a letter corresponding to their role in the case, *V* for victim, *W* for witness, *S* for suspect, and so on. Some of the names necessitated more than one designation. Any relevant information was added to the right of each player. When he had finished, Brock stood back to look at the information. The one name glaring at him was Albert. Brock had intentionally not filled in the last name. He knew he would need to advise Cumberland of the obvious conflict, but he also knew it could wait.

"Reminds me of the board game Clue," Chloe said.

"You're not wrong," Brock said. "Except I'd be surprised if Professor Plum makes an appearance in this case."

Chloe laughed at the comment, and Brock felt something loosen inside him. He hadn't intended to be funny. It was an insignificant thing, really, but the brief moment of levity felt like a step toward clearing the air between them.

Having finished with the board, Brock and Chloe turned their attention to the boxes of Owen's belongings. After laying out a clean sheet of butcher's paper across the table and donning latex gloves, Brock carefully removed and examined each item before placing it on the table. Chloe photographed and documented everything on an inventory sheet. The boxes contained assorted clothing, a used marijuana pipe, a half a pack of cigarettes, a small broken piece of bluish plastic that looked a bit like an electronic circuit mounting board, a half-empty box of latex condoms, two sets of keys, several TracFones—two of which were still sealed in plastic—and a book of matches with Marlintini's logo on the cover.

Brock paused as he studied the matchbook. They had missed something obvious.

"What is it?" Chloe said.

"How did Lee Owen get to Phinney's house to steal the snowmobile in the first place?" Brock said. "I mean, it's all the way over in Sargentville. He couldn't have walked there."

"Maybe someone gave him a ride," Chloe said. "Maybe The Bear."

"Yeah, maybe. Except when Owen's girlfriend filed the missing person report, she said he drove off that night to meet someone. So where is Owen's vehicle?"

"Good question," Chloe said. "I'll run his name through BMV for registered vehicles."

"Run Melinda's too," Brock said.

At that moment, Art Wheeler rolled into the conference room.

"Hey, Wheels," Chloe said.

"I can do that if you'd like. Run the Bureau of Motor Vehicle's stuff."

"Thanks. That would be great."

"Seriously, anything you need, just ask."

"Thanks," Brock said.

"What we really need is something from ERT," Chloe said. "Like cell phone info."

"And the handcuffs," Brock said absently.

As if in response to their comments, Brock's phone vibrated in his pocket. He removed the phone and checked the display. "Speak of the devil."

"Which one?"

"Fuente." Brock swiped the screen to answer the call. "Tell me you've got something, Mike."

"It's more of a good news, bad news scenario," Fuente said.

"Great," Brock said facetiously. "Let's start with the bad."

"Okay, Owen's cell phone is a bust."

"Damn," Brock said, earning a raised brow from Chloe.

"The lake water damaged the internal electronics beyond repair."

"Is that it?"

"Nope. I couldn't recover any usable prints from the handcuffs either."

Brock sighed in frustration. "What's the good news?"

"I've managed to dry out the SIM card from Owen's phone, and it appears to be fine. All I need to search it is a warrant."

"We'll get on it straight away," Brock said, casting a glance at Chloe. "Anything else?"

"Yeah, I spoke with a rep at Smith & Wesson about the cuffs. Name's Stuart Albertson."

"And?"

"They do keep records on sales by serial numbers. The problem is, these are old handcuffs. The serial number goes way back. Thirty-five years at least."

"Okay."

"I'm talking pre-computer days."

"Don't they have paper files they can search through?"

"They do. Might take a few days, though. The rep told me those records are maintained off-site. I gave Albertson your direct contact info and told him to contact you if he finds anything."

"Thanks, Mike. We'll start on the warrant ASAP."

"Tell me again why I'm doing all this work?" Chloe said as she banged away on the computer keyboard. "I mean, the phone belongs to Lee Owen, right? And last I checked, he was dead. At least he looked dead, and if he wasn't, he certainly was after Dr. Isleborn finished dissecting him. Why should we worry about the Fourth Amendment rights of a dead guy?"

Brock fought back a smile as he recalled making a similar argument himself as a new detective. "Two problems. The first is you're assuming the phone actually belonged to Owen."

"Who else would it belong to? We found it on his person."

"We also found him at the bottom of a lake riding someone else's snowmobile."

"Good point. What's the second problem?"

"Even if the phone belonged to Owen, how do we know it wasn't shared by Melinda Hamilton? And if it was a shared phone, wouldn't she still be entitled to privacy protections as part-owner?"

"It's only the SIM card. Can't we just get her to sign a release or something? It'd be quicker than going through the hassle of obtaining a warrant."

"And if Hamilton withdrew her consent as we were downloading the records? What then?"

Chloe didn't respond.

"Trust me, on homicide cases, it is always easier in the long run to get a warrant signed by a judge than to risk a Fourth Amendment challenge later in court. We've already got probable cause to believe the SIM card contains information that might be relevant to the murder, right?"

"We know from Melinda that someone called Owen late that afternoon and the call caused him to leave the house."

"And?"

"And the next time he was seen was when we found him at the bottom of Second Pond."

"Good," Brock said. "Now we get the court's approval. I know you can't see it yet, but erring on the side of caution every time will save you countless headaches when your cases finally get to trial." *Headaches you can't begin to fathom*, he thought.

"Fine," Chloe said as she resumed typing.

18

Chloe continued to grumble as she slogged through the affidavit and search warrant for Owen's cell records while Brock busied himself with compiling background information on Harold "The Bear" Perreault. Researching another possible suspect in Owen's murder was necessary, but it also provided Brock with a temporary escape from thinking about how he would need to approach Albert about Dr. Phinney's alibi at some point. A face-to-face meeting with the senior Justice wasn't something Brock wanted to deal with, but it wasn't something he could palm off on Chloe. It had to be done, and he had to be the one to do it.

Brock found the MSP database packed with information about Perreault, likewise his Triple I history. Triple I is the moniker used by law enforcement for the Interstate Identification Index, an electronic database maintained by the Federal Bureau of Investigation. The Bear had an extensive Triple I history, dating back to 2010, that included all the greatest hits: aggravated assault, weapons violations, strong arm robbery, armed robbery, and trafficking in scheduled drugs. And Deputy Hanscomb was right, Perreault had been part of a Maine-based outlaw motorcycle gang called The Enforcers. The club was based out of the town of Harrison in the southwestern part of the state. Ironically, at least according to what Brock found in several old reports, Perreault had been one of the gang's enforcers at least until he'd had a falling-out with the club's president and founder, a guy named Hap Bayard. Perreault departed from the group shortly after Bayard went missing. According to reports from two different state police investigators, Perreault was considered a prime suspect in Bayard's disappearance, but beyond simple suspicion, nothing solid was ever developed against Perreault, and the case had gone cold. Nobody inside the gang was talking, and truth be told the state detectives had other more pressing cases to work than that of a missing outlaw biker. Brock didn't need it spelled out for him; he could read between the lines easily enough. The truth was no one really cared. The Enforcers moved on, electing a new president, and Perreault relocated to northeastern Maine where—assuming the rest of Hanscomb's information was solid—he had gone into business for himself. The pharmaceutical business.

"I think it's ready," Chloe said, pulling Brock from his research rabbit hole.

"Let's take a look."

Brock went through every page of the document, looking for missing facts or inconsistencies, but there weren't any. Even the standard boilerplate legalese used by all Maine law enforcement investigators was correct. While Chloe might have wanted to take the easy route, this clearly wasn't her first search warrant. She was good at it.

"Nice work," Brock said. "Let's attach copies of some of the supporting documents and go find us a judge."

The Hancock County Courthouse was situated at 50 State Street in Ellsworth, the same building where the sheriff's office was housed. Perched high atop a grassy knoll, the tall brick-and-granite columned building seemed to command an elevated importance. A massive two-tiered flight of granite steps led to an imposing three-story façade. Surrounded by manicured hedges and mature deciduous trees, the leaves of which were still more than a month away from making an appearance, the courthouse was topped by Old Glory flapping in the breeze. Brock wondered if shoehorning the sheriff's department into the basement of the building like last year's holiday ornaments had been someone's idea of making a statement or something else entirely. As if the enforcement branch of the legal system commanded less respect than the hallowed halls of Lady Justice herself.

After fortuitously locating a vacant two-hour parking space on State Street directly across from the courthouse, Brock and Chloe ascended the stone steps and entered the building.

Justice Alexander Weymouth agreed to squeeze the detectives in during his lunch hour. Brock and Chloe sat across from him in leather club chairs while the judge alternated between bites of his turkey sandwich and studying Chloe's affidavit. Weymouth's wire-rimmed bifocal readers only added to his professorial appearance. A tall, balding man, he wore a close-cropped beard of white, a white buttoned-down shirt and tie, and a tweed vest.

Brock noticed the black robe hanging off a nearby wall peg and tried to picture Weymouth wearing it. Having known several southern Maine judges personally, it had always amazed him how much one single garment could alter a person's outward appearance, transforming them from a mere mortal attorney to an esteemed symbol of jurisprudence. Although Brock had also crossed paths with several ethically challenged attorneys whom a black robe would not have benefited in the least.

"And you say this is your first search warrant application?" Weymouth said as he peered over his glasses at Chloe.

"Yes and no, Your Honor. It isn't my first, but it is my first connected to a homicide investigation."

Chloe looked to Brock for guidance as Weymouth's eyes returned to the document. Brock gave her a slight affirming nod.

Weymouth picked up an expensive-looking ink pen and began scribbling his name across the pages. "I'm impressed by your thoroughness, Detective Wright. If this is any indication of your investigative abilities, I'm glad you're not chasing after me."

"Thank you, sir," Chloe said.

Weymouth's gaze shifted to Brock. "I must say, this is a most unusual method of murdering someone. I've been on the bench for a long time, and it's definitely a first for me. I'll be waiting to see how this case shakes out. Best of luck to you both."

"Thank you, Your Honor," they said in unison.

19

"Is it always so damned nerve-wracking?" Chloe said as they climbed back inside Brock's unmarked.

"No," Brock said.

"Thank God."

"Sometimes it's worse," Brock said, delivering a sideways grin.

As Brock pulled away from the curb, Chloe's cell buzzed with an incoming call. She placed the phone in the dash cradle and answered the call using the speaker option.

"Detective Wright."

"Good afternoon, Detective. Tommy Hanscomb here. Thought you'd want to know I found the guy who skedaddled on you yesterday."

"Franklin Desmond?" Chloe said.

"The one and only," Hanscomb said.

"How did you know we were looking for him?" Brock said.

"I mentioned it," Chloe said.

"Where is he?" Brock said, biting his tongue.

"At this very moment, he's in Blue Hill, seated in the back of my patrol vehicle wearing charm bracelets."

"We don't have any reason to hold him," Brock said, glaring at Chloe. "We only wanted to talk to him about Lee Owen."

"Oh, the jewelry isn't for you, Detective," Hanscomb said. "I spotted him operating his ATV right down the center of the road. And when I went to stop him, he tried to elude me. It ended badly. Patch of ice, phone pole, you get the idea. Anyway, I have a nice stack of charges you might be able to leverage to get Frankie to be a bit more—loquacious."

"Thanks, Tommy," Chloe said. "Be there as quick as we can."

"En route from Ellsworth," Brock said.

Brock and Chloe stood on the shoulder of Hinckley Ridge Road surveying the twisted ball of metal and broken plastic that had previously been Frankie Desmond's all-terrain vehicle.

"Does he need medical treatment?" Brock said as he glanced at Desmond through the rear window of the deputy's cruiser.

"He refused it," Hanscomb said. "He'll be fine. Nothing but a few bumps and scrapes."

"He was lucky to walk away from that," Chloe said.

"Some folks are just too stupid to kill," Hanscomb said.

"Or lucky," Brock said.

"Anyway, he's all yours if you want him," Hanscomb said. "I told him he either cooperates with you guys or I'll stack up the charges, starting with eluding a police officer, criminal speed, driving to endanger, operating an unregistered motor vehicle on a public way, and pretty much anything else I can think of."

They removed Hanscomb's cuffs and relocated Desmond to the front passenger seat of Brock's unmarked.

"So, am I being charged or not?" Desmond said as he rubbed his wrists.

"That's up to you," Brock said. "Just so you understand you're no longer in custody. Not with us, and not with Deputy Hanscomb."

"You mean I'm free to go?" Desmond said as he reached for the door handle.

"If that's what you want," Chloe said from the back seat. "It is too bad, though."

Desmond loosened his grip on the door handle. "What's too bad?"

"You're going to have a pile of driving charges against you," Brock said. "Probably looking at jail time and the loss of your license for a while too."

"Whatever. Those are just misdemeanors."

"I could have sworn the deputy mentioned something about eluding an officer, didn't he, Detective Wright?"

"I believe he did," Chloe said.

"Granted, it's been a while since I worked traffic enforcement, but eluding a police officer is still a felony, isn't it?"

"It certainly is. Class C," Chloe said.

"What's that, like a year, maximum?" Desmond said. "I'll be out in a couple of months. Big deal."

"Sorry to be the one to break it to you, Evil Knievel, but Class C crimes in Maine come with a five-year max," Brock said.

"Unless they consider the injuries," Chloe said.

"What injuries?" Desmond said. "I didn't hurt anybody."

"Yours," Brock said. "Look at you. You're all banged up. Which reminds me, we should get some pictures of your injuries. Did Deputy Hanscomb call an ambulance for you?"

"Yeah. But I told those rescue guys I didn't need to be transported anywhere. It's nothing but a couple of scrapes."

"I see where you're going with this, Detective Justice," Chloe said. "I'm sure the EMTs filed paperwork."

"I'm sure they did," Brock said. "It's routine."

"What does that mean?" Desmond said. "What the hell are you guys trying to do to me?"

"Should I tell him?" Chloe said.

"Might as well," Brock said.

"Tell me what?"

"The problem is, Frankie, if someone gets hurt while you're eluding a police officer, the penalty goes up. The injuries are what they consider an aggravating factor in the crime."

"Goes up to what?"

"Class B," Brock said.

"And that's a ten-year maximum, Frankie," Chloe said.

"But I'm the only one who got hurt," Desmond protested.

"I'm not sure it matters in the eyes of the law," Brock said.

"That isn't fair."

"Life isn't fair, Frankie," Chloe said.

"Your call," Brock said. "If you don't want to talk with us, don't. You're free to go."

Brock watched as Desmond's hand dropped away from the door handle and his head slumped forward.

"What do you want to know?" Desmond said.

20

As they drove Desmond to the Troop J barracks in Ellsworth, it became obvious to Brock that they would save a lot of time working out of Troop J rather than wasting time with the back-and-forth commute into Bangor.

Troop J's interview room was equipped for double duty. At one end of the room stood a laminated wooden table with four chairs. On the other was a long built-in counter equipped with an intoxilyzer and a fingerprinting station for processing OUIs. The large wall-mounted whiteboard would merely require repopulation of the murder board information they'd already started at Troop E.

Before they undertook further questioning, Brock decided to err on the side of caution by reading Desmond the Miranda warning. Though he was still free to go if he chose, Brock and Chloe had driven him to the barracks, which meant he was without means of transportation.

"What gives?" Desmond said. "Why are you reading me my rights? Thought I wasn't in custody?"

"You're not, technically," Chloe said. "But you know how devious those lawyers can be."

"You're telling me," Desmond said.

Brock read the warning verbatim from a printed sheet, careful to obtain a verbal acknowledgment of understanding from Desmond after each section had been completed.

"Yeah, yeah, I got it," Desmond said. "Give me a pen already, and I'll sign it. I probably know this stuff better than you guys, anyway."

"I wouldn't be a bit surprised, Frankie," Brock said.

"Do you believe him?" Chloe said after they deposited Desmond at his mobile home in Surry, leaving him in the capable hands of his angry-looking wife.

"I'm inclined to," Brock said. "Mostly because he has nothing to gain by telling us what he did. In fact, if Perreault is as big and bad as everybody says, Desmond just put himself in The Bear's crosshairs."

"Interesting that he told the same story as Deputy Hanscomb about Owen shorting a load of fentanyl."

Brock had the very same thought.

"Have you had a chance to read the file on Perreault?" Brock said.

"I did. Strange how the club president, Hap Bayard, went missing just prior to Perreault leaving The Enforcers."

"Exactly what caught my eye," Brock said. "That and the fact they never found a trace of him."

"You're wondering if Perreault did it again, only this time with Lee Owen?"

Brock nodded. "I am. And if you and your warden buddies hadn't chosen Second Pond for a training dive, we might never have found Owen either."

As he turned out of Desmond's driveway and headed back toward Ellsworth, Brock wondered which of York County's many lakes Hap Bayard might be occupying at present.

"Where to?" Chloe said.

Brock had been thinking about the next steps all day. One of those involved his father, Albert. They needed to check with him regarding Dr. Phinney's alibi for the night the snowmobile was stolen, but Brock knew too well what kind of shitstorm would accompany that interview. And he had no intention of dragging Chloe into that part of his life.

After dropping Chloe off at her car, Brock toyed with the idea of phoning Albert rather than just showing up at the camp unannounced, but with his thumb hovering over the call button, he relented and pocketed the cell. It had been Albert's decision to cut Brock out of his life after the trial, not the other way around. Hell, the truth of the matter was they hadn't been all that close when Brock's mother, Jolene, was still alive.

Cut from two different sets of cloth, Albert and Brock couldn't have been more dissimilar if they tried. Albert had been raised as an outdoorsman. Big and burly, fearless, a storyteller, a fighter, a hunter, a charmer, and a drunk. He was the kind of man other men wanted to be around. Smaller men who hoped some of Albert's charisma might rub off on them. As if his mere presence might be the catalyst for changing their fortunes.

Albert had always hoped one of his sons, either Brock or Brock's older brother, Jacob, might follow in his footsteps and join the US Marines or the ranks of the Maine State Police. He had dragged both boys along on numerous hunting and fishing trips with his cop buddies, hoping the experiences might bond them more closely to the law enforcement life. Of the two brothers, Jake had always been the fearless one, the adventurer, the protector, very much like Albert. While Brock, having never warmed up to that life, had chosen a more scholarly path for himself. He saw himself more as a teacher, or perhaps even a novelist, having always loved reading. Looking back now, Brock supposed his love of storytelling might be the only thing he truly shared with the old man.

Albert, realizing that only Jake shared his passion for adventure, had focused all his efforts on grooming his oldest boy to enter the field of law enforcement. He was over the moon the day Jake announced to the family that he had enlisted in the Marines and would be applying to the Maine State Police after completing his service. The pride Albert felt for his oldest son was etched upon his face as clearly as his disappointment in Brock. But like all best-laid plans, Albert's had come to an abrupt halt two years later.

Jake had been serving his second overseas tour in Afghanistan when he and two other members of his unit were killed in an explosion after driving their Humvee over a roadside IED. Despite their differences, Brock and Jake had always been close, and the news of his brother's death left a giant hole in Brock's heart, one that would never completely heal. But the news had destroyed Albert, turning him into a different person. He began drinking heavily and was quick to anger, his temper flaring seemingly at nothing. It was as if Albert's entire world blew up right along with his eldest son.

As Brock entered college, his relationship with his father devolved even further.

It had been Jolene who kept the two men from killing each other. She was the common bond that kept the family cohesive. And it was Jolene who, on her deathbed, made Brock promise to at least give law enforcement a try.

"It would mean so much to your father, Brock," she said. "And to me."

Her last words pierced his heart like a dagger. Like he'd been some great disappointment not to just Albert but to both of his parents.

Jolene had died the following day, taking with her any hope of redemption. And any chance Brock's life would continue along the path he'd been taking. Jolene's final words had changed his destiny from one of his own making to that of one of his parents. Six months later, Brock reported to the Maine Criminal Justice Academy, what his friends jokingly referred to as the "Justice" Academy, to begin his new life as a Maine State Trooper.

Brock knew the way to the camp so well he could have extinguished the headlights and driven the road in total darkness. He had spent so much time here as a boy. Every summer as soon as school ended, he and Jake would be whisked away to Down East Maine. Camp was the place where his father was never more at home and where Brock had never truly felt he belonged.

As Brock rounded the final turn, the Ford's headlights swept over the dooryard, illuminating Albert's F-250 and the camp porch beyond. Light spilled from the windows of the camp, and Brock caught the pleasant scent of wood burning in the stove. Had he been an outsider simply stumbling onto the place, the scene might seem warm and inviting. But for Brock, who knew better, it was anything but.

21

Albert Justice stood silhouetted in the open doorway of the camp, holding a rifle loosely in one hand.

"Dad," Brock said as he stood on the porch, waiting to see which way things were about to go.

"You're lucky I didn't shoot you, BJ," Albert said, the slur in his words only mildly detectable. "Shoulda called first."

"I thought about it."

"Well, I guess you'd better come inside. Before you let in a shit ton of these damn black flies."

As Brock stepped into the cabin, a tidal wave of memories came flooding back. Despite all the improvements Albert had made, the smell of the place hadn't changed one bit since he was a child. It was a heady, outdoorsy mixture of pine, tobacco, woodsmoke, and gun oil.

"Get you something to drink?" Albert said as he leaned the rifle against the wall beside the woodstove.

Brock's eyes settled on the bottle of whiskey on the floor beside his father's chair and the half-full glass on the arm. "Nah, I'm good, thanks. Working, actually."

Albert's steel-blue eyes rose to meet his. "And here I thought this was just a father-son social call."

Brock said nothing but held the old man's gaze.

"Go on, then," Albert said, gesturing toward the couch. "You might as well sit."

Brock watched as Albert settled into the chair then took a sip of the amber-colored liquid. Neat, as always. Brock hated how disarmed he felt sitting here. He had conducted thousands of interviews since becoming a trooper, locked up some seriously despicable creatures and faced death square in the eye, but somehow returning home was always different. Harder. Just as he'd known it would be. Coming home stripped away the façade of adulthood and left him feeling vulnerable. And it was precisely why he hadn't brought Chloe along.

"Saw you at the trial," Brock said, not knowing what else to say.

"Felt like I needed to be there," Albert said.

Brock waited to see if the old man would say more. Perhaps something along the lines of how proud he was of his son for standing up and doing the right thing, but he didn't.

"Thanks for coming," Brock said before he could stop himself, regretting it instantly.

Albert said nothing.

"I did what I had to do, Dad," Brock said, his voice betraying him as it cracked slightly. "What I thought was right."

Albert took another sip, his eyes drifting back to the stove, where the flames danced behind the glass door.

"I caught a murder case," Brock said. "Right here in Blue Hill."

"Lee Owen," Albert said. "A local shit bird they called Spike."

"You heard about that?"

"I hear about everything."

"Did you know him?"

"Knew of him. He worked down at the marina. But no, I didn't know him personally."

"Did you hear what happened to him?"

Albert's gaze returned to Brock. His eyes were cold and distant. "Heard he anchored himself to the bottom of Second Pond. Always good fishing in that pond."

"If you heard all that, you must also know what he was anchored to."

Albert nodded. "The sled he stole from Keith Phinney. Least, that's how I heard it."

"Mind if I ask where you heard that?"

"Saw it in the local paper, same as everyone else. Why? Were you hoping I would give up one of my friends?"

Brock ignored the comment, refusing to rise to the bait.

"Dr. Phinney's snowmobile was stolen the night of January 27," Brock said. "My understanding is his wife was out of town that night and Keith played in an all-night poker game. A game you were present for."

"Is that your understanding?" Albert said.

"That's what I was told. I was hoping you could either confirm or deny it for me."

"Well, I'd have to consult my social calendar to be sure, but that sounds about right. There's a group of us who meet fairly regular for poker, and I remember hearing someone broke into Keith's house one of those nights."

"On January 27th?"

"If you say so. Like I said, I don't keep records."

"And this group of yours? Always the same people?"

"Not always, but the core group I expect you know already. Me, Keith, Gene Parlin, Tommy Hanscomb, along with a few others."

"Parlin tells me you won big on the night in question," Brock said.

Albert grinned but said nothing.

Brock pressed on. "You know a guy named Perreault? Outlaw biker."

"The Bear? Everyone knows The Bear. And as far as I know, he's currently unaffiliated. That what you came to ask me about? My poker winnings? And if I'm friendly with any unaffiliated outlaw motorcyclists?"

Brock hated how easily Albert could manipulate him. It was as if the gun, the badge, and his years of police work simply evaporated in his father's presence, transforming him into the scared, intimidated kid from his youth. All of Brock's authority withered under Albert's Legendary Trooper Award–winning stare.

"I'll tell you two things before you go," Albert said. "First, no, I didn't have anything to do with killing Spike Owen. If I had, you can bet your boots you and your rookie partner, Chloe Wright, wouldn't have found him so easily."

Brock could feel the temperature in the room rising, and he knew it wasn't the heat emanating from the stove.

"And the second?" Brock said.

"I was playing poker with those guys all night at Parlin's place. The next morning, after breakfast, I took home my winnings. You might wonder how I remember that night in particular. I remember it because I made just a hair over twenty-five hundred dollars."

Brock said nothing as the two men stared at each other.

Albert pushed himself up and out of the chair, grabbed the empty glass, then headed for the kitchen. "You can show yourself out."

22

Brock tossed and turned in bed for hours, replaying the visit with Albert in his mind like one does after a crucial meeting, pointlessly dissecting each and every word spoken as if there were some nuanced meanings hidden within. But Brock knew most of that was probably in his head. The only important thing to come out of the visit, at least as far as the case was concerned, was that Albert had backed Phinney's alibi for the night his shed had been burglarized and his sled stolen. Meaning if Lee Owen had met his demise on the night of January 27th, which seemed more than likely, Keith Phinney likely had nothing to do with it. An all-night card game in the company of one legendary former lawman and two active ones made for one bulletproof alibi. Perhaps less important, at least as far as the Owen homicide was concerned, but lying just beneath the surface of Brock's conversation with the senior Justice, was Albert's disapproval of Brock's decision to testify against a fellow trooper.

Brock's visit to the former family retreat, now Albert's full-time residence, only reaffirmed that he and his father were nothing alike and never would be, not that he needed further proof. Albert had sprung from another time, another place, and another way of life, one so alien to Brock it might well have been on another planet. It was no wonder they were like strangers. In fact, the only thing that had ever bound the two men together in any meaningful way was Brock's mother, Jolene, and his brother, Jake.

He missed both of them terribly, but especially Jolene. At times like these, Brock was reminded just how strong his mother's presence had been. Jolene the peacemaker. Brock still experienced those self-pitying moments when he hated her for guilting him into becoming a police officer. Asking your son to change the trajectory of his young life from your deathbed seemed an almost unforgivable sin. But there were other times when he felt maybe she had possessed a deeper insight than he knew. Perhaps Jolene had seen something in him that he himself could not. Some innate need to help others that could only be sated by choosing the field of law enforcement. Where he would experience things he would never see as a teacher or writer. Maybe it was the same something Jolene had observed in Albert. God knew Brock had never grown close enough to his father to see it, whatever *it* was, but perhaps Jolene had.

He rolled his head to one side and stared at the digital clock seated atop one of many unpacked moving boxes scattered throughout the small apartment. The red numbers 3:20 glared back at him. It was too early to be thinking about anything so profound as family dynamics. He rolled onto his other side and punched the pillow. He closed his eyes and forced his mind to clear itself of all conscious thought. Slowly he drifted into a deep, dreamless slumber. The 5:30 alarm shattered that slumber to pieces.

Brock had agreed to meet Chloe in Bangor at 7:00 a.m. at a diner called Judy's, not far from the barracks. As he drove along Main Street past a giant thirty-foot statue of a plaid-shirted Paul Bunyan, directly across from the Hollywood Casino, Brock was once again reminded of his father. The famed fictional character stood strong, tightly gripping the handle of a peavey in one hand and slinging a double-bladed axe over his right shoulder with the other. Bunyan represented the rugged, larger-than-life outdoorsman. A mythical creature as impossible to compete with as Albert Justice, the statue symbolized everything that was wrong between Brock and his father. Brock, a mere mortal, versus the legend of Albert Justice. For Brock, Paul Bunyan was simply another bridge too far.

Judy's Restaurant, the eating establishment Chloe had chosen, was located at the corner of State and Essex Streets in an oddly shaped two-toned, two-story building. The white-over-beige structure's flat roof and wraparound marquee-style sign, complete with obligatory red-and-white Coca-Cola squares, effectively camouflaged the restaurant contained within, giving it more of a corner tavern or convenience store vibe.

Brock scoured the nearby streets until he located a vacant parking space a block and a half away on Essex. Following a brisk walk, he stepped inside the crowded eatery and found Chloe seated on a stool at the bar. She gave him a wave as he approached.

"I took the liberty of ordering your morning jolt," Chloe said as she slid the ceramic mug in front of him.

"Thanks," Brock said as he draped his overcoat across the stool and sat down.

"How did it go last night?" Chloe said after Brock had gotten settled. "Did you speak with Albert?"

Brock nodded as he splashed a bit of creamer into his coffee. "I did. And he backed the alibi Parlin provided for Dr. Phinney."

"Then Phinney's in the clear."

"So it would seem," Brock said.

Brock didn't care for Phinney, but not liking someone and liking them for a murder were two entirely different things. Handcuffing a man to a snowmobile before sending him to the murky depths of a frozen pond to die was sadistic. Not behavior one might associate with someone who had taken the Hippocratic Oath. On the other hand, Harold Perreault, the outlaw biker and suspected drug smuggler, was precisely that kind of person. Vengeful, ruthless, cruel, and driven to the point where those who knew him had nicknamed him The Bear. But even more important than his personality traits, Perreault had a motive, a business to run, and reputation to uphold. The Bear couldn't allow someone like Lee Owen to steal his product and go unpunished.

"What's our next step, then?" Chloe said.

"I want to focus on the SIM card from Owen's cell. Mike Fuente said he'd download all the information today."

"You think there'll be a text or phone number on there that will help us?"

"Maybe. But I'd be surprised. Since we're dealing with people smart enough to use burner phones, at best we might find a phone number or two, or a couple of coded texts."

"Why the urgency on the phone, then?"

"Because Owen's real phone, even broken, has a provider account associated with it. And all the records should still be retrievable from the phone company."

"Let me guess, you want me to get a subpoena for those records."

"That's exactly what I want. But more specifically, I want Owen's last known locations. What towers he was pinging off during the overnight of January 27th into the 28th."

"How will that help us? We already know he stole the snowmobile from Dr. Phinney's house."

"True, but we still don't know how he got there. And we still don't know where his vehicle is."

"Which reminds me, Wheels got back to me with the information from BMV."

"Wheels?"

"Art Wheeler. You met him yesterday."

"Sorry. I'd forgotten his nickname. Any luck?"

"Yup. Lee Owen only had one vehicle registered to him. A green 2015 Chevy Silverado."

"Makes sense if he was plowing for the Phinneys," Brock said as he retrieved his notebook and recorded the plate number and description of the pickup. "I think the cell provider information might just lead us to where Owen left the truck. And just maybe who he met with before he was murdered."

"In other words, The Bear."

"Never make those kinds of assumptions," Brock said, even as he realized he'd been doing the same thing. "We take it one step at a time and just see where the case takes us. Let the evidence point toward the truth. Never try to make the facts fit a theory. That type of thinking only leads to two possible outcomes."

"Which are?"

"We end up focusing on the wrong person."

"Bad," Chloe said.

"Very," Brock said. "Google 'wrongful conviction.'"

"And the other?"

"We end up at a dead end. Look up 'cold case.'"

Chloe nodded. "Got it."

Their waitress appeared on the other side of the counter. "Sorry about the wait. You folks ready to order?"

After a large breakfast of eggs, slab bacon, and home fries, they drove directly to the Troop E barracks; Chloe to contact Mike Fuente and start work on the subpoena to Owen's cellular provider, and Brock to bring Cumberland up to speed.

"I haven't got but a second," Cumberland said as she slid into her coat and grabbed her bag. "I'm late for a command meeting in Augusta. Walk with."

As Brock trailed Cumberland out of the bureau, he caught a side-of-the-eye glance from Chloe and a knowing smirk from Zimmerman. Whether she'd intended to embarrass him or not, the lieutenant had managed to make Brock look like her lap dog, and he didn't like it.

"So," Cumberland said as they stepped outside the barracks. "How is Chloe working out?"

"She's got a lot to learn, but she's catching on quickly," Brock said.

"Any problems? Between the two of you, I mean."

"Nothing we can't work through."

"Good. I'm glad to hear it. And the case? Where are we with solving that?"

"We're making good progress, I think. We'll get a look at the victim's cell phone records today."

"Great," Cumberland said as she reached for the door to her SUV and opened it. "I see you met Zimmerman and Wheeler."

"Yesterday," Brock said.

"Zimmerman is an acquired taste, but he works hard."

"And Wheeler?" Brock said.

"You know his story?"

"Only what I read."

"He's an IT pit bull. He was one hell of a street cop before the accident left him paralyzed. That same street cop's heart still beats inside him, it's just that it now resides in a broken man. Honestly, if he didn't have this job to come to every day, I think he might have given up and ended it years ago. Be good to him. And put his skills to good use."

"Understood," Brock said.

"Good."

"There is one little snafu I should probably mention."

Cumberland, who had been preparing to close the door, stopped. "What?"

"Albert, my father, lives in Blue Hill."

"Yes, I know. Figured the two of you would probably cross paths."

"It's more than that, I'm afraid. He's actually part of this case."

"Part of? Don't tell me he's a suspect."

"No, nothing like that."

"Then what?"

"He has provided an alibi for one of our original suspects. The owner of the stolen snowmobile. A doctor named Keith Phinney."

"Please tell me Albert isn't Phinney's only alibi."

Brock shook his head. "He isn't. But you asked to be kept in the loop. I just wanted you to know about the conflict."

Cumberland paused a moment as if thinking it through. "Unless something changes, I don't have any issue with you continuing as primary on this case. Anything else, Detective?"

"That about does it."

"Good. Then I'll talk with you later."

Cumberland shut the door and drove away, leaving Brock standing in the parking lot wondering why he'd even bothered to mention Albert's involvement.

"How'd it go with the Dreadful One?" Zimmerman said as Brock returned to the detective bureau.

"You'd better be careful throwing that nickname around," Wheeler cautioned.

"Yeah," Office Assistant Andrew Webber said. "The last trooper she caught calling her Penny Dreadful still hasn't been found."

23

Brock made the decision to split up for the remainder of the day, allowing them to check off more items on their ever-growing to-do list. He left Chloe to her own devices in Bangor while he drove south, hoping to salvage whatever remained of his reputation within the state police faction of the Maine Drug Enforcement Agency.

Detective Corey Hincks had worked alongside Brock for several years following Brock's first patrol assignment in York County as part of Troop A. The two men had covered the southwestern part of the state west of the Maine Turnpike to the New Hampshire border. During that time, they had bailed each other out of numerous dangerous situations, several of which were armed standoffs. Brock figured if there was any goodwill left within the state police rank and file, Corey would be his best bet.

Brock headed toward Augusta after firing off a text message to Corey asking if he was available to meet. The response came several minutes later.

10:30 @Camp Chamberlain

Brock wasn't surprised. Corey had been in the National Guard since before they'd first met. His long-time friend currently held the rank of captain.

"Hey, brother," Corey said as their handshake morphed into an awkward embrace. "How's The County?"

Corey was of course referring to the tongue-in-cheek term of endearment locals normally associated with the northern reaches of the Pine Tree State. A straight line drawn from Montreal to Halifax on any map of North America would basically bisect the state of Maine into two equal halves. Brock's current assignment put him squarely in the half of Maine that intruded into Canada. Anyone native to the state knew exactly where The County was located.

"Not quite as slow as I had imagined," Brock said.

"Maybe not," Corey said. "But it's still a million miles from Troop A."

"True story," Brock said. "This a good time to talk? I figured you might be busy doing that soldiering stuff you do."

"Or that I might not want to talk to you at all," Corey said.

"Yeah, maybe that too."

"Relax, brother. I know it probably seems like everyone has been avoiding you since the trial."

"Because everyone has," Brock said, a bit more forcefully than he'd intended.

"Don't take it too personally. There will always be detractors, but most of us get how tough it was to do what you did. Hell, I respect the shit out of you for doing it. Not sure I could have done it."

"Thanks," Brock said.

"That distance thing is just a self-defense mechanism, and it isn't unique to police work. The military has its own code too, amigo. It really isn't personal, though it probably feels like it. If it helps, think of it more like you caught career COVID and your coworkers are afraid if they get too close, they might catch it."

Brock stared at Corey, waiting for the telltale smirk. Corey's mustache partially hid it, but it was there.

"You're so full of shit," Brock said, punching him in the shoulder.

"Yeah, but luckily my good looks make up for it. Come on. Let Captain Hincks show you around Camp Chamberlain. If you're good, I might just treat you to lunch, flatfoot."

Half an hour later, Brock and Corey were seated in the mess hall.

"What is this?" Brock said after taking a bite of the sandwich and returning it to his tray.

Corey shrugged. "Your guess is as good as mine. I find the food here tastes better if I don't think about it too much. Aren't you the guy who wanted to be a novelist? Make something up."

"My imagination has its limits."

"So, spill it. I know you didn't drive all this way just to hang out with Captain America."

"I did reach out for a reason," Brock said. "I know you're still tied to MDEA."

"For now, at least. You know how that crap goes, jealousy from the upper echelon at never pulling such a sweet assignment."

Brock nodded.

"So, it's a drug thing, then?" Corey said.

"Maybe. Caught a homicide in Blue Hill. Not sure about the drug angle yet."

"I read about it in the paper. Did someone really cuff the guy to a Polaris?"

"Arctic Cat, actually. But yeah, somebody did."

"Shit, brother, maybe The County won't be so bad after all."

"Why don't I believe that?" Brock said. "Anyway, I caught wind of an outlaw biker guy in the area named Perreault. You know the type."

"Indeed, I do. Got a couple of those on my radar currently. Can't say I know Perreault, though."

"Apparently, the guy is a former member of The Enforcers motorcycle club out of Harrison. Goes by the nickname 'The Bear.'"

"Perfect."

"The intel I got was that he's been moving fentanyl into Maine by way of the Canadian border. I don't suppose you can poke around and see if there's anything to it."

"I'll ask around. How does that tie into your murder? You like this Perreault guy for it?"

"Too early to say. But if what I'm hearing is true, my vic may have been working for The Bear."

"And got caught with his hand in the sugar bowl?"

"Something like that. I need to pay this Perreault guy a visit, but I've got nothing aside from the fact they knew each other. Anything you can find out would really help me."

"Leave it to me," Corey said.

"I appreciate it, brother."

"Hey, how about dessert?"

Satisfied with the warrant, Mike Fuente printed paper copies of all the cell phone provider records in addition to burning the results onto a computer disk. Everything was ready and waiting by the time Chloe arrived at the state crime lab in Augusta. Fuente set her up in an empty office, and Chloe got to work identifying known telephone numbers, dates, and times of calls and texts leading up to the time Lee Owen had gone missing. Next, she plotted out points on a printed map of the Blue Hill Peninsula, trying to trace his last known movements. The last four cellular tower pings on the night Lee Owen disappeared put him, or at least his phone, near his apartment in Blue Hill, Marlintini's Grill, and Dr. Phinney's house in Sargentville. The last recorded GPS tower ping occurred between Brooksville and Second Pond in Blue Hill at 2:13 a.m. on Sunday, January 28th.

Chloe sat back and rubbed her eyes. The dates lined up perfectly. Phinney reported the break-in late Sunday morning, January 28th, the same weekend Owen disappeared. So where was his truck? The pond? Chloe found it difficult to believe she and her fellow divers wouldn't have tripped over something as large as a full-sized pickup when they located the sled. Not to mention sinking his truck in the lake wouldn't make any sense. If someone wanted to get rid of evidence associated with the pickup, why hadn't they simply sunk the vehicle with Owen inside? Why go to all the trouble to steal Phinney's snowmobile? It didn't make sense. They were missing something.

Her cell chimed with an incoming message from Brock.

Where r u?

I'm doing your grunt secretarial work, she thought. *While you're out being a real homicide* dick. Chloe grinned as she envisioned sending that exact message to Brock.

She typed: *Crime lab. Got some good stuff from cell records.*

Great! I'm in Augusta too. Making progress. Meet up in B H later?

He's in Augusta? Chloe thought. Then why go to the trouble to split up? Again, she fought with the urge to type something that would only land her in hot water. She settled on the lamest possible response.

Sounds good.

24

Penny Cumberland gathered her belongings as the staff meeting finally adjourned. Aside from giving the state's rising stars a chance to roll out "Effective Policing with Fewer Resources," which in her opinion was just as lame as the title implied, she had no idea why they were required to drive to Augusta for these meetings. If the state police powers that be had wanted to waste an entire day for each of the state police commanders, they could just as easily conduct this clown show by Zoom. Perhaps it was to give the upper echelon an opportunity to see if their Class A uniforms still fit around their bloated egos. She wondered if every agency was as top-heavy as the Maine State Police.

She headed for the door, trading nods with Lt. Yvonne Crawford, the commander of Troop A and only other female lieutenant in the ranks. Penny liked the way Yvonne handled herself but didn't know her well enough yet to call her a friend. At this point, Crawford at least presented the possibility of an ally in the vast wasteland of the good old boys' club.

Penny had just started down the corridor when she heard her name called from the far end.

"Lieutenant Cumberland. Might you have a moment?"

She knew even before turning around that the voice belonged to none other than Ronald Morgan, one of the slimiest members of the command staff and likely the sole reason she had ended up banished to MCU North. Penny painted on her best smile and turned to face him.

"Of course, Major."

"I'll meet you in my office," Morgan said. "Say, five minutes?"

"Perfect."

She hated the way Morgan made her feel. His mere presence felt like a burning cigarette deep in her guts. Even when they had been equals on the hierarchal ladder, both holding the rank of lieutenant, he'd always acted as though he was superior to her in some way. Not even rising to the level of passive-aggressiveness in their interactions, Morgan was more subtle than that. He always managed to use just the right word to burrow as far under her skin as was humanly possible. Like a goddamned tick. To anyone observing, Morgan's behavior would probably go unnoticed, but to Penny, there was no bigger condescending asshole within the ranks of the MSP.

Additionally, Morgan had swooped in and taken her promotion, utilizing a healthy dose of brown-nosery and a chaser of outright sabotage. She couldn't prove it was Morgan, but someone sent an anonymous letter to the colonel's office just before the interviews for major were held, and she would stake her life on it having been him. There were only a handful of people who knew her secret.

Penny hit the washroom first as her bladder was nearly bursting with bad coffee.

Morgan's office was like some narcissistic shrine he'd constructed unto himself. If there was ever any doubt as to the high regard in which he held himself, the myriad of wall-mounted awards sealed the deal. Penny knew many high-ranking members of law enforcement displayed what she thought of as "walls of me," but Morgan took his self-aggrandizing to an entirely stratospheric level with not one but four walls. She wondered if he'd ever inquired about the possibility of using the back of the office door or maybe raising the height of the ceiling by a couple feet to gain additional wall space. As she surveyed the room, it became apparent that Morgan hadn't accomplished much of anything. Much of his shrine consisted of framed photographs of the major standing alongside celebrities and high-ranking politicians, people who had fought their way to the top of their professions. Morgan had earned his position on the backs of others.

"Sorry to keep you waiting, Lieutenant," Morgan said as he breezed into the room amid a cloud of aftershave.

Penny knew he wasn't the least bit sorry. Everything about the man was a power play, even down to his addressing her by her rank instead of her given name as he had for years when they had both been equals. It was just another of those subtle knife jabs in the ribs Morgan was so famous for.

"Not a problem, Major," she lied.

"So, how are things going up in The County?"

She struggled to maintain a pleasant expression while wondering if shooting Morgan where he sat might negatively impact her future chances for promotion.

"Never better," she said.

"I understand that the homicide in Blue Hill was a bit unusual. Handcuffed to a snowmobile, was he?"

"Definitely a first for me."

"And you assigned the case to a brand-new detective?" Morgan said with a slight frown.

"Her name is Chloe Wright, and she's working the case as a secondary to Brock Justice."

"Ah, yes, Detective Wright. And how close are we to an arrest?"

"It's early days," she said, immediately picking up on his sleight of hand. When Morgan second-guessed her decision about assigning the homicide to Justice and Wright, it was *you*, but as soon as there was a chance at shared credit for an arrest, the pronoun became *we*. Maybe there was some truth to the old saw about top cops being nothing more than politicians with shields.

"Speaking of Brock Justice," Morgan continued. "How is he working out? Any problems I should know about?"

She had wondered if Brock would be part of their discussion. Perhaps Brock was the real reason she was sitting here instead of driving back to Bangor. Another sleight of hand.

"No," she said. "He's been a model detective thus far."

Morgan placed his elbows atop the desk and leaned forward, tenting his fingers together as if he might be about to pray to the Heavenly Father. Having seen this well-rehearsed maneuver before, she knew he was about to proselytize about Brock solely for her benefit.

"The colonel and I have been discussing Brock as of late, and we are of similar mind about what we would like to see happen."

"And what might that be, sir?"

Morgan held her gaze a little longer than necessary. She assumed either he was attempting to make her uncomfortable or trying to gauge the level of sarcasm contained within her question.

"We'd like MCU North to be Brock's swan song from the Maine State Police. Do you understand, Lieutenant?"

"I'm afraid I don't, Major. Justice is a highly decorated trooper with an unassailable homicide clearance rate. Are you asking me to run him out of town?"

"Of course not," Morgan said, his face reddening at the accusation. "Look, no one thinks more highly of that young man than I, but you must understand how bad it looks to the rank and file for him to still be on the job as if nothing happened."

"Aside from Justice and Mathers going into that arrest like a couple of cowboys, I don't see the issue. Mathers stepped over the line, and Brock did what we taught him to do. What we pay him to do. He told the truth."

"Well, the jury didn't see it that way, and the truth of the matter is we lost a good trooper because of Brock."

"Whose truth?" Penny said before she could stop herself. "With all due respect, Major, there is a monumental difference between a jury not wanting to put a decorated police officer behind bars for putting down a violent felon, and Brock Justice telling the truth under oath. It seems to me we still have the *good* trooper."

"Let me put it another way, Penny," Morgan said, attempting the softer approach as if they were the best of friends. "We just think it would be best for all concerned if you could help Brock transition."

"To what?"

"Something outside of the MSP. In the private sector, perhaps."

Penny said nothing, though she felt the anger welling up inside her.

"This is something the colonel really wants to see resolved to the benefit of everyone involved. I'm sure his gratitude to the commander who could quietly accomplish this will not go unrewarded, if you understand my meaning."

She absolutely got his meaning, and it pissed her off to no end. Before walking into his office, she couldn't imagine having a lower opinion of Major Morgan. She had been wrong. He had just hit a new low.

Morgan made a show of checking his watch before he stood and came around the desk. The time he'd allotted for her ambush was apparently over.

"So, can I report back that we have an understanding?"

"We definitely understand each other, Major," she said as she rose from the chair.

"It's great to have you on the team again, Penny."

25

Brock stood outside the rear door to the medical examiner's building, waiting for someone to answer the delivery buzzer. At last, the steel door swung open, and the face of a young woman appeared. He recognized her as Dr. Isleborn's assistant from Lee Owen's autopsy.

"Detective Justice, isn't it?" she said with a sly smile. "Debra Skilling. It's good to see you again."

"I apologize for showing up unannounced," Brock said, trying hard not to trip over his words as he spoke. "I was in the area, and I thought I'd stop in and see if the tox results were back yet." He hoped the line didn't sound as phony as it felt. The truth was he'd been hoping to run into her again.

"Why don't you come in, Detective?" she said. "I'll check."

Brock followed her up to the administrative offices on the second floor.

"Got 'em right here," Skilling said as she passed him several sheets of paper from a plastic tray.

He flipped to the back page where the lab results were listed. The alcohol level was .07, identical to the preliminary number Dr. Isleborn had already shared with them. Below the alcohol level, a single word jumped out at him like it had been typed in neon. *Fentanyl.* The powerful opiate was also present in Owen's system. The same drug Deputy Hanscomb believed Owen might have been importing into the country on behalf of someone else. Maybe Perreault. Coincidence? Brock wasn't a big believer in coincidence. Experience had taught him wherever there was smoke, fire almost certainly followed.

"Helpful?" Skilling said.

"Very," Brock said. "I don't suppose Dr. Isleborn is around? I'd like to run something by her."

"I'll see if she's available."

"Thanks. Also, would it be possible for you to—?"

"Make you a copy of the report? Of course." Grinning, she snatched the pages from his hand and turned toward the hallway. "Be right back."

"Thanks," Brock said as he watched her walk away.

Back on the road, armed with the toxicology results and Isleborn's take on the manner in which Owen may have met his demise, Brock headed toward Blue Hill. It was time to pay a visit to Harold "The Bear" Perreault. The fentanyl connection was a sure sign, not that he needed one.

Brock's visit with Corey Hincks had set off a series of uncomfortable memories. Their discussion about what had happened following the shooting in York County moved one of those memories front and center in his mind.

Albert Justice was known for waxing poetic about the thin blue line for as long as Brock could remember. He talked about the importance of belonging to something greater than the self or the individual. Brock had never quite been able to embrace the concept. Not as a boy and not even after deciding to honor his dying mother's wish that he trod in his father's sizable footsteps.

The police academy had been about what he'd expected. A lot of boot camp bravado combined with the breaking down of the individuality possessed by every cadet, instilling in each of them the importance of teamwork. There was a lot of study and physical agility required as well, neither of which had presented even the slightest challenge for Brock. He excelled at both. He'd made friends easily during his time at the academy and afterward during his first assignment to Troop A. But despite these things, he'd still never bought into the cult-like thin blue line mentality so many cops espoused. He was proud of his chosen profession and of the job he had done thus far, but in his mind, it was still only a job. Nothing more, nothing less. Certainly not a calling as he'd heard some officers describe it. Brock figured that kind of depiction should be reserved for the priesthood. He wasn't sure what was behind his reluctance to accept the us-versus-them theology, but it had always bothered him to hear those words spoken by anyone on either side of the badge. If asked to explain his resistance, he would have been hard-pressed to define it, at least until the day his former field training officer appeared at his house following the shooting.

Trooper Elmer Moore had been Brock's field training officer, or FTO. Assigned immediately following Brock's graduation from the Maine Criminal Justice Academy, Moore had been Brock's teacher, mentor, and his biggest cheerleader. In fact, Brock had grown so close to the veteran trooper, he'd even asked Moore to be the best man at his wedding to Carmen, the former Mrs. Justice. To say Brock respected everything about the man would have been a gross understatement. Brock worshipped Moore.

Following the shooting in York County, before he was whisked away to the Southern Maine Health Care Hospital in Biddeford, Brock's weapon was seized. Already on duty, Moore had immediately responded to the scene, even riding with Brock in the back of the ambulance. Brock was in shock, having lost a great deal of blood from the facial wound he had suffered at the hands of Terry Kirke and from the stress of the incident. Brock couldn't remember exactly what Moore had said to him during that time, mostly because he was in and out of consciousness, but he remembered feeling confident that everything would be okay because Elmer told him so. Everything Elmer had ever said or done came with conviction. A conviction Brock believed in.

Moore visited Brock repeatedly following his release from the hospital, offering words of encouragement and doing his best to minimize the importance of the ongoing investigation by the state police and the Maine

Attorney General's Office. Moore told Brock to stay strong and to keep his thoughts to himself.

"You feel like you're ready to give a statement, talk to your attorney," Moore said. "You start feeling emotional about something, talk to me. Capisce?"

Brock nodded, stopping as soon as he felt the pull of the stitches in his cheek.

Moore had been a godsend, his presence a comfort. All Carmen had been able to do was cry and tell him he needed to get as far away from police work as possible. Brock knew she meant well, and that she was scared too, but her words only added to the stress he felt.

The day Brock confided in Moore about seeing Evan Mathers shoot Kirke's brother after the man had already surrendered his gun, everything changed.

Moore had come directly to the house with a bag full of tall boys. And not the low-alcohol-content stuff either. These were strictly high-test brews from Mast Landing. Brock knew they'd be talking some serious shit for sure. The visit was well timed, as Carmen was back at work and Brock had the house to himself. No meetings scheduled, no doctor visits, no attorneys, just two cops hanging out and talking shop.

Moore had arrived as his usual jovial self. His opening salvo consisted of nothing but war stories, most of which Brock had heard repeatedly. But as the two men skirted the real reason for the visit, Brock came to realize Moore's stories were leading to a point.

"You're a good man," Moore said. "An honest person and a cop's cop. And sometimes you wear your heart on your sleeve. Don't you listen to what anyone says, either. Wearing your heart where everyone can see it beating doesn't make you weak, it just means you give a damn."

Brock remembered nodding, not wanting to break Elmer's train of thought. He remembered hearing the stupid cuckoo clock sound off in the living room, the one Carmen's aunt had gifted them as a wedding present. He remembered his face itching something terrible. And the taste of the beer as it slid down his throat. And the sting of the alcohol as it burned the inside of his wounded cheek. But more than anything, he remembered the confusion he felt hearing the strange words spoken by his mentor.

"Now you need to listen closely to what I'm going to say. You've got a brilliant career ahead of you, son. You are a rising star in this business. I'm damn proud of you. And whether that stubborn SOB of a father tells you so or not, Albert is proud of you too. But you've got to tread lightly with this Evan thing. Your shooting of Terry Kirke is unassailable. He's a bad MF-er who shot at you first and got exactly what he deserved. You and Evan probably should have waited until you found some other backup before you approached the house, but that's just Monday morning quarterback BS. But what you saw, or believe you saw, regarding Evan killing Kirke's brother is another thing altogether. A game changer. Once you put what you just told me in writing, once those words are immortalized on some attorney general investigator's digital recorder, your life is gonna change in ways you can't possibly fathom."

Brock remembered shifting nervously in his chair while staring at the faded stain of red wine on the beige dining room tablecloth. He remained silent.

"There's a whole generation of young folks who think we're all evil. A racist horde in blue looking to stomp the rights of anyone stupid enough to cross our path. But you know better than that. I've seen you in action, Brock. The fact that you still give a damn makes you a better person than I'll ever be. But people will use this. They'll twist your words. They'll protest. People who would have crossed the street to avoid Terry and Darrell Kirke will demand justice for them. Before this thing is over, both you and Evan will be portrayed as murderous thugs who only went to that house to kill two men. The truth will get lost like it always does, replaced by the ever-popular anti-cop crap that's prevalent everywhere you look. People with political aspirations will make their careers off you. The image of the state police will be forever tarnished. You understand what I'm telling you?"

"But it's the truth," Brock said. "I know what I saw, Elmer."

"The truth doesn't matter much nowadays. Society won't see this as holding one man legally responsible for a bad shooting. They'll see this as an opportunity to bring down everything good you've ever done. Everything we've ever done. You'll be hung out to dry. And the few people who aren't looking to make their careers off you, the ones you believe in, they'll turn their backs on you. Your own brothers and sisters in blue won't trust you anymore."

Brock's eyes watered with emotion, and he wiped the tears away with the back of his hand. He was confused and angry. Feeling betrayed.

"There is no upside to this, and I'm sorry. I'm sorry you got put into this shitty position. But what I'm telling you is the truth. I'm speaking from experience, son. I don't want to see the same thing happen to you."

"What are you asking me to do, Elmer?" Brock said, the words catching in his throat as he said them. "Lie?"

"I've never asked you to lie, and I'm not about to start now."

"Then what?"

"All I'm asking is for you to think very carefully about what you intend to say. You've been under a great deal of stress. You're probably still suffering from the shock of everything that's happened. Getting shot, shooting a man, watching another man get killed. This isn't a job for sissies. But even the best of us get things wrong sometimes. See things differently from the way they really happened. Stress does some crazy stuff to a man's head. It is possible in that moment you got things twisted up. A couple of seconds either way and Evan shooting Darrell Kirke looks entirely different. Darrell would have shot and killed your partner in a heartbeat if given the chance. Shot you too, just like his brother did. The world is a better place with one less Kirke and the other behind bars. But the world can't afford to lose two good cops over this."

Brock had seen Elmer several times since but never to speak with. He knew the betrayal he'd felt following that visit would never dissipate. Brock would always wonder if Elmer had come that day of his own volition or if someone else had sent him. Everyone knew that Elmer and the state police colonel had gone through the academy together, served together, and been as close as brothers even after they were separated by promotion. Brock knew asking Elmer for the truth would be pointless. Elmer was loyal. If the colonel had sent him, Elmer would never give him up. Besides, what did it really matter? Whether Elmer had been speaking for himself or on behalf of another, his words to Brock couldn't be taken back.

The fact that Elmer's prognostication had been spot-on changed nothing. A betrayal was still a betrayal.

Brock's cell phone chimed with an incoming text message from Corey Hincks.

Perreault owns a service station right in BH. u might want 2 check it out

Brock typed a quick response. *Business name?*

Perreault's LOL

26

Armed with the cellular information Mike Fuente had provided, Chloe headed straight to Blue Hill. Her first stop was the in-town apartment of Lee Owen's ex-girlfriend, Melinda Hamilton. Hamilton hadn't been all that helpful during the last visit when Brock had been present. Chloe wondered if the scorned woman might reveal a bit more if she came alone.

"What are you doing back here, Detective?" Hamilton said as she opened the door.

"I came to return the list," Chloe said, handing her the pages.

"What list?"

"The itemized list of Lee's belongings."

"Told you I didn't care about any of this."

"I know. It's just something we have to do."

"That it?"

"Actually, no. I was hoping you might be able to answer a few more questions about Lee."

For a long moment, Hamilton simply stood there staring back at Chloe, hand on the door. Chloe was certain she was about to have the door slammed in her face, but surprisingly, Hamilton stepped back and allowed her to enter.

"Take your shoes off, if you don't mind. I just Swiffered the floor."

"Of course," Chloe said, figuring her compliance might at least buy a modicum of goodwill.

"And keep your voice down. The baby's napping."

Chloe followed her into the living room, then sat opposite Hamilton on the only chair not littered with toys or food.

Hamilton tossed the inventory sheets on the coffee table, then refilled her glass of Pepsi from the two-liter bottle sitting beside it. Her failure to offer Chloe anything to drink seemed a clear indicator of exactly how threadbare this détente was.

"Ask your questions," Hamilton said.

"Okay," Chloe said. "The last time I was here, you mentioned you suspected Lee of having an affair."

Hamilton laughed. "I never said any such thing, sweetheart. I said he was banging everything in town. Most of them married too. You know, it almost seems funny now. He wouldn't marry me, but nearly every other woman he slept with was."

"My apologies," Chloe said. "You said you might know who some of these women were."

"What? You think some swinging dick got his nose out of joint after finding out my Lee was shagging his wife and killed him?"

"We always look for motive in these types of cases, Melinda. I just thought if you knew who Lee was with, we might be able to talk with some of them."

"Well, I can give you one name for sure. Cammie Russo."

"And where would I find her?" Chloe said, quickly jotting the name in her notepad.

"Cammie ain't hard to find. She and her husband, Rick, own Marlintini's Grill."

"Is Cammie her real name?" Chloe said.

"No. I think it might be Camilla, like that woman who broke up Charles and Diana."

"Bowles?" Chloe said. "You mean the Queen of England?"

"Yeah, that's the one."

"Anyone else?" Chloe said.

"Ain't that enough?" Hamilton said with a sigh. She looked up at the ceiling as if trying to recall Lee's other conquests. "I told you he did odd jobs for Dr. Phinney, right? Well, Mrs. Phinney is a looker. I don't know for a fact he tried anything there, but maybe Lee was plowing more than just the driveway."

Chloe ignored the distasteful comment but couldn't disagree with Melinda's assessment of Emily Phinney. Still, she had a tough time believing Emily would risk everything to have an affair with the handyman. She scribbled Phinney's name down anyway.

"You said on the night Lee disappeared, he received a phone call from someone just before he went out. Any idea who might have called?"

"No, but whoever it was, that two-timing bastard didn't waste any time running out of here. I assumed maybe one of his conquests called to say she was on her own for the evening."

"Any idea who Lee's guy friends were?" Chloe said, making another quick note.

"Friends? I don't know if I'd call any of Lee's acquaintances actual friends. They were all good-for-nothing users. I know he palled around a lot with that Frankie guy from the boatyard."

"Desmond?"

"Yup. Another worthless loser."

"Anyone else?"

"The scary guy from the garage?"

"What scary guy?"

"The one they call The Bear. Biker type. Harry Perreault. His father owns a service station in town. I know Lee spent too much time down at the garage, and he sometimes drank with The Bear."

Chloe did her best not to react as she wrote Perreault's name in the notebook and underlined it. Twice.

"Anything else you can think of that might help me?" Chloe said. "Something important I haven't asked?"

"I can't think of anything at the moment, but if you leave me your number, I'll—"

Before Hamilton could finish her thought, the piercing sound of a baby wailing came through the electronic monitor sitting atop the end table.

"Goddammit," Hamilton said as she dragged herself up off the couch. "Guess my break is over. You need to go now, Detective."

"Thank you for—"

"Yeah, yeah, just leave your card on the table on your way out. If I think of anything else, I'll call ya."

Penny Cumberland was steaming mad by the time she jumped on I-95 toward Bangor. If the colonel and his minion thought they could use her to extract a problem tooth, they were sorely mistaken. Brock's public testimony might have been embarrassing for the state police, but it seemed to her Morgan should have been far more concerned about Trooper Mathers's behavior.

Brock Justice was a good cop. A detective who got results. And Penny wasn't about to sit on her hands and watch while the powers that be torpedoed another brilliant career. She knew from personal experience what it felt like to be shoved aside. The politics of policing was an ugly business, but two could play this game. Leverage was what she needed. The upper hand. And she could think of no better way to gain an advantage over this situation than to have Brock succeed on his first case in MCU North.

She had told him to lie low, that she didn't want him to work on any high-profile investigations. But now she was rethinking that line of attack. If this case stayed out of the public eye, it might well be his last. Brock's career would simply flicker out and die as quickly and efficiently as yesterday's lead story. No, what she needed was to turn up the heat on this case. The circumstances surrounding the murder were unique enough to warrant further coverage. She just needed to find someone who would help her rekindle the embers. And when it came to the Fourth Estate, she knew of only one person she trusted enough to get it done.

Penny reached into her bag and fished out her cell phone. She scanned through her contacts until she found the name she was after, then punched the cell phone number. She placed the phone in the dash-mounted charger and hit the speaker button. It had been a while since she'd spoken to her contact at the *Bangor Daily News*, and she wondered whether the reporter was still on the job.

"Newsroom, Amy Tavanian speaking."

"Amy, it's Penny Cumberland."

"Whoa, it's been a long time, Lieutenant. To what do I owe the honor?"

"Are you available to meet?"

"Oooh, important stuff, huh? Sure, I can meet you. Name it."

The large pole-mounted sign out front read "Perreault's Service Station." Brock drove past without stopping, hoping to get a look at the business in its natural state of operation. He knew if anything untoward were occurring at Perreault's, it would cease long before he stepped foot outside the SUV. Unmarked or not, the Ford Interceptor had never fooled anyone.

The station looked exactly like the scores of others Brock passed each day. The concrete block building was divided into two sections, one for the service counter and waiting area, the other consisting of two garage bays with lifts, one of which was in use, for repairs and general maintenance. It was what his father called a workingman's garage for people who didn't fancy the high-end screwing most dealerships were infamous for handing out.

The parking lot was also divided into sections. Two gas pumps, set beneath a small steel canopy, occupied the front section, while the right side of the property appeared to be designated for customer parking. Bordering the road, in the spaces along the sidewalk, sat a couple of late-model vehicles with "for sale" signs prominently displayed on their windshields.

As soon as the roadway was clear of traffic, Brock executed a three-point turn and drove back to the service station and into the lot. He parked perpendicular to the parked cars, making sure to only block the two that were for sale, and got out.

As Brock walked past the pumps, he was greeted by the staccato blast of a mechanic's air wrench from inside the service bays. A dark-haired man wearing navy coveralls stood at the edge of the nearest overhead door, smoking and wiping his greasy hands on a red shop towel while eyeballing Brock. Brock nodded and continued toward the customer entrance, opened the door, and stepped inside.

Standing behind the counter with a phone handset trapped between his shoulder and ear stood a slim, balding middle-aged man. He held up an index finger, indicating he'd be with Brock shortly. Brock wandered over to a small flat-screen television in the corner. The TV was tuned to one of the national twenty-four-hour news channels; the sound was muted. The chyron at the bottom of the screen was alerting people to an earthquake in Indonesia.

"Help you," the counterman said as he hung up the phone.

Brock approached the counter. "I hope so. I'm looking for the owner, Mr. Perreault."

"You found him," the man said, surprising Brock.

"Guess I was misinformed," Brock said. "I was told Harold Perreault owned the place."

"That's me. Harry Jr. is my son, but he ain't here. Can I help you?"

"I don't suppose you know when Junior's due back?"

"I might, but why would I share that information with someone I don't even know?"

Brock displayed his credentials and watched as the man's expression shifted from curiosity to one of disdain.

"Figured you were probably a cop," Perreault said. "Didn't peg you for a statie, though, Detective Justice."

"So, any idea when he'll be back?" Brock repeated.

"Not until later tonight. He's making an out-of-state wrecker run for a couple of cars I bought at auction. If you leave me a card, I'll be sure to have him contact you."

Brock scribbled his cell number on the back of his business card and handed it to the senior Perreault.

"Can I ask what this is about?" Perreault said as he studied the card.

"Thanks for your time. I'll let your son know what it's about when he calls."

27

Chloe departed from Hamilton's apartment and drove straight to Marlintini's Grill. Hamilton might not know where Lee had gone after receiving the phone call, but the cell tower information clearly pointed to Marlintini's as one of the last places Owen had gone the night he disappeared. As she pulled into the lot, her cell chimed with an incoming text from Brock.

U back in Blue Hill yet?

"Yeah, working on some real homicide stuff, no thanks to you, *partner*," Chloe said aloud before typing out a reply.

Just pulled into Marlintini's

Meet u there

"Can't wait," Chloe said with an eye roll.

Not wanting to give the appearance she was waiting for Brock's next instructions, because she wasn't, Chloe locked the unmarked and headed inside to find Camilla Russo.

Brock spotted Chloe's SUV as soon as he pulled into the lot. He parked beside it mildly pissed to find she had already gone inside without him.

Every time he felt like they were beginning to show signs of moving forward, Chloe did something unexpected.

Brock heard a live band playing as soon as he exited his vehicle but had no real sense of how loud they were until he stepped through Marlintini's front door. His eyes did a quick scan of the tables and booths, but he didn't see Chloe sitting anywhere. He strolled around the bar, thinking perhaps she commandeered a pair of stools, but she wasn't there either.

"Brock," Chloe hollered from behind him.

He turned and held his palms up in a "what gives" gesture.

"Come on," she said.

He followed her past the kitchen doors toward the back of the tavern, still unsure what she was up to.

"Chloe, what are we do—"

She stopped at the door marked "Office," knocked once, then opened the door and entered. Brock followed.

"Cammie, I'd like to introduce you to Detective Brock Justice. This is Cammie Russo. She owns this business along with her husband, Rick."

"Nice to meet you," Brock said to the woman seated behind the desk.

"Likewise," Cammie said before her attention returned to the computer monitor.

Brock lowered his voice and leaned close to Chloe. "What are we doing here?"

"Recovering the surveillance video from the month of January," Chloe said at full volume.

"Why?"

"Almost done," Cammie said.

"I'll fill you in when we leave," Chloe said dismissively.

Brock opened his mouth to fire back but thought better of it, especially with Cammie present.

"There you go," Cammie said as she handed Chloe a thumb drive. "It's formatted to play on just about any computer you guys might have."

"I can't thank you enough," Chloe said.

Brock and Chloe returned to the dining room and grabbed an empty booth as far from the small stage as they could get.

"Now would you mind telling me what you're up to?" Brock said.

"As soon as I order," Chloe said, smiling at the waitress approaching their booth.

They ordered soft drinks and the house burger plate special.

"Well," Brock said with his arms crossed. "You mind telling me what you're doing freelancing my case?"

"Oh, is that what I'm doing, Mr. High and Mighty? Freelancing *your* case? See, because I was under the distinct impression I was the second detective on this homicide, not some gopher who writes warrants and analyzes printouts. You could get anyone to do what you've got me doing."

Brock opened his mouth to respond, but Chloe cut him off before he could.

"And another thing, why the hell did we separate today if you were just going to drive down to Augusta anyway? Are you trying to dump me? Because I mistakenly thought we were working together. Last I checked, people working together don't dump each other."

"Here are your drinks," the waitress said, clearly embarrassed at having overheard part of the conversation.

"Thanks," Chloe said as she yanked the paper from her straw before stabbing it into the tumbler and taking a long pull of Coke.

"Finished?" Brock said.

"I guess," Chloe said. Now it was her turn to cross her arms in defiance.

Not wanting to make a volatile situation worse, Brock took a moment to carefully organize his thoughts before speaking.

"I didn't dump you, but I can see how it may have looked that way. I went to talk to an old friend who is wired into the drug world. And I—well—I just wanted to meet him alone is all. As for dumping you with the less glamorous stuff, you're right, I did. But it wasn't intentional. All this stuff needs to be done, and I figured—"

"You figured you could keep me out of your hair by assigning me the busywork. Plus, how bad could that new detective I got stuck with fuck up my case, it is only paperwork after all, right? I mean, it's not like she's interviewing anyone." Chloe uncrossed her arms and took another long pull from the straw.

Brock let out a deep sigh. "Point taken. Guess it's been a while since I had to be in a training role. I might be a bit rusty."

Chloe looked out the window and nodded. "A bit."

Brock took a sip of his own soda, letting the air clear for a beat as they awaited their food.

"I stopped by the ME's office today," Brock said. "The tox results were back. Guess what else Lee Owen had in his system?"

"No idea," Chloe said.

"Fentanyl," Brock said.

Chloe's head whipped around. "Is that what killed him?"

Brock shook his head. "Isleborn didn't think there was enough in his system to kill him, but she did have a theory."

"Do tell."

"It's possible he was drugged. Someone could have slipped some in his drink to knock him out. Would have made handcuffing him to the snowmobile a lot easier."

"What about the head injury? Why wallop him in the back of the head if he was already unconscious?"

"I asked her that question. She said the fentanyl might have worn off before they sent him into the pond, or he may not have ingested enough to render him unconscious. Owen was a big boy, probably capable of putting up one hell of a fight once he realized what was in store for him."

The waitress returned with their food just as the band announced a short break.

"Thank God," Chloe said before taking a healthy bite out of her burger. "I'm starving."

28

After finishing their meals and comparing notes, both detectives agreed they had enough work to justify an all-nighter. They split up again, a mutual decision this time, hoping to cover more ground. As Chloe got to work reviewing a week's worth of surveillance video from Marlintini's, Brock decided to tackle another one of the case's many angles. Now that they had definitive proof Owen had fentanyl in his system, Brock wasn't about to wait around for Perreault to contact him, not when they had Phinney's snowmobile impounded. If Deputy Hanscomb's intel was correct, perhaps there was another reason, besides jealousy, someone had sent Lee Owen to an icy grave at the bottom of Second Pond. Either way, if Perreault was part of a network using all-terrain vehicles and snowmobiles for trafficking illegal narcotics into the US from Canada, and Owen had worked for him, then just maybe Dr. Phinney's stolen snowmobile possessed a hidden compartment. There was only one way to find out.

"You sure you want us to tear this whole thing down, Brock?" the overnight state police mechanic said as he stood beside Brock in the heated bay of the state garage in Augusta. "I mean, won't the owner be pissed?"

"It's not his machine any longer," Brock said. "The insurance company already paid off on the claim. Besides, if there are drugs inside this thing, I want 'em found."

Brock knew the insurance company might have something to say about it, but he would cross that bridge when he came to it. Right now, he needed answers.

"You're the boss," the mechanic said. "Might take me the better part of the shift, though. There's a lot of places you could hide drugs inside one of these."

"Take all the time you need."

It was raining again as Brock walked out of the garage and across the parking lot past a couple of orange DOT dump trucks with snowplows still attached, a sure sign of respect for Maine's fickle weather patterns. He couldn't remember who it was who invented the phrase about April showers being responsible for May's flowers, but given the amount of rain they'd been receiving, if there was any validity to the saying, Maine was about to be inundated with brightly colored flora. Regardless, rain was better than snow.

Brock was halfway inside the unmarked when his cell phone vibrated with an incoming message. He slid the phone from the pocket of his coat and unlocked the screen. The text originated from a blocked number. The message read:

If U want 2 know what happened 2 Lee Owen come to 2nd Pond 2night at 10

As he was reading the text, a second message came through.

Come alone

Who would be sending him messages from a blocked cell number? Brock took a moment to consider the possibilities but came up empty. He had given out his cell number to multiple people over the past few days. People who were in some way connected to the murder of Lee Owen. Whoever had sent this text knew the significance of Second Pond, even if they couldn't spell it. Was this a trap? Or simply someone afraid of being caught assisting the police? Without more information to go on and no way to respond, it was impossible to say.

Brock pulled up his call history, his thumb hovering over Chloe's mobile phone number. Should he call her and let her know what he was up to? He'd have been pissed if the shoe were on the other foot. Especially since he had just lit into her for freelancing the case. But if the text turned out to be nothing or just somebody screwing with him, he'd risk looking like an idiot, or worse, like he was afraid to meet a possible witness without backup. Not to mention the fact he'd be wasting Chloe's time. Time better utilized going through the security video from Marlintini's Grill.

He returned to the phone's text screen and read the messages again.

...2night at 10

Come alone

He checked the time. It was 8:25. Even if he took Route 3, it would still take him over an hour and a half to make the eighty-mile trek from Augusta to Blue Hill. He'd be cutting it close, but if he didn't at least try, he would always wonder if he'd missed an opportunity to break the Owen case wide open.

He pocketed the phone, started the Ford, and raced out of the lot.

Brock made it to Second Pond with three minutes to spare. He turned off the dirt road onto the pond access road, riding the Ford's brakes as he descended the steep muddy track. The rain had made quick work of whatever frost still existed below the ground's surface, leaving nothing but deep ruts and running water on the surface of the access road. For the second time in as many days, he realized he'd forgotten where he now worked, having left his L.L. Bean boots in the rear of the SUV, where they were all but useless. He wondered how accommodating Lt. Cumberland would be if he kept filing paperwork for new gear reimbursement.

The narrow beach bordering the edge of the pond was deserted, a stark contrast to what he had observed upon his arrival the day Owen's body was recovered. As his headlamps swung around the gravel turnout, he caught a flash of bright yellow coming from the tree line. He repositioned the SUV until the beam of light allowed him to identify what he was seeing. It was remnants of the crime scene tape still tied around the trunk of a birch, fluttering in the breeze like a warning beacon. After scanning the area for other vehicles, Brock repositioned the unmarked until it was back to the wood's edge and he was directly facing the access road. Anyone arriving by vehicle would be at a disadvantage if they were planning to surprise him. Brock lowered his window a crack, then killed the headlights and engine, giving himself both a visual and auditory advantage.

He sat in the dark, listening to the tick of the engine as it cooled and the patter of rain on the pond. The warmer air combined with the leftover patches of ice and snow created a thin layer of ground fog that hung over the water like a ghostly sheet. He checked the time on the dash clock. 10:05. No sign of anyone nearby. The rain had all but stopped again, reduced to nothing more than an annoying drizzle that required him to intermittently activate the wipers to keep the windshield clear.

Despite the unseasonably warm night air, there was still a damp chill seeping through the open window. Brock turned the collar of his overcoat up. He opened the console and rummaged around blindly through stacks of fast-food napkins for some chewing gum, something to pass the time while he waited for his mystery texter to show. He was about to give up the hunt for gum when his hand brushed up against a small package wrapped in cellophane. He instantly recognized the familiar size and shape of the object and the craving that accompanied its discovery. He sighed as his fingers closed around the small cardboard pack, and he lifted it from the cubby. Marlboro. The same brand Albert smoked. He supposed it made sense, seeing as how it was swiping smokes from his old man that got him hooked in the first place. He held the pack in front of the lighted dash clock for a better look. Only two cigarettes remained. Further inspection revealed one had broken, spilling tobacco inside of the pack. The other appeared whole though bent. He removed the only serviceable cigarette and dragged it under his nostrils, inhaling deeply. Brock tried to remember when he had smoked his last as he wondered how long the forgotten pack had been there. He had vowed to quit at the urging of Carmen, his wife. *Ex-wife*. But that only lasted about a month. His second attempt had come following his promotion to detective, largely because the department was cracking down again on personnel smoking inside the cars. His most recent attempt to swear off the habit came during therapy following the shooting. He could thank the department therapist for that alteration. Perhaps the only thing the guy had done to improve Brock's life, before being canned by Brock himself as soon as he realized the confidentiality only went so far. Brock fought for and ultimately was granted permission to go out and find his own psychotherapist, one who didn't answer to the state police powers that be.

Brock looked up from the cigarette after massaging it back into shape and performed another quick scan of the area. Deserted. The clock read 10:10.

He desperately searched the pockets of his trench coat for a lighter or perhaps a forgotten book of matches but came up empty. He leaned over the console and popped open the glove box again. He removed the stack of paper napkins and several sets of plastic-wrapped utensils and the unread owner's manual. Lying at the bottom of the glove box was the plug-in cigarette lighter that had come with the Ford from the factory. Brock felt a smile crease his lips as he swapped out the phone charger for the cigarette lighter, pushing it in and waiting to see if it still worked. After a moment, the lighter popped out. He removed it and checked the business end. The coil glowed bright orange. He lit the cigarette, inhaled deeply, then slowly let it out. He grinned as he watched the bluish smoke envelope the passenger compartment, and the familiar sensation of calm enveloped him. Brock paused to relish the moment.

Chloe, he thought. *Shit. She'll know I've been smoking in here.*

He reached for the door handle as he rechecked the time. 10:13.

"I'm giving you until I've finished this cigarette to show yourself, asshole," Brock grumbled as he stepped out of the car into the mud.

He studied his shoes for a moment before dismissing them. They were just shoes, after all. Besides, the thrill of the nicotine coursing through him and the familiar smell of burning tobacco made everything all right again.

He carefully pushed the door shut, making as little noise as possible, then leaned against the side of the SUV. His eyes swept the area for lights or movement, but there was still nothing. Whoever had sent those texts was simply fucking with him. Perreault? Maybe. The Bear certainly hadn't made any attempt at contact yet. One of his former Troop A compatriots? It was possible, but he wondered if any of them would be dicks enough to screw with him over a case. It didn't seem likely, no matter how great their disdain for Brock. Not even Evan would stoop that low. Would he?

Brock took another long drag off the cigarette, closing his eyes as he did so, exhaling slowly. His eyes popped open to the sound of something whistling past him. A moment later, the crack of a rifle tore through the silence, the sound echoing across the pond, making it impossible to determine the origin of the shot. Brock dove for cover, landing in the mud and pine needles. He tossed the cigarette, and he drew his sidearm. A second shot rang out. This one connected with the front fender of the Ford several feet from where Brock lay.

He felt everything closing in, as if he were stuck in some kind of tunnel instead of where he was. His heart raced, and he clearly felt the first flutters of panic setting in. He fought to remember what Kimber had said about high-stress incidents and what to do about them.

"Go to your training, Brock. Muscle memory. Move."

He took a deep breath, then struggled to focus on both the problem and solution. Cover. He needed to find cover or at least concealment. There was no way to know the shooter's exact position, but he knew from the round striking the fender he was hiding on the wrong side of the vehicle. Another shot. This one showered him in glass as the window on the driver's door exploded. Brock rolled onto his stomach and low-crawled past the rear of the SUV toward the trees.

Unseen branches from low-lying vegetation pulled at his clothing and clawed at his hands and face, but he pushed forward until he was safely concealed among the shadows of the woods. He rolled onto his back, peering out at his vehicle and the darkness beyond as he awaited another shot. He could still make out the glowing cigarette butt lying on the ground beside the Interceptor.

Stupid, he thought. *Nice going, idiot. You gave them something to shoot at.* He knew it was only the stress, but he had to fight the urge to laugh out loud as he thought back to the first counselor telling him how bad cigarettes were for his health. *Yeah, no shit, Sherlock.*

Minutes passed while Brock waited for the shooter to emerge from hiding. He remained on high alert, gun at the low ready position, his back in a semi-reclined position, the leafless shrubbery holding him up. His eyes were laser focused while his ears listened for the slightest sound, but nothing further happened.

He wondered if anyone had heard the shots and called them in. It was possible, right? But the more he considered it, given the time of year, the more unlikely it seemed. He was in the middle of nowhere. And this was Maine. Guns were beyond plentiful here, and Mainers tended to keep to themselves. The likelihood of anyone dialing 911, even if they had heard the shots, was low, he reasoned. No, likely he was on his own. And because he foolishly hadn't told anyone where he was going, no one would be looking for him. He released his left hand from the butt of the .45 and reached inside the pockets of his overcoat for his cell phone. Empty. He searched through the breast pockets of his suit coat but again came up empty. The phone must have fallen out when he dove to the ground. Brock shifted as quietly as he could, trying to elevate his torso into more of a seated position. Peering out over a pine bough, toward the spot where he'd been standing only minutes before, not far from the slowly dying ember of his cigarette, Brock caught a faint light spilling out from edge of his cell phone screen where it lay facedown in the mud.

Once again Brock fought back the panic threatening to engulf him as he considered his situation. He was well concealed, armed, and—assuming the temperature didn't drop any more than it had—clothed well enough for the conditions. If necessary, he would simply hunker down and wait out the shooter. Also in Brock's favor was the fact that the shooter had no way of knowing if the cavalry was on its way or not. It seemed more likely the reason the shooter was no longer firing at him was because they had already fled the area. At least Brock hoped that was the reason.

He readjusted his grip on the H&K, then pulled the collar of his coat up around his neck again and settled in for the long haul. As the light from his cell phone extinguished, the drizzle turned into a downpour.

29

Chloe's eyes felt like they might pop right out of her head and roll across the desk. She had consumed so much coffee her hands were literally shaking as she moved the mouse around the pad.

Marlintini's surveillance video, obtained from Cammie Russo, only covered the week Lee Owen had disappeared, and Chloe had wrongfully assumed reviewing it would be a piece of cake. Trouble was, the tavern had a total of sixteen interior cameras set up to record in sequence at five-second intervals, meaning the time delay created gaps in coverage. Someone appearing at the bar in one shot might have moved by the time the camera system cycled back. That anomaly, combined with the sheer number of patrons, made finding and keeping track of Lee Owen much harder than it should have been. Adding to the problem was the fact that the player she was using to review the footage wasn't the same one that came with whatever system the Russos were using. Chloe had downloaded a generic player from the internet, and it was acting wonky. She'd worry about the tantrum the state IT people would likely throw about the unauthorized download later.

Chloe had created a desktop file folder to store every screenshot in which Owen appeared. She categorized each image based on the corresponding time stamp, keeping a chronological record of Owen's comings and goings. She began her search by skipping ahead in the file until she was viewing the Saturday night in question. Starting at 6:00 p.m., it had taken her a while before she finally clocked Owen's arrival at the tavern just prior to nine o'clock, but once she found him, he walked directly to a booth where several other people were already gathered. One of those people was Harold Perreault, The Bear.

She had been at it most of the night, sitting alone in Troop E's darkened detective bureau. In fact, the only sign there was a world beyond the one she inhabited was the occasional sound of an aircraft taking off or landing next door at the Bangor International Airport. After a while, she stopped noticing those too.

"Good morning, sunshine," Detective Zimmerman said, shattering the silence and startling Chloe from her self-induced video coma.

"You scared the bejesus out of me, Zim," Chloe said as she turned and stretched, lifting her arms in the air and yawning loudly.

"Whatcha watching? Reality closed-circuit television?"

"Yeah, a little too much reality, if you ask me."

"That your snowmobile caper?"

"Yup."

"Find anything worthwhile?"

"Got some nice shots of our vic having drinks before someone sent him to the bottom of a lake."

"That's nice. Hopefully, they bought the round first."

Chloe checked her watch. It was only 6:05. "What are you doing in so early?"

"District court appearance in Houlton," Zim said as he tugged a maroon necktie off his coat stand, looped it around his upturned collar, and began tying it into a Windsor knot. "Don't want to be late. What do you think of my suit?"

She eyed the camel-colored three-piece. "How many decades has that thing been hanging in the back of your closet?"

He scowled. "Come on, it isn't that bad. Still fits. Besides, I remember Gene Rayburn wearing something similar on *Match Game 75*."

"Gene who?"

"Kids," Zimmerman said. "How goes the battle with St. Justice?"

Chloe thought for a moment before answering. "Not too bad, actually. I think maybe Brock and I are beginning to understand each other."

Zimmerman shook his head. "Not sure who I feel sorrier for."

"I think I hear Houlton calling," Chloe said.

"Okay, I'm going, I'm going. Good luck with your video—thingy."

Chloe was returning to her desk from the restroom when her cell phone rang. The caller ID read State Police Dispatch.

"Chloe?"

"Hey, Micki," Chloe said, recognizing the woman's voice instantly. "What's up?"

"Have you heard from Brock Justice within the past few hours?"

"Now you mention it, no. Why, is he not returning calls again?"

"Actually, he isn't. And we've been trying to reach him since about four thirty to pass along a message."

Chloe felt the hairs prickle on the back of her neck.

"Do you have any idea where he is?" Micki said.

"I don't," Chloe said, thinking how dumb it was they hadn't shared a planned itinerary. Or at least Brock hadn't. He knew she was planning to work through the night on this and wasn't going anywhere. "Last I knew, he was heading to the public works garage in Augusta. We split up to work on various aspects of the case. I kinda lost track of time. Have you tried him on the radio?"

"I have, but he's not answering there either. Think I should call Lieutenant Cumberland?"

"Hell, no," Chloe said. "She'll scalp us both. Let me try contacting the garage. They may know where he is."

Before she could hang up, Micki stopped her.

"Hang on a sec, Chloe. We're getting a 911 call from the Blue Hill area. Sounds like it might be Brock."

Chloe could hear the operator relaying the message to Micki from across the room. She couldn't understand every word, but the inflection in the operator's voice was unmistakable. Something was wrong.

"He's asking for backup," Micki said. "And an ambulance."

Chloe snatched up her coat and hurried toward the door. "Where is he?"

"Second Pond."

30

Brock sat on the rear bumper of the ambulance, holding a thermal blanket around his shoulders like a cape. The violent shivering brought on by prolonged exposure to the lower nighttime temps and frequent downpours had finally begun to subside. He had waited until dawn before crawling from the bushes to retrieve his cell. Despite having less than five percent left on the battery, only a single bar of service, and fingers too cold and stiff to function, somehow Brock had managed to successfully call for help.

It had taken less than ten minutes before the first trooper arrived, preceded by the comforting wail of their siren. Brock surveyed the crowded beachfront parking area. In addition to the ambulance, there were nearly a half dozen volunteers from the local fire/EMS crew, another half dozen marked county and state police vehicles including a K9, several unmarked state police vehicles, and the state evidence van. The cavalry had truly arrived.

For the second time in the past week, crime scene tape surrounded the area in a wide rectangle, encompassing his SUV. Fuente was busy documenting the bullet damage to the Ford with a digital camera that in all probability cost more than Brock made in a month.

Chloe, who was visibly pissed at him, had brought him an extra-large to-go cup of coffee. The hot beverage felt good as it warmed his insides, but he was still having difficulty holding the cup in his hands. He watched conversations taking place in little hushed clusters. He knew some were discussing strategy, while others appeared to be opining about how lucky Brock had been as their attention switched back and forth between the damaged unmarked and Brock himself. But the easiest faces to read belonged to two of his fellow troopers. Brock may have survived death at the hands of a sniper, but his fate was still up in the air as far as Chloe and Lt. Cumberland were concerned.

The frenzied sound of muffled barking and whining drew his attention away from the angry glares to the side of the ambulance.

"Hey, Brock," Trooper Reagan, the K9 handler, said as he fought to restrain his overly excited German shepherd, Cassie. "How're you holding up?"

"All things considered, not bad." Brock exchanged a silent nod with two members of the state police tactical team, neither of whom he knew. The men were dressed in BDUs and holding rifles, and judging by the looks on both their faces, neither one was happy at having drawn a short-straw assignment. Brock wondered if their grim expressions were about traipsing through the muddy forest and bogs to protect Reagan and his overzealous K9 during the impending track, or perhaps they were simply disappointed the shooter had missed.

"I saw the side of your car," Reagan said. "You are one lucky bastard, Justice."

Brock couldn't disagree.

Cassie whined and yanked forward in her harness, tugging Reagan slightly off-balance.

"We're getting ready to attempt a track."

"It looks like she's ready," Brock said.

"Right? Look, I know your shooter is probably long gone, but I'm hoping for either shell casings or tire prints. Anything we can use, really."

"Fingers crossed."

"Any idea where the shots originated?"

Brock shook his head. "I never saw a muzzle flash of any kind. And once I realized I was hiding on the wrong side of my car, I put my head down and made for the woods. I never saw where any of the shots came from, sorry."

"No worries. Hell, they may have used a flash suppressor."

"I suppose."

"I wanted to ask about a cigarette butt Fuente found near the driver's side of your unmarked. Did the shooter—?"

"No. It's mine."

"I didn't know you smoked," Chloe said, having approached unseen.

"I don't," Brock said, earning a perplexed look from her.

"Well, I'll get out of your hair," Reagan said. "Wish us luck."

"Good luck," Brock said.

Chloe sat down beside him on the bumper. "How's the coffee? Hot enough?"

"Yeah, thanks. Almost too hot."

"Good," Chloe said.

"Look, I know you're pissed at me for not telling you about the text, but—"

"I'm not pissed about that," Chloe snapped. "I'm pissed you came out here without telling *anyone* where you were going, Brock. You could have been killed. Did you bother thinking about me for even one minute?"

Brock bit his tongue. It was clear he hadn't given that subject much thought at all. "I didn't want to drag you all the way down here on a wild goose chase. I honestly thought it might be just—you know, someone yankin' my chain."

"And what do you think now?"

Brock said nothing, his attention momentarily pulled to a nearby conversation between Cumberland and a polygrapher from the MCU named Tisdale. Brock had yet to meet the man, but he already knew he wasn't likely to be a fan. Detective Howard Tisdale had been an academy mate of Evan Mathers.

"So, who do you think wants you dead?" Chloe said, asking the obvious question.

"No idea," Brock said with a shake of his head. "The originating number was blocked, and I've given out quite a few business cards this week with my cell number on them. And it isn't like I haven't made more than my share of enemies as of late."

"But they picked Second Pond specifically," Chloe said. "There must be some relevance to our case."

"Maybe. But there were photos from the day we recovered Owen's body in all the local papers. Remember? It isn't like someone wouldn't know this location was important to our investigation."

"We might still be able to trace the originating phone those texts were sent from through the carrier."

Brock wasn't holding out hope on that angle. "If I was going to lure someone out into the middle of nowhere to kill them, I'd use a burner."

"Good to know," Chloe said, her expression indicating she was thawing out a bit.

"Was that a joke?" Brock said.

"Don't push your luck, Justice. I'm still pissed at you."

"Join the club," Lt. Cumberland said as she approached, wearing a scowl. "You feelin' any better, hot dog?"

"I'll survive," Brock said.

"Good. Glad to hear it. I want you to know I've asked Howard Tisdale to head up the investigation into the shooting."

"Chloe and I can handle this," Brock said.

"I'm sure you can," Cumberland said. "But you're not going to. Neither of you. In case it slipped your mind, *you* are the victim here, Brock. And victims don't investigate their own cases."

"But this is probably connected to the Lee Owen murder," Chloe said, echoing Brock's very thought.

"My point exactly, Detective Wright," Cumberland said. "And your inability to separate those two things is exactly why I don't want either of you working the shooting. Stay in your lane. That means both of you. Work the Owen murder, and let Detective Tisdale handle the shooting. You got it?"

"Yeah," Chloe said. "I got it."

"Brock?" Cumberland said.

"You're the boss," Brock said as he caught a glimpse of Tisdale's smirking face standing just beyond the lieutenant.

"Don't forget it," Cumberland said.

The K9 track through the woods lasted nearly thirty minutes, ending at an icy off-road woods trail on the opposite side of Second Pond. The trail was a patchwork of snowmobile and ATV tracks left in the mud and what little snow remained. According to Reagan and Fuente, they had managed to locate the area where the shooter had been firing.

"It looks like they were standing up on a knoll behind and slightly above the tree line," Reagan said.

Fuente weighed in, "Not sure whose land it is, but there's 'no trespassing' signs posted everywhere. Looks like some old abandoned industrial site."

"Shell casings?" Brock said.

"I already told How Weird," Fuente said.

"How Weird?" Brock said.

"Tisdale," Reagan chuckled. "Howard Tisdale. Around here, he's known as Detective How Weird."

"Do I want to know why?" Brock said.

"Probably not," Chloe said.

"Good to know," Brock said. "Now what about shell casings?"

"I'm guessing the shooter must have gathered them up before departing," Fuente said. "I couldn't find one, let alone the three you said were fired."

"Tell me you found boot prints at least," Brock said.

The ET shook his head. "It looks like they wore some type of covering over the soles. Crampons, maybe."

"But there must be partials we can cast," Chloe said.

"The crampons held the tread up just high enough to keep the marks faint, and it looks like they may have added a layer of Tyvek in between."

"You mean like our crime scene booties?" Brock said.

"Exactly. It would be impossible to recover any comparable patterns. The shooter, whoever they are, knew exactly what they were doing."

Brock considered Fuente's comment. The shooter had prepared for the ambush. They'd found a way in and out that didn't require the roadway, leaving only a minimal risk of being spotted. They had altered their footwear. Even baited Brock in for the kill, then waited for him in the woods until the perfect moment to take him out. Except they hadn't taken him out. They hadn't finished the job, assuming that had been their intent. Or had they only hoped to scare him? Deliver a warning. His exhausted brain was having difficulty focusing enough to give the situation its proper due. What he needed was rest. Rest and a new left front tire.

After a moment, Brock said, "What about recovered rounds? I heard at least three shots."

"As far as I can tell, only two rounds penetrated your car," Fuente said. "One through the left front fender and the other clean through the windows of both front doors."

"And the third?" Brock said.

Fuente shrugged. "Must have sailed wide. I wouldn't hold out hope for locating that one. A rifle round can travel quite a distance, and based on the trajectory from where the shooter was firing, that missing round likely traveled across the pond."

Brock's eyes scanned the long body of water, and he nodded his understanding.

"We'll be towing your SUV to the garage for further processing. If I find anything, I'll let you know."

"Come on," Chloe said. "I'll give you a hand transferring your gear into my car."

31

Lt. Cumberland had called ahead to the state police garage and arranged for Brock's replacement vehicle. Chloe drove him to Augusta to pick it up. Brock trained the dash vents directly on his hands and cranked the heat, basking in the warmth as the miles passed. He was dressed in borrowed clothing, consisting of an insulated plaid chamois jacket, a faded Boston Celtics tee, a pair of Carhartt overalls, and the Bean boots from the back of his SUV. He felt like a backwoods hick.

They had been on the road for about twenty minutes when Chloe broke the silence.

"That's such BS."

"What is?" Brock said.

"Cumberland telling us to back off. We're not really going to hand over the shooting to How Weird, are we? Hell, he's the polygraph examiner. He's not even supposed to be a primary."

"You heard the lieutenant. She wants us to stay out of it."

"That wasn't really an answer, Brock."

"Nope. It wasn't."

"So, we *are* going to investigate it?"

"Not officially," Brock said. "But if the cases should happen to overlap, well, we'd be obligated to look into them, wouldn't we?"

Chloe turned toward him and grinned. "Is this part of my training?"

"The unofficial part. But if we get caught, you were acting at my direction, understood?"

"Gotcha."

Chloe pulled up perpendicular to the loaner vehicle and put her Ford in park. Brock stared through the side window at what was obviously a high mileage repaint.

"You've got to be kidding me," Brock said.

"It's a pretty color, anyway," Chloe offered.

Brock turned in time to catch her wry smile. "Really?" he said.

"What? Lavender's nice."

"I'm glad you think so. Wanna trade?"

"Not on your life. All I'm saying is it could be worse."

Brock couldn't see how.

"Come on," Chloe said as she opened her door and stepped outside.

After obtaining the keys from one of the mechanics, it only took them a few minutes to transfer his gear to the loaner vehicle. A quick inspection of the interior revealed that despite its putrid color, the Ford was at least clean and—according to the brand-new inspection sticker gracing the windshield—serviceable.

"What about your wet clothes?" Chloe said as she held up his trench coat, suit, and ruined shoes.

"Toss them in the back, I guess," Brock said. "I'll deal with them later."

Chloe closed the SUV's hatch, then turned to face Brock. "What's next, boss?"

Brock let out a loud sigh. "For me? A couple hours of sleep, or I'll be useless."

"I was thinking more about what you might want me to do on the Owen case."

Brock considered it for a moment before answering.

"I want to shore up Emily Phinney's alibi for the weekend Owen took the snowmobile, and we still need to locate Owen's truck. It didn't just disappear from the face of the earth. I don't suppose you happened to notice a full-sized pickup lying around at the bottom of the pond."

Chloe laughed. "Think I would've noticed. Sorry."

For a split second, something not quite fully formed jogged Brock's brain, but it was gone as quickly as it had come.

"What?" Chloe said. "Did you just think of something?"

"No, that's the problem. I'm too tired to complete a thought. Whatever it was will eventually come back to me." He hoped.

"You sure you're okay to drive?" Chloe said.

"Yeah, I'll replenish my caffeine level on the way home."

"Okay. Then I'm off to track down Doc Phinney's better half. Get some rest, okay? And I promise not to call you unless it's an emergency."

"I'll hold you to it."

After watching Chloe drive off, Brock headed inside the garage to check on the progress the mechanic had made. The brightly lit bay was littered with snowmobile parts, most of which Brock had never seen and couldn't have identified if asked.

"All done," the mechanic said proudly.

"There's a lot to one of these, huh?"

"That's the understatement of the year."

"So?" Brock said. "Any luck?"

"I didn't find any drugs, if that's what you were hoping for," the mechanic said.

"Nothing?" Brock said, trying hard to hide his disappointment, as he had been growing more confident that narcotics might have played a part in Owen's murder.

"I didn't say I didn't find *anything*," the mechanic said. "I said I didn't find drugs."

"Then what did you find?"

"The hiding place. And it's pretty impressive." The mechanic walked to a nearby bench and retrieved a large, molded piece of sheet metal.

"What is it?" Brock asked as he took the part from him and began to examine it.

"That, my inspectorial friend, is what they call the tunnel. At least in motorsport parlance. It's a cover that protects the underside of the seat assembly. See the two pieces of squared tubing running along both sides?"

"Yeah. What are they?"

"Those tubes house the coolant that keeps the engine from overheating.

The covers may look a little different, but all sleds, regardless of the manufacturer, have one."

"Okay," Brock said. "I still don't get it."

"One," the mechanic said as he held up a greasy finger and grinned. "That's the operative word. But this baby has two covers." He led Brock over to the tarpaulin and pointed to the collection of parts. "There's the other one. As you can see, it is nearly identical to the one you're holding."

Brock studied the two plates. To his untrained eyes, they looked identical.

"Ay-ay-ay," the mechanic said as he retrieved the panel from Brock. "You never took shop class, I'll bet."

Brock shook his head. "Majored in English and history."

"Figures. Well, you should have studied the history of drug smugglers. The way this works is this plate would have been mounted directly over the other one using friction mounts." He turned the false bottom over and pointed out the metal slots to Brock. "See these slots? They are manufactured to receive the male slots mounted underneath the real tunnel cover. Any ICE guys or any other law enforcement types that get nosey and have a look up under the seat would see exactly what they expected to see. A genuine tunnel cover. Look, it even has an identical finish. But if you knew how to separate these two panels, you would likely find bundles of illegal drugs."

"How big a space are we talking about?" Brock said.

"See for yourself," the mechanic said as he held the pieces together. "The rear of the assembly, the only one visible when this sled was still in one piece, looks whole. But if we turn it around, you can see there's a gap of about an inch and a half running the entire length of the tunnel."

"That could hold a lot of drugs," Brock said.

"Indeed, it could. I see all kinds of stuff up here, but even I'm impressed with this. Someone with an expansive knowledge of metallurgy went to a lot of trouble engineering this. My guess is they made a lot of these, probably for different kinds of sleds too. This particular sled is one expensive toy. At least, it was before I tore it apart. But the amount of drugs someone could smuggle in this hidey-hole, depending on the value of the drug being transported, could easily eclipse the total cost of the sled."

Brock wasn't sure how he felt about this revelation. On one hand, it still allowed for the possibility that Owen had broken into the Phinneys' garage to steal hidden drugs and not just a snowmobile. On the other hand, it could mean Keith Phinney was part of a drug smuggling operation. Or that Phinney had purchased the used sled not knowing it was rigged for smuggling. And yet another possibility was that the drugs were still hidden inside the snowmobile the night it was stolen, then removed by the killer before dumping both the sled and Lee Owen's body into Second Pond.

"What exactly is the look you're going for here, Brock?" the mechanic said as he surveyed Brock's clothing.

"Long story," Brock said, having completely forgotten how he was dressed.

"I'll bet."

Brock departed the garage intending to drive to his apartment for a hot shower and a couple hours of sleep. He had traveled less than five miles when his cell phone rang.

"Justice," he said.

"Hello, Detective. Stu Albertson here."

Brock didn't immediately recognize the voice or the name.

"The Smith & Wesson rep your evidence guy called. Fuente said it was okay to contact you directly."

"Sorry, it's been a long day," Brock said. "Thanks for getting back to me, Stu. Any luck?"

"Let's just say you're never going to believe where I traced those handcuffs back to, Detective."

Brock, not in the mood for twenty questions, did his best to play nice. "Hit me with it."

"The Maine State Police."

"Say again?" Brock said.

"The serial number your guy sent me came from a block of fifty handcuffs shipped to a first responder uniform supply company in Gardiner, Maine, called Eastern Law."

Brock struggled to recall any business by that name. "Never heard of them."

"That's because they're not in business any longer. Which means, of course, getting records from them would be impossible."

"And you're sure this isn't some kind of mistake?" Brock said.

"I double-checked. Eastern Law placed the order in 1987 as part of a new equipment invoice they received from the state police."

Brock sat there, stunned. How would a set of handcuffs originally purchased by the Maine State Police end up on the wrist of a murder victim? Something was very wrong here.

"That's it, then?" Brock said, more to himself than to Albertson.

"It is from my end. The rest is up to you."

Brock thanked Albertson, then ended the call. As he returned the phone to the charger, he considered the latest information and what he'd have to do to track the serial number to the assigned trooper. 1987 was a long time ago. Would the state maintain equipment records back that far? He didn't know. That time frame would have predated the internet and all of today's computer platforms. Images of dusty files and floppy disks filled his head. He reasoned the state would probably have records, assuming the trooper in question was still on the job, but how likely was that? He performed a quick calculation in his head. Assuming his math was correct, that same trooper would now have amassed thirty-eight years of service. It was unlikely, but there were still a few dinosaurs roaming the state.

He considered the problem from another angle. How likely was it a trooper still on the job would use cuffs assigned to him to kill a man and risk putting himself in the crosshairs for a murder? It didn't seem likely at all. Not unless the trooper was totally unhinged.

32

Brock had just climbed out of the shower and was wearing only a towel wrapped around his waist when someone began banging on the door to his apartment. He quickly donned a pair of jeans and a T-shirt, then opened the door to find Jeanne Anderson standing there.

"Oh, thank God," she said, wrapping him in a bear hug.

"I'm afraid I don't understand," Brock said.

Anderson released her grip on him and stepped back. "Don't play coy with me, young man. I worried when you didn't come home last night. And then when I turned on the news this morning, I heard all about someone shooting at a state police detective, and I just knew it was you. Then I saw the strange car parked in the drive, and, well, it was all too much. I had to come see for myself. Are you okay?"

"I'm fine," Brock said.

She squinted up her face in disbelief.

"Really," Brock said. "They only injured my car."

"Well, I should think they'd give you a better one than that awful-colored thing down there. It's hideous."

Brock grinned. "I don't disagree."

"Have you had anything to eat? I could fix you up some food."

What he really needed was a few hours of sleep, but he knew now it wasn't going to happen. "That's nice of you, Mrs. Anderson, but you don't need to go to any trouble on my account."

"It's no trouble at all, and it's Jeanne. Besides, it has been a long time since I had someone to cook for."

Brock could see the longing in her expression. The loneliness. This was more about his company than breakfast.

"Let me finish getting ready, and I'll be down in a few minutes."

Anderson's face lit up. "I'll just go put on the coffee."

Chloe turned into the rear lot of the Blue Hill Public Library off Parker Point Road. The handsome colonial-style brick building was trimmed in white with white shutters. Two pairs of faux Greek columns highlighted the façade of the main building, framing the entryway doors. Protruding from either side of the two-story building were identical single-story wings with flat roofs. The overall appearance of the building reminded Chloe of a schoolhouse from her hometown in Presque Isle.

Chloe made her way to the circulation desk, where a bespectacled middle-aged woman with short graying hair was seated.

"May I help you?"

"I hope so," Chloe said, removing her credentials from her coat pocket and holding them up for inspection.

"State police?" the woman said, clearly taken aback. "What brings you to our library, Detective Wright?"

"I'm looking to speak with Emily Phinney."

"Do you have an appointment to see Director Phinney?" the woman said.

"It's okay, Ginny," a voice said from behind Chloe.

Chloe turned to find Emily Phinney standing there holding a small stack of books under each arm.

"Nice to see you again, Detective Wright," Emily said, giving her a pleasant smile.

"Likewise," Chloe said, surprised by the warm greeting. "I wonder if there might be someplace we could chat in private?"

"Of course. Let's go to my office. Ginny, would you please see to it we are not disturbed?"

Chloe followed Emily downstairs to a nicely furnished but hardly ostentatious space. Chloe hadn't been sure what to expect, given the extravagant nature of the waterfront home Emily shared with her husband. The room featured a large window overlooking a well-manicured lawn that led to the woods behind the library. Situated in front of the window beneath the usual clutter was a large antique desk. Facing the desk were a pair of walnut-colored Windsor-style visitor chairs. Both side walls were lined with bookcases and detailed nautical maps of the Blue Hill Peninsula.

Emily set the books down atop one of the bookcases, then gestured for Chloe to sit. "Can I get you anything before we start? Coffee, perhaps, or tea?"

"Thank you, but that isn't necessary," Chloe said as she sat in the chair to the left, allowing her a peripheral view of the office door.

Emily sat in a teal-colored ergonomic chair across from Chloe. The chair, looking more like something that belonged to the bridge of the starship *Enterprise*, was the only thing in the entire office that looked out of place.

"I want to apologize for my husband's behavior the other night," Emily said. "That was totally uncalled for, and so unlike him."

"Not necessary," Chloe said. "Given the circumstances, I might have reacted similarly. While it certainly wasn't my intention, I'm afraid I may have given you both the impression we were looking at you as suspects in Lee Owen's death."

"Honestly, your visit did come as a bit of a shock to both of us. But it doesn't excuse Keith's behavior."

"You understand in cases like this, we have to talk to everyone who has a connection to the victim."

"Of course, everybody is a suspect until you rule them out, right? I'm addicted to all those British mystery shows, and isn't that what the inspectors always say?"

"Something like that," Chloe said.

"So, what do you need from me, Detective?"

"You mentioned you were away the weekend your carriage house was broken into."

"That's right. I knew Keith would be playing poker, so I made the trek out to Vermont to visit my sister, Georgia. I left right from work on Friday and didn't return home until late Sunday night."

"I'll need Georgia's contact information to verify."

"Of course," Emily said as she grabbed a pad of notepaper from the pile atop her desk. She quickly scribbled down the information, then handed it to Chloe. "I heard on the news that someone shot at a state police detective last night, right here in town. I hope everyone is all right."

"Yes, everyone's fine. We're still looking for the shooter."

"You weren't involved, were you?"

"No, my partner was." The word caught in Chloe's throat, but she wasn't about to refer to Brock as her trainer.

"Detective Justice, right?" Emily said. "I hope he's okay."

"He's fine."

"Thank God. Well, I do hope you catch the person responsible."

"I'm quite sure we will."

Following an artery-clogging but wonderful brunch consisting of crispy slab bacon, home fries, spinach quiche, and homemade blueberry scones, Brock returned to his upstairs apartment and changed into a clean suit and tie. His brain was now fully functioning, and he knew sleep would not come until it was good and ready. Besides, Jeanne Anderson had forced enough caffeine into him to last the remainder of the week. It wasn't until Brock clipped on his sidearm and extra magazine that he remembered his ruined dress shoes were still lying on the floor of his loaner's trunk next to the soaked ball of mud-covered clothing from last night's ordeal. He combed through several moving boxes marked "work clothes" before he located a serviceable pair of brown penny loafers to match his Van Dyke–colored suit. Before leaving the apartment, he made a quick check of his appearance in the hallway mirror. It wasn't great. The striped button-down could have benefited from some ironing, but it was a vast improvement from the overalls, Bean boots, and the plaid chamois he had been wearing.

He grabbed his briefcase and headed down to the unmarked. It was time to find out where the old state police uniform records were kept, and he knew just whom to check with. He had driven less than a mile from his apartment when a memory he'd been struggling to recall popped into his head. He placed the cell in the dash-mounted charger and activated the speaker setting, then dialed Chloe.

"Hey, I thought you were gonna try and get some sleep," Chloe said.

"Where would you get such a crazy notion?"

"This stubborn guy I know."

"Don't listen to him. He's sleep deprived."

"Don't worry, I won't. Okay, so if you're not sleeping, what *are* you doing?"

"I've got a lead on the handcuffs I want to chase down."

"Care to share the deets?"

"Not until I know more. How about you? Any luck with Mrs. Phinney or locating Owen's truck?"

"Is that how it works? I share what I've been up to, and you keep secrets?"

He could hear the anger rising in her tone. Chloe was right. Besides, he'd kept her out of the loop on the bogus overnight meeting, and they both knew how well that turned out.

"You're right," Brock said. "I heard back from Smith & Wesson."

"And?"

"And the handcuffs we removed from Lee Owen were part of a large order placed through a local uniform supply company called Eastern Law."

"Never heard of them," Chloe said.

"That's because they're no longer in business. The order shipped in 1987."

"Jesus, I wasn't even born yet. Who placed the order?"

"I'm working on that. Any luck connecting with Emily Phinney?"

"Yeah, I spoke with her about the weekend in question. She claims to have been in Vermont visiting her sister."

"Did the sister verify her story?"

"I'm waiting on a call back from her."

"Good. The reason I called is because I need you to check on something for me. You still in Blue Hill?"

"Just left the library. What do you need?"

"Do me a favor and check the parking lot at Marlintini's."

"What am I looking for?"

"I'm just spitballing here, but I'm almost positive I saw a sign in the lot saying they tow any vehicles left overnight. There should be contact information for a wrecker company."

"And we care about this why?" Chloe said.

"You said the cell records listed one of the locations Owen went to the night he went missing was Marlintini's Grill, right?"

"Yeah, I've got him there on video. I meant to tell you about it this morning, but things got a little crazy, if you remember. So, you're thinking, what? They might have towed Owen's truck from there?"

"Why not? You said there were no exterior cameras, right?"

"Right. But if they towed his truck, how did Owen get to Phinney's to steal the snowmobile?"

"One thing at a time. Can you check it out for me?"

"I'm on it."

33

Chloe slowly circled Marlintini's parking lot, locating not one but three identical signs posted at intervals along the far edges of the property, each clearly stating vehicles left overnight would be towed at the owner's expense. Wondering how she hadn't noticed the signs previously, she copied down the information from the signs, which included a phone number and the name of the wrecker company, J & P Towing, into her notebook. The business name sounded familiar, but she couldn't place it. After snapping a photo of one of the signs, she took a moment to consider the best way to approach this. She knew wrecker companies were required by law to reach out to registered owners before they could begin the civil process to transfer ownership. Chloe reasoned if Lee Owen's truck had been towed from Marlintini's on the night of his disappearance, it would have been in the wrecker company's possession for less than ninety days. Odds were, they would still have it.

She decided the best way to confirm the wrecker company still possessed the vehicle, without raising suspicions that the police were interested in it, was to play the part of the owner's wife. She changed the settings on her cell phone to block her number from view, then dialed the number of J & P Towing.

The phone rang close to a dozen times before a gruff and bored-sounding male answered.

"J & P Towing. Norm speaking."

"Norm, I'm hoping you can help me. I think my truck may have been towed by your company, and I'd like to find out how much I owe to get it back."

"Plate number?"

Chloe read the registration number aloud directly from her notebook.

"Make and model?"

Chloe provided the description of Owen's truck, including the color.

"And you say this is your vehicle?"

"Well, it's registered in my husband's name, but I bought it, so I guess that makes it mine. Do you still have it?"

"Yeah, we got it. It's in our impound lot, where it has been since the end of January."

Chloe grinned as she scribbled the month into her notebook.

"You owe us quite a bit of money, lady," Norm continued. "Those storage charges really add up after a couple of months. Didn't you get the letters we sent?"

"My husband isn't too good at keeping our mailing addresses up to date. Sorry. Can you tell me when and where you towed it from?"

As Norm relayed the details, Chloe recorded everything into her notebook. "And you're sure it was January 28th?"

"Yeah. Towed it myself. We take care of overnight towing from Marlintini's. Bar owners get kinda pissed about people leaving their cars in the lots, especially during the winter months, with plowing and such."

"I can imagine," Chloe said. "So, where should I meet you to get my truck back?"

Brock drove through the lot of the old Augusta barracks toward the rear of the property where the evidence garage was located. He figured if anyone working for the state police knew where to find old records, it would be Clarence Snyder. Clarence was a civilian now, but years ago—prior to the traffic accident that left him with pins in his back and a permanent limp—he'd been a trooper assigned to the Maine Turnpike.

"Holy shit, look what the cat dragged in," Clarence said by way of a greeting. "Man, I haven't seen you in a month of Sundays. How you doing, Brock? Or should I say Detective Justice?"

"Okay, all things considered."

"Rumor has it they stuck you way up in the willy-wags."

"True story."

"Well, I've been stuck here since God was a toddler. Sometimes that's just the way it goes, right? Guess I'm lucky to still have a job."

Brock supposed he was too.

"So, what can I do for you, Detective?"

"Caught a homicide in Blue Hill. I was hoping you might have some old SP records at your disposal."

"I heard about that one. Some poor slob took a snowmobile for a swim, right?"

"I don't think it was his choice."

"What kind of records you lookin' for?"

"Issued equipment from the late 1980s."

"Late '80s, huh?" Clarence said as he pushed up the bill of his state police ball cap and absently scratched his crinkled forehead.

"I would imagine those would be handwritten files," Brock said.

Clarence laughed. "Sonny boy, all my files are handwritten. I don't trust these computers as far as I can heave one, and that ain't very far. I figure when the day comes and all this stuff crashes, I'll be way ahead of the game."

Brock nodded. "Sound logic."

"Follow me."

"You know where those files are, then?" Brock said as he fell in behind him.

"Nope, but I know where all the *old* stuff is. I'll leave the searching part to you, youngster."

Brock followed him at a respectful distance. Clarence's limp had worsened in the time Brock had known him, and he didn't want the man to be any more self-conscious than he probably already was.

"You see much of your old man?" Clarence said.

Brock carefully considered his response. He didn't know specifically what, if any, history existed between the two men, but he did know there were more than a few veteran troopers who still held Albert in high regard.

"Saw him the other day, as a matter of fact," Brock said.

"Well, you tell that old son of a gun I said hello."

"Will do," Brock said.

"I know he's all highfalutin now, what with winning the Legendary Trooper Award and everything, but I still remember him as a greenhorn back when he first joined the ranks. Didn't know his asshole from his elbow back then."

Brock said nothing as he followed Clarence into the service elevator and watched him punch the button for the basement.

"Someday I'll have to tell you the story of how Al and I met."

The elevator doors slid open, revealing a large, caged-in storage area. Ten-foot-high sections of cyclone fencing were bolted together to form a secure pen in which to store anything the state wanted to protect and preserve. Clarence pulled out a retractable cord on his belt that held a ring of keys the size of Brock's fist. After fiddling with the brass-colored lock for a moment, he opened it and removed it from the hasp. He swung open the cage door, then flipped on an entire bank of rocker-style electric switches, bathing the entire area in fluorescent light. There were rows of steel shelving packed with uniforms, cruiser accessories, and file boxes as far as Brock could see. It was like walking into a Chapter 11 warehouse.

"We keep damn near everything you could ever want down here."

"Where are the sofas and love seats? I just moved into a new apartment."

Clarence threw a playful elbow into Brock's ribs. "Living room section won't be ready until next year, wise guy."

"Good to know."

"Now, what year were you looking for?"

"From 1987 to 1988."

Clarence moved farther down the center aisle of the cage, mumbling to himself and pointing at each row they passed as if he were solving a mathematical problem. Despite his limp, Clarence moved swiftly, and Brock momentarily forgot about keeping his distance until Clarence came to a sudden halt and Brock nearly ran him over.

"I think what you're looking for may be down this aisle," Clarence said, pointing to the left. "The file boxes are all marked by year, but as you'll see, they're not in any particular order."

A loud electronic buzzer sounded from somewhere nearby.

"What's that?" Brock said.

"That's my high-tech doorbell alarm system. State spared no expense. Tells me someone is in dire need of my services. Think you can handle the rest of the hunt on your own?"

"I'll give it the old college try."

"Attaboy. Leave you to it, then. Let me know when you've finished."

"Thanks, Clarence," Brock said as he began scanning the shelves.

After several minutes of searching, it became clear Clarence had made absolutely no attempt to follow anything resembling chronological order. Neither forward nor backward. Adding to the problem, some file boxes were stacked behind others, hidden from view. Brock sighed as he removed his suit coat and tie and hung them from a peg protruding from one of the powder-gray industrial shelf stanchions. This was going to take a while.

34

Chloe stood outside the gate of the impound yard, looking through the cyclone fencing at Lee Owen's pickup. The vehicle sat in a far corner of the lot tucked between a construction dumpster and a bright yellow VW conversion van. The roof and hood of Owen's truck were still covered in a thin layer of ice. Chloe wondered how long after Lee's murder the Chevy had been towed. Minutes? Hours? Or even simultaneously? It was odd to think about the truck having been here ever since.

"There it is," Norm said. "The plow blade's the nicest thing on it. Not sure the truck is worth the money you owe me."

Chloe wasn't sure it was either, but its evidentiary value, which had the potential of being far greater, was still unknown.

"Like I told you on the phone, we did send letters to the address listed for the registered owner. Your husband, right?"

Chloe looked over at him and slid her hand inside her raincoat. "Actually, Norm, I wasn't entirely honest with you when I phoned earlier."

"Now, why doesn't that surprise me?"

She opened her badge case and held it up for Norm to see.

"Detective, huh?" Norm said as he frowned. "Suppose this means I'm not getting my money after all."

Brock pulled box after dusty box from the shelves, stacking them wherever he could find space along the aisle. It didn't take long before his hands and clothing were covered in black soot. He tired quickly, the exertion a reminder of just how badly he needed rest. He was beginning to think he was on a fool's errand when he happened upon a box at the bottom of a stack at the rear of a shelf marked *Equip. 1987–88.*

"Bingo," he said as he leaned in and pulled the heavy box toward the front of the shelf.

The glue holding the carton together had dried out long ago, and the cardboard was caved in slightly from the weight of the boxes stacked atop it. Deciding not to chance lifting the box from the shelf and having its contents spill onto the floor of the aisle, Brock went searching for something that would allow him to examine the contents where they sat. He returned several minutes later carrying a beat-up metal step stool. He leveled the stool on the concrete floor, then climbed up. The musty smell of the old files was nearly overpowering as he flipped open the flaps, releasing a flurry of dust motes that made him sneeze. It was clear from the stains he saw on several folders that water damage might also be a factor.

The contents appeared to have been placed chronologically from one end of the carton to the other, but somewhere along the way someone had misfiled a number of folders. Brock had searched through nearly all the files before his hand finally fell on the one he'd been looking for. The thick green folder was dated November 1987. Moisture had damaged some of the papers contained therein, causing the typewriter ink to run nearly to the point of illegibility. He paused when he spotted an invoice from Eastern Law. The pages were held together by a rusty staple. The company's logo, a silhouetted police officer, was displayed atop each page. The order was for batons, handcuffs, campaign hats of assorted sizes, and breast badges. It looked to Brock as if an entire academy class of recruits had been outfitted. Apart from the hats, none of the items ordered were size specific and could have been issued to anyone. But the number of items seemed far too large for a single academy class. Brock wondered if the state might have placed the larger order to cover two different classes of cadets, one about to graduate and the other about to attend the state police academy in Waterville—which had since relocated to Vassalboro just outside of Augusta—thereby taking advantage of a bulk discount. Brock flipped through the remaining pages but couldn't find any records pertaining to the issuance of the equipment. He set the invoice aside and continued to the next folder in the box. Having exhausted the box's contents, Brock was disappointed at failing to locate a single folder that could account for who received any of the purchased equipment.

He descended the step stool and resumed his hunt for containers marked 1987–1988 but was unable to locate any other boxes covering those years. He sighed loudly as he surveyed the thirty or so file boxes scattered along the floor up and down the aisle. None of them contained the records he was searching for, and they all needed to be returned to the shelves.

Wondering if Chloe was faring any better, he checked his cell phone for messages. The home screen displayed the words "no service." The concrete and steel of the garage had eliminated all contact with the outside world. As he returned the phone to the pocket of his trousers, his eyes caught a glimpse of a cardboard box lying on the floor underneath the bottom shelf. There was a two-foot gap separating the shelves between the aisles, and it appeared as if the box he was looking at might have tumbled off the back of the shelf at some point. He activated the flashlight app on his cell phone and crouched down. He shined the light under the shelf to get a better look at the wayward box, but the end of the box was facing away from him. The clearance wasn't great, as the shelf only sat about two feet above the floor, just enough to house the row of boxes he had already moved. Brock realized he would have to crawl under the shelf and retrieve it. He stood and looked at his pants and shirt. They were already disgusting; he didn't suppose crawling on the floor could make things much worse than they already were. Regardless, he needed to see the contents of the file box. If there was any truth to Murphy's Law, what he'd been searching for might well be inside that carton.

He got down on his hands and knees and crawled beneath the bottom shelf. He stretched his right arm to try and reach the handle at the end of the box, just managing to hook his fingers into it. As he tugged on the handle, the cardboard tore, splitting the box at one corner and spilling the files across the dusty concrete.

"Goddammit," Brock grumbled.

He inched closer, then scooped up the errant files and shoved them back inside. Wrapping his arms around both ends of the box, he pulled it along with him as he backed toward the aisle. He managed to move the entire container into the light despite smashing the back of his head against the steel shelf support. He stood erect and rubbed the back of his skull as he eyed the prize. The end that had torn open had nothing written on it, but upon the other someone had written *1987–1988 cont.*

No longer worried about his clothing, Brock knelt directly on the concrete, righted the box, and lifted the flaps. He followed the same front-to-back procedure he had before, making every attempt to be thorough so as not to miss something important that may have been misfiled. He was halfway through the folders when he found it. A battered green file folder containing lists of new troopers along with their issued equipment. Typed in the header of each sheet was the trooper's name followed by rows of equipment. Sidearms, handcuffs, anything with a serial number was recorded along with all identifying information. Beside each item were the trooper's handwritten initials. Brock retrieved the notebook from the pocket of his coat and flipped it open to the serial number he had recorded from the handcuffs removed from Lee Owen. He memorized the number, then began flipping through the equipment log sheets until he found a match. He held the notebook up beside the sheet, confirming it was the same number. His attention shifted to the top of the page. The rookie trooper who had been issued the handcuffs used in the murder of Lee Owen was none other than Albert Justice.

35

Chloe watched Owen's pickup winched onto the back of J & P's flatbed and secured with canvas straps. She followed the wrecker in her SUV back to the state police garage in Augusta for processing. The owner of the wrecker company hadn't been happy about losing two months of storage fees, but his consolation prizes were an empty space in an already overflowing impound lot and not needing to go through the hassle of fighting for ownership of yet another abandoned vehicle.

Chloe stood beside Mike Fuente as Owen's truck, plow blade still attached, was lowered onto the floor of the garage where it would be impounded and thoroughly examined for fingerprints, hairs, fibers, bodily fluids, anything else that might help identify a suspect or tie Owen's killer to the pickup.

"You're telling me this thing has been sitting in an impound since the day Lee Owen was murdered?" Fuente said.

"Crazy, right?" Chloe said.

"That's one word for it. Any idea who you guys like for the murder? Make my job a whole lot easier."

Chloe shook her head. "Still too many suspects to count. Besides, why would I want to make your job easier?"

"Touché."

Brock returned the file boxes to the shelves, signed for the documents, and thanked Clarence before returning to his loaner vehicle armed with the information he'd come for. The time he had spent in the dimly lit basement had taken a toll on his eyes, and the bright sunlight forced him to squint. He removed a pair of dark glasses from his pocket and slid them on, taking a deep breath of fresh air as he did so. Brock was halfway to the SUV before his cell phone reacquired service, immediately populating the notification screen with a half dozen missed texts. One was a message from Chloe telling him she had located Owen's missing truck and was waiting on Fuente to give it the once-over before towing it to a secure location. The time stamp indicated her message had come through more than an hour ago.

Forward progress, he thought.

As he continued walking, he thought about the implication his discovery might have for the case. If Cumberland learned what he had found, she might well pull him from the Owen murder, and he couldn't have that. Not after all the hard work he and Chloe had already put in on the case. And not after being shot at, not once, but three times. Besides, there was no way he really believed Albert would've had anything to do with the murder of a lowlife like Lee Owen. At least he hoped not.

Another problem was sharing the discovery with Chloe. Despite his repeated warnings to her about keeping each other in the loop, if he let her in on this find, she would be in serious jeopardy if Cumberland ever found out she'd been privy to such sensitive information and didn't apprise her superior. Not exactly an auspicious beginning to her detective career. No, it would be far better for Chloe's longevity if she had deniability. He would keep the discovery from Chloe for now, consequences be damned.

One thing was certain, alibi or no, Albert Justice had some tough questions to answer.

Brock unlocked the SUV and climbed inside. As he reached for the seat belt, his cell rang. The call originated from a number he didn't recognize. Blocked numbers usually earned an ignore, unrecognized numbers were always toss-up. Deciding to risk it, Brock answered.

"Justice."

"You must have ESP or something," Corey Hincks said.

"How do you figure?" Brock said.

"Because my counterparts at MDEA North have been working on a secret squirrel fentanyl smuggling operation from Canada into Maine for nearly six months now, but they haven't managed to make even a single bust."

"How did you find out?" Brock said, chuckling at the secret squirrel comment. For as long as he'd known him, Corey referred to all organizational compartmentalized secrets as secret squirrel stuff. Brock had learned from experience when it came to keeping a lid on investigations, nobody did it better than the DEA, not even the FBI.

"What? You think anyone in law enforcement is wily enough to keep a secret from Captain Hincks? I'm deeply wounded by your lack of confidence, Detective Justice."

"You pulled rank, didn't you?" Brock said, grinning.

"You're damn straight. Any idea how many Maine cops serve in the National Guard? It's good to have a little pull."

"Thanks, Corey. I appreciate you running it down."

"Does this mean you found out something I can use to further my career in the glamorous world of drug enforcement?"

"Sorry, brother," Brock said. "I can't risk compromising *my* case."

"Now who's getting all secret squirrel? Come on, dawg, spill the beans to Captain Hincks."

"You're forgetting something, Corey," Brock said.

"What's that?"

"I'm not in the Guard."

Chloe was en route to Ellsworth when she received a call from Georgia Toothaker, Emily Phinney's sister.

"Thanks so much for getting back to me," Chloe said.

"Not at all," Georgia said. "I must admit your message worried me a little. Is Emily in some kind of trouble?"

"No, nothing like that," Chloe said, confident that Georgia already knew why she was calling. If the two women were anywhere near as close as Emily had intimated, Georgia would have phoned Emily before returning Chloe's call.

"I am merely trying to confirm Emily's alibi for the weekend of January 27th and 28th. Emily said she wasn't home that weekend because she had gone to Vermont to visit you. Is that accurate?"

"Um, I think so," Georgia said. "Give me a minute to bring up the calendar on my phone."

"Certainly," Chloe said, wondering if Georgia was pretending to look up the date.

"If you don't mind my asking, why would my sister need an alibi?"

"We are investigating the death of a man we believe may be connected to the theft of your brother-in-law's snowmobile."

"I had heard about the theft of Keith's snowmobile, but not about any death. Can you tell me what happened?"

"It's a long story, Mrs. Toothaker, one I'm not at liberty to share. Suffice it to say, the man we believe to be responsible for stealing the snowmobile is now dead."

"How awful."

"Any luck with the calendar?" Chloe prompted.

"Oh, right. Sorry. Okay, here it is. Yes, Emily came and stayed with me the weekend of January 27th and 28th."

"Do you remember the exact date and time she arrived and left?" Chloe said.

"Not down to the minute."

"As accurately as you can, then."

"Okay. Well, I know she arrived on Friday evening, the 26th of January, because we went out for dinner to a lovely Italian restaurant nearby and I made reservations ahead of time. On Saturday we shopped and drove around the state a bit, trying to take advantage of the nice weather because we'd barely had any snow. Sunday morning, we ate breakfast at a diner in Burlington not far from my home. I think Emily must have packed up already because she was ready to hit the road as soon as we got back to the house."

"Do you remember what time she left?"

"This is only a guess, but I'd say sometime between eleven and eleven thirty Sunday morning. It was definitely before noon."

Chloe thanked her for her help and ended the call. It was clear after speaking with Georgia Toothaker that whatever happened to Lee Owen hadn't involved Emily Phinney. At least not directly.

36

It was late afternoon when Brock pulled into the dooryard of Albert's camp on the lake, the gravel crunching loudly beneath the tires of the SUV, effectively removing the element of surprise. Not that Brock had been going for that, but not telegraphing his arrival might have been nice.

Spring was a fickle lady capable of lulling even lifelong Mainers into believing summer was nearby, when in fact nothing could be further from the truth. The sun had already dipped behind the thick canopy of evergreens, and along with it, the temperature had plummeted a good fifteen degrees from the day's high, bathing everything in shadow and giving the crisp spring air a more seasonable nip. Brock remembered many chilly Mays and Junes. It wasn't usual for the steady summer warmth to hold off until as late as July.

He parked next to his father's pickup, then climbed out of the Interceptor. He caught a whiff of woodsmoke as he snatched his trench coat off the passenger seat and shrugged it on. He approached the camp, keeping one eye peeled for Albert as he went. The last visit hadn't gone particularly well, and now here he was, unannounced, returning to question his father about his possible involvement in a homicide, however unlikely that involvement might seem.

Weathered boards snapped loudly beneath his shoes as he ascended the steps to the porch. He rapped on the screen door, then stood back and waited. Several moments passed before he knocked again, but no response came. He moved over to a nearby window and peered inside. The flicker of flames was visible through the glass door of the cast iron stove, but the fire was dying down, a clear indicator it hadn't been tended recently. Adding to Brock's suspicion that his father had gone out was the fact that none of the camp's interior lights were illuminated. He surmised Albert had either gone for a walk in the woods or had taken the boat out for a ride on the lake.

Brock opened the screen door, then tried the inside door handle. It turned freely. He pushed the door open and stepped inside. The warm air emanating from the stove was a welcome contrast to the outdoor chill.

"Dad, it's Brock. You here?"

Again, there was no acknowledgment. Brock took one last look back toward the driveway before closing the door.

Renovated or not, the smell of the camp remained unchanged. Brock remembered having read somewhere that odors were the most powerful link to the past. Colors tended to fade, faces of acquaintances and loved ones blurred, even our recall of places became muddled, but the olfactory senses remained strong, possessing an almost mystical power, as if they were capable of rewinding time. He stood just inside the door, transfixed as his eyes wandered throughout the space. Every object conjured up a childhood memory, some pleasant, others less so. Despite the camp's overstated masculine decor, glimpses of Jolene's influence, like the flowered lampshade, showed through.

He wandered the first floor, touching nothing as he took it all in. Despite having received new legs, the dining room table's wooden slab top still retained the same scarred patina he remembered from years before. The stainless-steel kitchen sink and corresponding hardware were new, but the knotty pine cupboards, wood countertops, and plank flooring remained.

Brock moved toward the rear of the first floor, toward Albert's den. Upon reaching the doorway, his cell buzzed, startling him. He removed the phone from the pocket of his overcoat and checked the caller ID. Lt. Cumberland.

Great, he thought. Given where he was, Penny Dreadful was the last person he wanted to talk to. She was probably seeking another case update, but Brock knew if she had even the slightest inkling where he was, or what he was doing, she would lose it. He briefly considered the consequences, then thumbed the ignore button and returned the phone to his pocket. He froze to the sound of a shotgun slide being racked directly behind him. There were few sounds more terrifying than a live round being chambered into a pump shotgun.

"Twitch and I'll splatter you all over the wall," his father's baritone voice commanded.

"Dad, it's me," Brock said quickly in a voice at least an octave higher than normal.

"Goddammit, Brock. What the hell are you doing sneaking around my house?"

"I'm not sneaking," Brock said as he turned to face him. "I came here to talk. I didn't know you were out."

"I would have thought my not answering the door would have clued you in. Guess you thought it would be okay to just let yourself in, huh?"

"Last I checked, this camp belongs to the family," Brock said.

"Funny, I was under the impression this is my home now. When was the last time anyone besides me stayed here?"

Brock opened his mouth to say something but thought better of it.

Albert wore a plaid insulated jacket, faded state police ball cap, blue jeans, and L.L. Bean boots with the laces untied. Brock wondered how the old man had managed to sneak up on him so easily. He hadn't been able to navigate even the front porch without a board snapping in protest. Yet somehow his father had managed it without a sound. Was Brock losing his edge? Or was his father really the wily outdoorsman he had always claimed to be?

Brock observed his father's index finger shift to the side of the trigger guard, reengaging the safety before he lowered the shotgun barrel toward the floor.

"Don't suppose you bothered to stoke the fire," Albert grumbled as he moved over to the wood box beside the stove. "You could have made yourself useful before you started snooping around."

Brock said nothing as he peeled off his overcoat and slung it over a wall peg beside the front door.

Albert refilled the stove with several pieces of hardwood, positioning them to his liking. He left the door to the stove ajar to help the wood catch, then stood up and stretched his back. He gave Brock the once-over before snatching up the shotgun and returning it to the wall cabinet in the corner of the room.

"You eaten?" Albert said as he brushed past Brock on his way to the kitchen.

"I haven't," Brock said. "But that isn't why I'm here."

"Didn't figure it was," Albert said as he opened the refrigerator door. "Whatever it is, will it keep until after we've eaten?"

"Yeah."

"Good, then give me a hand."

37

The two men ate at the dining room table in front of a large picture window overlooking the lake. Brock couldn't remember the last time they had done that. It seemed like there had always been someone else at the table, either Jolene, or Jake, or Carmen, his ex. Brock did his best to try and make conversation, but most of Albert's responses tended to be of the singular-syllable variety.

The food was delicious. Two-inch-thick porterhouse steaks grilled to perfection, mixed greens with olive oil and pepper, and baked potato. Albert drank scotch neat while Brock had ice water. After they'd finished the meal, Brock helped by clearing the table. He carried the dirty dishes over to the sink and began to rinse them.

"Leave 'em," Albert said as he donned his jacket and cap. "I'll clean up later. Right now, I want a smoke. And you can say your piece."

Brock grabbed his coat and followed Albert out onto the deck. They sat across from each other in unpainted Adirondack chairs angled slightly toward the water. Brock watched as Albert tapped a cigarette from the pack and lit it. He extended the pack to Brock.

"I quit," Brock said, shaking his head as he stared longingly at the offering.

Albert fixed him with a knowing grin but said nothing as he returned the pack to the breast pocket of his jacket.

"I'm still working the Owen homicide," Brock said matter-of-factly.

"Figured you were."

"I learned something today that I need to ask you about."

"So, ask," Albert said.

"Did you kill Lee Owen?"

Brock watched as his father's head slowly swiveled toward him. Albert appeared to be studying him as if trying to confirm he was serious.

"Why would you ask me such a dumb question?"

"Because the handcuffs used to secure Owen to the snowmobile were state police issue."

"And?"

"They were issued to you."

Albert's unblinking blue eyes held Brock's. His expression gave nothing away. After several long moments, Albert's attention returned to the lake, and he took a long drag off the cigarette. Brock couldn't imagine how difficult his old man would be to read in a poker game.

"So, did you?" Brock said.

"Did I what?"

"Have anything to do with Lee Owen's murder?"

"My cuffs were stolen, along with a few other items from the camp last fall," Albert said at last.

"I don't suppose you filed a police report, did you?"

"I did not. Stuff they took didn't amount to anything, no real value, aside from sentimental, maybe."

Brock had never met a less sentimental man than Albert Justice. But the absence of a police report documenting the theft was potentially a huge problem. It meant his father was in the frame for the murder no matter how ludicrous the idea might sound to him, or to anyone. It also meant Brock's name would adorn the very top position on Cumberland's shit list as soon as she found out.

As the two men sat in uncomfortable silence, punctuated only by the gentle lapping of waves against the shoreline, stars gradually punched holes in the darkening canopy of a cloudless sky. The only other light emanated from the glowing ash at the end of Albert's cigarette.

Upon reaching the pavement at the end of the camp road, Brock stopped the unmarked car and shifted the transmission into Park. His mind was already replaying the conversation with his father. He pulled out his phone and looked at the missed call notification again. He briefly toyed with calling Cumberland back and filling her in on the latest. She would lose her mind when she found out about Albert's handcuffs. He could easily imagine her response.

"You've got to be kidding me," Cumberland would say. "What happened to keeping me in the loop?"

And Brock would lie and tell her that he was keeping her in the loop. That he had literally just learned about the cuffs belonging to Albert. And while that wasn't entirely true, the less she knew about Brock's investigation the better. Besides, hadn't she been the one who told him that Albert's part in Phinney's alibi wouldn't present a problem?

Brock held the phone out, studying the glowing screen as he considered his next move. The truth was Albert had dropped him right in it. If Brock told the lieutenant the latest she would undoubtedly yank him off the case so fast he'd get whiplash. Chloe too. As for Albert, the alibi he had provided for Keith Phinney now worked both ways. The two men needed to have spent the entire night at Sheriff Parlin's home for their alibis to mean anything, and according to Parlin and Deputy Tommy Hanscomb, they had. Brock realized those alibis were the only thing keeping him on the case. The handcuffs would be a bridge too far.

He was reaching for the shifter when the phone rang. He checked the ID, expecting it to be Cumberland calling back, but it wasn't her. In fact, it wasn't a number Brock recognized.

Against his better judgment, he punched the speaker button.

"Justice."

"I understand you're looking for me," a baritone voice said.

"Who is this?"

"Harold Perreault."

38

Despite Brock's exhaustion, sleep did not come easily. As usual, his brain was completely immersed in the investigation. The leads they had followed thus far and the leads that still needed fleshing out occupied his every thought. He tossed and turned until nearly two in the morning before sleep overtook him at last. But it wasn't restful. His mind was plagued by a series of related nightmares. A confusing patchwork of real life and altered reality played out over the widescreen of his subconscious. There were pieces taken from his previous night spent shivering at the pond while targeted by an unseen assailant combined with other bits pulled from the memory of Terry Kirke's compound in Bar Mills. Try as he might to climb out of the chaos of imagined danger, Brock's exhaustion kept him firmly entrenched in the ever-shifting dreamscape.

In one scenario, Evan Mathers was killed in the backyard by Terry Kirke's brother, Darrell, while Brock watched helplessly through the grimy second-story window. In another version, Brock himself was gunned down in the upstairs hall by Terry, except it wasn't a hallway at all, it was the beach at Second Pond. As Brock lay there bleeding out on the frigid muddy ground, his father stood over him in his state police uniform, holding a shotgun and grinning.

"Guess you were cut out for this life after all," the dream Albert said with a tip of his campaign hat.

Brock awoke with a start. He sat up in bed as the remnants of the dream slowly began to dissipate, separating and breaking apart like a spider's web. His entire body was covered in a sticky sheen of perspiration, and the bedcovers lay pooled on the floor. He grabbed his T-shirt from the bedpost and used it to wipe the moisture from his face and torso. He retrieved his cell phone from the nightstand and checked the time. It was nearly 5:45 a.m. He wasn't scheduled to meet with Perreault until ten o'clock, meaning he still had time to grab a few more hours of sleep. But Brock had no intention of returning to the nocturnal hell from which he had just escaped. He rose from the bed and headed for the bathroom.

"Jesus, Brock, you look horrible," Chloe said as they drove toward their meeting with Perreault. "When was the last time you slept?"

"Last night," Brock said abruptly, hoping to cut her off.

"What, for like an hour?"

He didn't bother responding.

"Are you pissed at me or something?" Chloe said.

"No," Brock said, surprised by the question.

"So, you're just one of those brooding guys who likes to let it all build up inside, huh?"

Brock considered letting her in on the conflict but decided focusing on the upcoming interview with Perreault was a much better use of their time. Besides, he knew how upset she'd be that he held back on her yet again. Especially when she learned what he had held back.

"How do you want to approach The Bear?" Brock said.

"Are you really asking for my input, or are you just screwing with my head?"

"I really want to hear your thoughts."

"Okay, I think we should play to his personality," Chloe said.

"How's that? We don't actually know him."

"Oh, I think I've got him pegged. He's a forty-something, anti-establishment type, who sees himself as a badass, probably a ladies' man, and he likes his motorcycle more than his friends."

"And how do you propose we play to that?" Brock said.

"Easy, let me do all the talking. I'll act like I'm impressed, to get him talking, and we'll go from there."

"How do you know you'll even be able to get him talking?"

"Trust me, I can turn on the charm when I need to. Besides, I've known lots of guys like Harold Perreault. And the one thing they all love is the sound of their own voices."

Brock thought Chloe was probably right about the ego. Especially considering the man's nickname was The Bear.

"Just keep something in mind, whether this guy had anything to do with killing Lee Owen or not, he might still be responsible for at least one other murder," Brock cautioned.

"You're talking about the missing motorcycle club president?" Chloe said.

"Perreault was the club's enforcer at the time," Brock said. "He would have had access and, based solely on their falling-out, motive."

"I'll keep it in mind," Chloe said.

39

Brock parked the SUV in a roadside space directly across from the diner. Chloe was the first to spot Perreault's motorcycle not far from the entrance, leaning on its chrome kickstand. Besides having been painted an obnoxiously loud shade of purple, the Harley-Davidson Fat Boy wasn't hard to spot, as it was the only two-wheeled mode of transportation in sight. One look at the exhaust and Brock knew it had been modified to be as loud as possible.

"You'd think if The Bear was involved in smuggling narcotics, he might want to maintain a lower profile," Chloe said as they crossed the road toward the diner. "No way that thing is street legal."

"Neither is smuggling," Brock said.

"Good point," Chloe said.

Brock held the door for her, allowing her to put the plan into action by taking the lead.

They found Perreault sitting alone at a four-top in the far corner of the dining room, nursing a mug of coffee and playing with his cell phone. Back to the wall and facing the door, he gave them a slight nod as they moved toward the table.

"Mr. Perreault?" Chloe said, turning on the charm. "Thanks so much for meeting with us."

"Didn't know I had a choice," Perreault said, making no attempt to stand up.

"I'm Detective Wright, and this is Detective Justice."

"Justice, huh?"

"That's right," Brock said as he settled into the chair, positioning his sidearm as far from Perreault as possible. "Why do you ask?"

"No reason," Perreault said, his eyes shifting between the detectives. "What can I do for the state police?"

"I thought we might grab a coffee and have a chat," Chloe said, signaling the waitress by holding up her mug and two fingers.

"You folks gonna order food?" the waitress said.

"Just coffee for now," Chloe said.

The table fell silent while the dour-faced woman filled their mugs.

"Top you off?" the waitress said to Perreault with slightly more enthusiasm.

He held up his mug, and she obliged.

After the waitress departed from the table, Chloe pounced.

"The Fat Boy out front is a beauty," Chloe said. "Yours?"

"Yup," Perreault said. "Did all the mods myself."

"Paint too?"

"Of course. No self-respecting owner's gonna let someone else lay a hand on his hog."

Brock watched as Perreault fixed Chloe with a salacious grin as he made the crude comment. The attempt to rattle her was clear. It was all Brock could do to remain silent.

"That's a good one, Harry," Chloe said. "I'll have to remember that one for my youngest brother. He's a big fan of juvenile bathroom humor."

The grin disappeared from Perreault's face, and the blush of embarrassment spread across his cheeks.

Brock fought against the urge to show any emotion at Chloe's smooth and efficient verbal neutering of the biker.

"You got questions or what?" Perreault said, his annoyance now clearly on display.

"Let's start with an easy one," Chloe said. "How well did you know Lee Owen?"

Brock was impressed by the way she phrased the question. It took not knowing the victim entirely off the table, as if their relationship had been common knowledge, leaving Perreault only the degree of familiarity as a possible answer.

"Let me guess, you're harassing me because some guy was murdered," Perreault said.

"How did you hear about the murder?" Chloe said.

"Come on. It's been all over the papers."

"You don't strike me as a big newspaper guy."

"It's a small town, okay?" Perreault said. "And yeah, I knew of him. Hell, I probably know everyone in this shitty little town."

"So, you're telling us you didn't know him very well?"

"That's right. I'd just see him around town."

"When did you see him last?"

Perreault shrugged. "I can't say off the top of my head."

"A few days?" Chloe said. "A week? Last month? Last year?"

"Sometime last year, maybe," Perreault said. "Last fall."

Chloe looked over at Brock and set her jaw.

"What?" Perreault said, clearly picking up on the nonverbal communication.

Brock weighed in. "Mr. Perreault, why would you lie about something as simple as when you saw Lee Owen last?"

Perreault's eyes narrowed. "Who says I'm lying?"

"I do," Chloe said. "We know you were out drinking with him on the very night he went missing."

"Says who?"

"Says the surveillance video we took from Marlintini's Grill."

Brock watched as Perreault's expression softened from one of intensity to something far less readable. He guessed the leather-clad biker was recalculating his answers.

"Okay, so I was drinking with him at the tavern," Perreault said. "So what? I must have forgot which night it was."

"Let me help you, then," Chloe said. "It was Saturday night, January 27th."

Perreault crossed his arms defensively. "If you say so."

"Did you leave the tavern together or separately?"

"If you've got video, then you know I left after Spike did. Which means I didn't kill him."

Brock exchanged another look with Chloe. He knew she had also picked up on Perreault's use of Owen's nickname.

"Actually, it doesn't," Chloe said.

"Where did you go when you left the tavern?" Brock said.

"Shit, I don't know. It's been two months, man. Probably back to my place."

"And where is that exactly?" Chloe said.

"Next town over. In Surry. I got a mobile home on my old man's property. But I imagine you guys already know that, don't you?"

"Anyone live with you?" Chloe said. "Someone who might be able to verify what you're telling us?"

"I live alone," Perreault said, leering at Chloe as he said it. "I like to play the field, if you know what I mean. You should come by sometime."

"Why would you try to hide the fact that you were with Lee Owen the night he went missing?" Chloe said, ignoring the comment.

Again, Brock was impressed with her line of questioning and confidence. Chloe was keeping Perreault off-balance by changing the direction of the conversation at will.

"Probably because I know how you cops work."

"Detectives," Chloe said.

"What?"

"I know how you *detectives* work. We're detectives."

"Whatever. I know how you *detectives* work, okay? I figured if I told you I was with Spike, you'd automatically assume I must have done something to him."

"And you thought lying about it would make you seem less suspicious, Harry?" Chloe said.

Perreault's face reddened again. Chloe was clearly getting under his skin with the overly familiar use of his given name.

"I got a long history with you guys."

Chloe's eyes shifted to Brock. "You don't have a history with me. How about you, Detective Justice?"

Brock shook his head. "Nope. First time I've ever met him, Detective Wright."

"You know what I mean," Perreault said. "Not you guys specifically. Just —cops in general."

"We understand Lee might have been doing a bit of work for you," Chloe said.

Perreault's brow furrowed. "What do you mean? I haven't got any business. I work for my old man at the garage."

"That's funny," Chloe said. "I could have sworn someone told us you had a side hustle going on outside of the garage and towing business." She looked at Brock again. "Do you remember what the business was?"

"Um, I think it was an importing business of some kind," Brock said. "Pharmaceuticals, if memory serves."

"Drugs?" Perreault said.

"Yeah, Harry," Chloe said. "That's what 'pharmaceuticals' means. We heard you might be back in the drug business."

"Who told you that?"

"That's not important. What is important is whether it's true or not."

"Well, it ain't."

"See, because if it is true, you might have a motive to want Lee Owen dead."

"How do you figure?"

"Maybe he threatened to go to the cops if he didn't get a bigger cut? Or maybe because he helped himself to some of your *pharmaceuticals*. Is that what happened, Harry? Did Lee get greedy?"

"You're whacked. Both of you. I've got no idea what the hell you're talking about."

"No?" Brock said. "Because there are numerous references to trafficking all through your Triple I history."

"What's a triple-eye?"

"Interstate Identification Index, Harry," Chloe said. "It's a database maintained by the FBI where criminal activity gets reported. You know, arrests, convictions, sentences, stuff like that. It's a rap sheet, and you've got a long one."

"I was set up on the drug stuff, okay?"

"Really?" Chloe said. "By whom? One of the biker guys you ran with when you were with The Enforcers?"

"I don't run with those guys anymore."

"Why is that?" Chloe said. "I thought motorcycle gangs were for life."

"Maybe on some bullshit TV show where they wear sneakers, but not in real life. I left because I had a disagreement with one of the other club members."

"That wouldn't be the missing club president, would it?" Chloe said before turning to Brock. "What was that guy's name?"

"Bayard," Brock said without missing a beat. "Hap Bayard."

"I don't know anything about that," Perreault said, but Brock caught his eyes widening ever so slightly.

"That's funny," Chloe said. "Because the way we heard it, you were the club's enforcer."

Perreault set his jaw, glaring at her. "Don't believe everything you hear, *Detective*."

"It is strange, though," Chloe continued.

"What is?" Perreault said.

"By my count, that's two people close to you who've gone missing."

"Spike's not missing," Perreault countered.

"True, only because we found him at the bottom of Second Pond."

Perreault shrugged again. "Like I said, nothing to do with me."

"Maybe we should have the York County guys start searching underwater for old Hap," Chloe said, turning her attention to Brock again. "What do you think?"

"Not a bad idea," Brock said.

"Yeah, well, I had nothing to do with what happened to either of those guys. And I think I've answered all the questions I'm going to," Perreault said as he stood and shoved the chair back into the wall, donning his tough-guy persona for the benefit of anyone watching. He walked around Chloe and headed for the door.

"Oops," Chloe said. "Don't forget to pay for your coffee. Wouldn't want to see you get jammed up on a petty theft charge."

Perreault scowled as he dug several crumpled one-dollar bills from the pocket of his jeans and tossed them on the table.

"We'll probably want to talk with you again, Harry," Chloe said. "So don't go leaving town."

Brock fought back another grin as Chloe gave her best Western sheriff impersonation.

"I ain't going anywhere," Perreault said. "And the next time either of you want to accuse me of something, you better have proof."

40

"Well?" Chloe said as she and Brock exited the diner carrying to-go breakfast sandwiches and coffees. "How'd I do?"

"Not bad," Brock said as they walked across the street toward Brock's SUV. "Guys like Perreault aren't easy to handle, and you handled him."

"I grew up with three older brothers," Chloe said as she opened the passenger door and climbed inside. "Testosterone doesn't impress me."

"I picked up on that," Brock said. "So, what's your take on Perreault? Think he is involved?"

"I can't tell," Chloe said. "He did try to hide that he'd been with Owen the night he disappeared, but like he said, it might have been because he knew we would suspect him."

"Maybe," Brock said as he thought about reaching out to Corey Hincks again or even Deputy Hanscomb. Perhaps they could get someone from the area to poke around a bit now that they'd rattled Perreault's cage. "Either way, we need to keep a close eye on him now he knows we're watching."

"You think he might do something stupid?" Chloe said as she unwrapped the foil covering her bacon, egg, and cheese bagel and took a large bite.

"I'm counting on it," Brock said. "Why else do you think I let you crank him up like that?"

Chloe reached into the bag and handed Brock his sandwich.

"Thanks," Brock said as he set it on the dash and checked the time. The meeting with AAG was in ninety minutes. "Hang on to your coffee. We gotta get going."

Brock backed out of the space and headed toward Augusta.

They'd only been on the road for a few minutes before Chloe brought up the briefing.

"I've never attended one of these before. And if I'm being honest, I'm a little bit nervous about it."

Brock glanced in her direction and shook his head. "I don't get you. You just went toe-to-toe with a convicted felon who might well turn out to be a murderer, and you never once flinched. Now you're about to lay out our case progress to one of the state's attorneys, and a few members of the state police brass, and you're nervous?"

"Hey, you've done this before, quite a few times, I imagine, but I haven't. What if I say something I shouldn't? Or something stupid?"

"Like what?"

"I don't know, do I?"

"Look, you're second on this investigation, Chloe. No one expects you to have all the answers. And no one expects you won't have a few butterflies."

"More than a few," she said, tossing her half-eaten breakfast sandwich back into the bag and picking up her coffee.

Brock's eyes returned to the road. "You'll be fine. You just lay out the case and—"

"Whoa, whoa, why am I laying out the case? You're the primary. Why don't you do it?"

"Because they all know me. And I'm quite sure none of them are fans. This meeting is all about you. Cumberland will want to show you off to the team."

"Great," Chloe said, not sounding like she meant it in the least. "Can't wait for that."

"As I was saying, you'll lay out the case and our progress, and they'll pose the occasional question. If anyone asks something you don't know the answer to, or if you're worried you might say the wrong thing, just look at me and I'll take it. All right?"

"Okay."

"The important thing to remember is don't overshare. Oversharing is a rookie mistake. It's far better to hold something back than to see it being fed to the media on the six o'clock news."

Chloe nodded.

"And don't speculate. Lay out the facts as we know them and what we've done so far. You start speculating and some of them will take what you say as gospel."

"Just the facts, ma'am," Chloe said.

"Exactly," Brock said. "The only other advice I can offer is don't argue. This meeting isn't the place."

"Argue? Why would I argue? About what?"

"Trust me, someone will try to insert themselves into our investigative strategy. It always happens."

"Who?"

"No idea," Brock said with a shrug of his shoulders as Major Morgan's mug popped into his head. "But someone will. Usually, somebody who's never investigated a single case in their entire career, let alone a homicide."

"How do I respond to that?"

"You don't. Just smile and nod a lot. It will make whoever is doing the talking feel important." Which, as Brock knew too well, was the whole point. "Stick to that and you'll keep them off our case. I like to think of it as pleasant condescension. They'll feel like we're receptive to the advice, while verbally we've agreed to nothing. Get it?"

"So, basically it's reverse psychology for our superiors."

"I'm not sure how superior they are," Brock said. "But yeah, that's basically it."

The conference room was packed with bodies and much too warm for Brock's liking. Despite being the reason everyone had gathered, Brock and

Chloe felt a bit like outsiders as Lt. Cumberland, Major Morgan, and AAG Grover were all chatting with Dr. Isleborn. Brock couldn't recall ever seeing the chief medical examiner so chatty. There were several other people milling about in suits, none of whom Brock recognized. He assumed they were support staff for Morgan or Grover.

Several tables were set up in a horseshoe pattern with the open area facing a bare wall used to project PowerPoint presentations from a ceiling-mounted projector. Brock was glad they were spared that bit of a dog and pony show today. Not that they had time to prepare such a presentation, anyway.

"Is this what these are normally like?" Chloe whispered to Brock. "I feel like a pariah."

"Remember what I told you about the powers that be. Just remember your job while we're here, and you'll do fine. Use lots of bullshit phrases like we're 'casting a wide net' and 'we're narrowing the pool of suspects.' Don't ask me why, but they eat that stuff up. And don't let anyone get under your skin."

"And if someone does?"

"Don't let them see they're getting to you."

"How do you do it?"

"Me?" Brock said. "When it comes to bottling up aggression, I'm a pro."

"Detective Wright," Lt. Cumberland hollered from across the room. "When you have a second, I'd like to introduce you."

Chloe glanced at Brock, wide-eyed.

"Showtime," Brock said.

The briefing started at 11:30 sharp. As usual, Major Morgan took the opportunity to thank everyone for their professionalism and interagency teamwork on solving another heinous murder.

Brock wondered if Morgan might be honing his public speaking skills for a political run. He briefly considered mentioning the error, as they hadn't actually solved the case yet, but didn't imagine his commentary would be appreciated.

Chloe spent the next fifteen minutes or so laying out the entire case, from the discovery to the physical evidence, to the growing list of suspects.

She provided details but nothing too specific. Even with the occasional curveball question thrown at her, Chloe hadn't wavered.

"Would you say you're narrowing in on a prime suspect?" Morgan said.

Brock glanced at Chloe to see if she recognized the trap or if she might need assistance, but she didn't hesitate in delivering her response.

"It's still too early for that, Major," Chloe said. "We're still casting a wide net until we've got a better picture of what exactly happened here and who the players are."

Brock fought back a grin. He couldn't have done better himself.

41

The sun had disappeared again by the time they exited the building. Dark clouds were threatening additional rain.

"Jesus, that was brutal," Chloe said. "Is it always like that?"

"You'll get used to it," Brock said. "But you did great. Even managed to work in that 'casting a wide net' line, I noticed."

Chloe laughed. "I gotta admit, I thought you were screwing with me when you gave me that lame-sounding advice. But it actually worked."

"Like a charm," Brock said. "Come on, let's go grab some lunch."

"Where are we going?"

"I know a place."

The Downtown Diner was located on Water Street in Augusta in the space formally occupied by Hersey's Shoe Store. The previous tenant's name still graced the marquee above the front door. Sandwiched between a row of brightly painted three-story flats of varying heights, the block resembled something from an Old West mining town.

"A shoe store?" Chloe said as they approached on foot from Oak Street.

Brock turned and kept a straight face. "Where else would you find soul food?"

Chloe groaned at the bad joke.

They grabbed a corner table away from the thinly scattered late lunch crowd. After placing their orders, Brock got down to business.

"I want to go over what we've got so far."

"Come on, I just did, didn't I?"

"What you did was a dog and pony show solely for the benefit of our bosses. This is a creative meeting."

"Okay, where do you want to start?"

"Let's look at what we know for sure about Owen," Brock said.

"Well, he was only seasonally employed at the boatyard. Supplemented his income doing handyman work during the winter months. We know he did some work for the Phinneys, and it looks like he paid them back by stealing one of their snowmobiles. There is also the possibility he may have been doing something illicit on the side for or even with Harold Perreault."

"Though at this point, that's only rumor," Brock said.

"Granted, but we also have the rumor that Owen was sleeping with half the married women in town. At least according to his live-in baby mama."

"I feel like there might be a bit more validity to that one," Brock said.

"Why?"

"Jealousy is a powerful motivator. And because a woman usually knows, doesn't she?"

Chloe thought it over for a moment before nodding. "Okay, yeah. I'd say that's probably accurate."

"Who do we have on the list of likely conquests from Owen's known associates?" Brock said.

Chloe counted on her fingers. "Dr. Phinney's wife, Emily. Cammie Russo from Marlintini's."

"So, our known suspects are Keith Phinney and Rick Russo."

"Don't forget about Owen's baby mama, Melinda Hamilton."

"How is Hamilton a suspect?" Brock said.

"You said it yourself; jealousy is a powerful motivator."

"You're right," Brock said.

"So, Dr. Phinney and Rick Russo are both strong on motive, assuming

Owen was in fact sleeping with any of their spouses and they found out. And Melinda Hamilton because Owen was cheating on her with half the town.

"Keith Phinney has an alibi for the night in question, so he's out," Chloe said. "We don't yet have an alibi established for Russo, or for Hamilton."

Brock jotted several notes on the to-do list.

"Plus, we still have the drug angle," Chloe said. "I can check in again with Tommy Hanscomb, if you want."

"All right. And why don't you pay another visit to Marlintini's and talk with Cammie Russo again. Sounds like she took a shine to you."

"She did," Chloe said.

"You're more likely to get something out of her than I would. I'll follow up with Corey Hincks, my buddy at MDEA. He might be able to shed more light on Perreault."

"What about the snowmobile?" Chloe said. "You think Phinney knew about the modifications?"

Brock had been mulling it over in his mind. There was no question the Phinneys appeared to be doing well financially, and while he had no idea how much the good doctor hauled in from his practice, their wealth certainly hadn't come from whatever the town paid Emily to be the librarian. While he might have owned an expensive sled, Phinney claimed to have purchased it used.

"I don't know," Brock said.

"We need to find out where he bought it," Chloe said.

"Why don't I take that," Brock said as he scribbled another entry into his notebook and thought about how well Chloe and Phinney had hit it off during their first encounter.

"Perfect timing," Chloe said as their waitress appeared with their orders.

"Who gets the BLT?"

Following lunch, Brock dropped Chloe at the Blue Hill Fire Station where she had left her vehicle. She was about to drive over to Marlintini's when a

Hancock sheriff's vehicle pulled into the lot. It was Tommy Hanscomb. Chloe killed the ignition and got out.

"Hey," Hanscomb said as he exited the black SUV and approached.

"Hey, yourself," Chloe said. "What's up?"

"Nothing much," Hanscomb said as he lit a cigarette. "I saw your vehicle parked here earlier, and I wondered where you'd gotten to."

"Brock and I just got back from a meeting in Augusta."

"Heads of state?"

"Hancock County has those too?"

"Oh, yeah. Not with homicides, obviously, but we have them. Parlin loves that shit. I figure they were invented by some self-aggrandizing ass so the upper echelon of every police agency in the world could tell us what to do."

Chloe laughed. "You summed it up perfectly."

"Now you and Brock have your marching orders?"

"I guess. Brock isn't one for following the crowd or taking orders."

"And you are?"

"Touché."

"I can always spot a nonconformist. I'd say you were both of that ilk."

She gave him a sly grin. "You may be right."

"Heard about what happened to Brock the other night," Hanscomb said. "He doin' okay?"

"Seems to be," she said, though she knew he wouldn't tell her either way.

"That's good. I figured it might be too much, what with him just coming back from a shooting and everything."

"He seems okay to me, but then he doesn't share too much personal stuff with me anyway."

Hanscomb nodded. "I get it. Any thoughts on the identity of the shooter?"

"None. The case isn't assigned to us, anyway, for obvious reasons. Tisdale has it."

"How Weird?"

"Yup."

"Well, I'll keep my ears to the ground. Let you know if I hear anything."

"Thanks, Tommy."

"How about the Lee Owen case? You guys making any headway?"

"You mean have we narrowed in on a specific person of interest yet? No. We aren't there yet, but we're trudging forward."

"Did you get a chance to run down the lead I gave you on Perreault?"

"We met with The Bear this morning. Real charmer, that one."

Hanscomb chuckled. "He didn't get that nickname by being personable. He give you anything?"

"You mean did he come out and confess to running a drug smuggling ring and killing Lee Owen? Not by a long shot. But it was our first chance to sit down with him. We were just feeling each other out."

"Did he have an alibi for the night Owen went missing?"

"He was a little vague on that one. I don't suppose you might be willing to give us a bit more information about your source? You know, where you got the intel about the fentanyl smuggling. It might really help us if Perreault turns out to be our guy."

Hanscomb regarded her for a moment before answering. "I can't burn a source, Chloe. You know how it works."

"Obviously. I just wondered if maybe you'd be willing to reapproach. You know, on our behalf."

Hanscomb exhaled a plume of bluish smoke through his nostrils as he considered it.

"I'd understand if you're not comfortable doing that," Chloe said, attempting to give the impression she was letting him off the hook.

"Nah, I'll reach out and see if I can get something more concrete for you. No guarantees, though."

"Appreciate it, Tommy."

The base radio squawked from inside Hanscomb's SUV, followed by the dispatcher calling his unit number.

"That's my cue," Hanscomb said as he took one last drag off the cigarette before tossing it to the pavement and grinding it out under his boot. "I'll let you know if I hear anything."

42

The fancy sign on the front lawn identified the business as Down East Medical Associates, Dr. Keith Phinney's practice. Brock drove past the sign and turned into the newly paved side lot, consisting of a dozen or so spaces, the majority of which were occupied. The building was a large square single-story structure with a flat roof that sloped from front to back. The façade was a combination of red brick and weathered cedar shakes. The windows and doors were trimmed in white. The landscaping had been professionally designed, right down to the custom fieldstone walkway, bordered on one side by a manicured row of boxwoods, shaped to match the curve of the path, which led from the sidewalk to the covered glass entryway. Everything appeared to be in good repair.

Upon reaching the entryway, Brock pulled open the door and held it for an elderly couple who were exiting. He stood back, allowing them to pass before continuing inside.

A reception window sat directly ahead, flanked on either side by identical waiting areas. Brock performed a quick head count as he glanced each way. On his left sat a harried young woman attempting in vain to negotiate with three hyperactive toddlers intent on destroying the furniture. At the opposite end of the lobby sat a gray-haired couple of similar age to the people who had just exited. The woman was perusing a periodical through bifocals while the man, who Brock guessed was her husband, sat beside her, transfixed by something on the screen of his cell phone.

"May I help you?" a voice said from the opposite side of the reception window.

"I hope so," Brock said to the young brunette as he stepped up to the counter. "I'm here to speak with Dr. Phinney."

"Do you have an appointment?" she said, her eyes shifting to a desktop computer screen where Brock assumed the day's schedule was displayed.

"I do not," he said as he removed his credentials from the inside pocket of his suit coat.

A look of worry creased the woman's brow. "State police?"

"Yes, ma'am."

"Dr. Phinney's with a patient right now, and he does have several others waiting," she said, gesturing to the waiting areas.

"Not a problem," Brock said. "I'm happy to wait."

He could tell she wasn't used to dealing with law enforcement as her face telegraphed her relief at his response.

"Thank you for understanding, Detective," she said, giving him a smile. "I'll inform the doctor you're here. I'm sure he'll find a way to squeeze you in."

Brock turned away from the window and surveyed the waiting room options again. The mother attempting to wrangle her own three-ring circus wasn't faring any better than she had a moment ago. One of the children had gotten caught beneath a chair while another kicked the stuck child in the rear end, causing them to wail. The woman fixed Brock with a look of helplessness as she hurried into the fray. Brock turned to his left and walked over to the calmer of the two waiting areas, the one inhabited by the elderly couple. He concealed a grin as he imagined a similar scenario playing out between the two of them.

He selected a seat that allowed him a view of the entire lobby. It wasn't that he was expecting trouble to break out, but experience had taught him to always be alert to his surroundings.

Brock pulled out his cell and drafted a quick text to Corey Hincks about the possibility of another meet up. After sending the text, he opened a search engine on his phone and queried nearby snowmobile dealers. There were at least a half dozen motorsports dealerships listed in the greater Bangor area, and two more in Ellsworth. The only establishment located anywhere near Blue Hill was a company called Morehouse Motorsports & All-Terrain in Surry. Brock clicked the link to the company website to see if they sold previously owned models as well as new.

Brock looked up as the receptionist called out a name. A young nurse propped open a door to the inner sanctum, and the elderly couple stood and approached her. Brock followed their deliberate progress until they disappeared as the door closed behind them. His attention returned to the phone.

After several minutes of navigating pop-up ads while searching through the menu, Brock made a discovery. Not only did Morehouse Motorsports sell previously owned snowmobiles, but they specifically listed Phinney's sled under the models sold and serviced. Brock didn't know whether Phinney was going to tell him he purchased the snowmobile in a private sale or if he bought it from Morehouse, but he figured it was better to go into it with all the available facts. Even if Phinney had purchased it in a private transaction, Brock reasoned he would still need occasional service, and there was nothing closer than Morehouse Motorsports.

Brock had gotten so lost in his own research he hadn't noticed the interloper standing nearby until they tugged on one leg of his trousers. Brock lowered his phone and saw that one of the mischief-makers from the opposing waiting area, the same one previously kicking her sibling in the derrière, had absconded with a stuffed rabbit, presumably from the large basket of toys situated on the floor beside her mother.

The child smiled at Brock and reached up toward him with the rabbit in hand. It appeared to be meant as a peace offering.

"For me?" Brock said as he reached for the toy.

The girl squealed with delight as Brock held the rabbit out to look at it.

"I am so sorry," the mother said as she hurried over with her youngest slung on one hip and a children's book in the other hand.

"No worries," Brock said. "I have no idea how you even manage three at once."

"Neither do I," she said. "Come on, Lexi. Let's leave the nice man alone. I'll read you a story."

"Story," Lexi parroted before snatching the rabbit from Brock's hand and racing back to the other waiting area, where the third child stood precariously balanced atop a chair while reaching toward a wall-mounted potted ivy.

"Detective Justice," the nurse called out. "Dr. Phinney will see you now."

Brock followed the woman down a long corridor past several examination rooms, stopping at the last door on the right. She stepped to one side and gestured for Brock to enter.

Keith Phinney sat behind his desk, a telephone receiver pressed to one ear, giving instructions to someone at the other end of the line. He gestured for Brock to sit.

Brock was only half listening to the conversation as he studied the many framed diplomas and certifications hanging behind the doctor. After finishing with the "wall of me," Brock moved on to the framed art prints on the adjoining wall. He recognized the prints as Norman Rockwell paintings. They depicted a young boy and a girl during doctor visits. Brock carried a vague memory of having seen these same prints adorning the walls of his own pediatrician's office, and likely the walls of every family doctor across the country for the past half century.

"Sorry to keep you waiting, Detective," Phinney said as he ended the call. "It has been a crazy day, and it isn't over."

"I completely understand," Brock said.

"I'm afraid I can only give you a few minutes."

"That's all I need."

"How can I help you?"

"When we last spoke, you mentioned you had purchased the snowmobile used."

"Correct."

"Can I ask was this a private sale?"

"Actually, it wasn't. I bought the snowmobile from a dealership in Surry. Um, the name escapes me at the moment."

"Morehouse Motorsports?"

"That's it," Phinney said.

The doctor seemed surprised Brock already knew the name of the dealer.

"Do you think there is some connection between the murder and Morehouse?" Phinney said.

"I don't know yet," Brock said. "But we have to look at everything."

"Of course."

"How long had you owned the Arctic Cat before it was stolen?"

"Ah, let me think. I'm pretty sure we bought it in late fall 2022. Maybe October, or November? The paperwork should be back at the house. I'm happy to bring it in if you need it."

"If you wouldn't mind."

Phinney scribbled a quick reminder on a notepad. Brock didn't need to see what he wrote to know it was probably in the same illegible cursive all doctors seemed to use when writing prescriptions for their patients. He often wondered how anybody ever managed to get the correct prescription from the pharmacy.

"Did you make any modifications to the snowmobile?" Brock said.

"Modifications? I'm not sure what you mean."

"I know it's an unusual question. Let me put it another way. Did you customize anything from stock?"

"Oh, you mean like, exhaust or engine upgrades," Phinney said.

"Anything."

"I didn't customize a thing. I purchased it just the way it was. If there were any modifications, they were done before I purchased it."

Having expected that answer, Brock nodded and made a note of his own, likely far more legible.

Phinney made a point of checking his watch. "If you don't have anything else, I really must get back to my patients."

"Just one more question," Brock said. "You said Lee Owen had been doing odd jobs for you for a couple of years. Did you or your wife have any issues with him?"

"With Lee? Not at all. I know he has—had his share of legal troubles over the years, but he was a great worker for us. In fact, I would have recommended him to any of my friends, had they needed someone."

"Well, thank you for your time," Brock said, intentionally holding Phinney's gaze a bit longer than necessary.

"Not at all," Phinney said as he rose from his chair and walked around the desk. “Listen, before you go, I want to apologize for the way I behaved the other night when you and your partner—”

“Detective Wright.”

“Yes, Detective Wright. When you both came to my house. I guess I was in shock. I shouldn’t have reacted the way I did. I know you were just doing your jobs. And I know from talking with your father just how difficult the job can be at times. Please convey my apology to Detective Wright.”

Brock wondered if the mention of Albert had been meant as a jab or an olive branch. “Let me know when you locate the paperwork for the snowmobile. I’ll swing by and pick it up.”

“Will do.”

43

Marlintini's Grill was nearly deserted when Chloe walked inside looking for Cammie Russo. Dining room chairs stood upside down atop the tables as if they were at attention. And all the wall-mounted television screens were dark. Aside from the acne-plagued teen—who barely looked old enough to be employed—mopping the dining room floor and a female inventorying the shelf stock behind the bar, Chloe saw no one else in the dining room.

"Detective Wright, isn't it?" Cammie said as she appeared around the corner from the hallway that led to the kitchen.

"Hello again," Chloe said.

"What can I do for you?"

"I wondered if this might be a good time to chat."

"Honey, I own a restaurant. There is never a good time to chat. I work. I sleep. I work again. That pretty much sums up my life. But as you can see, there are no happy-hour customers yet. Won't be for another twenty minutes or so. So, now's as good a time as any. Come on. We can talk in my office."

Chloe followed her down the corridor to the rear of the establishment.

"Can I get you a coffee?" Cammie said as they passed through the swinging kitchen doors with porthole-styled windows.

"I never turn down caffeine," Chloe said.

"How do you take it?"

"Black is perfect."

"Black it is."

Cammie poured a mug for each of them, then led Chloe to her office. She slid two chairs over to the center of the room, removing the desk from the equation. Chloe took it as a good sign.

"All righty then," Cammie said. "What do you want to talk about?"

"Your relationship with Lee Owen," Chloe said matter-of-factly, hoping to trigger a reaction.

For a long moment, the woman regarded her over the brim of her mug, saying nothing. Chloe wondered if she was debating tossing her out on her ear. Finally, she spoke up.

"I guess it's good you caught me here while my husband's out getting supplies, huh?"

Chloe said nothing, waiting to see where she would take the conversation.

"I don't know where you heard about it, but yes, I did have an affair with Lee, though I'm not sure 'affair' is the right word. 'Fling' might be a better description of what we had."

"What happened?" Chloe said.

"What always happens? Rick and I were going through a bad patch, business pressures, overworked, overtired, communication bottomed out, the usual marital bullshit. In walked Lee Owen, ridiculously attractive, always the charmer, and available."

"But he had a live-in girlfriend and child," Chloe said.

"Honey, I wasn't thinking about either of them. And Lee certainly wasn't. Like I said, it wasn't an affair, it was two people acting like teenagers whenever and wherever we could hook up. I'm not proud of it, but I'm not going to apologize for it either. We had what we had, then it was over. I went back to trying to be the loving and supportive wife while running a restaurant."

"And Lee?" Chloe asked. "What about him?"

She shrugged. "I assume he moved on to other conquests."

"So, the split was amicable?"

"There was nothing to split. One day we were fucking, and the next we weren't."

"Did your husband ever find out about the relationship?"

"I don't know if Rick ever knew for sure, but he may have suspected it. He's not stupid. And let's be honest, it's tough to hide something like an affair in a small town. And Blue Hill is a small town."

"Has Rick ever made any threats against you or Lee?"

Cammie turned and eyed a picture of her and Rick hanging on the wall. "For all his faults, my Ricky is a big teddy bear. He would no more threaten me than anything. It's just not who he is."

"And Lee?" Chloe asked.

"If you're asking me if my husband might get jealous enough to punch a man like Lee, sure. I could see him going toe-to-toe with Lee. But handcuffing him to a snowmobile and sending him to the bottom of a lake is something else entirely. And that's definitely not my husband."

Chloe wondered how many other spouses believed the very same thing only to later learn they had married a killer.

There was a sharp knock at the door.

"What is it?" Cammie shouted.

The door opened slightly, and the bartender stuck her head inside.

"Sorry to interrupt, Cammie, but the customers are starting to trickle in."

"Thanks, Jenny. I'll be out in a second."

Chloe waited until she was sure the bartender had departed before saying anything further.

"Look, Detective, I expect Rick will be back at any minute, so we really need to wrap this up. Do you have any other questions?"

Chloe smiled disarmingly. "No, that's all I have for now. Thank you for your honesty."

"That's me, Honest Cammie."

Morehouse Motorsports & All-Terrain was located on Route 172 in the town of Surry. The building, an elongated white single-story concrete block structure, was fronted on the showroom side almost entirely in plate glass, while the opposite end of the business featured a half dozen garage bays. Four of the bays were standing open. Brock figured if the motorsports business was anything like the automobile industry, then service after the sale was where the real money existed.

As he turned into the patron parking lot on the right side of the building, Brock noticed a man dressed in tan chinos with a light blue dress shirt and tie standing between the building and a dumpster, having a smoke. Brock parked on the opposite side of the lot and exited the SUV. He watched as the man tossed the remainder of his cigarette to the pavement, painted on a shark's smile, then began walking in Brock's direction. The predatory demeanor clued Brock in immediately that the man was more likely a member of the sales staff than the owner or manager.

"Good afternoon," the man said, extending a nicotine-stained hand in greeting. "Welcome to Morehouse Motorsports. I'm Tim."

"Tim," Brock said, playing along but not providing his own name.

"Great spring day for toy buying, isn't it?" Tim said.

"I guess so," Brock said.

"You look like an ATV man to me. Am I right?"

"Not exactly," Brock said. "Actually, I'm here about a snowmobile." He watched the confusion glide across Tim's face like a cloud.

"Not exactly snowmobile weather, friend. I'm afraid that season has already passed by. Hell, the black flies will be here before you know it. Am I right?"

Brock flashed his credentials, taking immense pleasure in watching disappointment register on Tim's face as his imagined sales commission dissolved into mist before his very eyes.

"Detective, huh?" Tim said. "Guess that means you're not here to make a purchase."

"Good guess," Brock said, returning the wallet to his pocket. "Who would I speak with about used snowmobiles?"

"Follow me," Tim said.

He led Brock inside to the showroom floor where two other employees were busy hanging a large brightly colored banner above one corner of the sales floor. The banner advertised spring ATV sales and special financing.

"As you can see, we've moved on," Tim said. "It's gator season. That, along with three- and four-wheeled ATVs and dirt bikes. Best way to get a kid off the internet? Buy 'em a dirt bike. Am I right?"

Brock was beginning to wonder if Tim knew any other catchphrases.

"You got kids?" Tim said, turning the page on his sales playbook.

Brock shook his head.

"Well, what about you?" Tim said, his hopeful smile returning. "You're never too old for a dirt bike. You sure I can't interest you in something that would put a little fun back into your life? Maybe a toy for the little woman."

"I'm divorced," Brock said, intentionally maintaining a stoic expression.

Tim's phony smile faded.

"What I'd really like is to talk to someone about a snowmobile you may have sold?"

"Yeah, okay. Hang on a sec. I'll go and fetch the sales manager."

"Thanks," Brock said, projecting more enthusiasm than was necessary as Tim slunk away.

44

Chloe was halfway to her SUV when she noticed a woman hurrying toward her from the other side of the lot. It took a moment before Chloe recognized her as the waitress from the first visit to Marlintini's.

"Hey," the woman said. "Can I speak with you, officer?"

"Of course. You waited on my partner and me the other night."

"I wasn't sure you'd remember me. I'm Judy Babbage."

"What can I do for you, Judy?"

Judy looked around nervously before she spoke again. "I can't talk long because I'm expected inside, but I've been listening to people talk about what you guys are up to."

"What people?" Chloe said.

"Just townsfolk. Everyone is talking about you and your partner and what happened to Lee Owen."

"And what are they saying about it, or us, Judy?"

Judy checked the lot again before answering, but nobody appeared to be paying them any mind. "I know you guys have been looking into who Lee might have been sleeping around with."

"And you'd be in a position to help with that?" Chloe said.

"Maybe," Judy said. "It is possible Lee may have upset some of the married men around here."

"Like whom, specifically?" Chloe said.

Judy paused, staring at Chloe as if she was trying to decide whether she really wanted to get further involved.

Chloe considered pressing her to do the right thing. If Judy wavered now, they might never learn what she wanted to tell them.

"If you're worried about getting someone in trouble, you won't," Chloe said, attempting to disarm the woman with a friendly smile. "At least not unless they've done something criminal. We're not the marriage police, Judy."

"It's not someone else I'm worried about. It's me."

"I don't understand," Chloe said. "Are you worried someone will find out you talked to me?"

Judy looked as if she might bolt as a dark-colored sedan pulled into the lot.

"I can tell you're nervous about something," Chloe continued. "Anything you tell me in confidence will remain that way."

Judy's head whipped around to face her again. "You guarantee that, can you?"

"I promise to do my absolute best. Obviously, I'd still need to independently confirm anything you tell me, but nobody will know the information came from you."

Judy paused a long moment before taking a step away from Chloe.

"Look, I've gotta get back to work."

"Seriously, Judy," Chloe said. "Just tell me whatever it is you've got to say."

"You're looking in the wrong direction," Judy blurted out at last.

"I don't understand," Chloe said.

The waitress shifted nervously from one foot to the other like a child needing to use the bathroom. "Y'all are too busy focusing on Lee's conquests."

"I'm not sure I understand you, Judy. Who do you think we should be looking at?"

"Lee's girlfriend, Melinda Hamilton," Judy said before she spun on her heels and hurried inside the tavern.

Brock checked his cell phone for missed messages as he wandered the showroom floor. The only text was from Chloe.

Ran into Tommy. He'll reach out 2 source again.

Brock frowned. He thought he had been very clear with her about wanting to speak to Deputy Hanscomb himself. He couldn't help wondering if the meeting between Chloe and Hanscomb really had been happenstance as her text seemed to indicate.

"May I help you, sir?" a voice boomed from the other side of the showroom.

Brock looked up and pocketed his phone. Unlike the tall, thin salesman with the bad skin and shark-like smile, the man approaching him was as big around as he was tall, reminding Brock of a sea turtle standing on its hind legs.

"Name's Curtis Smith," he said as he shot out a hand in greeting. "I'm the general manager."

"Detective Justice," Brock said as he gripped the sweaty offering while trying not to grimace.

"I understand you need some information about snowmobiles."

"That's right."

"Well, follow me, and we'll see if we can't fix you right up, Detective Justice."

Smith led the way to a sun-filled office that overlooked the woods to the rear of the business. A scarred wooden chair rail extended along the entire circumference of the room. Beneath it was dark-stained faux paneling straight out of the 1970s. The upper half of each wall consisted of painted drywall covered in cheaply framed colored photographs of various local children's sports teams sponsored by Morehouse Motorsports.

"Looks like you do a lot for the community here," Brock said, pointing to the pictures.

"The owner really likes giving back to the kids," Smith said, beaming proudly as he pointed to several pictures on an adjoining wall, each one depicting children racing dirt bikes. "We sponsor several local motocross events each year."

"Cool," Brock said.

"Now, let's see if we can't find what you're looking for. You say the snowmobile you're searching for was sold by us?"

"Yes," Brock said. "According to the owner, he purchased the snowmobile from this dealership in 2022. He wasn't positive on the date, though. Could have been late fall of '22."

Smith sat down at his desk, donned a pair of reading glasses, and turned to a desktop monitor. His pudgy fingers hovered over the keyboard as if he were a pianist about to take a request. "What is the name of the customer?"

"Phinney," Brock said. "Keith Phinney."

"Doc Phinney?" Smith said, surprised. "Indeed, he did buy that sled here. Handled the sale myself. Gave him a nice discount too, on account of his being a sponsor of some of our teams and all."

Brock waited as Smith punched up the details of the sale.

"Here we are," Smith said, leaning back in his chair and lacing his fingers together atop his substantial belly.

Brock heard Smith's chair creak alarmingly as if the wood might simply break apart. Smith seemed oblivious to the sound.

"Keith Phinney purchased the Arctic Cat from us on October 24th, 2022. Reason I remember it so well is because we had literally just taken it in trade from the previous owner on a newer model Cat. I don't know how much you know about sleds, Detective, but those ZR 9000s still command a pretty hefty price tag."

"I've heard," Brock said as he jotted the date in his notebook. "I don't suppose you have the previous owner's information, do you?"

"Of course we do. Let me just switch screens here. Would you like me to print out copies for you?"

"I'd appreciate it," Brock said.

"Happy to help."

Brock listened and watched as the ancient dot matrix printer next to Smith's desk came to life and began to noisily feed paper in from a box on the floor beneath the credenza.

"Never actually seen one of those," Brock said, pointing to the printer.

"This old printer has been here as long as the company," Smith said.

"The owner wanted to toss it out, but I said I wanted it for the office. Pretty cool, right?"

Brock, surprised to see anyone could still locate paper for the antique electronic, had to admit it was.

Smith continued to test the chair's durability as he leaned his heavy frame to one side, then tore off the printed sheet and handed it to Brock. "Now, let's get you the details of the previous owner."

Brock perused the information outlined in the transaction with Keith Phinney while Smith typed. The "nice discount" Smith alluded to was five hundred dollars. Five hundred was nothing to sneeze at, Brock figured, but given that Phinney had still paid sixteen grand for a used snowmobile made the discount seem paltry by comparison. Though Brock had no way of knowing how much the previous owner had received for the trade-in, he was confident Morehouse Motorsports had made a "nice profit."

"Just out of curiosity," Brock said. "Do you know if any modifications were made to the snowmobile before you sold it to Phinney?"

"Modifications?" Smith said. "How do you mean?"

"Some type of custom add-on. An exhaust, maybe, or something along those lines."

"No, we wouldn't do anything like that here. Not without the customer specifically requesting it. And that Cat is a top-of-the-line machine. Anytime we take something like that in trade, we give it a quick spruce-up, then turn right around and resell it. Not to mention any aftermarket stuff like you're describing would raise havoc with the manufacturer's warranty, adding to the price I would have had to charge Phinney."

Brock nodded his understanding and made another note.

"Got it," Smith said at last. "The previous owner's name is Parlin. Gene Parlin."

It was all Brock could do to keep his jaw from striking the floor.

"Helluva nice guy. He buys all his toys here."

Brock kept his expression impassive as he scribbled Parlin's name in his notebook and underlined it, followed by the word "toys."

"Would you like a printout of this too?"

45

Brock departed from the dealership carrying the printouts and an uneasy feeling in his gut. Something wasn't right about these coincidences, if that's what they were. He wasn't a big believer in coincidence to begin with, but he did believe patterns were often a good indicator of something being amiss, especially when investigating homicides. Learning that the handcuffs used to bind Lee Owen to the snowmobile had previously been issued to Albert Justice was bad enough, but learning that the snowmobile in question, the one reported stolen by Dr. Phinney, had previously been owned by Sheriff Parlin was a bridge too far. Brock didn't know about Denmark, but he was beginning to suspect something was rotten in the state of Maine. Particularly within the Blue Hill Peninsula.

He was reaching for his cell, intending to place a call to Chloe, when it rang.

"You must have ESP," Brock said.

"Why is that?" Chloe said.

"I was about to call you. You available to meet?"

"Just leaving Blue Hill. Name it."

Twenty minutes later, Brock pulled into the lot of Freshies in Winterport. The restaurant/deli had previously been a Sunoco gas station, but the missing pumps, combined with the backhoe parked unattended behind a temporary cyclone fence, gave away the change. If that wasn't enough of a hint that Freshies was no longer in the gas business, the one cent price per gallon displayed on the electronic sign for fuel was a dead giveaway. Freshies was exactly the kind of place Brock frequented when he'd worked uniform patrol in York County. While not known for their ambience, places like Freshies often served the best food around.

He found Chloe sitting alone in a far corner of the dining room with her laptop open. She was typing madly but apparently still had one eye on the door as she paused long enough to wave him over. Having worked alongside younger troopers before, Brock was impressed with Chloe's survival skills. Not every law enforcement officer was as aware of their surroundings. Lack of situational awareness was right up there with tombstone courage when it came to getting yourself killed in this business. Brock remembered his training officer, Elmer Moore, uttering those very words.

He crossed the room and sat down across from her.

"Here," Chloe said as she slid a cardboard to-go cup of coffee toward him. "Figured you might need the pick-me-up."

"Thanks," Brock said before taking a sip of the steaming liquid. "What are you working on?"

"Just trying to catch up on my supplemental reports," she said before saving her work. She closed the laptop and slid it inside her leather briefcase. "It's amazing how much more writing is required when the investigation is a homicide."

"And this is just the beginning," Brock said.

As a new detective, Brock's mentor had hammered that very point home. Building a successful murder case is like building a literal mountain of evidence. Facts, eyewitness accounts, physical evidence, analysis, continuity, and logic must all point overwhelmingly to the person responsible for taking the life of another. The larger the mountain constructed by detectives, the more impervious the case will be to the onslaught of attacks mounted by the defense. It was inevitable that evidence would be suppressed during future judicial proceedings for any number of reasons.

Graphic photos of a particularly gruesome scene might be deemed too prejudicial by the presiding judge. Analysis of physical evidence could be called into question. The evidential chain of custody might be broken. Regardless of how well any homicide case is constructed, no matter how diligent and thorough the investigators are, there are always weaknesses, things that could have been done better. Things missed. The goal is always the same, to keep those weak points to an absolute minimum. Brock knew this from experience. His job now, in addition to solving the murder of Lee Owen, was to impart that knowledge to Chloe.

He squinted at the wall-mounted food menu as he carefully considered his next words.

"How'd you happen to run into Deputy Hanscomb?"

"Actually, he ran into me," Chloe said. "I was just getting ready to leave the fire department when he pulled into the lot."

Brock noticed Chloe's pinched expression as she regarded him for a second.

"I wasn't stepping on your toes, if that's what you're implying," Chloe said.

"Not at all," Brock said, feigning innocence. "I was just curious."

She didn't look convinced.

"So, what did he have to say? Will he help us?"

"Tommy's pretty protective of his sources, obviously, but he promised to reach out and see if he could find out anything more."

Brock hated the idea of depending on someone else to act as a go-between. Things had a tendency to get lost the longer the information chain got.

"Any luck with Cammie Russo?" Brock said as he removed a paper menu from the next table and gave it the once-over.

"She admitted to having an affair with Owen," Chloe said. "But told me it was over and had been for months."

"You believe her?" Brock said, wondering how many unfaithful spouses had uttered those very same words. And believed them.

"Yeah, I think she was being straight with me," Chloe said. "About the affair, anyway."

"And her husband?" Brock said. "Did he find out?"

"Rick," Chloe said, shaking her head. "She doesn't think so, but she also said Rick isn't stupid. He may have suspected something."

"Did you ask her how she thought he might react?"

"I did. She said he would have no reservations getting in Lee's face about it and confronting him man-to-man."

"What about killing him? Did she think he'd have any reservations about that?"

"She seemed convinced he wasn't capable."

"Everyone is capable, Chloe," Brock said. "If the right buttons are pushed."

They both went to the counter to place their orders. Mash potato pizza for Chloe, a buffalo chicken wrap for Brock, and more coffee for both.

After returning to the table, Chloe spoke up again.

"I did have another unexpected encounter, though."

"Oh?" Brock said. "With whom?"

"Judy, our waitress from Marlintini's. Remember her?"

Brock quickly scanned his memory banks for a mental picture of the woman Chloe was referring to, but he came up blank. "Which waitress?"

"The redheaded woman who waited on us the very first day we were in town. The day we recovered Owen's body."

"Okay, I guess," Brock said, thinking the redhead apparently hadn't made much of an impression on him, as he was unable to conjure up an image. "What did she want?"

"She wanted to let us know we may be looking in the wrong place for our killer."

Brock nearly choked on his coffee. "So, the waitress is a part-time amateur sleuth?"

"I don't know about that, but it sounds like she might have her fingers on the pulse of Blue Hill. She definitely keeps her eyes and ears open."

Brock had his doubts. During his years in Major Crimes Unit South, he had run across more than his share of busybodies. And, though many of them were well intentioned, most saw only what they wanted to see.

"The town gossip, then," Brock said. "And what exactly does Judy the waitress/amateur sleuth think we should be focused on?"

"She heard we've been running down the jealous-husband angle, looking at some of Owen's married conquests," Chloe said.

"And she doesn't think that's a good use of our time?"

"Actually, she suggested we might want to consider another angle."

"Which is?"

"Lee wasn't the only one fooling around."

Brock let the comment hang in the air for a moment while he tried it on. "The waitress is suggesting that Lee's live-in girlfriend w—"

"And baby mama," Chloe said, interrupting him mid-thought. "Don't forget baby mama."

"Right," Brock said. "Owen's live-in girlfriend and baby mama was having an affair of her own?"

"That is what she was getting at," Chloe said.

"I don't suppose she provided you with something useful, like a name."

"She didn't. But she did suggest that we might want to talk to Melinda Hamilton again."

Brock thought about the baby. "I don't suppose she mentioned anything about the child possibly being fathered by this other man?"

"Nope, but it's something to consider."

The cook arrived and slid the orders onto the table in front of them. "Careful of the plates," he said. "They're hot."

"Looks great," Chloe said.

"Bon appétit," the man said.

"I love these French places," Brock said. "So high class."

Brock watched as Chloe pried a slice of pizza from the steaming pie and took a healthy bite. As she chewed, she maintained eye contact with him. Though they hadn't worked together long enough to read each other the way long-time partners do, Brock knew something was off. Something she had kept hidden until now. It would have been hard to quantify if he'd been asked, but he knew just the same. It was in the tone of her voice, her expression, and the way she positioned herself in the chair.

Even during his brief marriage to Carmen, Brock had learned to read the signs of trouble brewing. He was aware that women are far better at concealing their feelings than their male counterparts, at least in Brock's experience. But once you knew what to look for, the warning signs flashed like neon. And those signs often meant trouble. Chloe's tell meant she knew something he didn't.

"Something wrong?" Brock said.

"Why do you ask?" Chloe said.

There it was again. An almost imperceptible snippiness to her tone. She was pissed at him; he was sure of it. He pressed on.

"Chloe, if you've got something to say, just say it."

She continued to stare at him, as if sizing him up, or maybe trying to decide the best way to broach the subject.

"I got an interesting phone call a short time ago," Chloe said at last.

And there it is, Brock thought. He'd been busted. A break in the secret chain he'd been forging. Not quite as destructive as a break in the evidentiary chain, but it might have a chilling effect on their fledgling partnership nonetheless, assuming that's what this was. Would Clarence really do him up like that?

"Who from?" Brock said.

"Clarence Snyder," Chloe said matter-of-factly.

"Oh?" Brock said, trying to project innocence as he dipped a hot fry into the congealed tomato puddle passing as ketchup he'd squeezed onto the plate. "What did he want?"

Chloe's face remained stoic. She wasn't going to make this easy.

"He was trying to get a hold of you but wasn't having any luck, so he called me. Something about handcuffs and old issued equipment. Guess he must have figured, since we were supposed to be working this case together, that I already knew about your visit down to Augusta to peruse the property archives. I can only imagine what kind of an idiot I sounded like when Clarence figured out I didn't know what the hell he was talking about."

"Look," Brock said. "I was going to—"

"No, you look," Chloe said, her face flushed with anger. "Is this how you work a case? Is it your standard MO to cut whoever you're working with out of the loop while you run your own shadow investigation? Is that what you're teaching me?"

"Chloe, I—"

"I might not be half as pissed if we hadn't done this dance already, Brock. If you hadn't just read me the riot act about freelancing. So, is that how this works? You can keep secrets and do whatever the hell you want, and I have to report every move to you. Or worse, run it by you for your goddamn approval?"

"May I speak?" Brock said as he looked around the room to see whose attention her raised voice was grabbing. The cook quickly looked away.

Chloe grabbed another slice off the plate without breaking eye contact. "Don't let me stop you. Not like I could anyway."

Brock let out a deep sigh before speaking. "Look, I get that you're pissed. You have every right to be. I did tell you we should keep each other in the loop. And then I did just the opposite."

"Yup, you did," she said. "Again."

"I had a very good reason," Brock said.

Chloe tore another large bite off the slice. "I can't wait to hear this," she said around a mouthful of food.

"I was trying to give you deniability," Brock said.

"Deniability? For what?"

"I managed to trace the cuffs we removed from Owen to a bulk order placed by the Maine State Police back in 1987."

Chloe stopped chewing as her eyes widened. "You're telling me those handcuffs belonged to a trooper?"

Brock nodded.

"Who?"

"That's the thing. I had to keep this from Cumberland too. If I let her in on this, she'd likely yank us both off the case."

"Jesus, Brock, spit it out. Whose handcuffs are they?"

Brock glanced at the nearby tables before answering.

"Well?" Chloe said impatiently.

"They belong to my father."

46

"You can't be serious," Chloe said as she dropped the pizza crust back on the plate and wiped her hands on the napkin. "You don't think Albert killed Lee Owen, do you?"

"I'm not sure what I think," Brock said.

"Have you confronted him?"

Brock nodded. "Last night."

"And?"

"He told me the camp was burglarized last fall. Said his handcuffs were stolen along with a few other things."

"Then there'll be a police report, right?"

"Told me he never filed one."

"What? Why the hell not?"

"He figured the sheriff's department had more important things to do than to chase down his old memorabilia."

Chloe sat there without speaking for a long moment. At last, she said, "So basically, he's dropped you right in it, hasn't he?"

Brock nodded. "Yup."

"What are you going to do?"

"Nothing, for now. Albert still has an alibi for the night Owen disappeared, remember?"

"Then you should come clean with Cumberland."

"Do you want to see us pulled off this case? Because that's exactly what will happen as soon as she finds out."

"Of course I don't. We've worked too hard on this. It's ours."

Brock was pleased to see Chloe taking a personal interest in her first homicide investigation. That passion would bode well for her future as a detective.

"I'm keeping this close to the vest for now," Brock said. "And if Cumberland asks, I never mentioned anything to you."

"I'm not all that keen on lying to her, Brock."

"Trust me, it beats the alternative."

Chloe snatched up the last remaining slice of pizza from her platter, then looked at Brock before biting into it. "Damn, you're on a roll. Any other bombs you want to drop on me?"

"Actually, there is one more. I just found out who owned the snowmobile prior to Keith Phinney."

"Oh, let me guess," Chloe said. "The Bear?"

Brock shook his head. "Sheriff Parlin."

They departed Winterport going their separate ways with a plan to regroup first thing in the morning. Chloe told him she was looking forward to getting at least one good night's sleep. Despite the exhaustion he was feeling, Brock wasn't looking forward to sleep given that his post-shooting nightmares had begun again. He decided to take a drive out to Second Pond. Cumberland had ordered him to stay out of the sniper investigation, and he knew Detective Tisdale had most likely already canvassed the area. Just the same, Brock wanted another look.

It was nearly dusk by the time Brock turned off Route 176 onto Douglass Loop Road. He parked at the top of the road where the loop intersected with the access road leading down to Second Pond. Between the recent rains and the heavy vehicle traffic, the access road had become almost impassable. He could see deep muddy ruts traversing the middle of the road and the tire impressions of large SUVs and trucks lining both sides.

Brock popped the hatch as he got out of the Ford, having finally learned the value of his all-weather boots. He laced up his Bean boots, then descended the muddy track to Second Pond.

As he neared the water, he felt an invisible barrier pushing back against him. An indescribable force attempting to prevent him from reaching the site of the shooting. It was impossible not to feel it. Brock fought through the sensation knowing that it was merely a symptom of PTSD, and he couldn't allow himself to succumb to it.

Though the sun had set, the sky above the pond appeared much lighter. Lit by the sun from below the tree line to the west, deep lavender clouds drifted across a pale sky, the bottom edges of each painted an intense pink color, reminding Brock of cotton candy.

The humidity had dropped again, leaving the night air feeling crisp. The remnants of ice and snow had completely vanished, replaced by the organic smell of lake water and decomposing vegetation. He paused at water's edge and gazed upon the distant shoreline. There was something odd about the land on the opposite side of the pond. He could just make out the dim flat shape of the ground beyond the trees. It was as if whatever was above the slope had been blanketed with a large gray tarp covering acres of ground. He hadn't noticed this before. Not during the recovery of Lee Owen's body and not while getting shot at. But now as the light quickly faded, the distant shore seemed to glow.

As he stood there thinking, Brock caught another scent carried by the breeze. Tobacco. And not from a cigarette or a cigar either. This was a sweeter smell. Someone was smoking a pipe. He turned to his right and squinted, trying to make out where the smell was originating. Through the swaying bows of evergreens, Brock caught sight of a distant light that he presumed was coming from one of the seasonal homes dotting this side of the pond. He turned and started back up the road to his vehicle. Lt. Cumberland had warned him to keep his nose out of How Weird's investigation, but now, thanks to the smell of pipe tobacco, his nose was leading him directly into it. *Oh, the irony*, he thought.

Brock climbed into the SUV, then drove slowly along the loop road, trying to locate the source of the smell. He was nearing the next curve in the road when he saw a vehicle parked to his left in the driveway of a small two-story Cape. A shadowy figure was struggling to secure a tarpaulin over a large tractor. Brock parked the unmarked and got out.

As he approached, the figure turned toward him. Brock could just make out the elderly man's features in the glow of the pipe.

"Evening," the man said.

"Good evening," Brock said, removing the ID case from his pocket. "I was hoping you could answer a couple of questions."

The man studied the ID for a moment, then looked back at Brock. "State police, huh? Aren't you the guys that have been making such a mess of my boat launch?"

Brock nodded as he pocketed the wallet. "I guess that would be us. I am sorry about that, sir. But between recovering a body and getting shot at, it really couldn't be helped."

"You want to get back on my good side, give me a hand with this tarp. Damn wind is making this job harder than it needs to be."

Brock grabbed a hold of the tarp and secured one corner to the rear frame of the tractor with a bungee cord while the old man performed the same maneuver on the opposite side.

"That okay?" Brock said as he stood back to check their work.

"It'll do. Name's Wilber Stubbs."

"Brock Justice."

"You got questions, you said."

"A few," Brock said.

"Better come inside, then."

47

Brock departed after spending over an hour talking with Stubbs. The conversation had left his thoughts a swirling jumble of possibilities. The old man hadn't spoken with Detective Tisdale or anyone else about the shooting or the body recovery, but he knew a great deal about the history of Second Pond, Blue Hill, and the strange glow Brock had seen across the water.

"The glow you saw is the old mine," Stubbs said.

"I didn't know there was any mining taking place in Blue Hill," Brock said.

"There isn't, at least not for the past fifty years. The mine closed around 1970. Guess they figured they'd exhausted it."

"Exhausted what?" Brock said.

"Minerals, copper, manganese, stuff like that."

"Who owns the land now?"

"It's changed hands several times. The current owner is a company out of Portland, but the name escapes me. The original owners set aside seven or eight million for site maintenance, then turned it over to another company. Hard for me to keep up, but it's always another private firm."

"The money was for cleanup?" Brock said, making a note to check on the current ownership.

"No. No, the cleanup is done. Now it's about keeping the site secure and keeping people out of it."

"They've got their own security?" Brock said.

"I'd imagine. Last time I was over there, I was still a young man. Dangerous place, though. Not someplace you'd want someone poking around."

Brock couldn't disagree.

"You say someone shot at you from over there?"

"I'm not sure where the shot came from exactly, but it originated from that side of the pond."

"You might check with them for security video and the like. I'm sure they monitor the area. Great place to take a shot from too."

Brock stopped writing long enough to look up at Stubbs. "What do you mean?"

"Just what I said. I told you I used to sneak around over there as a young man. If you were looking to shoot something near the boat launch, like a deer maybe, the old mine is a great place to set up. You'd have a direct line of sight straight across the pond."

Stubbs's last words echoed in Brock's head as he drove north in the dark.

The Troop J barracks were deserted, the lone exception being a young uniform trooper who was working on an operating under the influence report.

"Hey," Brock said. "Didn't expect to find anyone else here at this hour."

"That makes two of us," the trooper, whose name tag read *A. Chandler*, said.

"Brock Justice," he said, extending a hand.

"I know who you are," Chandler said, making no attempt to accept the offering.

Brock grinned. "Guess that answers that question."

"And what question is that?" Chandler said.

"What you think about my being here."

Brock hesitated for a moment, awaiting a response, but Chandler said nothing, returning instead to his paperwork. Brock continued toward the conference room he and Chloe had commandeered for the investigation.

"Why'd you do it?" Chandler said to Brock's back.

Brock stopped in his tracks and turned to face the trooper. "Do what?"

"You know. Why did you testify against Trooper Mathers? Why would you do that to one of your own?"

"Because he shot and killed an unarmed man," Brock said.

"As I heard it, you were the only witness," Chandler said.

"Your point?"

"Nobody would have ever known is all I'm saying."

"I'd know," Brock said.

"You ruined Mathers's life, Justice."

"Evan ruined his own life. Anyway, don't assume you know everything about what happened that day."

Chandler appeared to consider Brock's comment before nodding. "Fair enough. All's I'm saying is I don't think I could have done it."

"Let's hope you never have to find out."

Brock left the young trooper to his own devices and continued down the hall to the conference room. He opened the door and switched on the light. The room was hot and stuffy, having been shuttered for a couple of days. Brock decided to work with the door open.

A quick scan of the murder board confirmed that he and Chloe had filled in many of the gaps over the past two days, but there was still much to do. As in every homicide investigation, each new piece of information gleaned only led to more questions. His conversation with Stubbs opened the door to all kinds of new questions, and the timeline they had been constructing for Lee Owen's last day still had gaps that couldn't be accounted for. The biggest of which was how he had gotten from Marlintini's to the Phinney home to steal the snowmobile. Had someone given him a ride from the bar? Or had he phoned someone to come pick him up? There had to be a reason Owen had left his vehicle in the parking lot, but what was it? Was he intending to have the same person give him a ride back to Marlintini's after he'd finished dropping off the stolen snowmobile?

Brock absently ran a palm over the whiskers on his face as he thought about how much they still didn't know. He paused as his fingers brushed against the scar on his cheek. A constant reminder of just how close Terry Kirke had come to ending him. *Maybe it would have been better if he had,* Brock thought, and not for the first time.

Brock shook off the negative thought and refocused his attention on Owen's murder. Where was Owen taking Phinney's snowmobile, anyway? Did he think it had drugs hidden inside it? Of course, this question led to an entirely different thought. Who installed the false compartment on the snowmobile in the first place? Had Phinney done it? Or hired it out? Or was Phinney even aware of it? Sheriff Parlin's knowledge of the false bottom seemed too implausible. If Parlin had been responsible for the modification, would he then trade the snowmobile in and risk having the compartment discovered? Brock reasoned Parlin could just as easily have sold it to Phinney in the first place, cutting the dealership completely out of the equation.

So many unanswered questions. Brock's head was beginning to ache. He was overtired and overcaffeinated. His six-month leave had clearly left him out of practice.

He was rifling through his briefcase for Ibuprofen when his cell phone vibrated. He checked the screen and found a text from Kimberly Millick.

Heard about the shooting. U ok?

Brock pursed his lips as he considered the question. Sometimes Kimber felt less like his therapist and more like his conscience prodding him to do the right thing. He typed out a short response.

Yeah. They missed.

Very funny. U want 2 meet up?

Meet up? he thought, the idea filling him with excitement as he thought about their last encounter. Where was she? Her response came before he could ask.

I'm in Bangor for a conference. Hollywood Casino Hotel.

Brock checked the time. It was nearly ten thirty. If he left now, he could be there in half an hour. If he drove like he was in an unmarked state police unit, he could probably be there in twenty minutes.

Where R U exactly?

Casino Bar. Losing.

C U in 20

Brock encountered little traffic as he sped along Route 1A, wondering if this was a good idea. Kimber had been very good for him to begin with. She had helped him untie some of his knots, and she had kept him from becoming victimized by the state police therapist, who had turned out to be nothing more than an informational conduit to the colonel's office. Hell, the colonel might just as well have sat in on Brock's sessions for all the confidentiality he'd had.

No there was no question she had been good for him initially. But now it was different. They had crossed an ethical line neither of them was fully prepared for. He could have blamed his state of mind during the trial, or perhaps his pending divorce, or even the alcohol they'd both consumed that night. But the truth was they were physically attracted to one another. In the medical code of ethics, he was sure there was a rule about therapists sleeping with patients. In fact, she had said as much, but this was the real world, and in the real world, shit happens. He told himself that he was going to continue seeing her professionally only when he needed her counsel. Their night of bad decisions was a one-off. At least that's what he wanted to believe. But it wasn't the truth, and he knew it. He suspected she knew it too.

As he neared the hotel, Brock wondered what Kimber told herself.

Kimber looked just as good to Brock as she had nearly a month ago when he'd last seen her. Dressed in blue jeans and a thin white sweater, she sat alone on a stool at the far end of the bar, nursing a dirty martini and a small stack of poker chips. He knew she liked to gamble; it was one of her admitted vices. Brock guessed he might be one of the others.

"There's a sight for sore eyes," she said, a knowing smile warming her features as he sat down beside her. "What took you so long, Detective?"

"You won't believe it, but traffic was a bear," Brock said.

"You're right, I don't believe a word of it," Kimber said as she leaned over and kissed him square on the lips, lingering for several beats before she finally withdrew. He could taste the alcohol on her lips and see the desire in her eyes. "I missed you."

"I missed you too," he said as he signaled the bartender over and ordered a double whiskey, neat.

The bartender placed Brock's glass on a napkin and slid it toward him. "Would the lady like another?" he said to Kimber.

"Why not?" she said. "And put these on my room."

The bartender took her empty away and moved down the bar to mix her drink.

Kimber's attention returned to Brock. "What do you think we should do about it?" she said, placing a warm hand on his thigh and leaning in close.

"About what?" Brock said.

"All this missing," she said, her voice husky.

"Well, I thought maybe we could discuss it over a drink and then see where it leads."

"Oh, I think we both know exactly where it will lead," she said.

Their conversation lasted exactly fifteen minutes, both finishing their drinks in record time before departing the casino for her hotel room. They were all over each other in the elevator, and Brock wondered what might have happened had they been in a taller building.

Forty-five minutes later, they both lay naked and spent amid a tangle of bedding.

"Oh, my God," Kimber said. "Tell me again why we aren't together?"

Because you're supposed to be my therapist, a thought Brock wisely kept to himself.

"I'm not sure that's a complication either of us need," Brock said.

"Or maybe it is," she said as she ran a fingernail seductively across his chest, then downward.

As Brock felt his excitement stir, he wondered what they were doing. She was risking her license to practice, and he was complicating his personal and professional life.

As Kimber rolled on top of him and kissed him deeply, Brock stopped thinking.

48

Brock awoke to the shrill sound of a ringing cell phone. Disoriented, he reached for the wall shelf above the headboard where he kept his phone to charge. There was neither a phone nor a shelf but something hanging that he only managed to knock askew. His eyes sprung open, and he pushed himself up into a sitting position in the bed, momentarily confused by the unfamiliar surroundings. He was still in Kimber's hotel room at the Hollywood Casino in Bangor. He looked over to Kimber's side of the bed. Empty. The cell phone kept shrilling like some kind of lunatic siren from over near the desk. He forced himself up and stumbled across the room, finally locating his cell in the pocket of his suit coat, which was draped over the desk chair.

"Justice," he mumbled.

"Brock, where are you?" Chloe said. "I've been texting you for like twenty minutes."

Brock held the phone away from his face and checked the text messages. He had missed a half dozen in all.

"Well, you've got me now," he said. "What is it?"

"I just swung by Gene Parlin's house to see the poker den, and you'll never guess who I saw arguing with the good sheriff."

Brock rubbed a hand over his face as he surveyed the room. All of

Kimber's personal effects were gone. She had snuck out and left him without so much as a goodbye. He walked toward the bathroom, thinking maybe she had moved her things into the bathroom so as not to wake him, but it was empty. Kimber was gone.

"Brock, are you listening to anything I've said?" Chloe said.

"Yeah, yeah. I heard you. You ran into Sheriff Parlin."

"I knew you weren't listening. Where are you?"

That's a long story, he thought. And one he wouldn't be sharing with her. "I'm listening now. Something about Parlin in an argument. Did you ask him about it?"

"Of course not. I didn't want them to see me, so I kept driving."

"Them? Who's them?"

"Parlin and your dad."

It took Brock the better part of an hour to drive to his apartment, shower, shave, change into fresh clothing, then meet up with Chloe at Denny's in Bangor.

"You look like hell," Chloe said.

"Exactly the look I was going for."

"Like you've been on a bender," Chloe said as she reached out and wiped something from under his chin. "You missed some," she said, holding up a bit of dried shaving cream on one finger.

Brock took a throat-searing gulp of hot coffee. His mind was a jumbled mess of thoughts. What had been a long and pleasurable but highly inappropriate night was now apparently about to be followed by a day-from-hell chaser.

"Where were you when I called? You didn't go home, did you?"

"Doesn't matter," Brock said as he took another gulp, this time burning the roof of his mouth. There was no way he was about to share his dark and dirty secrets with her. Not that he could have adequately explained it anyway. Brock forced himself to focus. The coffee helped. "Tell me again what you were doing at Parlin's house."

"I already told you. I thought I'd pop around under the guise of picking up his written statement alibiing everyone the night Owen disappeared. But what I really wanted to do was to check out the house where these poker nights take place. Nice house. A little too nice, if you know what I mean."

Brock didn't know what she meant. "Pretend I don't," he said. "What do you mean?"

"Remember what Phinney's house looked like?"

"Yeah, okay, I got it."

"Parlin's is nicer than that. I don't know what a sheriff in a small Maine county makes, but I can't believe it's enough to pay for what I saw."

Brock searched his scrambled brain for an explanation. "Maybe his wife has a real job," Brock said, thinking back to how the former Mrs. Justice, a medical doctor, brought in two-thirds of their joint income. At least.

"He's divorced, remember?" Chloe said.

"Meaning?"

"Meaning he should have even less money."

"Can we get back to what you saw?" Brock said.

"Anyway, when I got there, I was intending to pull into the driveway, but there was already a pickup parked there. It was at a weird angle, and it was running with the driver's door hanging open. Parlin and Albert were standing on the front lawn. They were faced off and having what looked like one hell of a heated argument about something."

"How do you know it was Albert?"

"Um, because I'm a detective. I ran the registration. Then found a picture of him online."

Brock nodded. "What did you do?"

"What could I do? I kept driving. I pulled over down the road and continued to watch them in my rearview."

"Did they see you?"

"I don't think so, though the woman whose house I stopped in front of came outside with her Shih Tzu. They gave me the stink eye."

"What happened?"

"Nothing. She and her five-pound guard mutt went back inside."

"I mean what happened between Parlin and Albert?"

"Oh. Well, they kept at it for a few more minutes. I really thought they were gonna come to blows, but eventually your dad stormed back to his truck and sped off. He backed over the lawn and took out Parlin's mailbox in the process. Drove right past me and kept going."

Great, Brock thought. Albert was probably driving drunk too. He wondered if Parlin would make a complaint.

"What do you think that could be about?" Chloe said, clearly excited.

"No idea," Brock said. "They're friends, right? Friends fall out sometimes." Even as he spoke the words, he thought of Evan Mathers.

"Want to know what I think?" Chloe said.

"Not really," Brock grumbled. "But you're going to tell me anyway, aren't you?"

"I think the heat is getting to be too much and they are starting to turn on each other."

"What heat?"

"Our investigation. The closer we get to finding out what happened to Lee Owen, the worse it's going to get for—"

Their waitress stopped by, interrupting Chloe. "What can I get you?" she said.

"Eight more hours of sleep," Brock said matter-of-factly, causing the waitress to laugh out loud, hurting his head in the process.

"That's a good one," she said.

"I'll just take some more coffee," Brock said as he held up his mug.

"He'll have a breakfast bagel," Chloe said. "Bacon, egg, and cheese on a plain bagel and a big glass of ice water."

"And you?" the waitress said to Chloe as she topped off both of their mugs.

"Same."

Brock watched the waitress depart, then turned to Chloe. "What's with the water?"

"One of the key problems accompanying a hangover is dehydration," Chloe said. "You need to hydrate, and coffee won't do it. Plus, you need to eat. Get something in your stomach."

"I'm not hungover," Brock said. "And I'm really not hungry."

Chloe gave him a look he couldn't decode. "What did you have for supper last night?"

Brock scanned his memory for the last time he'd taken in any sustenance, but all he could conjure up was coffee, alcohol, and the previous night's sex. "I'm sure I ate," he said at last.

"Sure you did."

He gave up and retreated into his mug of coffee.

"So, back to Parlin and your dad," she said. "I want to know what they were fighting about."

So did Brock, but he wasn't sure how best to approach it. He'd already had two visits with Albert, and neither interaction had yielded anything more than half-truths and resentment for things long past. But he wouldn't wish Albert on his worst enemy, let alone a fledgling trainee. On the other hand, Chloe seemed to have an in with the Hancock County sheriff, one he couldn't begin to match.

"You still want to use the ruse about the written statement with Parlin?" Brock said.

"Why not?" Chloe said.

"Then use it, but pay him a visit at the office instead of his home. Act like nothing has happened and see how he responds. If he saw you in the vicinity of his house, you'll know."

"And if he's still riled up from his interaction with Albert?"

"You'll likely know that too. Regardless of what they were fighting about, Parlin should still be angry enough to have made a complaint about the damage to his lawn and mailbox."

"And if he didn't?"

"Then we'll *know* he's hiding something."

49

Brock left the restaurant fully intending to drive to Albert's camp. He had barely driven a mile when his cell phone rang with a call from Corey Hincks.

"Is this the world-famous State Police Detective Justice?" Hincks said. "I hear you're making waves again."

"What can I say," Brock said. "It's a gift. You got something for me?"

"Always right to business, huh? Okay, I was given a super-duper peek behind the curtain."

"I assume you didn't tell them who was asking."

"I'm not that dumb, brother. They think I've got a case that might overlap."

"I appreciate it. So, what did they tell you?"

"It looks like you might have staggered into something bigger than we thought. According to the intel I saw, there is an organized crime group smuggling fentanyl into the US from Canada."

"That's similar to the information we got from one of the county deputies through a snitch," Brock said.

"Yeah, but they didn't know this part, I'll bet. The fentanyl is being pressed into tablets using stolen presses taken in a pharmaceutical manufacturing company break-in."

"A pill press? What's that?"

"It looks like a giant silk-screen machine. They use it in combination with binding agents to make tablets, caplets, pretty much everything people take for medication that isn't in liquid or capsule form. Those pills you take are in powder form before they get pressed."

"Why bother going to all that trouble?"

"It's all about distribution. They simply manufacture look-alike pills using the fentanyl for the drugs they are manufacturing. This stuff could look exactly like alprazolam."

"Alprazolam?"

"Look who wasn't in the drug unit. Xanax, you flatfoot."

"Why didn't you just say that? So, this stuff could look like anything, right?"

"Not necessarily. Their intel says the stolen plates are used specifically for making the oval-shaped Xanax pills."

"Don't they come in more than one color?"

"Yeah, white is a quarter milligram, orange is a half, and blues are the biggie at one milligram. But all they need to copy the pills is to tint them to the correct color. Presto, counterfeit drugs."

"So, any random person caught with these wouldn't raise an eyebrow if they were stopped," Brock said.

"As long as the counterfeit pills were in a prescription bottle, who would be the wiser? Even worse than that, if they fell into unsuspecting hands, like some high school kid, they could be fatal."

"Damn," Brock said.

"Exactly. Now we just need to find out who is running this and where the pills are being manufactured. You find anything that might help me?"

Brock filled him in on the false bottom discovered when Phinney's snowmobile was disassembled.

"Doesn't surprise me," Corey said. "These guys are pretty resourceful when it comes to finding new ways to smuggle drugs."

"But would it be worth it?" Brock said. "I mean, how many tablets could someone smuggle inside that snowmobile panel?"

"It doesn't take much, brother. The street value per gram of fentanyl ranges between one-fifty and two hundred bucks. I couldn't tell you how much they could stash inside the snowmobile you found without seeing the cavity size, but I can tell you a pound of those pills would go for about ninety grand."

Brock whistled.

"Yup. Think about it. Two or three guys make a weekend snowmobile run up to Quebec and back, each of them stuffing, say, five pounds of fake Xanax into their sled could net a cool one-point-three mil."

"Jesus," Brock said, his jaw dropping open.

"You can say that again. You said you were looking for motive for your dead guy getting cuffed to a sled and sent to the bottom of a fishing pond. I don't know about you, but one-point-three million just might be enough to make me turn on a business associate."

Brock was thinking the very same thing.

"I don't suppose you could hook me up with someone involved in this investigation, could you?" Brock said.

Corey sighed. "I knew you were gonna say that. Look, this is some serious secret squirrel shit here. You can't talk about this with anyone, capisce?"

"What are you, Italian now?"

"I'm serious. Don't go spreading this around."

"Okay, I got it. Can you hook me up with someone on the inside or not?"

"Give me a few hours, and I'll see what I can do."

"Thanks," Brock said. "I'm going to owe you one."

"Oh, you'll owe me more than that, brother."

Chloe sat in traffic, the left turn signal of her SUV flashing, as she waited for an oncoming line of cars to pass by. When it was clear, she turned onto the drive of the Hancock County Sheriff's Department, a place she had been to many times.

As she slid the unmarked into an empty space, she noticed Parlin's black SUV was parked in its usual reserved spot. There were several additional county patrol vehicles in the lot, leading her to wonder if Parlin might have been holding some kind of staff meeting.

At the reception desk, she saw a familiar face. The recognition was twofold. The woman seated behind the glass jumped up and hurried over to open the security door.

"As I live and breathe," she said.

"How are you, Martha?" Chloe said.

Martha embraced Chloe in a bear hug. Chloe felt her face redden with embarrassment as she caught the glances of several onlookers inside the lobby.

Nearly a foot shorter than Chloe, with curly hair dyed so black it was nearly blue, the middle-aged matron had worked the weekday shift at the county's front desk for as long as Chloe had been with the state police. As the gatekeeper, she and she alone decided who made it past the front desk and who might just be doomed to wait in the lobby for all eternity. Nobody with any sense messed with Martha.

After a long moment, Martha released her grip on Chloe and stepped back. "Let me get a look at you. I can't believe how different you look out of uniform. You look so grown up in your suit. Just like that woman detective I love so much on that TV show."

"Which one?" Chloe said, silently hoping she wouldn't say Vera Stanhope.

"That Captain Olivia Benson from *Law and Order*. You know I just love that show."

"I'll take that as a compliment," Chloe said.

"You should. I meant it as one. So, Detective Wright, what brings you here today?"

"I was hoping to speak with Sheriff Parlin."

"Oh. I'm afraid Gene is in a meeting right now. Is there anything I can do for you, hon?"

"Actually, I've been waiting on a written statement from him. Maybe he left it somewhere. I could just pick it up and be on my way without bothering him."

Chloe faked her disappointment in the hopes her relationship with Martha might cause her to yank Parlin from whatever meeting he was in. In addition to finding out whatever had transpired between Parlin and Albert

Justice this morning, she also wondered who Parlin might be meeting with now, and if the meeting might be related.

"You just hang right on a minute, Chloe. I'll see if I can pull him free. Gene's never been too busy to see you."

"Thank you, Martha. You really don't need to bother him on my account, though. Honestly, all I need is the statement."

"Nonsense," Martha said. "Be right back."

And with that, Martha disappeared through the security door to the inner sanctum of HCSD.

Chloe exchanged an awkward glance with one of the lobby attendees as she waited. The young man was smirking at her knowingly. The familiarity between her and Martha had stripped Chloe of any remaining semblance of professionalism her suit and badge might have projected. It conjured up a grade school horror of being kissed by her mother while being dropped off in front of her classmates. Teasing by a group of boys had immediately ensued. It was relentless and didn't end until she'd bloodied the lip of the biggest offender. The fighting had resulted in a three-day suspension from school. But no one messed with Chloe after that.

She suppressed a smile as she stared down the young man smirking at her. He eventually looked away.

"Chloe Wright," Parlin's voice boomed through the open doorway.

"Sheriff," Chloe said as she moved toward him.

"Come on in."

50

Brock's cell rang less than forty-five minutes later. The call originated from a number he didn't recognize, but as he'd been on perma-hold for over ten minutes with a company out of Portland that might or might not be the current holder of the abandoned mine at Second Pond, he opted for the sure thing. Dumping his call, he accepted the incoming.

"Justice."

"Brock? Gabe Higgins, Maine Drug Enforcement Agency. I just spoke with Corey Hincks about your drug smuggling theory, and he asked me to give you a call."

"Thanks for reaching out, Gabe," Brock said. "I really appreciate it."

"Yeah, well, Corey's a good man."

Brock paused a beat to analyze the comment. He had begun to weigh the start of any conversation by how the person reacted to speaking with him. Higgins certainly knew what Brock's role in Mathers's trial had been. There weren't many in state law enforcement who didn't. The only question remaining was whether Higgins had reached out to help a fellow LEO or if it was some obligation he owed Corey? Brock was beginning to worry he might be seeing things that weren't there. So soon after returning to the job, it was nearly impossible not to read into the nuances of every conversation.

When Brock didn't immediately respond, Higgins pressed on.

"I understand you might have a lead on Canadian drug smuggling," Higgins said.

"Maybe," Brock said. "At this point, it's just one of several theories we're looking at that might be motive in a homicide investigation. Corey mentioned you guys have been trying to crack a fentanyl smuggling ring."

"Yeah, we have. I'm assigned to the Mid-Coast District, and as you might imagine, we've already got more than we can handle. Like everyone else, our resources have been stretched mighty thin. That fentanyl thing has got a bug up the boss's ass, but none of our snitches have given anything up, and I'm not sure what that means. Could be new players, could be one or more of our snitches are involved. So far, all we really have is a few pills showing up that aren't what they are supposed to be."

"Corey mentioned they might be using a stolen pill press," Brock said.

"Or a good counterfeit one," Higgins added.

Brock filled him in on Phinney's stolen snowmobile and the false bottom discovery.

"That's a pretty good transportation method," Higgins said. "How good was the false bottom?"

"I'm not much of a snowmobile guy," Brock said. "But I wouldn't have spotted it. It looked exactly like the real cover."

"Which probably means we've got an engineer or machinist in the mix. Most of these yahoos aren't sophisticated enough to do more than avail themselves of the car door panel ruse. Though every once in a while they manage to surprise us with a trapdoor or a fake catalytic converter. The problem for most smugglers is they like to brag. Post a couple of YouTube videos showing their genius invention and then everyone knows about it, including drug agents. Play stupid games, win stupid prizes, right?"

"Right," Brock said.

"I don't suppose you'd be willing to share the names of your suspects, would you?"

Brock thought about it before saying anything further. Here he was asking for help from a fellow cop he didn't know. The man was sharing some of his intel. The least Brock could do was return the gesture of goodwill.

"I already told you about Keith Phinney," Brock said.

"Yeah, the name doesn't ring any bells. He's the guy who owned the snowmobile?"

"Yup. Claims he knew nothing about the secret compartment."

"If he bought the sled used, he could be telling the truth. I'll run his name up the flagpole anyway."

On that point, Brock still wasn't convinced. He opened his mouth to provide Sheriff Parlin's name to Higgins, then stopped. The last thing Brock needed was for word to get out that he was looking at another cop. Fresh off the shooting debacle and Mathers's trial, another debacle, his go-to list of police insiders was still in tatters. He decided to hold back on Parlin for now. And he certainly wasn't about to share his suspicions about Albert. Even if Albert wasn't his father, training his sights on a legendary trooper wouldn't help his stock either.

"I guess the only other name we have is Harold Perreault. Goes by—"

"The Bear," Higgins said, finishing his thought. "Yeah, yeah, I know him. Used to be an enforcer for the outlaw motorcycle gang The Enforcers. Is that the definition of irony, or what? I'll have my people poke around. Anyone else you can think of?"

Brock provided the names of Camilla and Rick Russo, the owners of Marlintini's Grill, and Ralph Dixon, the foreman at the boatyard where Lee Owen had been employed seasonally, though none of them had criminal records in the databases Brock had searched.

"Okay, I'll poke around and let you know if I find anything useful."

"I appreciate it," Brock said.

"You happen to run into a deputy up there named Hanscomb? Tommy Hanscomb?"

"I have," Brock said. "He's been helping with the case. He's actually the one who suggested the drug angle."

"Good man. Tommy and I went through a bunch of narcotic training sessions together at the academy. He worked out of Division 2, mostly Down East District, and a couple of years out of Aroostook. You be sure and tell that asshole I said hello."

"Will do," Brock said. "Thanks again."

"Don't mention it."

Brock had barely disconnected from his call with Higgins when his cell rang again. This time it was Chloe.

"What happened with Parlin?"

"Hello to you too," Chloe responded. "Nothing. I spoke with him, and he gave me his signed statement, but he seemed as jovial as ever. No mention of any run-in with Albert. If he was upset about anything, it didn't show. Having someone run over my mailbox would've pissed me off royally."

So much for the direct route, Brock thought.

"Martha did have to pull him from a meeting, though."

"Who's Martha?" Brock said.

"Sorry. I keep forgetting you're not from around here."

Brock bristled at the comment, unsure if she'd said it as a matter of course or if she'd meant it as a dig.

"She's the keeper of the front desk at the sheriff's office. Anyway, he was in a meeting with someone, but I couldn't see who."

Brock took a beat to consider this. "You think it had anything to do with what happened between him and Albert?"

"Who knows. It might have. Could be why he closed the door to his office, to prevent me from seeing inside."

"Any indication he saw you drive by this morning?"

"If he did, he didn't let on."

"Any guesses who he was meeting with?"

"Not really. I did notice Tommy Hanscomb's vehicle in the lot outside, so it might have simply been a staff meeting."

"Then why close the door?" Brock said, thinking out loud.

"Good question," Chloe said. "So, what's next?"

"Has Hanscomb gotten back to you about his snitch?"

"Not yet. You want me to follow up?"

Initially Brock hadn't wanted her to deal with Hanscomb directly, worried that maybe she was too close to the deputy to maintain objectivity, but Hanscomb's comfort level with Chloe might provide some leverage.

"Yeah, go ahead," Brock said. "And see if he mentions anything about meeting with Parlin."

"You want me to spy on a friend?"

"What were you doing with Parlin?" Brock said.

"Touché."

Brock considered telling her what he'd learned about the old mine from Wilber Stubbs but then thought better of it. The mine had nothing to do with Lee Owen's death, which meant he was disobeying Cumberland's order even talking to Stubbs. He decided to give Detective Wheeler a try. If anyone could get inside information, it would be MCU North's IT detective. Plus, it would be a good test to see if Wheels could be trusted.

"What about you?" Chloe said.

"I'm gonna try and track down Albert. Before he murders any more mailboxes."

51

Brock knew his father's pickup was missing even before the camp had come fully into view. This early in the season, and this far north, the deciduous trees were still leafless, not showing much more than the occasional bud, allowing for more visibility through the woods than was possible during the summer months.

He parked in the empty dooryard and climbed out of the SUV. Standing in the middle of the gravel drive, Brock turned in a slow circle to take it all in.

Could Albert have somehow gotten mixed up with the likes of Lee Owen? Brock found it unlikely and difficult to imagine. His father made his career putting guys like Owen behind bars. And while Albert had his faults, being a less than nurturing father among them, he was a man who had always thought in terms of black and white, good and evil, right and wrong. There was no wiggle room in Albert Justice's mind when it came to lawbreaking and victimizing others. His dedication to those values was one of the reasons the Legendary Trooper Award had been bestowed upon him.

Brock took a hard look at everything within view. It was the same old camp. Though his eyes detected several recent updates, mainly windows and a new roof, even those had been modest. Apart from one new outbuilding, the property looked largely the same as Brock remembered.

He followed the path around the camp toward the lake. The well-worn trail was carpeted by a deep layer of pine needles, crisscrossed by tree roots waiting to trip up unsuspecting visitors. The wooden dock looked to be in good repair, but it was homemade, nothing special. Certainly not what Albert would call one of those fancy-schmancy preassembled, overpriced sectional docks all the seasonal folks were so enamored with.

"Those folks from away hardly know the business end of a fishing rod," he could hear his father saying in that deep growl with just the faintest tinge of a Down East accent.

Albert's trademark attention to detail showed clearly in the workmanship. If there was something he didn't know how to build or fix, he would figure it out. His father had always been handy. It was what set him apart. Brock often wondered if problem-solving might have been the only thing he had inherited from his old man.

He continued down the path to the boathouse, though "boathouse" was too grandiose a term for what was really nothing more than a small cedar-shingle-clad post-and-beam barn built from logs harvested off the property. Brock and his brother, Jake, had always referred to it as the boathouse. Even Jolene had thrown the term around, tongue in cheek, as if they were one of those highfalutin families from Rhode Island or Cape Cod.

Brock found the double doors of the boathouse secured with a shiny new padlock, the kind requiring a key. He stepped off the ramp, then moved around to the side of the building, spooking a red squirrel in the process. He watched as the tiny animal scurried up the trunk of the nearest pine onto a low-hanging branch, where it sat scolding him loudly. Ignoring the chatter, Brock moved closer to the window. The olive paint on the outside sill was nearly obscured by a layer of pine needles, and the corners of the frame were encased by thick spider webs. He picked up a small branch from the ground and used it to clear away the webbing. It wasn't arachnophobia motivating him. Not exactly. It was more a fear of having a spider crawl across his face. He cleared the glass to his satisfaction, tossed the branch, then leaned in close. Cupping both hands around his eyes, he peered inside.

The interior of the boathouse was too dark to see much of anything beyond silhouettes, an overlay of the large, featureless items stored inside.

One of the shapes toward the rear of the space appeared to be Albert's bass boat, trailered and covered in canvas. Closer to the front, near the double doors, was a dark shape that looked a lot like a covered snowmobile. Given what Brock was working on, the sight gave him an uneasy feeling. Though the sight of his father's sled wouldn't have meant anything had he not recently seen Lee Owen's corpse handcuffed to a snowmobile as it was pulled out of Second Pond.

Hoping for a better look, Brock dug out his cell and activated the flashlight app. Holding it up to the glass, he attempted to illuminate the interior. Between the filthy panes and the glare of reflected light, the phone did little more than confirm the shapes he'd already identified.

Finding nothing and growing tired of the constant chatter above his head, Brock pocketed the phone and moved to the front of the shed.

He paused on the mossy ramp to survey the front of the camp. He studied the weathered deck and Adirondack chairs where he and Albert had sat several evenings prior.

Brock sighed in frustration. Nothing he saw gave the slightest indication Albert had come into any kind of illicit windfall. In fact, the property looked exactly like the property of a widower living on a police pension. The year-round camp of a man trying to maintain his love of the outdoors while supplementing his meager income by fleecing a few well-to-do out-of-staters with glimpses into the hunting and fishing life of a real wilderness man.

While awaiting a response to the voicemail she had left for Deputy Hanscomb, Chloe drove toward Blue Hill thinking about her next move. She and Brock had checked off a great many boxes on their investigation into the murder of Lee Owen, but there were still as many unanswered questions about what had happened as when she first made the gruesome discovery at the bottom of Second Pond. The case was frustrating and pretty much all she could think about. She was beginning to understand why so many homicide detectives had such shitty home lives.

Chloe considered herself lucky she was still untethered from a significant other. A life partner who would most likely end up resenting her for making them feel as if they were playing second fiddle to a corpse. And in truth, they would be.

By all accounts, Lee Owen was a player who had spent most of his adult life, and his good looks, preying on anyone who could advance his situation. Whether it was money, or the married wife of a "friend," Owen appeared to have no qualms about helping himself to whatever he desired. Was he the kind of guy who would steal a snowmobile from his employer? *Of course he is*, Chloe thought. Owen was also the kind of guy who might have helped himself to Dr. Phinney's wife if the urge hit him. Assuming Emily had been willing.

"You're looking in the wrong direction," Judy, the waitress at Marlintini's Grill, had said. "Y'all are too busy focusing on Lee's conquests."

What exactly had she meant? The waitress hadn't been inclined to speculate further about her meaning. But she had been willing to plant the seed with Chloe. Was she right? Was the answer somewhere outside of Lee's playing field?

Chloe adjusted her grip on the steering wheel and refocused entirely on the road in front of her. She knew what her next step would be. It was time to pay another visit to Melinda Hamilton. Maybe she *was* holding something back. Maybe she'd been holding back all along.

Chloe parked just down the street from Hamilton's apartment. She had planned to use the driveway, but there was a medium-sized box truck backed in with its cab sticking out into the road.

Chloe climbed the steps to the second floor and knocked on the door to Hamilton's apartment. After a moment, the harried-looking mother snatched the door open.

"Oh, it's you," Melinda said. "Now isn't the best time."

Chloe could see past Hamilton's shoulder into the apartment where a couple of people were moving items around.

"What's up?" Chloe said.

Melinda stepped into the hallway, partially closing the door behind her, intentionally blocking Chloe's view of the other occupants.

"It's moving day."

"Oh?" Chloe said. "I didn't realize you were planning to move."

"Neither did I. But now that Lee has been found, by you guys, the landlord is pretty sure he won't be helping with the rent anymore. And as I am already two months behind, it's adios."

"I'm so sorry," Chloe said.

"Don't be. Not like the landlord is ever gonna see a dime of the back rent. Besides, this place is a shithole."

"Do you need any help?" Chloe said, not because she had any intention of assisting but because she was hoping for a quick peek inside the apartment to identify the other occupants.

"Nope. I've got enough help, *Detective*."

Chloe noticed Hamilton's emphasis on the word "detective," an obvious warning to the other occupants about who was at the door.

"Like I said, this isn't the best time."

"I only have a few questions," Chloe said. "Why don't you give me your forwarding address, and I'll stop by after you're settled in. Maybe tomorrow."

Melinda fixed her with a knowing grin, letting Chloe know they were both aware of the cat-and-mouse game being played.

"Actually, I've got a better idea, Detective Wright. Why don't I call you after I get settled. Maybe tomorrow."

"Okay," Chloe said, forcing a smile with absolutely nothing behind it.

"Great," Melinda said. "I gotta go now."

She stepped back inside and closed the door, leaving Chloe standing out in the hallway.

Chloe retreated to her vehicle, fired the ignition, and was preparing to drive off when another thought occurred to her. She drove past Hamilton's apartment building and continued up the road and out of sight before making a U-turn and backtracking. She pulled into a vacant parking spot about a quarter mile up the road, giving her a direct sightline to the truck occupying Hamilton's driveway.

She hadn't been waiting long before the moving truck rolled out of the driveway and headed toward her. Following the truck was a bright purple Harley-Davidson with an exhaust as loud as its paint job. The motorcycle was driven by none other than The Bear himself, Mr. Harold Perreault.

Chloe did her best to slide down low in the seat as the vehicles passed.

She didn't recognize the man behind the wheel of the truck, but neither he nor Perreault seemed to pay her any notice.

As Perreault's bike blatted past, Chloe wondered where he had parked it. She hadn't seen it on the roadway, and it wasn't visible in Hamilton's drive. The only other possibility was he'd intentionally parked it behind the apartment building. Why would Perreault and Hamilton try to hide their relationship? Owen had been out of the picture for months. Who would care if she and Perreault were seeing each other? Was their relationship the reason Melinda hadn't wanted Chloe to have a look inside the apartment?

She took a moment to process the new information. If the relationship between Hamilton and Perreault was such a well-guarded secret, had it been going on before Lee Owen was murdered? Was this relationship what Judy, the waitress at Marlintini's Grill, had been referring to when she said the police were looking in the wrong place? That it wasn't one of Lee's affairs they should focus on, but Hamilton's. Was Perreault responsible for Owen's murder? Tommy Hanscomb had suggested as much, but his suspicions had revolved around the idea that Owen might have been skimming drugs, or proceeds, from The Bear. But now, given this previously unknown connection, perhaps Perreault's motive, assuming for a moment he was the killer, might have been totally unrelated to drug smuggling. The motive might simply have been the oldest motive in the book. Jealousy.

Chloe shook her head as she pulled away from the curb. There were still more questions than answers.

52

Brock had just departed from Albert's camp when his cell rang with a call from a number he recognized as belonging to Howard Tisdale. Brock had been awaiting an update from the detective but wasn't expecting much, especially from the man Chloe referred to as How Weird.

"Justice," he answered.

"Brock, it's Tisdale. I'm calling to let you know I may have a lead on the cell phone that led you to Second Pond the night of the shooting."

"Don't keep me guessing," Brock said as he felt the hair on the back of his neck bristle. "What do you have?"

"It's definitely a TracFone, and I've managed to trace the sale to a variety store in Bangor. A place called Silly's off Hogan Road. Looks like it was purchased about three days before you received the text message."

"Any idea who made the purchase?" Brock said.

"No, but I'm on my way over there now to check their security footage. I'll let you know what I find out. If the video is any good, I'll try sending you a still image of the purchaser's mug."

"Thanks, How—Howard," Brock said before ending the call. He had nearly slipped up and called him How Weird. MCU North's penchant for unflattering nicknames would come back to bite him if he wasn't careful. Speaking of nicknames, he wondered if Wheels had gotten anywhere in tracking down the current owner of the mine and if there might be some connection to the person who bought the phone.

Before he could do more than think about calling Wheeler, the phone rang again. It was Chloe.

"Can you meet me?" Chloe said.

"Name it. I'm headed back to Blue Hill from Albert's camp."

"How about Marlintini's?"

Brock and Chloe exchanged information as they broke bread at what was fast becoming their new haunt.

"How many times have we eaten here now?" Brock said as he plopped what remained of his cheeseburger onto the plate.

"Four?" Chloe said. "I've lost track. Why?"

"Because I'm getting tired of eating the same thing every day."

"Just one of the many drawbacks of working cases in Northern Maine," Chloe said with a smirk. "We don't have all those five-star dining options like you big-city detectives have in the south. You could order something else from the menu, you know."

Brock ignored her comment and scanned the dining room. "Where's the waitress who gave you the lead about Hamilton?"

"Judy? I don't think she's working. Why?"

"Because I want to know if she actually knew about Hamilton and Perreault or if she just knew the woman was fooling around on Owen."

"Guess it would be good to know," Chloe said. "What do you make of Melinda trying to keep it a secret?"

"I don't know," Brock said. "Given Lee's propensity for alley-catting, it wouldn't seem like her relationship with Perreault would make much difference. Certainly not a motive for murdering Owen."

"Unless her child was fathered by Perreault," Chloe said absently.

"Even then," Brock said. "I'd think it might provide more motive for Owen to want Perreault out of the picture than the other way around."

"Maybe," Chloe said, sounding unconvinced. "So, your friend, what's his name, thinks there's a drug angle in this?"

"Corey. And yeah, he agreed with Hanscomb. He didn't know how Owen factored into any of it other than he may have been acting as a mule for Perreault and got caught with his hand in the cookie jar."

"Any luck with Albert?" Chloe said.

"He wasn't there, and he's not answering his cell."

"You don't really think your father's involved in drug smuggling, do you?"

"No, but I can't explain what you saw between him and Parlin this morning. Nor can I explain the handcuffs. It's a little too convenient that they were stolen, and he never filed a report."

"You know, even if we manage to identify Owen's killer and make a case, those cuffs are going to be a problem if this thing ever goes to trial," Chloe said.

"You think I don't know that?" Brock snapped a little more forcefully than he'd intended.

Chloe looked up from her plate, wide-eyed. "I didn't mean—"

"No, I know you didn't. Sorry. I shouldn't have jumped on you like that. I'm just a bit on edge about the link to my father."

"I don't suppose you've heard from How Weird?" Chloe said.

"Actually, he called this afternoon."

"Really? Any progress on identifying your shooter?"

"He managed to trace the sale of the TracFone used to send me the text. It was purchased at a variety store in Bangor."

"That's great," Chloe said. "Video of the buyer? Sale info?"

"Don't know. He was headed over there when he called. As for sale info, I'm gonna guess it was a cash transaction."

"Most likely."

Brock also knew there was a possibility the phone might not have been purchased by the shooter. Still, locating the point of purchase was something.

Brock was debating sharing the information about the Blue Hill mine when his cell vibrated across the tabletop. He wiped his greasy hands on a napkin, then picked up the phone and checked the display.

"Good news?" Chloe said.

"Hardly," Brock said. "It's a text from Cumberland."

"Looking for an update?"

"Yup."

"Well, maybe you can put her off until tomorrow," Chloe said, sounding hopeful.

"Not likely," Brock said as he typed out a quick response.

"Why not?"

"Because she's in town."

Chloe's eyes widened. "What? Like, in town in town?"

Brock nodded.

"Where are you meeting her?" Chloe said.

"Right here."

"What? When?"

"She just pulled into the lot."

53

Brock was livid as he drove away from the meeting with Lt. Cumberland. It wasn't that she was still angry with him, he'd fully expected that, it was more that she seemed to take his breach of protocol personally. He had no idea why she had reacted that way. There had been nothing personal about his decision to keep her out of the loop for as long as possible when it came to Albert's involvement in the case. As far as he was concerned, the decision to hold back was simply self-preservation as the case lead.

The one surprise was that the lieutenant didn't immediately remove him from the case. At least for now. He had no illusions about how quickly that might change, depending on whether the facts swung toward Albert or away from his possible involvement in the murder of Lee Owen. Brock found it ironic that the one thing keeping him on the case was the alibi supplied by some of the most likely suspects. Only the sheer number of attendees at Parlin's poker game were keeping Albert off the proverbial hook. To believe otherwise was to invite conspiracy.

As pissed as he was at the way she had laid into him, Brock was grateful the lieutenant had shown enough professionalism to keep Chloe out of it. If he was to have any chance of developing her into a top-notch detective, Brock would need to retain what little authority he had over her training. And given his reputation as a lone-wolf investigator, and his recent press coverage concerning Evan Mathers, he was amazed he held any sway over Chloe. Brock could already tell she possessed the necessary traits to be an effective homicide investigator. She was highly intelligent, driven, fearless, and methodical. All traits she would need going forward. But perhaps the most important quality he'd seen from her was empathy. There was no question Chloe cared. In direct opposition to Albert, a highly competent trooper who had lacked empathy for anyone. Brock had seen firsthand how callous his father could be, at times downright cruel, especially when he'd been drinking.

Brock was less than five miles from Bangor when he received a call from the Ellsworth Emergency Communications Center—in other words, the Hancock County Sheriff's Department.

Brock pressed the accept button and put the phone on speaker. "Justice."

"Detective, this is county dispatch calling on behalf of one of our deputies. Are you available to respond to a traffic stop?"

Brock checked the time. It was nearly ten o'clock.

"I don't suppose you can tell me what it's about, can you?"

"Stand by, Detective."

Brock listened as the voice of the person he was speaking with made radio contact with someone to clarify the nature of the stop and why he was needed. The response was garbled, and Brock only caught part of it.

The dispatcher came back on the line. "Did you copy?"

"I only caught part of the location," Brock said.

"Deputy Hanscomb has a vehicle stopped on Route 1A near Green Lake. He has requested and is currently awaiting a K9 unit for a search. Deputy Hanscomb advises you'll be interested in the vehicle operator."

"Who is it?" Brock said.

"Harold Perreault."

As he crested the rise, Brock saw a cluster of emergency vehicles about a quarter mile ahead. The night was ablaze with red and blue strobe lights mounted on roofs, rear decks, marker lights, and grilles. Every conceivable location was flashing. Brock couldn't help but wonder what Perreault had done, and what he himself was being dragged into.

He pulled onto the right shoulder, activated his own vehicle's emergency lights, and radioed that he was on scene. He turned off the headlights on his unmarked so as not to blind the other officers, then grabbed the flashlight from the charger. Before he could do more than open the door, two uniformed deputies approached. He immediately recognized Tommy Hanscomb. Brock didn't know the other man.

"Welcome to the party," Hanscomb said.

"Tommy," Brock said. "What do you have?"

"Only the jackpot," the other deputy said. Brock caught a glimpse of *S. Pratt* on the deputy's name tag mounted directly above the K9 patch.

"This is Sam Pratt," Hanscomb said.

"Nice to meet you," Pratt said.

"Likewise," Brock said as he offered his hand. His attention shifted to Harold Perreault, who was seated on the ground, hands cuffed behind his back. The Bear did not look happy. "So, what's this jackpot you're talking about?"

Hanscomb grinned. "You mean why did I drag you out here in the middle of the night?"

"Yeah, that too."

"Come on," Hanscomb said. "We'll show ya."

Brock followed the two men past marked vehicles belonging to Hancock SO and Ellsworth PD. Several uniformed officers from the corresponding agencies stood in a small cluster adjacent to Perreault. One of them nodded to Brock as they passed. Up ahead, Brock observed a late-model black sports car that clearly wasn't a cruiser. Leaning against the open trunk was a long-haired guy smoking a cigarette. He wore a closely trimmed goatee and a stud earring and looked to be about thirty. Brock made him as an undercover drug agent even before the introductions. Goatee pushed himself off the bumper and stepped to one side, allowing Brock an unobstructed view of the trunk's interior. The floor felt had been pulled back and the spare tire removed, revealing several large clear plastic ziplock bags in the empty well.

"You shoulda seen Gypsy hit on that," Pratt said proudly. "I thought she was gonna tear the bumper off."

"What is it?" Brock asked.

"Tested positive for fentanyl," Goatee said.

"Which is very interesting," Hanscomb said.

"Why's that?" Brock said.

"'Cause all these pills look like Xanax."

The MDEA agent, named Jim Blaney, was on loan from Sanford PD. According to Blaney, he'd received a telephonic tip that Perreault was moving a large number of counterfeit pills inside his wrecker.

"Who called in the tip?" Brock asked.

"Came in anonymously," Blaney said with a grin.

The grin told Brock two things. One, that this was a bullshit stop known in law enforcement circles as a fishing expedition that may not have been called in at all, or the call may well have been made by another cop. The second thing it told Brock was that they would have needed another reason to make the stop on the off chance they located any drugs. Lose the stop, lose the case. Fruit of the poisonous tree.

"You pulled him over on an anonymous tip?" Brock asked.

"Hell, no," Hanscomb said. "Wrecker has a headlight out."

"Yeah," Blaney said. "And you troopers know how unsafe that is."

Brock stared at Blaney. The comment had been an attempt to get a rise out of Brock, but he wasn't about to give the smug agent the satisfaction. After a long moment, Brock's attention returned to Hanscomb.

"Is Perreault talking?"

"Said he didn't know anything about it. Told us he was just picking up a car after getting a call from a woman about needing a tow."

"Have you tried to locate the woman?" Brock said.

"Can't," Hanscomb said.

"Why not?" Brock said.

"Perreault said he took the call on a landline at the shop. The name and number she provided are fake. And the plates on this heap are stolen."

Brock turned toward Blaney again. The drug agent remained silent but gave him a knowing smirk. Brock was positive now. This entire stop had been manufactured. A setup.

"I want to talk to Perreault," Brock said.

"Figured you would," Hanscomb said. "That's why I had the dispatcher contact you."

"Good luck getting him to say anything," Blaney said. "The Bear thinks his shit don't stink."

"Doesn't," Brock corrected.

"What?"

"He thinks his shit *doesn't* stink. Looks like the two of you have something in common."

54

The interview room at the Hancock County sheriff's department resembled a 1970s Hollywood movie set. Dominating the center of the cramped, windowless space was a scarred and worn wood-top table surrounded by four mismatched chairs. The video camera mounted in one corner of the ceiling was inoperable, and the room's only egress was a steel door that could only be locked from the outside. The air inside the room was stale and reeked of sweat, body odor, and nicotine. Brock's keen sense of smell picked up on the cigarettes instantly. It always came with a sense of longing. As he pulled out one of the chairs across from the muscular biker, Brock wondered how many of the detected odors were emanating from The Bear himself.

With his hands still cuffed behind his back, Perreault sat staring back at Brock. In the harsh overhead lighting, Brock could see several bloodied scrapes on Perreault's right cheek along with the first faint traces of bruising. Brock wondered how much resistance The Bear had offered the deputies during his arrest.

Surprising everyone at the scene of the traffic stop, Brock included, Perreault had agreed to waive his rights and give a statement on one condition. He would only talk to Brock. Hanscomb had balked initially, but following a heated conversation with Brock, the deputy finally relented.

"You know how this works, right?" Brock said as he removed a sheet of paper from a case folder. Typed onto the sheet was the Miranda warning in its entirety.

"Yeah," Perreault said.

Brock read aloud each section of the warning verbatim, making a written note of Perreault's verbal responses after each one of his rights was explained.

"Now, having all those rights which I just explained to you in mind, do you wish to answer questions at this time?" Brock said.

Perreault nodded.

"I'll need a verbal response, Harold."

"Yeah, I'll answer your questions."

Brock scribbled Perreault's response at the bottom of the page, then signed and dated the document, now officially part of the investigation, before sliding it back inside the folder.

"Didn't think I'd be seeing you so soon," Brock said.

"Me either," Perreault said, sulking.

"Looks like they caught you holding quite a quantity of illegal narcotics."

"That's bullshit," Perreault said. "None of that stuff is mine. All I did was respond to a call."

"Tell me again how you received the call?"

"I already told those other assholes."

"I need you to tell me," Brock said. Hoping to maintain their shaky détente, Brock allowed the inclusive derogatory comment a pass.

"I was working at the garage when a woman called in and said her car had broken down on Route 1A north of Ellsworth. Though it ended up being all the way up near fucking Green Lake. She gave me her callback number, the registration and description of the car and told me she needed it towed. That's it."

"She give you a name?" Brock said.

"Cheryl Smith."

"Did you try calling Ms. Smith back before you drove to get the car?"

"She sounded legit."

"Would it surprise you to know that the number she gave you comes back to a burner phone?"

Perreault sighed deeply. "Guess I should have called back, huh?"

"What did Ms. Smith say she wanted done with the car?"

"She asked me to tow it back to the garage and leave it. She said she'd get a ride out to see us in the morning."

"Did you get a credit card number or anything?" Brock said.

Perreault shook his head. "Naw, man, I wasn't really worried about it. I figured if we had her car, she'd pay to get it back."

Brock scribbled another note in the notebook, then sat back in his chair. "Why did you agree to talk to me, Harold?"

"Because I can't trust anyone else. These fuckers are obviously setting me up."

"Who do you think is setting you up?"

"Hanscomb, and his buddies. That sawed-off little prick has had it out for me since I moved up here."

"What makes you say that?"

"What makes me say it? 'Cause he's been dogging my ass every time I turn around. I can't drive through the county without having him pull me over on my bike. Loud exhaust, inspection violations, speeding. It's all bullshit."

"I don't know about the other stuff," Brock said. "But speeding seems like a reasonable reason to stop you."

"Five over. That sound reasonable to you?"

It didn't, but Brock kept it to himself.

"Okay, so maybe Deputy Hanscomb doesn't like you," Brock said. "But that's a long way from setting you up on a trafficking charge."

"Is it?" Perreault said. "I haven't had anything to do with drugs since I left The Enforcers. And that's the God's honest truth."

"Find Jesus, did you?" Brock said.

"No, man, I just like my freedom a whole lot more than getting high and selling shit to losers."

"Let's say, for argument's sake, you are telling me the truth and someone went to all this trouble just to set you up. What makes you think Hanscomb had anything to do with it?"

"Because the dude's bent."

"How would you know that?" Brock said.

Perreault leaned forward in his chair until his chest was pressed up against the top edge of the table. He was so close Brock could smell the nicotine on his breath.

"When I was still in the club, I got caught dealing to a narc. I was introduced to the guy by a fellow biker who vouched for him. I was stupid. It was the first time I'd ever dealt with the guy, and I got greedy."

"Did the narc charge you?" Brock said.

"He didn't. Gave me a choice. Either I snitch for him, in which case he'd lose the evidence, or he'd bust me on the spot. With my priors and an added weapons charge, I was looking at some serious time. Maybe even federal."

"So you started snitching for him?"

"Yup," Perreault said as he slumped back in the chair. "I should have done the time."

"Hanscomb?" Brock said after a moment.

"Bingo," Perreault said with a nod. "And I've been owned by that asshole ever since."

"Rumor has it you're seeing Melinda Hamilton," Brock said.

Perreault shrugged. "Guess your partner did see me, huh? So what?"

"So, Hamilton was living with Lee Owen. How long have you been seeing her?"

"Started about a month after Spike went missing."

"You weren't seeing her before he went missing?"

"I just said that I wasn't, didn't I? Why do you care, anyway?"

"I don't, but if you were seeing her when Owen was still alive, it might have given you motive to want him out of the picture."

Perreault didn't respond right away, but he maintained eye contact with Brock. Finally, he spoke up. "So, now you're gonna stitch me up too?"

"Not how I work, Harold. But you've given me nothing to work with. When we asked you where you were the night Owen disappeared, you played fast and loose with your answer. Something about being with a lady friend that night, if memory serves. I don't suppose it was Melinda, was it?"

"I told you I wasn't seeing her yet."

"Then who were you with that night?"

"Judy. Judy Babbage. She works at Marlintini's."

Brock fought to keep from showing any emotion as he scribbled her name into his notebook.

"And she'll back you up?"

"I was with her that night. All night. Go ahead and ask her if you don't believe me. I didn't kill Lee Owen."

55

Brock departed the sheriff's office without sharing a single word of the conversation with the deputies. Hanscomb demanded to know the nature of Brock's discussion with Perreault, but Brock shut him down, telling him it was about Lee Owen and had nothing to do with the drug charge.

As he drove through the night, Brock replayed his conversation with The Bear over and over, trying to find an angle. The fact that Perreault denied any knowledge of the drugs wasn't surprising; it was standard MO for most dealers when they got caught holding. The theory being to make the cops prove the case. But Perreault's detailed account about having a history with Hanscomb was unusual. And Perreault wasn't stupid. He had to know Brock would check out his story, at least in so far as Hanscomb's assignment to MDEA was concerned. And Perreault's alibi for the night Owen was murdered, assuming it was true, made perfect sense. Judy Babbage was jealous The Bear had left her for another woman. Why else would Babbage have led Chloe to Hamilton?

Brock reached up and absently rubbed the scar on the side of his face. Things were beginning to get complicated. He'd been holding back information from Chloe. Holding out on his boss, who was likely still pissed at him. He was beginning to feel a bit like Perreault in that he wasn't sure whom he could trust.

Between learning Albert's handcuffs had been used in Lee Owen's murder, the heated mystery argument between Albert and Sheriff Parlin, and Perreault's contention that Deputy Hanscomb had set him up, something was definitely amiss here. But given his recent infamous testimony against former Trooper Evan Mathers, Brock knew any suspicions he verbalized about Hanscomb would only make him look like he was targeting another cop. Chloe had said as much when he'd told her the handcuffs had belonged to Albert. Accusing a deputy, on the word of a convicted felon no less, would endear Brock to no one. It might even make him appear unhinged to Cumberland. As if Brock saw dirty cops everywhere. No, he would need to be careful going forward. Play his cards close to the vest. Brock knew of only one person he trusted who had access to inside information and would be discreet about looking into it. And that person was Corey Hincks.

His fellow trooper picked up on the second ring.

"Geez," Corey said. "People are gonna start thinking we're an item."

"Sorry to bother you at this hour, brother. This a bad time?"

"Not at all. I'm sitting here with the dog, watching the replay of the Masters and trying to stay awake."

"How's Tiger doing?"

"Not too bad. Coupla birdies. One under after thirteen. Looks like he might be back in form. Only the first day, though. Still early. So, what's up?"

"I'm hoping you might be able to help me with something sensitive."

"Oh, goodie. You mean I get to snoop around? That's what I do best. Who do you need checked out?"

"That's the thing. I'm not sure how much you're going to want to involve yourself."

"Now I'm really intrigued. Come on, man, spill it."

"It's a cop."

There was a moment of hesitation at the other end of the line. Brock wondered whether he'd lost the cellular connection or if maybe Corey had simply hung up on him.

"You still there?" Brock said.

"I'm here. Now I understand the cloak-and-dagger routine. Who do you need me to check out?"

"A deputy named Hanscomb. Tommy Hanscomb. Works for Hancock SO."

"I've heard the name, but I don't really know anything about the guy. Why do you think he's dirty? And why come to me?"

"I think Hanscomb may have worked an undercover assignment while with MDEA."

"How long ago are we talkin'?"

Brock didn't know. He hadn't thought to ask Perreault when he'd had his initial run-in with Hanscomb.

"I'm not sure exactly," Brock said. "It would be a few years back. You think you could find out on the QT for me?"

"I can't promise anything, but I'll do my best."

"That's all I can ask."

"Mind if I ask why you want to know?" Corey said.

"I'd rather not say at the moment, just in case this turns out to be a wild goose chase."

"Okay, I'll do some poking around tomorrow."

"Thanks, Corey. I owe you one."

As Brock disconnected the call, he thought about Chloe's relationship with Hanscomb. She was too close to him to confide in. If there was anything at all to Perreault's story, Brock would need to flesh it out before bringing Chloe in on it. If he'd learned anything during his years as a state trooper, it was not to accuse a fellow cop until there was undeniable proof of wrongdoing. Hell, he personally witnessed Mathers shoot an unarmed man only to see his own recollection and reputation called into question by those he once trusted. No, he would keep whatever he uncovered on Hanscomb to himself as long as he could. If Hanscomb really was dirty, and Corey could help him substantiate it, then and only then would he bring Chloe onboard.

As if reading his thoughts, Chloe's name popped up on his cell phone screen with an incoming text message.

What time do U want 2 meet in the AM?

Brock considered their next official move. They needed to put some time in on the murder board. They had checked off several additional boxes, but there was still much to do. Updating the board would help both of them see the path forward.

Make it 9. Troop J.

C U then.

56

Brock sat in the conference room of the Troop J barracks, staring at the whiteboard. His takeout coffee had gone cold, and he grimaced as he swallowed the last of it. Caffeine be damned, there was nothing worse than cold coffee.

He'd come in at seven, two hours earlier than he'd told Chloe to meet, due to his ongoing insomnia, and would have arrived sooner were it not for the six inches of wet, heavy snow that had fallen overnight. Poor man's fertilizer, the farmers called it. Brock called it an annoyance that would likely melt away within a day or two.

Using the extra time to his advantage, he had populated the board with information garnered from the previous day's work. Brock intentionally omitted his overnight contact with Perreault for two reasons. First, there were the prying eyes from Troop J that he suspected were keeping tabs on their progress. He knew there were other keys to the room floating about. The second reason was Chloe, though he knew she would find out he'd questioned Perreault soon enough, likely by way of Hanscomb himself. But when that happened, Brock would simply tell her it had no bearing on the Lee Owen case and leave it at that.

The other name he'd omitted from the board was Albert's. It was clear to Brock that his father was avoiding him. But the fact that he hadn't been seen since running down Parlin's mailbox was concerning. What was he up to? And what were he and Parlin arguing about? And why hadn't Parlin mentioned it to Chloe when she stopped by his office? It couldn't have been more than a few hours after the incident at his home, so why hadn't he said anything? Brock needed to check the camp again. And maybe it was time to pay Parlin a visit too. Chloe's discretion hadn't worked. Brock needed to be a whole lot less discreet with the sheriff.

He was startled by a knock on the door. "Come in," he said.

The door opened, and Mike Fuente stuck his head inside. "Thought I might find you here."

"Hey, Mike," Brock said. "Come on in."

Fuente entered the room and closed the door behind him. He sat down across from Brock and eyed the whiteboard.

"Can you believe that snow? I thought we were past that already."

"You know what Mark Twain said about New England weather, right?" Brock said.

"Yeah, but I don't have a minute to wait, brother," Fuente said, his eyes shifting back to the board. "Damn, you two have done a lot of work on this."

"Long way to go yet," Brock said. "What's up?"

"Not much. They've had me chasing down a bunch of commercial burglaries. Think I've inhaled more fingerprint powder in the last week than I have in my entire career."

"That can't be healthy."

"It isn't," Fuente said as he placed a high-definition photo of a single bullet on the table.

Brock picked up the image and studied it. "What's this?"

"That is a slug from a .308 rifle that I dug out of a tree trunk not far from where your SUV got shot up. I think it might be the round that took out your windows."

"Seriously? That's great news. Any match in NIBIN?"

Brock was referring to the National Integrated Ballistic Information Network maintained by The Bureau of Alcohol, Tobacco, Firearms and Explosives. NIBIN is a one-stop-shop digital database used to make ballistic comparisons in much the same way law enforcement agencies match fingerprints.

"Would have been too easy, right?"

Brock sighed. "Well, at least we know the caliber."

"And it's in the system now. By the way, I hear tell that you had an off-the-books with Harold Perreault last night."

Brock turned around to face him. "That didn't take long."

"The grapevine is strong in these parts."

"Apparently," Brock said as he studied Mike's face, wondering if he really was an ally. "And what does the grapevine think we talked about?"

"Nobody knows, but it put more than a few people's noses out of joint."

"Don't suppose any of those noses mentioned that I was called to the scene of the stop."

"Actually, they did, but I think they were hoping to be included in your interview."

Brock didn't respond, but he clearly heard Albert harping his favorite old saw about hoping in one hand, shitting in the other as you wait to see which filled up first.

"Well, it didn't work out that way," Brock said before turning back to the whiteboard.

"Any closer to identifying Owen's killer?" Fuente said.

"We're making progress, but it's slow going."

The awkward silence continued for close to thirty seconds before Fuente finally got up.

"Well, I gotta get back at it. Good talking with you, Brock."

"Yeah," Brock said as he watched Fuente depart. He picked up the empty cardboard coffee cup and tossed it in the general direction of the wastebasket in the far corner of the room. The cup bounced off the wall, missing the wastebasket entirely, and clattered across the linoleum floor.

"Nice shot," Chloe said as she breezed into the room carrying two to-go coffees.

"Exactly why I went into law enforcement," Brock said.

"The NBA wouldn't have you?"

"Can you believe it?"

"I can," she said, handing him one of the coffees.

"Thanks," Brock said.

"You're welcome," she said as she sat down beside him. "I'd have been here sooner, but I got stuck behind a plow."

Brock nodded his understanding.

"You've been busy. What time did you get in?"

"A while ago. I couldn't sleep."

"The Bear?" Chloe said.

"You heard?"

"Two calls so far. Is there a reason you didn't call me?"

"I figured at least one of us needed the rest."

"Anything come of your private interview with him?"

"He may have an alibi for the night Owen was murdered."

"Who?"

"Judy Babbage."

Chloe's eyes widened. "The waitress from Marlintini's?"

Brock nodded. "Can you run that down?"

"Of course," Chloe said. "Anything else?"

Brock took a sip of the hot coffee before he answered. "How well do you know Tommy Hanscomb?"

Brock departed from Troop J headed for Albert's camp. Chloe had taken the news about Hanscomb about as well as Brock had predicted. She wasn't happy, telling Brock she'd worked alongside Tommy a lot longer than she'd known Brock. The implication being she trusted Hanscomb, a trust Brock had yet to earn.

"And why would you be inclined to believe a word that comes out of Harold Perreault's mouth?" Chloe had countered.

Brock wasn't entirely sure he did, but Perreault had brought up some interesting things concerning his history with Hanscomb. Some of which could be checked, and Perreault had to know Brock would. Then there was the alibi.

"I hate to tell you this, Brock," Chloe began.

"But you're going to anyway, right?" Brock said.

"You're beginning to get a reputation as a guy who targets his fellow officers."

"If you mean I don't like bent cops, you're right," Brock said. "Is this the part where you preach to me about the thin blue line? Us and them?"

"I happen to believe in that blue line," Chloe said after a long moment.

"So do I, Chloe. But it has a different connotation for me. I believe we represent the thin blue line protecting society from its own evils."

"So, what, you're a savior now?"

"Hardly," Brock said. "But I still remember the oath I made when I took this job. Do you?"

Chloe frowned. "Not verbatim, but of course I remember it."

"Well, I do remember it. Every word. And the most important line is about never betraying my integrity, character, or the public trust."

"And you think because Perreault made some random accusations about Tommy that you're now obligated to follow up? Jesus, Brock, the guy's a known drug trafficker and outlaw motorcycle gang enforcer. Why would you ever take his word over that of a decorated veteran cop like Tommy Hanscomb?"

Brock stared at Chloe for a long moment without answering, allowing her words to hang there.

"Ever work internal affairs?" Brock said.

"The rat squad? No way. Why would I?"

"You think anyone who comes to file a complaint against an officer is unsullied?"

Chloe didn't respond.

"Fact is, most of the people filing complaints have violated the law in some way. The very reason they ended up interacting with us in the first place."

"Your point?" Chloe said.

"My point is, even criminals have the right to be heard. If there is a bad cop out there, who would know better than another criminal?"

"Now you're comparing Tommy to Perreault?"

Brock sighed. He was getting nowhere. It was obvious she was allowing her friendship with Hanscomb to cloud her judgment, and nothing he said, short of handing her actual proof, would sway her opinion of him.

"All I'm saying is we need to keep an open mind until we know the truth."

Brock's attention was yanked back to the here and now as a black pickup pulled out of a side road directly in front of him, causing him to step down hard on the brake pedal to avoid a collision. He lay on the horn to get the driver's attention. The young man's middle finger popped up in automatic salute. Brock reached for the emergency light switches, intending to activate them and pull the young hot dog over, but after a moment's reflection, he decided against it. He wasn't a traffic cop anymore, hadn't been for some time. Besides, he had bigger fish to fry than some young punk. Brock slowly resumed his speed as he watched the rusty pickup race off into the distance.

That bigger fish was Albert Justice.

57

Chloe was hot under the collar after her conversation with Brock. She was glad he'd gone off on his own, as she didn't think she could stomach working with him today, not after he'd shared his suspicions about Tommy.

Brock didn't know him like she did. Tommy Hanscomb was a squared-away cop who'd had her back more times than she could count. Brock was nothing more than a spoiled glory boy who'd turned on one of his own. How long before he turned on her?

She sighed, then turned to the maps she had brought with her. There was still a case to investigate, even if she and Brock were focused in two different directions.

She had considered driving out to Second Pond and pulling up her GPS to see how far Owen had traveled the night he died. One of the many unanswered questions nagging her was his destination. Where exactly was Lee Owen headed with Phinney's stolen snowmobile?

She unrolled the map of the Blue Hill Peninsula on the table, then weighed it down at the corners with several of the thick file folders they were amassing. The map encompassed Blue Hill and several of the surrounding towns.

The oddly shaped peninsula reminded Chloe of Europe. Like most of the Down East coastline, the Blue Hill Peninsula jutted out into the Atlantic in a southeasterly direction. Separated from the western headlands by Penobscot Bay and to the east by the Union River, the Blue Hill area encapsulated more than a dozen towns with names like Castine, Surry, and Naskeag, the latter originating from the Abenaki tribe, meaning "the end." In addition to lengthening Maine's rocky coastline, the peninsulas made traveling between nearby towns much harder. While only fifteen miles separated Blue Hill from the popular tourist destination of Bar Harbor, an easy trek by boat, driving from one town to the other took nearly an hour by land. And far longer during the busy summertime season.

Chloe scrounged through the room for something that would act as a long straight edge but came up empty. She retreated into the hallway, expending her search to the nearby offices but found most of them locked up. She was thinking she might have to make a run to the local dollar store for a yardstick when she noticed a four-foot section of an aluminum radiator cover lying askew due to a missing end cap. It was perfect. She snatched it up and headed back to the conference room.

She set the makeshift straight edge off to one side of the table, then studied the map. The first thing she did was use a red marker to plot the locations of each of the addresses pertinent to the case, beginning with Second Pond, the site of Lee Owen's body recovery and Brock's shooting. Following that, she proceeded to add the locations of Keith and Emily Phinney's home in Sargentville, Albert Justice's camp, Harold Perreault's trailer, Perreault's Service Station, and Parlin's home on Woods Point Lane.

She stood back and surveyed the map and each of the plotted points, looking for any kind of pattern. Nothing jumped out at her. She picked up the radiator cover and placed one edge at Second Pond and the other at Phinney's home, then drew a straight line with a fine-point magic marker. She removed the straight edge and checked her work. She knew there were snowmobile trails crisscrossing the peninsula, and she could easily see where Owen would have had to travel to get from Phinney's to Second Pond. His route would have required him to cross Routes 15 and 175. She considered this. That made at least two points where Owen risked being spotted on the stolen sled. Though the late hour meant traffic would have been light, it was still a risky route for Owen to have taken. She was positive now. Owen wasn't out for a joyride on his employer's snowmobile; he was on a mission. Had Owen known about the false panel? Did he believe drugs were hidden inside? Was he driving to meet someone who could help him remove the drugs? Or was he going somewhere to remove them himself? Either way, Chloe knew Owen had a specific destination in mind. And he had chosen the one night that neither of the Phinneys were home. Ergo, he had to have known their schedules.

Chloe ran her finger back to the pond. "Where were you going, Lee?"

Half an hour later, Brock navigated the loaner SUV along the unplowed two-track path that led through the woods to Albert's camp. The previous night's wet, heavy snowfall had obscured the ground and strained many of the low-lying tree branches, bending them until they partially blocked the drive and scraped along the sides of the Ford. Whatever damage the branches were causing to the exterior of his loaner, he supposed it was better than the bullet holes his last assigned vehicle had suffered.

Brock wondered where How Weird Tisdale was in his investigation and how hard he was even trying to find the shooter. He still hadn't gotten back to him about the variety store video. Tisdale wasn't Brock's biggest fan, that much was clear. But whether it would prevent him from identifying the person who'd shot up Brock's ride remained to be seen.

Albert's truck was parked in the dooryard. The payload door was open, and it was stacked with firewood. His father was nowhere in sight.

Brock parked beside the truck and got out. The revving sound of a chainsaw coming from the front of the camp echoed through the woods. Brock locked the SUV and headed toward the lake on foot.

As he rounded the front corner of the camp, he could see the heavy toll of storm damage. A half dozen or so thick pine branches had broken off, littering the property at the water's edge. Albert was making quick work of a large section that had crashed down across the dock. Not wishing to startle him, Brock stood near the deck stairs and waited.

Chloe availed herself to the straight edge to follow along every conceivable path Lee Owen might have taken after reaching Second Pond. She alternated between the larger paper map and the digital map she had opened on her laptop. After about twenty minutes, she expanded the search zone for possible destinations in the direction of Surry. The one item she realized she was missing was a map of the snowmobile and ATV trails intersecting with the pond. Such a map would allow her to locate every off-road option available to Owen on the night he went missing. It was clear to her that Owen would have tried to avoid anything more than just a quick crossing of any paved roads.

She opened a new web browser and conducted a search for local ATV/snowmobile clubs and trails. After several minutes, she found what she was searching for on a site belonging to the BHP Trail Association. Searching through the site, she found the association was responsible for maintaining more than two hundred miles of trails throughout the Blue Hill Peninsula. Unfortunately, they hadn't posted more than a rudimentary map of the trails online. The digital map consisted of nothing more than a few squiggled lines of assorted colors, each one representing a different region or town. Chloe scrolled through the menu and clicked on the contact page where she located a phone number for the club president, Logan Cousins. She picked up her cell phone and punched in the number.

After waiting through more than a half dozen rings, Chloe fully expected the call to go to voicemail and was surprised when someone picked up.

"Yes," the phlegmy-sounding voice of an elderly male said.

"I'm looking for Mr. Logan Cousins," Chloe said.

"You found him," Cousins said after clearing his throat.

"Mr. Cousins, my name is Chloe Wright. I'm a detective with the Maine State Police, and I'm investigating a murder in the town of Blue Hill."

"How can I help?"

"I was hoping you could provide me with some information. I see you're the club president of the Blue Hill Peninsula Trail Association."

Cousins responded with a chuckle. "It's a pretty loose association, but yeah, that would be me."

"I wondered whether you might have detailed maps of the trails your club maintains. The one picture I found online isn't much help."

"You mean those blue and red squiggles won't help with your case?"

"No, not really."

"Well, I may have what you're looking for. Are you in the Blue Hill area?"

"I can be. I'm in Ellsworth now."

"You know where Marlintini's Grill is?"

"I do indeed," Chloe said, thinking she needed to speak to Judy Babbage anyway. "Been a frequent flier there just recently."

"Good. I can meet you there in about an hour if that works for you. I'll grab a booth."

"That would be great. How will I recognize you?"

Cousins chuckled again. "I'll be the old guy holding the big rolled-up map."

58

Brock didn't know what to say as his father stood there covered in sawdust, glaring at him.

"Happy now?" Albert said as he retrieved the chainsaw and carried it over to the dock.

"Not particularly," Brock said, following him. "Why would you lie about the poker game?"

"I didn't lie about it; I just don't remember all of it." Albert paused as he uncapped the fuel cover and began to refill the tank. "I told you, Tommy showed up late, said he got caught up dealing with a bad car accident in Surry, so we started playing cards without him. Gene made my drinks pretty strong that night, and I guess I put down more than I thought because I've got gaps in my memory I still can't piece together."

Brock knew about Albert's drinking problem, which had seriously worsened following the death of Jolene, Brock's mother, to cancer. The drinking had been one of the reasons Albert retired from the state police. He'd had his time in but was planning to stay on indefinitely, or until they forced him out due to his age, but he cracked up his cruiser and injured the other driver. The responding officers found him highly intoxicated. The colonel gave Albert a choice: retirement with full honors, or risk internal/criminal investigations and firing in disgrace. Albert had grudgingly chosen the former.

"What time did Tommy finally show up?" Brock said.

"Not sure," Albert said as he began to refill the chainsaw bar oil reservoir.

"But you said you won big that night. You said it was the most you'd ever won."

"That's what they told me the next morning while we were eating breakfast at Gene's. But I can't remember what happened."

"Is that why you were arguing with Parlin?" Brock said.

"Dammit," Albert said as he spilled some of the oil on the dock. His eyes narrowed into slits as he stood up and stepped toward Brock. "You spying on me?"

"My partner went around to Parlin's and saw you. Said it looked like you and Gene were about to come to blows. What was that about?"

"You seem to have all the answers. Why don't you tell me?"

"I think you know something is wrong here," Brock said. "And I think you're still holding back, putting your friends before doing what's right."

"It's called loyalty. Not that I'd expect you to understand it."

Brock felt himself rising to the bait. He wanted to take a swing at his father in the worst way, but he knew it was exactly what Albert wanted. He'd never laid a finger on his old man, but the same certainly couldn't be said of Albert.

Albert had been a big believer in corporal punishment when it came to raising Brock and his brother, Jacob, both of whom had felt the sharp sting of a leather belt frequently during their formative years. Brock hated his old man for those beatings, vowing to never raise a hand in anger against his own children. And now here he stood, toe-to-toe with his mentor and nemesis, ready to strike out in anger and relish the feeling of power that accompanied it.

The twinkle in his father's eyes was impossible to miss. Albert wanted this. Brock didn't know if he could take him or not; despite his age, the old man was still a bear, but Brock knew how good it would feel to finally release all those years of pent-up anger and humiliation. For Jake, as well as himself.

"You gonna man up or just stand there like a momma's boy?"

Brock balled up both hands into fists, forcing his fingernails into his palms until he thought they might bleed. He was ready to pounce and let the chips fall where they may, but something stopped him. Maybe it was the need to prove he wasn't like his father. Or maybe he didn't want Albert to feel like he'd successfully goaded him into physical violence. Brock wasn't sure. But he was sure that assaulting his old man, who was at a minimum a witness in this case, at worse a suspect, was a sure way to not only fuck up the investigation but possibly get himself booted off the job in the process.

"Come on, coward," Albert said as he drew closer, their noses nearly touching.

Brock stood his ground a moment longer, holding eye contact with the bitter, sweaty old man, neither speaking a word. Finally, Brock turned and trudged back to his SUV and drove away.

Chloe departed Marlintini's Grill armed with a large, detailed trail map provided by Logan Cousins and a solid alibi for Harold Perreault. Judy Babbage confirmed she was with Perreault on the night Owen had gone missing. She also admitted to pointing Chloe in the direction of Hamilton because she was jealous of the woman. Perreault had dumped her for Melinda after all.

Chloe was excited about the map. It meant she now had three different sources available to establish Owen's destination the night he was murdered. Using the information she'd already obtained, combined with Cousins's trail atlas and Google Maps, it took her less than half an hour to arrive at what she called a really good guess. What Chloe found was a self-storage facility on Route 172, the road that led from Blue Hill to Surry, aptly named Blue Hill Self-Storage. Following the discovery, Chloe made two phone calls. The second was to Brock.

"I've been looking at maps of the area, trying to figure out where Owen might have been going with the stolen sled," Chloe said.

"Good idea. Any luck?"

"Yup. Guess what I found rented in Lee Owen's name," Chloe said.

"Let me guess, a self-storage space?"

"Way to ruin my surprise," Chloe said. "It's on Route 172, and the owner said Owen paid up through October. You okay? Your voice sounds funny."

"I'm fine," Brock said. "You're sure that's where he was headed with Phinney's sled?"

"Not a hundred percent, but it is the most likely place for him to have been going that night," Chloe said. "And it must be more than a coincidence that he has a space rented there. Who knows what else he may have hidden. Should I start working on a warrant?"

"Did the storage guy say who was listed on the rental agreement?" Brock said.

"Just Owen. He paid cash."

"Then we don't need a warrant," Brock said. "Nice work, partner."

Chloe allowed herself to smile. It was the first time since they'd been paired up by Cumberland that he had referred to her that way.

"I'll see you there," Brock said.

Brock watched as Chloe used the bolt cutters from the utility bag she carried in the back of her SUV to cut the padlock on the storage unit leased by Lee Owen.

"We kind of encourage our lessees to use our locks," Leonard Happel, the manager of the self-storage facility, said to Brock. "But I get why they want to put their own on. Hard to trust people nowadays."

Brock grinned at the irony in that comment as he watched Chloe reach down to lift the overhead door.

The space was crammed along the left wall with random items stacked floor to ceiling on cheap plastic shelving. On the right side of the space, Owen had left himself more than enough room to drive several all-terrain vehicles inside. Lingering in the air was the faint odor of gasoline and oil. Brock noticed traces of dried mud on the concrete floor in a pattern suggesting it might have come from the rubber track of a snowmobile.

The rear of the storage area had been fashioned into a home away from home. There was a sleeping bag rolled out on a foam pad, a pillow, and a small battery-powered lamp set atop a cardboard box doubling as a nightstand of sorts.

"Pretty cozy," Chloe said.

"Looks like the kind of place a guy on the run might hide out," Brock said.

"You think some of this stuff might be stolen?" the manager called out from behind them.

"Thanks for your help, Mr. Happel," Brock said.

"Call me Leonard."

"We'll take it from here, Leonard."

"You know we don't condone any type of illegal storage in these units," Happel continued.

"No worries," Chloe said. "We'll let you know if we need anything."

Happel finally got the hint and wandered back to his vehicle.

Among the items they located were a set of tools and a drop light, the kind used by auto mechanics for working on engines or undercarriages.

"Are you thinking what I'm thinking?" Brock said.

"If you're thinking Owen used this space to unload the smuggled drugs, then yes."

Brock looked through the junk without touching anything. They would need to finish photographing all the contents in situ before moving anything. Among the items he saw were various nautical memorabilia. He wondered how many of the items had been taken from either the boatyard or the Phinney home.

"Betcha this would bring a pretty penny," Chloe said, pointing to a solid brass antique ship's compass on one of the shelves.

Brock nodded in agreement. He thought back to his conversation with Albert about the police memorabilia taken in the camp burglary. Owen had been involved with so many different people, both in his role as a handyman and a property maintenance guy, that it wouldn't have been a surprise to find something here that belonged to Albert.

Brock got down on his hands and knees and shined a flashlight underneath the bottom shelf, illuminating a mountain of debris consisting of leaves, dust, and cobwebs. But one item in particular caught his eye. A single pink tablet with the word Xanax imprinted on its side.

He got Chloe's attention and pointed under the shelf.

She hesitated for a moment. "You're not going to show me a dead rat or something, are you?"

"Nope. This is better."

She joined him on the concrete floor and followed the beam of his light.

"How much you want to bet that isn't Xanax?" Brock said.

Chloe sat up on her heels. "I think we just made the link we've been looking for."

59

"Okay, so we know that Lee Owen was involved in whatever this is," Lt. Cumberland said.

"In so far as he stole Phinney's snowmobile to try and recover the drugs," Brock said. "But we have no idea if he was involved in the smuggling or distribution."

"You don't think he was?" Major Morgan said.

"We can't be sure," Chloe said. "It may have simply been that Owen found out about the operation and wanted a piece for himself."

"Then Dr. Phinney must be the mastermind," Morgan said.

"We need to be damn sure about that before slinging that information around publicly or otherwise," AAG Grover said. "Phinney is a highly respected member of the Blue Hill community. He and his wife give a substantial amount of money to that town. Hell, they're major benefactors of the George Stevens Academy."

"And they just built the town's fitness center and gymnasium," Brock added.

"Phinney and his wife will slap us with a defamation lawsuit faster than you can say early retirement if we're wrong," Grover continued. "I am gonna need a lot more than a single pill in the storage unit of a known criminal."

"Phinney's got to be involved," Morgan persisted. "His snowmobile has the false panel and everything. There's no way he isn't aware of what's happening here."

"You willing to stake your career on that?" Grover said. "Because I'm not." He turned to Brock and Chloe. "Look, I think you're really close to breaking this thing wide open, but I'm going to need more."

Cumberland waited until after the meeting had broken up before asking Brock and Chloe to come to her office.

"Nice work, you two," she said after closing the door.

"Thanks," Brock said.

"I guess I thought the AAG would be more excited about our find," Chloe said.

Cumberland sat down at her desk and faced them. "He's a pragmatist, Chloe. You need to remember that it's his butt on the line if we don't do this right. As the attorney tasked with prosecuting Owen's murder, Grover will be the one holding the bag if we miss something or hand him a case that hasn't had every box checked."

Brock nodded.

"So how do we get one of these guys to give it up?" Chloe said. "No one's going to just admit they've been smuggling drugs into the country."

"This is where you earn the big bucks," Cumberland said, looking directly at Brock as she said it. Her gaze then shifted to Chloe. "Think of your investigation as a baseball field. Your investigation must stay on the diamond and in the outfield. Anything in foul territory is off-limits, i.e., outside of the law. Figure out a way to make the case in bounds, and you'll get there."

Cumberland hurried off to another meeting while Brock and Chloe returned to their desks, where Jordan Zimmerman was anxiously awaiting word.

"How'd it go with Penny Dreadful?" he said.

Chloe shook her head. "She told us to think outside the box."

The detective grinned. "She gave you the old baseball analogy, didn't she?"

Brock nodded. "I take it that's her go-to?"

"Like she was Joe Torre himself."

"Who's Joe Torry?" Chloe said.

"Ay-ay-ay," Zimmerman said with a shake of his head. "From the mouths of babes. He was only one of the best managers the Yankees ever had. The Bronx Bombers won four World Series titles under him, Chloe."

As they bantered back and forth, Brock's mind began to follow a thread that had been bothering him for some time. From the discovery of Owen's body, to the poker game, to the missing person's report filed by Melinda Hamilton, to the break-in at Albert's camp, one name had been right in the middle of all of it.

"Tommy Hanscomb," Brock said absently, stopping Chloe and Zimmerman in mid-discussion.

"What's that?" Zimmerman said.

"Deputy Hanscomb," Brock said again.

"Here we go again," Chloe said with a sigh of exasperation.

"I don't get it," Zimmerman said. "What about Hanscomb?"

"Brock has it in his head that Tommy is some criminal mastermind," Chloe said.

"What makes you think that?" Zimmerman said.

Brock looked at Chloe for a moment before diving into his explanation. Both detectives listened quietly until he'd finished speaking.

Chloe spoke up first. "Assuming for a second that you're right, and for the record, I think you are way off base, why would Tommy get involved in this in the first place?"

Brock shrugged. "Who knows? Money trouble? Extortion? Greed? Why does anyone ever get involved in something like this?"

"May I ask a question?" Zimmerman said. "Who was it that told you about this drug smuggling thing in the first place?"

Brock exchanged a glance with Chloe before answering. "Hanscomb," Brock said.

"I gotta admit it, Chloe," Zimmerman said. "Brock does have a point here. It sounds to me like Hanscomb deserves a closer look."

"I've worked alongside Tommy for years," Chloe said, her frustration clearly showing. "He's had my back more times than I could count. Now you're saying what, that he murdered Lee Owen?"

"Nobody's accusing Tommy of murdering anyone," Brock said. "But whether he did or didn't, I think he might be the key to all of this."

Brock and Chloe departed from the barracks in his SUV, headed back to Blue Hill Self-Storage to drop Chloe at her vehicle. Her silence was an indicator of exactly how pissed she was at him for mentioning Hanscomb again, not that Brock had needed an indication.

"I feel like you're forgetting one big thing, *partner*," Chloe said, putting specific emphasis on the last word as if she'd spat something foul out of her mouth. "Tommy Hanscomb was at Gene Parlin's poker game on the night we know Owen stole Phinney's snowmobile. Your own father vouched for him."

Brock looked over at her.

"Well, didn't he?"

60

Brock felt the exhaustion envelope him as he drove along a darkened stretch of Route 172 toward Surry from Blue Hill. The last week's work in combination with his ongoing insomnia was taking its toll. He knew fatigue was a recipe for disaster. Murder investigations tended to have multiple moving parts, and in this case, there had been the added trouble of a new and relatively inexperienced partner. Not to mention Albert's involvement, however deep that involvement might turn out to be. Exhaustion also meant unclear thinking and mistakes. And mistakes never played well in the legal sense. Ever. On the street they could get a person killed, but the courtroom could be every bit as treacherous.

He lowered the front windows of the SUV in the hopes that the crisp night air would revive him enough to complete the trip to his apartment. A check of the rearview revealed headlights approaching. Besides his Ford, the trailing vehicle was the only other on the dark and desolate road. Whoever was behind the wheel had to have been in a hurry, as they were closing the distance quickly. Before Brock could fully process what was happening, blue strobes and flashing headlights glared brightly in his rearview, harshly illuminating the interior of his vehicle, blinding him.

He glanced down at the speedometer, thinking that perhaps he'd been speeding, but the digital display read 49, only four miles an hour above the posted speed limit. Surely not enough to warrant stopping him.

He removed his foot from the accelerator and activated the right turn signal. He coasted to the side of the two-lane road, thinking that the cruiser would simply pass by, but it didn't. Brock stopped the SUV and put the transmission in park as the other vehicle slid in behind him at a slight angle. He lowered the driver's side window the entire way, then placed both of his hands on the steering wheel. It was as automatic as anything he'd ever been trained to do. As a former street cop himself, Brock knew there was nothing more dangerous than a nighttime traffic stop. Always the ultimate unknown, as the approaching officer had no idea who might be inside the stopped vehicle and what secrets they might be hiding, beyond the actual reason for the stop. He knew whoever was approaching him on foot would likely be on high alert. A remote location, in the dark of night, all alone with no backup nearby, any sudden or unexpected moves by Brock were a good way to get shot.

As he waited for the officer to make the approach, Brock glanced at the screen of his dash-mounted cell phone. No service. He shook his head. It wasn't as if the lack of cellular coverage hadn't been a thing in Southern Maine, because it was, but it was nowhere near as prevalent as it was in the Down East part of the state. He supposed it was just one more thing he would grow accustomed to.

His attention returned to the driver's side mirror as he heard a door shut on the other vehicle.

"Evening, Detective," a familiar voice said from behind the beam of a handheld flashlight just beyond Brock's sightline.

"Well, if it isn't Deputy Hanscomb," Brock said. "Mind telling me what I did wrong? Pretty sure I wasn't speeding."

"I clocked you at five over, but I can probably see my way clear of letting that slide," Hanscomb said with a chuckle that had zero warmth attached to it. "I understand you've developed some interesting theories about who your suspect in the Lee Owen murder might be."

Brock's mind scrambled to figure out what information might have gotten back to Hanscomb, and how. Had someone been talking out of school? Brock had warned Chloe of his concerns about the deputy. Would she have been foolhardy enough to share those concerns with Tommy? Would she have allowed her ongoing friendship with the deputy to cloud her judgment? Would Albert?

"I've got a few theories," Brock said. "But nothing solid enough to act on yet."

"That's good to hear," Hanscomb said as he extinguished the Kel-Lite and moved around to stand in front of the outside mirror. He was holding his flashlight in one hand while resting the other atop the butt of his sidearm. "You know we kind of depend on each other up here. It isn't like where you came from, where a backup was only a few minutes away. Nope, up here we're pretty much on our own. Might take as much as a half hour or more for a backup to respond to an officer's call for help. And that's assuming your radio is working and anyone is even available to respond. And don't even get me started on cell service. Nope, you're officially in the boonies now, Justice."

Brock felt a chill make its way across the surface of his skin as the two men locked eyes. Tommy was making a power play here, delivering a message. A veiled threat carefully thought out in advance. If Brock bothered to complain to Parlin about his most trusted deputy pulling him over in the middle of the night, he would come off looking like a whiny problem child, and he knew it. Hanscomb hadn't said one word that could be used against him. He would tell anyone who asked that he was just offering some friendly advice to a cop new to the area. But both men knew what was happening here. Tommy Hanscomb's intent couldn't have been clearer.

"Anything else?" Brock said, following a long, awkward moment of silence.

"Nope," Hanscomb said as he gently tapped the top of the mirror with his light. "I guess that just about covers it. You drive safe now, Justice."

Brock's heart was racing as he sat there watching Hanscomb's cruiser make a U-turn and head back in the opposite direction. Tommy had stalked him, waiting until Brock was all alone and out of cell coverage to pull him over and issue his warning. It was something a hunter would have done to his prey. Except a hunter wouldn't have given him a warning. Brock didn't imagine there would be another. Had Hanscomb delivered the message at the behest of another, or was he acting on his own? There was no way for Brock to know. Hell, he didn't even know whose side Chloe was on now. Or even Albert.

As Brock's heart rate began to slow, the anger welled up inside of him. If Hanscomb or anyone else thought they could intimidate Brock into letting this case simply fade away as another unsolved murder, they had another thing coming.

Steeled in his resolve, Brock moved the gearshift lever into drive and pulled back onto the roadway.

He had already faced death more than once in his career, a career he had nearly lost in the process. It would take a hell of a lot more than Tommy Hanscomb, or anyone else for that matter, to chase Brock Justice off the case. A lot more.

61

It was nearly noon the following day as Brock nosed the SUV to the curb in front of the Subway sandwich shop in Blue Hill. He had been craving a meatball sub with marinara and provolone since first waking. He couldn't imagine where that idea had originated, but he knew he wouldn't be able to focus on anything else until the urge was sated. He grabbed his cell phone and was reaching for the inside door handle when something caught his eye. Taped to the lower left corner of one of Subway's plate-glass windows was a faded missing person flyer. The photograph shown in the flyer appeared to be that of Lee Owen. Brock stepped out and approached the window for a closer look.

As he studied the flyer, Brock realized it was the first one he'd seen anywhere around town, which was odd. The second thing he realized was that whoever had posted the flyer had yet to take it down, which could only mean that they'd either forgotten about it or hadn't yet heard the news of the grisly discovery. Brock snapped a quick photo of the flyer through the window with his phone, then stepped inside.

"Help you?" the twenty-something male clerk said as he moved toward the end of the sandwich preparation counter.

Brock flipped open his state police identification and held it up.

"Detective Justice," Brock said. "Wondering if you might be able to help me with something."

"What do you need?"

"I am wondering about that missing person flyer in your window," Brock said.

The clerk stood up on his tiptoes to get a better look at the window. "Huh," he said. "Guess I didn't even notice it. Must be a new one."

"Actually, it isn't," Brock said. "The man in that flyer went missing around the end of January. Lee Owen."

"Oh, yeah," the clerk said. "I remember that now. Local guy, right?"

Brock nodded. "I don't suppose you remember who posted the flyer."

"Not really. We get so many requests to hang stuff. Usually it's business flyers, or someone selling something, or running for office." He rolled his eyes as if accentuating the last.

"Normally we don't allow any of that stuff to go up. Company policy. But if someone has a worthwhile cause, like a missing person, we try and help."

"I don't suppose you'd mind if I took that with me," Brock said as he cocked a thumb in the direction of the window.

"Guess that depends," the clerk said with a chuckle.

"On?"

"Whether or not he's still missing."

"We recovered his body last week," Brock said.

The clerk's face paled, and his eyes widened. "Tell me that's not the guy you all pulled from the lake."

"It is."

"Man, that's one effed-up deal, huh? I mean, who'd want to handcuff a guy to a snowmobile and send him to the bottom of a lake?"

Brock couldn't have summed the case up any better if he'd tried.

"By all means. Take the poster if you need it."

"Thanks," Brock said as he walked toward the window and donned a pair of latex gloves.

"Can I get you anything else?" the clerk said.

As he reached the window, Brock turned and said, "I'd kill for a meatball sub."

Brock carefully removed the flyer by slicing along the cellophane tape that held it to the window. The clerk confirmed that one of the employees had hung it, so Brock wasn't worried about the prints left on the tape. He did, however, want to check for any prints left behind by the person who'd created the flyer. While the clerk prepared his sandwich, Brock returned to the SUV and tucked the flyer inside a document envelope, then sealed it.

The sub was exquisite, and Brock sat in his SUV enjoying every bite. After he finished, Brock used a wet wipe from the glove box to remove all traces of marinara sauce from his fingers. He pulled out his cell phone and opened the jpeg of the flyer, blowing it up until he could read the contact information. The only thing listed was a phone number that Brock did not recognize. There was no indication that the flyer had been created by the Hancock County Sheriff's Office. In fact, the pixelated flyer appeared to have been printed using a cheap home printer on plain white paper stock. Brock removed the notebook from the pocket of his suit coat and wrote down the number from the flyer.

Whoever had created and posted the flyer had obviously cared about Lee Owen, which was more than Brock could say about most of the people they'd spoken with. Even his live-in girlfriend, Melinda Hamilton, hadn't been broken up by his disappearance, at least not beyond the financial hardship it had created. A hardship that she appeared to have rectified by hooking up with Harold Perreault. Brock studied the number again as he took another swig from his Diet Pepsi. Whoever the number belonged to was someone they really needed to speak with. Never one for diving in blindly, Brock made a quick call to Chloe. She answered on the first ring.

"What's up?" she said.

"Not much, just finishing lunch. I wondered if you could check a phone number for me through the SP system and see if it's ever come up on a case before?"

"Sure. Shoot."

Brock recited the number twice, then waited as he listened to the sound of Chloe punching keys.

"Um, it looks like that number isn't in our database. Who does it belong to?"

"Not a clue."

Brock proceeded to tell her how he had come across the number.

"Well, that sounds promising," Chloe said. "I haven't met too many people all that broken up by Lee's murder."

Brock grinned as he listened to her say nearly verbatim what he had been thinking.

"You want me to call them?" Chloe asked.

Brock hadn't been planning to have her do more than check to see if they had a name to go with the number, but he was rethinking that strategy. Something in his gut was telling him that the person who'd created the flyer was a woman. A woman who still cared about Owen. If he was right, Chloe might be less likely to scare off whoever it was. Especially if they knew that Owen had been murdered. A phone call from a strange man might just be enough to scare whoever this was away for good.

"That's a good idea," Brock said.

"I'm on it."

62

A tentative-sounding female voice answered the phone. "Hello?" The word came out seeming more like a question.

"Good afternoon, my name is Chloe Wright. I'm a detective with the Maine State Police. To whom am I speaking?"

During the silence that followed, Chloe could hear the faint whisper of breathing at the other end of the line. "Hello, are you still there?"

"I'm here."

"May I ask who you are?"

"My name is Cyndi," the woman said. "Cyndi Williams. I'm almost afraid to ask why you're calling me."

"I'm calling about the missing person's flyer you posted."

"Have you found Lee?"

Though only a fledgling homicide detective, Chloe knew enough to tread lightly here. If she came on too strong, she might lose Williams entirely.

"Yes, we did locate him," Chloe said. "May I ask your relationship to Mr. Owen?"

"He's—an old acquaintance," Williams said after a moment's hesitation. "Is he okay?"

Again, Chloe knew enough to take it slow. "I'm sorry to be the one to tell you this, Cyndi, but Mr. Owen is deceased."

Chloe heard Williams's sharp intake of breath. It was clear that Williams and Owen had been more than just acquaintances.

"Can you tell me what happened?" Williams said at last.

Chloe chose her words carefully, not wanting to give anything away, but she knew that Williams could, and likely would, conduct an online search to find out what had happened as soon as she ended the call, if not sooner. "As I said, I'm a detective, and we are trying to figure out exactly what happened to him."

"So, if you're a detective, was he murdered, then?"

"Yes."

Williams said nothing.

"Would you be open to answering a few questions for me? It might help with our investigation."

Williams proceeded to tell Chloe exactly how she knew Lee Owen. As Chloe suspected, they had been romantically involved prior to Williams moving away from Maine as a condition of her employment. According to Williams, they had maintained semi-regular contact with each other by cell phone and text messages. When Williams couldn't get a hold of Owen at the start of March, she began to worry. As the weeks passed, she became convinced that something bad had happened to him.

"Did you ever try to contact any of Lee's acquaintances?" Chloe said.

"I did," Williams said. "Called his girlfriend, Melinda Hamilton. But she wasn't any help at all. In fact, she was pissed to find out that Lee and I stayed in contact."

Chloe wasn't surprised. In Hamilton's shoes, she probably would have responded in a similar fashion.

"In the end, I just decided to make up a few posters and mail them to a few businesses in Blue Hill."

"And Subway was one of those businesses?" Chloe said.

"Yes. There were five in all. Did you see any of the others?"

"We weren't looking for them, to be honest," Chloe said. "My partner happened upon the poster hanging at Subway."

"The other businesses might have thrown them away, I suppose," Williams said. "Or never hung them at all."

Chloe was thinking the same thing.

"When was the last time you had contact with Lee?" Chloe said.

"Mid-January. He was all excited about some new venture."

Williams's comment gave Chloe pause. She wrote the quote verbatim in her notebook and underlined the passage. "Don't suppose he told you what this new venture entailed, did he?"

"He didn't. But he did say that things would be different. Maybe different enough for us to get back together again."

Brock listened without interruption while Chloe filled him in on her conversation with Williams. When she had finished, he took a moment to consider what this revelation meant.

"What do think?" Chloe said. "You think Owen knew about the drug smuggling operation? You think that's what he meant by a new venture?"

"Knew about it, or was directly involved in it," Brock said. "What I keep coming back to is why he felt the need to steal Phinney's snowmobile."

"What do you mean?" Chloe said.

"Well, assuming for a moment that Owen had been part of the smuggling operation, why would he need to break into Phinney's garage to steal it?"

"Maybe he was planning to rip off his co-conspirators by staging a break-in."

Brock let that idea percolate a bit as he played it out to its logical conclusion. "Why wouldn't he simply keep helping them smuggle? Unless they got busted, the cash would continue to flow. It would seem like a more lucrative option to me."

"Maybe," Chloe said. "But we don't know how much of a cut he was getting, assuming he was part of it. Besides, if he really was planning to reconnect with Williams, stealing a full load from Phinney would have made a nice golden parachute to start over somewhere else."

Brock couldn't argue with her logic as he reviewed the photos of the burglary in Phinney's garage. There was something bothering him about the whole thing, but he couldn't put his finger on exactly what.

"Let's assume you're right and Owen was part of the smuggling ring," Brock said. "If he broke into the garage that night to steal the sled and remove the drugs himself, where are they?"

"What do you mean?"

"Just what I said. If he stole the sled to empty out the hidden stash, where is it? The SP mechanics didn't find it, and they tore that sled apart looking for it."

"Maybe he got caught," Chloe said.

"Normally, I'd agree with you," Brock said. "But if we're right about the storage unit Owen rented, he would have driven directly to it to empty out the pills, right?"

"Right."

"Then how did he end up on Second Pond? There are quicker ways he could have driven."

Chloe slid several of the pictures over in front of her. "I see what you mean. Okay, then where do you think he was going?"

"I don't know, but he wasn't alone. Someone handcuffed him to the sled. Someone whacked him on the head. And if his truck was towed from Marlintini's, how did he get to Phinney's?"

"Maybe Perreault drove him," Chloe said. "We did see them drinking together just beforehand."

"Yeah, but they didn't leave together. Besides, Judy Babbage alibied Perreault. Said she went straight to his trailer after leaving the bar, right?"

"But they didn't get together at Perreault's place until after Marlintini's closed. If Owen left his truck at Marlintini's, someone had to drive him to Phinney's house. Why not Perreault?"

It made sense, but Brock still wasn't entirely sold on the idea. There were holes in that theory. The time frame would have been too tight. And Brock still wasn't sure he believed the entire Perreault story Hanscomb and his drug detective buddies were trying to sell. It wasn't that Brock had any reason to believe The Bear. After all, the man was a known trafficker and an outlaw biker gang enforcer. Not exactly résumé builders. But something about his most recent arrest felt too much like a stitch-up for Brock's liking. Suddenly an angle popped into his head that he hadn't considered before.

"What if Owen was set up to be killed that night?"

"How do you mean?" Chloe said.

"What if someone else planted the seed about ripping off Phinney, or whoever else was involved in the smuggling operation."

"How would that be any different than Owen operating on his own?" Chloe said.

"It wouldn't, not unless the drugs were never in Phinney's sled to begin with. What if the entire break-in to steal the sled had been to test Owen's loyalty to the group?"

"Okay," Chloe said. "I see where you're going."

Brock continued. "Somebody convinces him that he can make an easy score by stealing Phinney's sled on a night that nobody would be around. To the rest of the world, it will simply look like a burglary/motor vehicle theft. But the break-in will be the way Owen can steal the drugs without looking like he was behind it. He already had keys to the garage because the Phinneys had him on the payroll as a handyman."

"If you're right, wouldn't Owen also need an alibi for the night of the break-in? We haven't talked to anyone who can account for his whereabouts that night after he left Marlintini's."

"Maybe that's because his alibi never materialized. Maybe his alibi was part of the plan to remove Owen from the page."

"Like Melinda Hamilton?"

"You said it yourself, she got herself another man."

"Perreault," Chloe said.

"Bingo."

"And what if she'd already found out that Lee had been staying in touch with this Cyndi Williams?" Chloe said. "What if Hamilton learned he was planning to leave her? Along with the income she depended upon."

"And what if the baby isn't Owen's?" Brock said.

Chloe's eyes widened. "Hamilton and Perreault could have planned this entire thing to get the drugs and remove Owen from the equation."

"Stranger things have happened," Brock said.

"So, assuming your theory is right, how do we prove it?" Chloe said.

"The most effective way I know to out co-conspirators is to turn them against each other."

Brock stood and headed toward the restroom. He was halfway there when his cell phone rang with a call from Detective Tisdale.

"Justice."

"Hey, Brock, it's Tisdale. I know, I know. You thought I'd never call, right?"

"I figured you'd call when you had something," Brock said.

In truth, he hadn't been holding out hope. Between the detective's reputation as a slacker and his obvious disdain for Brock, Brock had assumed that he would do the absolute minimum in trying to identify the shooter.

"Well, the manager of the store is the only one who has access to the video system, and he's been away."

"And?"

"Anyway, he's back, and I just left the store. Where are you? Are you available to meet?"

"I'm at Troop E with Chloe."

"Good, stay there. I'll head over now. En route from the Bangor Mall."

"What did you find?"

"Oh, nothing much. Only a surveillance video of the guy who bought the cell phone used to lure you into an ambush."

"Seriously?"

"See you in twenty minutes."

Before Brock could ask any additional questions, Tisdale ended the call.

"Was that How Weird?" Chloe said. "What's he so excited about?"

"You wouldn't believe me if I told you."

63

Brock and Chloe stared intently at the computer screen while Tisdale blathered on about how he had tracked down the cell phone manufacturer, then the distributor, followed by the store where the phone had been delivered as part of a small shipment.

"There, right there," Tisdale said, interrupting his own story.

"Not a great shot of his face," Chloe said.

"Just wait. I didn't come all the way out here just to crow about the back of someone's head."

Brock wasn't so sure.

"Okay, he's just finishing up the transaction now. Wait for it, wait, wait. Boom-sauce, there he is," Tisdale said, using the mouse to freeze the frame. "Recognize that guy?"

"Holy crap," Chloe said. "That's—"

"Frankie Desmond," Brock said, completing her thought. "We've got to bring him in before something happens to him."

"What do you mean?" Tisdale said.

"The last time we talked to him, he nearly died while trying to outrun a county deputy," Chloe said.

Yeah, Brock thought. *Deputy Tommy Hanscomb.*

"You don't really think Frankie was the one who shot at you, do you?" Chloe said as they raced along Route 1A toward Ellsworth in Brock's SUV.

"No, I don't," Brock said.

"Frankie's nothing but a follower," Chloe said. "If he was the one who sent that text to lure you to Second Pond, you can bet it was at someone else's request."

"Who?"

"Maybe Frankie will tell us," Chloe said hopefully.

Brock had his doubts about that. He also had some specific thoughts about suspects, but he wasn't ready to share them with Chloe just yet, in part because one of the names on his mental list included Hanscomb, and Brock didn't want anything else getting back to him.

"Let's just say I think Frankie Desmond has been doing the bidding of someone around here for a while," Brock said.

"If you're right, whoever that is may be the brains behind the entire smuggling operation."

Brock was thinking the very same thing.

With weekday traffic in full swing, it took Brock and Chloe the better part of an hour to reach the Blue Hill Boatyard. They entered the yard, stopping directly in front of Ralph Dixon's office.

"Desmond?" Dixon said. "No, I haven't seen Frankie for a few days. He was supposed to be here at seven this morning, but he didn't show."

"Did he call in sick or something?" Chloe said.

"Nah, but that ain't all that unusual for some of these guys. Reliability isn't really their strong suit."

"When was the last time you saw Frankie?" Brock said.

"Couple of days ago when he clocked out. Give me a sec, and I'll pull his timecard for you."

They followed Dixon to the wall-mounted punch clock. Hanging beside the clock was a steel-gray metal rack with long, thin manila-colored cardboard time slips protruding from it. Dixon ran his finger down one of the rows before plucking a card from the rack.

"Here we are," he said as he lowered his reading glasses from the top of his head and peered through the lenses. "Frankie punched out Wednesday afternoon at five fourteen."

"And you've had no contact since?" Brock said.

"None," Dixon said. "Should I be worried?"

Ten minutes later, Brock and Chloe turned into the dooryard of the Desmonds' mobile home. The first thing they noticed was that the only vehicle present was Frankie's rusty pickup. The silver Toyota belonging to Mrs. Desmond was missing. Brock maneuvered the SUV in the direction of the pickup, then stopped short, giving them two separate barriers should things turn deadly. Chloe was already unclipping the rifle from the holder behind the front seat.

"I thought you didn't believe Frankie was the shooter?" Brock teased.

"I don't, but I'm not willing to die on that hill, partner."

Brock nodded and stepped out of the vehicle.

"You see what I see?" Chloe said, joining him at the rear of the Ford.

"I'm not sure what you're referring to," Brock said. "Are you talking about Mrs. Desmond's Corolla not being here?"

"No," Chloe said. "I'm talking about the yard and what else is missing from it."

Brock scanned the muddy yard again, trying to see what Chloe had picked up on.

"The toys," she said at last. "Last time we were here, the yard was littered with kids' stuff."

Brock looked again and saw that she was right. Even under the fresh layer of snow, he could see the children's playhouse was gone, as was the bike he had seen leaning against the trailer's skirting beside the front steps.

"You think she skedaddled?" Brock said.

"I can't think of any other reason the toys would have suddenly disappeared," Chloe said. "I don't like this, Brock. Nothing about this feels right."

Brock couldn't disagree. He'd had feelings of déjà vu since they arrived. This felt too much like the botched arrest of Terry and Darrell Kirke in Bar Mills.

"Shouldn't we get some backup down here?" Chloe said.

Her comment only heightened Brock's concerns. The last time he'd chosen to go it alone with Trooper Mathers, everything had gone completely to shit. Including his career. But this one was different. They weren't here to charge anyone with murder. This visit was only to talk to Frankie Desmond about his purchase of a burner phone. Besides, there were only two agencies that might be able to provide backup, the state police and Hancock County SO. The first agency wasn't exactly loaded with Brock Justice fans. Brock couldn't help but wonder how quickly any of the road troopers would even respond when they learned who it was requesting assistance. As for the latter, there were at least two prominent members of the sheriff's office who might be up to their eyeballs in this case, including Sheriff Parlin himself. While backup would normally be the prudent choice, Brock wondered if making that call might put him and Chloe in greater jeopardy.

"Well?" Chloe said.

"No, we've got this. We're just here to talk to him, right?"

Chloe didn't look convinced.

"Tell you what," Brock said as he studied the filthy trailer windows. "You stay here and cover me. I'll approach and see if I can get him to come to the door. If you so much as see the barrel of a rifle pointing in my direction or Cujo charging toward me, you know what to do."

Chloe nodded and drew a deep breath. "Be careful, partner."

"You too."

Brock braced himself for what would be a thirty- or forty-foot walk to the trailer's front door. Once he left the cover of the SUV, he'd be completely exposed, and there was nothing he could do about it. If things did go to hell, Chloe would be fine so long as she maintained her cover and a clear head. Brock, on the other hand, would be a sitting duck.

He pulled back the front of his jacket and rested one hand on the butt of his .45, then began moving slowly toward the trailer. Planting one foot carefully in front of the other, he made doubly sure of his footing. The last thing he needed was to slip on one of the hidden icy patches beneath the snow. With each step he took, the trailer seemed to draw back farther from him. Brock could feel his heart racing and the sweat forming atop his brow. He fought the feeling of panic that was trying to worm its way inside his head. It was the exact same feeling he'd had at the pond the night his unseen assailant took pot shots at him and his Interceptor. PTSD, Kimber had called it.

"It will happen at the most inopportune times," she had said.

No shit, Brock thought as he drew closer to the trailer. Much like their rendezvous at the hotel.

"You're still in the clear," Chloe whispered into the radio.

The last thing Brock felt like was in the clear. He continued forward, drawing a deep breath, then exhaling slowly exactly as he'd been taught. His eyes continued to scan the windows, the door, and the woods around the trailer. Aside from him, there was no movement anywhere in the yard. He strained to hear anything that might be a threat, a door opening, a sliding window, a growling dog, but the only sound was the pulse throbbing in his ears.

At last, he reached the rickety wooden steps that led to the trailer's side door. He reached out and grabbed hold of the railing, giving himself a moment to regroup. His legs felt shaky, but he was doing his best to project confidence, a confidence he didn't remotely feel, for Chloe's sake if not for his own.

"You good, partner?" Chloe said quietly.

Brock lifted his left hand and gave her a thumbs-up, never taking his eyes off the door as he gripped the handle of his sidearm with his right.

He took a deep breath, then carefully mounted the steps, sliding his handgun from its holster and holding it down at his side. When he reached what passed for a landing, he moved to one side, then reached out and knocked on the storm door with the knuckles of his left hand. His attention was entirely focused now. Chloe was safe, and he had to trust that she would have his back if it came to that. He had managed to get his heart rate down to a more normal level, and with it, his auditory senses improved. He listened for any sounds emanating from inside the trailer, but there was nothing. He waited for what seemed an eternity but was likely no more than thirty seconds before he knocked again. And again, there was no response from inside the trailer.

Brock moved to open the storm door when he caught sight of the doorjamb next to the knob of the inside door. The wood frame was heavily damaged, splintered as if someone had forced it open from the outside. His breath caught in his throat. Chloe was right, everything about this was wrong. Had Desmond kicked open his own door? Not likely. Had someone taken his wife and kids? Or had they fled at his request? Did Frankie know that the police were closing in? Or did someone else know? Someone like Tommy Hanscomb. Or Albert.

Brock signaled that he was about to make an entry. Chloe acknowledged with a single click of the radio.

He shoved the door open and quickly stepped inside.

64

Brock swept the business end of his handgun across the open space, crouching low to minimize the target he might offer to anyone lying in wait, but there was nobody in sight.

"Police," he called out. "Frankie, it's Detective Justice. If you're here, show yourself. I only want to talk."

He waited, but no response came.

"Your trailer is surrounded," he lied. "No point in running."

Again, no response was forthcoming.

The front of the trailer was laid out in an open concept. From his position, Brock could see the entire living room as well as the kitchen. Both spaces were empty, and neither appeared large enough to present a hiding place for an adult the size of Franklin Desmond.

Brock's attention shifted toward the darkened hallway that led toward the rear of the trailer, where he knew the bedrooms and at least one bathroom would be located.

"Frankie," he called again. "If you're here, show yourself. I don't want you getting shot by accident. I just want to talk about the burner phone you purchased last week."

Once again there was nothing but silence.

The trailer had an odd, closed feel to it, as if no one had been living there for some time. And there was the faint odor of spoiled food hanging in the air. Brock glanced around the living room again and couldn't help but notice that the room was as devoid of toys as the yard had been. Another thought occurred to him. Maybe Desmond's wife hadn't left him. Hadn't been taken. Maybe the entire family fled from whatever was happening here.

Then why is his truck still parked outside? Brock wondered. *Had Frankie planned to follow them? Had something, or someone, interfered with that plan?*

Brock's focus returned to the near end of the hallway, and he moved toward it, holding his gun at the low ready, index finger snugged tight against the outside of the trigger guard.

"Frankie," Brock called again. "It's Brock Justice. I just want to talk."

Again, his words were met by silence.

After taking a quick peek down the empty hall, Brock moved slowly but steadily down the narrow passage.

There were no doors to the right, as that encompassed the exterior wall of the trailer. To his left, he saw three open doorways, dim light spilling through them into the hall. At the far end of the hall was a single door, and it was closed. *Of course it is*, Brock thought. The door at the end represented the biggest threat to him. Impossible to clear without opening and the last place he would check. If Frankie Desmond, or anyone else, decided to throw a few rounds in his direction from the far end of the hall, even through the closed door, Brock would have zero cover until he reached the first doorway on his left. Assuming that room was clear, Brock would at least have the option of diving out of the line of fire.

He kept his head on a swivel and stepped forward, looking and listening for any signs of movement. A creaking floor, a passing shadow, even the sound of heavy breathing could give away the presence of another. Unfortunately, those same sounds could betray him just as easily.

Brock had nearly reached the first doorway when the floor beneath him gave a loud snap as he stepped down. He froze and waited for whatever response would come.

Brock slowly moved the gun back and forth between the nearest egress and the door at the far end of the hall while he waited. He counted to ten, slowly, intentionally taking his time. Rushing now would be foolhardy. He reached the number ten, but the situation remained unchanged. He started forward again, carefully planting his next step to the right side of the hall. This was a calculated move that accomplished two things. The first was that it meant his weight would shift more closely to the wall supports, meaning there was less chance of another snap like he had found in the heavily traveled center of the carpeted hall. The second thing it did was position Brock as far from the open doorway as possible, giving him the widest view into the room. As Brock inched forward, he would continually gain visual access to whatever lay beyond the doorway one degree at a time, until the entire room was visible, or at least as much as the opening would permit.

As the contents of the room slowly came into view, Brock could see it was the room of a child. A pink bureau, Disney's Ice Princess light fixture, and a forgotten tiara lying in one corner of the floor all tended to indicate a young girl's room. Brock stepped in and checked the room's blind spots, behind and under the bed, behind the door, and inside the closet, but the room was empty.

Before returning to the hallway, Brock steeled himself, then performed another quick peek, moving only the right side of his head through the doorway, then quickly withdrawing it. The quick peek maneuver provided him with a mental snapshot of the hall. As far as he could tell, nothing had changed. The corridor looked the exact same as it had before he'd entered the girl's room.

Brock repeated the process at each room he came to. The next room appeared to have been occupied by two young boys based upon the contents and the unmade bunk beds along the far wall. Again, the room was unoccupied. He felt the pain of nostalgia at the sight of the beds. He and Jake once shared such a room.

The final door on the left led to a bathroom, the easiest room to clear, as the only real hiding place was the shower stall, and it was empty.

The air inside the trailer was stale, and Brock was beginning to feel claustrophobic. His heart was racing again as he knew the greatest danger for him lay directly ahead on the other side of the closed door at the end of the hall. He leaned back against the bathroom wall and wiped the sweat from his face with a forearm and fought to slow his rapid breathing.

Get it together, trooper, Brock thought. *You've done this hundreds of times.*

It was true, he had performed this maneuver many times, but something about this one felt different. Was it Desmond's connection to the TracFone that had led Brock into an ambush? Or was it something closer to home, like residual PTSD from the Bar Mills shooting that had scarred him for life, dramatically altering the course of two careers? Brock wasn't sure what was spooking him. But he did know one thing: if he wanted to keep being a Maine state trooper, he needed to get it together, and fast.

He shoved himself away from the wall, then turned and crouched against the right side of the bathroom doorframe. Keeping the gun trained on the closed door, he leaned forward, and reaching out with his left hand, he turned the knob and shoved the door open as hard as he could. It swung inward and banged into the wall. No one behind the door.

The shades had been pulled, leaving the bedroom in darkness. As Brock waited for his eyes to adjust, he caught a whiff of something unpleasant emanating from inside the room. It was like the odor he had picked up coming from the kitchen, but different. Far worse than spoiled food. A smell that was all too familiar.

As Brock's eyes slowly adapted to the low light, large shadows began to take shape. Brock could make out a queen-sized bed, several bureaus, and something at the center of the room posed upright as if standing but not quite. He moved into the doorway and reached around the corner, blindly feeling for a light switch until his fingers brushed against the wall plate. Brock moved his fingers until he found the rocker switch, then pressed upward, filling the room with light.

Brock lowered the gun and rose to his full height as he studied the familiar scene before him. Frankie Desmond's body was hanging limp and lifeless from a belt that had been fashioned into a slipknot-type noose and tied to a ceiling fan. The leather belt had stretched from dead weight, and the fan had partially torn free of its mount, allowing Desmond's bare feet to contact the floor. His knees were bent, suspended inches above the rug. Brock entered the room and carefully finished checking for any other occupants, but Frankie and Brock were alone. Brock holstered his weapon and turned his attention to the body.

The skin of Desmond's face and hands were an angry bluish bruised color, as were his feet where the blood had pooled following death. The belt was cinched tightly under his jawbone with the buckle located just above the back of his head. Brock saw that Frankie's skin had begun to slip slightly as decomposition took hold. Estimating time of death would ultimately fall to the medical examiner, but Brock knew already that it had likely occurred days earlier.

Brock took one last look around the room, then backed out into the hallway and keyed his radio mic.

"All clear."

"Ten four," Chloe responded.

"I'll meet you outside," Brock said as he turned and headed back down the hallway.

65

Brock and Chloe stood at the end of the hall watching as the medical examiner worked alongside Evidence Tech Mike Fuente to cut the body down. Both wore gloves and Tyvek suits to avoid any possibility of contamination in case the death wasn't what it appeared. Once Frankie was freed from the ceiling fan, they laid his body on a clean tarpaulin that had been spread across the bedroom floor.

Chloe stood silently, taking it all in. Brock was grateful that she appeared to be getting the concept of slow is fast. The same principle used when clearing buildings and rooms applied equally well when it came to death investigations, or for that matter any investigations. Rapidity was often a necessity when dealing with life-or-death situations in real time but could become a hinderance during homicide investigations where something overlooked could bring an entire case crashing down. It was one of the hardest concepts for first responders-turned-detectives to embrace. The sooner Chloe accepted that reality, the better.

"Well, I can tell you definitively that death wasn't by hanging," Dr. Isleborn said.

"How can you tell?" Chloe said, leaning in through the doorway for a closer look.

Isleborn pointed to a reddish welt circling the neck of the victim. "See this?"

Brock and Chloe nodded.

"What is it?" Chloe said.

"It's a secondary ligature mark. The angle that the belt was wrapped around the throat is different. See?"

They both nodded again.

"What does that mean, Doc?" Chloe said.

"It means that your victim was strangled before being strung up by the belt."

"Then he was already dead when someone hung him from the fan?" Brock said.

"Not necessarily," Isleborn said. "He may have only been unconscious. Incapacitated by an assailant long enough to hang. I won't know for certain until after I've had a chance to perform a full autopsy."

The doctor leaned her face closer to the victim's neck. "And the belt wasn't used in the initial strangulation."

"How can you tell?" Chloe said, the tone of her voice betraying her newfound fascination with death investigations.

Isleborn turned her head to address Chloe. "Because the first ligature left behind a braided pattern. Something akin to a rope, maybe, but wider. This leather belt is smooth on the inside. As you can see, the pattern imprinted on the skin beneath is completely different."

Brock turned to Chloe. "We need to search the entire trailer for the other ligature."

"Wouldn't the killer have taken it with them?" Chloe said.

"Maybe. Maybe not."

Mike Fuente spoke up. "I'll forward a picture of the imprint to you. Might help you find whatever they used."

"Thanks," Chloe said.

Brock's mind continued to work the problem. Something was amiss here. He didn't like the fact that they'd found Desmond dead so soon after learning of his involvement with the ambush. Nor did he like the fact that the murder had been staged to look like a suicide, albeit an amateurish attempt. Hell, even the forced front door to the trailer was at odds with the pretense of suicide. It was as if the killer was always a step ahead of them, but when it came time to act, they messed things up. It was almost as if two different people were behind what had happened here.

"What do you think he weighs, Doc?" Brock said.

"I'd say one-sixty to one-seventy," Isleborn said as she looked to Fuente for confirmation.

"Sounds about right," Fuente said.

"Why would that matter?" Chloe said.

"Because it would have taken one very strong person to lift an unconscious or dead body and hang it from the fan," Isleborn said, answering the question before Brock could.

"So, we're probably looking for two killers," Chloe said.

"Very likely," Brock said.

"What do you think happened to Frankie's wife and children?" Chloe said.

Brock turned to look at her. "I'm thinking it's entirely possible his wife didn't leave him."

Chloe's eyes widened. "You think someone may have taken her and the kids?"

"It's a possibility we need to consider," Brock said.

"Well, if someone did grab them, whoever it is has a couple of days' head start," Fuente said.

Brock looked back at Chloe. "Let's find Mrs. Desmond's cell phone information and contact the provider for an emergency location track. If we can't find it here, try calling Dixon at the boatyard. He may have it as an emergency contact number."

"I'm on it," Chloe said.

"And have Wheeler start the paperwork. Tell the provider it's a possible abduction."

It was nearly three o'clock before Chloe made telephonic contact with Desmond's wife.

"She okay?" Brock said.

"Not about her husband being dead," Chloe said. "But yeah, she took the kids and got out of Dodge. Went to her sister's place in Massachusetts as soon as Frankie told her he might be in trouble."

"Did Frankie tell her why he thought that?"

"Said it had something to do with some money he was about to come into."

"Any luck finding the second ligature?" Brock asked Fuente.

The evidence tech shook his head. "No, and we've torn this place apart. We did make one interesting find, though."

"What's that?"

The evidence technician held up a rifle. "It's a .308."

"Any prints?"

"Wiped clean," Fuente said. "How much you wanna bet ballistics will match this gun to the round I dug out of the tree at Second Pond?"

Brock wouldn't have been surprised at all, but something else was still bothering him.

"What are you thinking?" Fuente said.

"I'm thinking this was too easy. Finding the rifle, assuming it is a match to the one used to shoot at me. Desmond had to know that every cop in the state would be looking for that rifle, and he just happened to keep it here in the trailer?"

Fuente shrugged. "Not every criminal is smart, Brock. Shit, if they were, we wouldn't catch half of them."

Brock paused to consider what they had so far. Everything about this case was beginning to feel like a setup. As if everything was staged. But for whose benefit? That was the real question. And what part did Tommy Hanscomb play in this? Brock was convinced that he was dirty; the bogus traffic stop all but confirmed it. But was the deputy some brilliant criminal mastermind? It belied belief. Even the traffic stop, and the accompanying veiled threat against Brock, seemed like the moves of an amateur. But if it wasn't Hanscomb, then who? Who was behind all of this? Sheriff Parlin? Dr. Phinney? Harold Perreault? Albert? There were simply too many suspects and not enough answers.

Of all the names on his list, Brock felt like Perreault was the least likely suspect. Especially after being set up by an anonymous phone tip to the drug squad. None of it worked unless Perreault had set up the whole thing to make himself look like the victim. But how likely was that? Even if he was eventually cleared of the charges against him, it still seemed like a bridge too far. No, it felt more like Perreault was being punished for something. As if he hadn't played ball the way his handlers wanted. The same way Frankie Desmond seemed to have crossed his superiors. The same way Lee Owen had crossed his.

"We've got to start over," Brock said as he breezed into the makeshift investigation room at Troop J.

"What are you talking about?" Chloe said.

"We've been thinking about this all wrong. Treating Owen's murder as if it was a singular event. Maybe even a result of petty jealousy by some husband who took exception to Owen sleeping with his wife."

"Um, I thought that motive was still on the table."

"No. This is bigger than that," Brock said as he taped a large sheet of white paper over the murder board. "And it all comes back to fentanyl."

Chloe sat back and crossed her arms. "I'm listening."

"This whole thing points to a well-run smuggling network. Drugs from Canada into the US. We've been thinking too small. Like maybe only a couple of good old boys doing weekend trips on snowmobiles or four-wheelers. But I'm beginning to think it's way beyond that and the players in our case, and the victims, might be nothing more than bottom dwellers in the supply chain."

"What chain?"

"I think there's a law enforcement link at the top of this."

"Please don't start with the dirty cop thing again, Brock. I get that you don't like Tommy, but you're—"

Brock shook his head as he began to populate a new list of names on the paper with a marker. "You're right, it isn't Hanscomb."

"I am?" Chloe said, clearly surprised. "But I thought—"

"He's involved, but I think he's nothing more than a foot soldier. And not an overly bright one at that."

For the next twenty minutes, Brock laid out his theory about what was happening and who was behind all of it. When he'd finished writing, he stood back to take it all in, looking for holes.

After several moments, Chloe spoke up at last. "Jesus, Brock. If you're right, this thing is huge. Way beyond anything we can handle. We'd need the feds and a shit ton of backup to bring in all of the people you've listed."

"Maybe not," Brock said. "We've still got the element of surprise on our side, right? Nobody knows that we've figured this thing out, so we act like we're still plodding along on Owen's murder with the added fun of a suicide that isn't a suicide."

"Speaking of which," Chloe said. "Isleborn is planning to conduct the post first thing in the morning. Are you okay with me taking it?"

"Are you?" Brock said.

"Yeah, and I can meet Mike Fuente at the ME's office."

"Okay. Have at it."

Brock waited as Chloe studied the board, looking for additional holes. "And your father? Where does Albert fit into this?"

"I haven't worked that out yet," Brock said. "He may only be a patsy for the poker game alibi. Maybe using his handcuffs to kill Owen was a way to keep him in line."

"We've got to share this with Cumberland," Chloe said.

"Absolutely not," Brock said. "If I've learned anything from investigating homicides, it's don't tell the boss if you want to keep something in-house."

"You don't really think Cumberland would blow up our case, do you?"

"Not intentionally, but there's always more at play when it comes to police hierarchy than you think. Trust me, the lieutenant is either seeking a promotion or a way out of MCU North. That's what I'd be doing in her shoes. The last thing she's going to do is put either one in jeopardy by keeping our discovery a secret. Not telling her gives her deniability, at least as far as her superiors are concerned."

"Meaning we'll fall on our own sword if this goes sideways?"

Brock grinned. "It's far easier to ask for forgiveness than permission."

"Another Brock Justice rule of investigation?"

"Yup. And you should write that one down."

66

This next morning, Brock drove straight to the Bangor barracks from his apartment. There were some things he needed to sort out before making his next move.

Despite what he had told Chloe, Brock was still worried about his father's role in all of this. Whatever else Albert Justice was, Brock had always known him to be an ethical man. Albert understood things in terms of black and white. As far as Albert was concerned, there was right and there was wrong. Period. Brock couldn't believe Albert would have ever willingly involved himself in something like this. And yet, he struggled with the thought of Albert not knowing, or at least suspecting, what these people were up to. There was a conspiracy happening in this town. A conspiracy that had resulted in at least two murders, and likely a third had Brock's shooter been successful. The only question remaining for Brock was, who was behind it?

He was about to head out to the SUV when his cell phone rang with a call from Corey Hincks.

"Hey, brother," Brock said.

"How goes the battle?" Corey said. "Making any headway?"

"Slow but steady, I think. What's up?"

"Nothing much. I just wanted to let you know that I'll be up in your neck of the woods today. Wondered if you might want to meet up. Maybe grab lunch or something."

"Damn," Brock said. "I'd love that. Only problem is we just caught another homicide."

"Well, that sucks. Separate case or related to your snowmobile swimmer?"

"Not sure yet. But both victims knew each other. My partner is down at the post as we speak."

"Got a name for me? I've been compiling a list of persons of interest for you."

"Desmond. Franklin Desmond. Went by the name Frankie. He worked at the Blue Hill Boatyard with Lee Owen."

"No shit? That's interesting because Desmond's name just came up."

"Seriously?" Brock said.

"Yeah. Hang on a sec. I gotta pull over to look through the file. Okay, got it right here. Franklin Desmond was stopped by Immigration and Customs Enforcement at the Canadian border crossing near Houlton on January 11th this year."

"Does the record give a reason for the stop?"

"Just says SOS."

"SOS?"

Corey laughed. "Suspicion of smuggling. You know how much the feds love those acronyms, brother."

"You're telling me," Brock said. "They find anything?"

"Nope. And it doesn't look like they actually caught him crossing the border. He was traveling with another guy on the Maine side, but ICE thought it looked suspicious, so they took a closer look."

"Don't suppose they listed the other person," Brock said.

"It's redacted."

"Seriously? Why would they do that?"

"Lots of reasons. Could be someone of political importance. Someone connected. Or maybe a CI."

"A confidential informant for who?"

"Your guess is as good as mine. You sure you can't make time to meet up? I can give you the rest of the reporting."

"You know what?" Brock said. "Yeah, let's meet."

"You pick the time, and I'll name the place," Corey said.

After scribbling down the address Corey provided, Brock ended the call. He thought about giving Chloe the heads-up but then decided against it. Corey was his source, not Chloe's. While it might have seemed a petty move to someone outside of law enforcement, most cops knew how hard it was to develop professional relationships that occasionally bore fruit when it came to gathering useful intelligence. As Brock knew too well, people lie, even people involved at the periphery of a police investigation. Lying was as deeply engrained in the human psyche as breathing or eating. Some folks just couldn't help themselves. Having someone on the inside of not one but two law enforcement agencies was a huge boon. Besides, even as a road trooper, Chloe likely developed her own go-to sources.

The meeting place Corey had chosen wasn't far from where Brock and Chloe had been working the case. He'd swing over quickly, meet up with Corey, and be back before anyone even knew he was missing.

He was halfway across the parking lot to his SUV when a familiar voice called out from behind.

"Hey, Brock," Zimmerman said.

Brock turned without breaking stride to see the lanky detective hurrying toward him, looking much too glib for Brock's liking. Brock had been hoping to reach the safety of his vehicle and get out of the lot before anyone saw him. *So much for best-laid plans*, he thought.

"Hey, Zim," Brock said. "What's up?"

"What's up is I'm coming with you."

"Because?"

"Because Penny Dreadful ordered me to. Guess she wanted you to have a partner since yours is out of town."

Brock tried hard to hide his annoyance but couldn't quite muster the necessary energy. He briefly considered jumping in the unmarked, locking the door, and driving off anyway, leaving Zimmerman standing there, but he didn't suppose that would fly. He was already dangling precariously from the end of Cumberland's frayed rope; another misstep wasn't likely to improve his standing.

"Don't look so glum, my brother from another mother. It'll give us a chance to bond."

"*Great*," Brock said as he yanked open the door to the SUV and climbed inside.

"Where to, Kemosabe?" Zimmerman said as he jumped in beside Brock.

Brock considered reminding him that they barely knew each other—and that Brock was hoping to keep it that way—but decided to at least pretend to play nice.

"Blue Hill Boatyard," Brock said. "I want to follow up on Frankie Desmond's last few days. But we gotta make a quick stop on the way."

"Let's hit it," Zimmerman said excitedly as he snapped his seat belt home.

It's shaping up to be a long day, Brock thought. A very long day.

67

As Brock followed the GPS directions to the address Corey had provided, he wasn't sure if the feminine computerized voice was more condescending than usual or if his tolerance was just stressed from being paired with a partner he didn't want. He was mildly surprised to find himself wishing that it was Chloe riding shotgun and not the boorish Jordan Zimmerman. Perhaps Chloe was growing on him after all.

"I hate the way these things try and get you to take roads that were never constructed in the first place," Zimmerman said. "One time my first wife and I were late to a wedding, and the damn GPS sent us down a dirt path onto a soccer field."

Brock suppressed his annoyance as he navigated around another muddy pothole, remaining focused on arriving at the designated meeting spot on time. He wished he had time to warn Corey about Zimmerman, but it probably didn't matter. He'd meet him soon enough.

"Maybe this is it," Zimmerman chuckled. "I mean, how many gravel roads that lead out to the middle of nowhere can there be around here?"

Brock was wondering the very same thing when a large, dilapidated warehouse loomed into view above the tree line. They continued along the road for another half mile or so before passing by a rusted metal gate that had been propped open. Brock noticed a shiny new chain and padlock hanging from the post. As they came around a sharp bend in the road, the forest opened, revealing a clearing that was several acres in size with the warehouse sitting squarely at its center.

"Geez, your friend couldn't have picked a more welcoming spot for a meet-up?" Zimmerman said, grabbing ahold of the windshield pillar in an attempt to keep from bouncing his head off the roof. "Maybe you need a new friend."

Brock ignored him and continued driving.

The property consisted of a half dozen brick-and-steel outbuildings scattered about the area with the main warehouse lording over everything. A pair of broken windows several floors up resembled dark eyes watching them. The property appeared to have been some type of industrial facility, but aside from several abandoned crimson-colored dump trucks, there was nothing else visible to hint at its former use.

"Does this friend of yours drive a pickup?"

"Not that I know of," Brock said. "Why?"

Zimmerman nodded toward the right side of the warehouse.

Brock followed his gaze. Parked unattended near a large overhead door sat a familiar-looking primer-gray four-by-four. Brock wasn't sure if he remembered the truck from somewhere specifically or if he'd just seen so many flat gray pickups in the last week that they all were beginning to look the same. This was Down East Maine, after all.

While Zimmerman continued to provide an exhausting play-by-play worthy of Tony Romo, Brock pulled up beside the pickup and stopped the SUV. He hesitated a moment before shifting the transmission lever into park. Something was wrong. This clandestine meeting with Corey was entirely out of character.

"So, we getting out or what? Where's this friend of yours, anyway?"

"Give it rest, would you, Zim," Brock said. "Let me think."

"Whatever you say, new guy."

Brock turned his head toward Zimmerman with every intention of laying into him when he spotted someone approaching from inside the gloom of the open garage bay. It was Corey, and he wasn't alone. Walking behind him were two stone-faced men wearing black BDUs, neither of whom Brock recognized. And both men were pointing short-barreled automatic weapons in their direction.

"Friends of yours?" Zimmerman said.

Chloe had just returned to her vehicle after attending the Desmond postmortem when her cell phone chimed with a missed call followed by a voicemail alert. She placed the phone in the dash-mounted charger and hit speaker.

"Hey, Chloe, it's your friendly gopher calling about your property search request. Call me."

Chloe rolled her eyes as she tossed her notebook onto the passenger seat, then reached for her seat belt. She knew Wheeler could have just as easily given her the details by way of voicemail. This was his lame attempt at making her call him back so he could talk to her directly. It wasn't that she wasn't flattered by his attention, but it could be annoying at times. Like now.

She started the Interceptor and put it in gear before punching the redial button. Wheeler picked up halfway through the second ring.

"Hey, Wheels."

"Sorry about the delay in getting back to you, Chloe. It's been a little crazy around here, and your stuff kind of got lost in the shuffle. And I don't understand why you're both requesting this information."

"Both?"

"Yeah, Brock made the same request."

Damn you, Brock, Chloe thought. He was still freelancing, and this time it was connected to How Weird's investigation into the shooting, not the Owen murder.

"Is that a problem?" Wheeler said. "Because I've got it now, and I thought you'd want it sooner than later."

"Nope, no problem. Don't keep me in suspense. What did you find out?"

"Okay, here goes. The site from where Brock was fired upon was formerly a copper and manganese mine called the Douglass Copper Mine, long since defunct. The place dates back to the late 1800s. They closed just before the turn of the century, then reopened two more times, but it doesn't look like the follow-up attempts were any more profitable than the first venture. The mining operation was closed for good in 1963, the property and all its holdings were turned over to a management company called E. B. Noyes. The original mining company, Douglass Holdings, set aside a trust fund for the express purpose of maintaining the site. From what I can tell, the company's job was to maintain site security and occasional testing to make sure none of the harmful by-products that normally come from mining leaked out into the surrounding area or groundwater. This is where things get a little convoluted as the property changed management companies at least five times during the decades that followed. So, let me speed it up for you and get to the point."

"Please," Chloe said as she turned onto Route 15.

"In addition to the actual mine near Second Pond, the original owners also had a second property holding in the nearby town of Sedgwick. I checked the town's tax records, and it looks like this second property was used to house their management office as well as a manufacturing and shipping facility for products connected to the mine. I'm guessing warehouse. It doesn't go into detail. Remember this was way before the days of internet."

"I'm assuming this Sedgwick property was supposed to be managed by the subsequent management companies with trust fund monies?" Chloe said.

"Um, that's the strange part. Up until a couple of years ago, it was. Then in the summer of 2020, it appears that this second property changed hands."

"To whom?"

"Hard to say. It looks like the purchaser set everything up through a corporation called New Age."

"Okay," Chloe said, taking the bait. "What can you tell me about New Age?"

"Well, that's the thing. I can't seem to get closer to the actual entity who owns it. Every time I've gotten close, all I manage to find is another shell company. Whoever this is has gone to a lot of trouble to stay hidden."

Chloe considered what Wheeler was telling her as she navigated the

SUV toward Blue Hill. If property controlled by the original mining company had been sold off to a new owner, then there had to be a link between the new owner and the original company. A close link. She wondered if that link was close enough to warrant trying to take out Brock. Was he getting too close to whatever had happened leading up to Owen's murder?

"So, what do you think, Chloe?"

"I think you did good, Wheels."

"Thanks. If you need anything else, I've got a whole lot more information about several neighboring mines, including one called the Kerramerican Mine. Fascinating stuff."

"Thanks. Maybe some other time. What I really need is for you to shoot me the address for that second property in Sedgwick."

68

Brock and Zimmerman were ordered out of the vehicle, then quickly disarmed. While one of the two men trained his weapon on them, the other thoroughly searched the detectives. Their weapons and cell phones were confiscated and handed to Hincks.

"What the hell, Corey?" Brock said after being shoved away by one of the two goons.

"Sorry about this, brother. I had really hoped you'd back off after getting shot at."

"That was you?" Brock said, unable to hide his surprise.

"Actually, that was me," a familiar voice said from behind them.

Brock turned around to find Tommy Hanscomb approaching them. He was accompanied by three more men dressed in black and carrying automatic weapons.

"Why am I not surprised?" Brock said.

"You were fucking everything up," Hanscomb said. "I wanted to take you out, but Corey wouldn't let me."

Brock turned back to Corey. "So, you're the brains behind this whole thing?"

"I wouldn't say the brains, exactly. More like the muscle. And you were never supposed to get this close. If only you'd backed off a little, Perreault would have gone down for the whole thing. The Lee Owen murder, the smuggling, all of it."

"You've done all of this just to smuggle in a few counterfeit drugs into the US?"

Corey grinned. "Oh, this operation is way bigger than that. Come on. I'll show you."

"What about him?" Hanscomb said, pointing to Zimmerman.

"Detective Zimmerman is welcome to join us," Corey said.

Hincks led them inside the warehouse to a substructure that had been constructed within the original building, hidden from view by the dilapidated exterior of the warehouse.

"What do you think?"

"I'll give you credit for creative thinking," Brock said. "It certainly is well camouflaged. But isn't this a bit of overkill for a smuggling op? Why do you need all this?"

"Smuggling, huh? You still think that's what all of this is about?"

"Well, isn't that what you're doing?"

Corey removed a biometric swipe card from his pocket. Then held it up to an electronic reader. Following the card's acceptance, he manually entered a code into a wall-mounted panel. Brock watched as the light on the panel changed from red to green and a heavy steel door popped open.

"Come on," Corey said. "I'll give you guys the five-cent tour."

Chloe wasn't surprised at all to find Brock not answering his phone. She'd left him a message about Wheeler's latest information on the mine and told him to call when he could. What concerned her a bit more was that she couldn't get through to Zim either. Could they both be out of cell coverage? It was super spotty in Down East Maine, as she'd discovered herself on more than one occasion. Chloe punched up the number to Andrew Webber, the office assistant at the Bangor barracks.

"State Police," he greeted.

"Andy, it's Chloe."

"Hey, Chloe. What can I do for you?"

"Actually, I'm looking for Zim. Have you seen him this morning?"

"He was in earlier, but he went back out. He paired up with Brock."

Chloe paused for a moment. "With Brock? Really?"

"Really."

"Did they happen to say where they were headed?"

"They did not. You want to leave a message for one or both of them?"

"No, I've already left voicemail messages. Guess I'll just wait and see which one calls me back first."

As she disconnected the call, Chloe thought more about the odd pairing. Why would the two men be together? Would Brock have invited Zim along? It didn't seem likely, not even if there was a new lead. Maybe it was something Cumberland cooked up to keep an eye on Brock. Either way, it didn't really matter. She paused to consider her next move. The way she figured it, there were two courses of action open to her. The first was waiting until she'd heard back from Brock. The second was to check out the Sedgwick address Wheeler had given her. She knew Brock would be pissed if she went rogue again, but it wasn't as if he hadn't moved the needle on their investigation without telling her until afterward. Again. Besides, she thought, she wouldn't have gotten this far in her career without jumping in with both feet, right?

She checked her phone again for a signal. Two bars of 5G service. Both detectives could certainly reach her if they needed to. Maybe they really were outside of the coverage zone. Chloe punched the Sedgwick address into the GPS on her phone. According to the application, the address for the mining company's former headquarters was less than thirty minutes away.

69

Brock looked around in amazement. He had dramatically underestimated the size and scope of the illegal narcotics operation they were dealing with. The hidden manufacturing facility was a full-scale pill mill. Rows of state-of-the-art digital pill presses and chemical mixers lined the space. It looked like a legitimate pharmaceutical factory.

"I still don't get it," Brock said. "If you're making drugs here, what were you smuggling in from Canada?"

"Plates," Corey said.

"Plates?" Zimmerman said, breaking his silence for the first time.

"Plates used to manufacture tablets," Corey said. "You see, we needed the original plates for the drugs we would be counterfeiting so we could mass-produce molds for making our own. Using 3D printers, we were able to create flawless molds from computerized scans of the original plates. From there it was just a matter of reproducing them."

"I don't get it," Brock said. "This seems like a lot of overkill for a pill mill. Surely you wouldn't need anything on this large a scale to supply illegal drugs to the state of Maine."

Corey laughed. "You always were of a conservative mind, brother. Who said anything about this being limited to Maine? We—that is, my benefactors and I—are building something that, when finished, will supply a global market. Countless countries will purchase our products."

Hanscomb spoke up. "You mean *we*, don't you, Corey? *Our* benefactors, right?"

The trooper stopped walking and turned to face the deputy. "You know, Tommy, I was wavering on when the right moment would be, but it seems we have officially arrived at it."

"What moment?" Hanscomb said, a confused look pinching his face.

"Your severance package."

Brock watched in horror as his longtime friend and fellow trooper drew and pointed a semiautomatic handgun at Hanscomb's head.

"Stop fucking around, Corey," Hanscomb said. "You don't want to do this. You need me."

"Do I?" Corey said before pulling the trigger twice in rapid succession, dropping the deputy where he stood.

Brock hadn't been entirely sure that Corey intended to kill them. In one fell swoop, that doubt had been erased.

Corey returned the gun to its holster, then readdressed Brock and Zimmerman. "There's an old saying about relationships. Something like, if they don't end badly, they don't end." He looked back at Tommy Hanscomb's lifeless body. "Guess it's true."

Brock remained silent. He couldn't think of anything to say. And clearly, by the example Corey had made of Hanscomb, saying the wrong thing came at a high price. His former friend and colleague was an unhinged sociopath.

"Who else wants to finish the tour?" Corey said with a smile.

Chloe managed to locate the unmarked road on her second pass. Bad cell coverage had caused the GPS to freeze up, delaying its final instructions until she had driven past the road. She turned onto the gravel road, and the GPS went silent again. She glanced down at her cell phone to see the words "no service" displayed on the screen, giving her second thoughts about her decision not to wait for Brock's callback.

"Way to go, Chloe," she said aloud. "You have no idea what you're getting yourself into, no cell service, and no backup. Oh, yeah, and no one has any idea where you are." She wondered if maybe Brock was beginning to rub off on her.

She brought the vehicle to a stop and scanned the heavily wooded area in front of her.

"This is totally stupid," she said as she considered backing out of the roadway and returning to the barracks. Before she could do more than think about it, a pickup truck pulled in behind her and stopped, blocking her in. Through the windshield she saw a lone male wearing a ball cap and dark glasses seated behind the wheel. Whoever it was already had the tactical advantage. No point in making it easy for them, she thought. Chloe reached down, unholstered her sidearm, and jumped out of the SUV.

"Show me your hands," she commanded. "Now."

Slowly the driver complied, placing both hands atop the steering wheel.

Just then, two full-sized black SUVs pulled in directly behind the pickup and stopped.

Chloe realized she was in deep. With her only exit blocked, there was no retreating from this situation. She kept her gun trained on the man in the pickup while her eyes darted back and forth between the three vehicles. The man in the pickup truck stared back at her, unmoving, his hands resting on the steering wheel. Her brain raced through the scenarios she'd encountered in the past, looking for a way out of this, but nothing had prepared her for this moment. Nothing could.

Before she could bark another order, a half dozen armed men dressed in camouflage BDUs exited the SUVs.

As Corey led them around the facility, boasting about the size of the operation, it became clear to Brock that whatever ethical boundaries the man might have possessed while in his early days in law enforcement had long since disappeared. Perhaps those boundaries had never existed. Or maybe Corey had simply returned from the war in the Middle East a changed man, warped from battle and determined to make his own rules as he had likely seen others do in that strange, faraway land. Whatever Corey may or may not have been, the man who Brock had once thought a friend was now nothing more than a criminal, drunk on his own power and the promise of wealth.

Brock glanced over at Zimmerman. The veteran detective seemed beyond capable of helping Brock find a way out of this mess. The wide-eyed man had been reduced to nothing more than a deer in the headlights. If they were to have any chance of escaping death at the hands of these men, Brock would need to figure something out on his own, and quickly. Stalling for time seemed their best option, as Corey clearly enjoyed bragging about what he'd already accomplished.

"So, who's bankrolling all of this?" Brock said. "Clearly you have a backer."

"Oh, I do, brother," Corey said. "I guess you'd call them more of an NGO."

"People you met overseas?" Brock said. "Afghanistan, maybe? Or Iraq?"

Corey grinned. "Aren't you just the inquisitive one."

"Must be the detective in me."

Corey seemed to ponder how best to answer the question. Finally, he said, "Actually, it's neither. My years with the DEA and HIDTA exposed me to a vast network of people willing to go up against Big Pharma and the government."

Brock knew Corey was referring to the Drug Enforcement Agency and the High Intensity Drug Trafficking Areas program, both of which were important tools used by the United States to combat illegal drug distribution networks around the country.

"But we *are* the government," Brock countered.

"Come on, Brock. Neither one of us *is* the government. We just do whatever they tell us. Follow whatever whim they currently believe in. Think about it. We fought for decades against the onslaught of marijuana shipments, and for what? Our own government finally realized how much money they could make by legalizing it and taxing the hell out of it. Think about it, our own government went into the weed business. How exactly does that square?"

"Yeah, but that's just weed. You're counterfeiting medications using fentanyl. That stuff kills tens of thousands of people every year. How do you square that?"

"Don't have to. Big Pharma is a multibillion-dollar industry, brother. They've made gross amounts of money by hooking people on the latest and greatest drug. Remember the oxy scandal? They hooked millions of people in this country alone. And they did it on purpose. Then they had the gall to sit there and force us to take their vaccines while their attorneys were still trying to settle the oxy scandal. That shit takes some serious balls."

Corey paused long enough to wave a hand at the operation surrounding them. "We're not developing drugs here, brother. Just filling a need. The people are already hooked. They want these drugs, need them, and they'll find a way to get them whether we do this or not."

"Sounds like you've already justified it in your mind anyway. But you still haven't told me who *we* are."

"Let's just say they're a like-minded group from the north."

Brock glanced at the faces of the five men holding weapons on them. "You're talking about Canadian organized crime, aren't you?"

"Like I said. My benefactors understand the value of a good business model."

"So, what does that make you? Their man in the States?"

Corey laughed again. "Not quite. Just their man in Maine. For now."

"And what makes you think these friends of yours won't dispose of you just as soon as this operation is up and running? The same way you disposed of Tommy Hanscomb."

"They won't because I'm loyal. Tommy was a fuck-up. A greedy and careless cop who got in way over his head."

"And what are you, *brother*?" Brock said.

The anger flashed in Corey's eyes. For the first time in all the years he'd known the man, or at least thought he'd known the man, Brock saw something inside Corey that he didn't recognize. Something dangerous and unhinged. Brock had assumed that Corey would have his men dispose of him and Zimmerman, but now he wasn't so sure.

"Load them into the truck," Corey said before readdressing Brock. "The tour is over, *brother*."

"Where are you taking us?" Brock said.

"To your final resting place."

"Like you did Lee Owen?"

Corey grinned again, but there was no warmth in his expression. "Owen wasn't my doing. If he had been, you would never have found him."

70

The driver of the pickup was none other than Albert Justice. Thanks to Brock's habit of going solo, Chloe had never actually met the man personally. Albert wasn't there for anything other than backup. The men in the SUVs were handpicked members of the state police tactical team and friends of Albert's.

As relieved as Chloe was, she still didn't understand what they were doing there or what exactly she had stumbled into.

"Brock and Zimmerman are in there right now," Lt. Holmquist, the TAC team commander, said.

"How could you possibly know that?" Chloe said. "I couldn't raise either one of them."

"Because they've been tracking Brock's SUV," Albert said.

"And mine?" Chloe said.

"Yours too," Holmquist said. "We knew about the drug operation. We just didn't know where they were operating from or who was running it."

"Who are they?" Chloe said.

"Sheriff Parlin, Tommy Hanscomb, Dr. Phinney, and a number of others you haven't met yet," Albert said.

"I don't get it. I thought you were tight with Parlin and the others."

“Playing poker with them was just a way to get inside the group, Chloe,” Albert said.

“We came to Albert about twenty months ago and asked for his help,” Holmquist said. “We didn’t dare go through the normal channels to work this because we had no idea how far it went, but we knew they had turned a few cops to be partners in this thing.”

“So, Brock and Zim are in there right now with these guys?” Chloe said. “Jesus, Albert, we’ve got to get them out.”

“And we will,” Albert said.

“I’m going in with you,” Chloe said.

“That’s not how this works,” Holmquist said. “My group functions as a unit.”

“And Brock is my partner. You just told me that you didn’t know how deep into law enforcement this thing goes. Pardon me if I don’t completely trust a group of men, half of whom I just met. I’m going in with you.” Chloe opened the right rear door to her SUV and removed the AR-15.

Holmquist gave Albert a look of exasperation.

“Chloe’s with me,” Albert said with a nod.

“All right, Detective Wright,” Holmquist said as he reached back into his SUV and retrieved a spare ballistic vest, tossing it to Chloe. “You’re Al’s responsibility, but you’re not going in unprepared. Suit up.”

The armed men marched Brock and Zimmerman through to the far side of the complex where several large white box trucks were lined up just beyond the building’s exterior. Each truck looked brand new, displaying the logo that Brock had seen on several pieces of manufacturing equipment inside. The logo was a red-and-white image of a phoenix. Below this was the company name BioMed.

“Classy name,” Brock said. “It’s almost like you’ve all convinced yourself that what you’re doing is somehow legitimate.”

Corey, walking alongside them, hadn’t said a word since giving the order to load Brock and Zimmerman into a truck. He stopped now and approached Brock until he was nearly toe-to-toe with him.

"You know that stubborn streak of yours is exactly why we didn't approach you to be a part of this, Brock."

"Don't you mean ethical streak? I swore an oath just like you did. Or are you so warped that you don't remember what you agreed to when you first joined the state police?"

"Oh, I remember. But I finally figured out that the government I work for is no different than some of the governments I fought against in the Middle East. I'm surprised you haven't realized it too."

The two former comrades stood squared off, glaring at each other. In another time and situation, they might have simply come to blows.

"Excuse me, sir," the tallest of the armed goons said, momentarily breaking the spell.

"What is it?" Corey said, maintaining his eye contact with Brock.

"One of our perimeter cameras has failed."

Brock waited to see how Corey would react. After a long moment, he stepped away from Brock and approached the guard.

"Which one?"

"The one at the half-mile marker."

Corey looked at the compact monitoring device before turning back to face Brock. "Cavalry?"

"No one knows we're here," Zimmerman said absently.

Brock could have throttled him for making such a foolhardy comment. If Corey had been worried that anyone besides Brock and his partner for the day was onto him, he wouldn't be worried now.

Corey's grin returned. "Adios, my friend. Sorry it had to end like this."

"Me too," Brock said.

As one of the shorter guards stepped forward and reached out to put his hand on Brock, the high-velocity whine of a rifle shot pierced the air a split second before the crack from the muzzle reached them. The man's head snapped back, and his body collapsed to the ground.

"Back inside!" Corey yelled as he sprinted around one of the trucks.

One of the men lunged toward the fallen guard, intent on retrieving the man's weapon. Brock saw what was happening and scrambled forward to try to intercept him.

Another shot rang out, this one striking the side of the truck and narrowly missing a fleeing guard. Another shot punctured the front tire of the same truck, rendering it unusable.

Brock reached the fallen man's weapon at the exact same moment that the other guard did, but the advantage went to Brock as he grabbed a hold of the stock. As Brock tried to insert his finger inside of the trigger guard and bring the weapon to bear, the other man twisted the barrel, trying to break the gun free from Brock's grip. It was a well-known maneuver designed to break Brock's trigger finger. As they continued to struggle for control of the weapon, Brock caught a glimpse of Zimmerman, who, after disarming one of the guards, knocked the man unconscious with the butt of his own rifle.

Brock's full attention returned to the man he was engaged in battle with as he realized that the weapon he'd been fighting over was suddenly free. The guard shoved him away, then reached down intending to draw the sidearm holstered on his hip. Before Brock could take aim, another rifle shot rang out, this one much louder and closer. It appeared to be coming from inside the warehouse. The bullet struck the guard from behind, but it didn't stop him from getting a round off. The bullet struck Brock in the left thigh. At first Brock didn't feel anything. The impact felt more like he'd been punched in the leg until the pain began to radiate out from the wound and his leg felt as though it were on fire. Gritting his teeth, he fought through the agony. Brock trained the barrel of the weapon on the guard's torso and fired repeatedly, dropping the man where he stood.

Brock was scanning the area for other threats when he heard an engine starting and a vehicle door slam shut. Corey had climbed into one of the trucks and was attempting to flee. Brock heard grinding gears as Corey struggled with the transmission as he accelerated toward the far corner of the warehouse. Several more shots coming from the nearby tree line kicked up gravel near the truck's rolling tires but missed the mark. As Corey neared the end of the warehouse, Brock saw two more camouflaged figures come into view and fire on the cab. The truck's brake lights illuminated as Corey slammed on the brakes and cut the wheel hard. The truck shuddered as the tires fought for traction. The box truck spun a hundred-and-eighty degrees until it was facing Brock. After finding the correct gear,

Corey hammered the accelerator, causing the rear tires to spin as the truck shot forward.

The box truck was gaining speed as it headed directly toward Brock. The two men made eye contact, and Brock could sense something unspoken passing between them. It couldn't have been more than a split second as the truck barreled down on him, but the moment seemed to stretch out as years of their shared history replayed. But that history no longer mattered, and both men knew it.

Brock's arms felt detached, as if belonging to someone else. Everything moved in slow motion as he raised the barrel of the rifle and took aim on the driver's side of the windshield. Something shifted in Corey's expression as the truck continued to close the distance. Brock cinched up the slack on the trigger and braced himself for whatever would come next. Before he could squeeze the trigger, he saw Corey's head rock sideways, releasing a spray of crimson coating the passenger side of the windshield. Corey's body slumped forward over the wheel, and it took Brock a moment to realize that he hadn't fired the fatal shot. It had come from the nearby woods.

The truck, now driverless, continued its forward momentum, engine racing. Brock broke toward the overhead doors and the safety of the warehouse's brick walls. He glanced over and saw the truck turning toward him as Corey's body slipped to one side, causing the steering wheel to turn in Brock's direction. Pain radiated out from Brock's wounded leg with each stride, and the engine roared in his ears as he sprinted toward the darkened doorway where Zimmerman stood over another fallen guard. Zim was frantically waving him on, hollering something Brock couldn't make out. At the last possible instant, he dove forward through the open bay door.

The sound of the truck colliding with the outer wall of the warehouse was deafening. Brock landed hard on the concrete floor amid a hail of bricks dislodged by the impact. Several of the bricks struck him, setting off new flares of pain all over his body. One final brick struck him squarely in the back of his head, knocking him unconscious.

EPILOGUE

Brock awoke in a hospital bed in the Intensive Care Unit of Bangor's Eastern Maine Medical Center. He was groggy from whatever painkillers they'd given him, and his mouth felt like it was full of sand. He glanced down at his wounded leg to see that it was elevated and wrapped in a fresh dressing. His eyes moved to a side table where a plastic cup of water stood with a straw protruding from it. He tried to reach out for the cup, but the straining set off a wave of pain in his torso, and he lowered his arm. The cup may as well have been on the other side of the room.

"Well, look who's rejoined the living?" a cheery voice said from the opposite side of the bed.

Brock turned his head slightly to find Chloe sitting in a bedside chair, grinning.

"Hey, partner," she said as she stood and walked around the bed.

"Hey," Brock croaked weakly.

"This what you're looking for?" she said as she picked up the cup and held the straw in front of his mouth.

Brock nodded before taking a long sip of the cool water. He laid his head back onto the pillow and closed his eyes.

"How long have I been here?"

"Couple of days."

"Really?"

"Yup."

"What happened?" he said.

"You want the long story or the abbreviated one?"

"Let's start with why I'm in the hospital and go from there."

"You got shot," she said.

"Thanks. I remember that much. One of Corey's goons. What else?"

"You busted a bunch of ribs with that swan dive onto the concrete floor of the warehouse. I think landing on the rifle probably didn't help."

"Remind me not to do that again," Brock said.

"And you have a concussion from trying to stop a brick with your head."

"Add that to my list. Did we get the bad guys?"

"Not all of them. But I'd say we made a significant dent in their organization."

"Who's we?" Brock said.

"Albert, Zim, about six of Albert's TAC team buddies, and me."

Brock opened his eyes again and turned his head toward her. "Seriously?"

"Yup," Chloe said, beaming with pride.

"You were part of the cavalry?"

"Of course. You didn't think they'd partner you with some desk jockey, did you?"

"I guess not," Brock said.

"Speaking of desk jockeys," a voice said from the doorway. "Have they told you how long you'll be out of commission yet?"

Brock looked up to see Penny Cumberland standing there.

"Hey, Lieu," Brock said.

"Hey, yourself," Cumberland said as she entered the room carrying a large bouquet of flowers in a glass vase. "What happened to keeping a low profile?"

"I've never been very good at following orders," Brock said as his fingers operated the remote, lifting the head of the bed a bit more.

"Like father, like son, I guess," Cumberland said.

"Was Albert really at the takedown?" Brock said after finding a comfortable setting.

"Right in the middle of it," Chloe said.

"I don't understand. He's been retired for years."

Cumberland placed the flowers on the windowsill, then stood near the foot of the bed. "A special task force has been operating in this area for the past eighteen months. By design, only a few of us were even aware of its existence. You see, we knew there was the high likelihood of corrupt law enforcement officers involved in the pill mill you stumbled onto."

Brock turned his head toward Chloe. "Did you know about this?"

Chloe shook her head. "Not until I got blocked in at the end of the warehouse access road by Albert and his friends."

"You followed me?"

"Of course not. I found the warehouse on my own. I am a detective, remember?"

"As you keep reminding me."

"Anyway," Cumberland continued, "when Lee Owen turned up murdered, we knew we had the opening we'd been looking for. It was a no-brainer to assign you and Chloe to the case. Chloe was a brand-new detective, and you had come from Southern Maine. Plus, Albert vouched for you."

"Seriously?" Brock said.

"Seriously," Cumberland said.

Brock wasn't quite sure how to feel about the news. Until this case, he hadn't had much of any contact with his father. Not since his mother's death.

"Weren't you worried about the history between me and Corey Hincks?" Brock said.

"We didn't know for sure that Trooper Hincks was involved until the last few days," Cumberland said. "It makes sense, though. We knew there had to be a DEA connection to this whole thing. The feds track things like pill presses shipped from other countries. But this counterfeiting angle was a whole new animal. Thanks to 3D printing, anything that can be copied and scanned onto a computer can be cloned. Drug manufacturing is now as vulnerable to counterfeiting as paper money."

Brock paused to let everything he heard sink in. He had so many questions.

"And Zimmerman?" Brock said. "You paired me and Zim up on purpose?"

"Of course. We knew you were getting close to flushing out the key players. We already suspected Sheriff Parlin, and we knew Hanscomb was probably dirty. But we needed the man on the inside who was working for the Canadians."

"Corey," Brock said absently.

"Correct."

An uncomfortable silence passed between them as Brock replayed the events in his mind.

"Well, I should get out of here and let you get on with your recovery," Cumberland said. "You're going to be answering a lot of questions in the coming days. Better get some rest."

Brock nodded.

Cumberland stopped at the door. "See? Not so dreadful after all."

Brock allowed himself the slightest of grins.

"And listen to your partner. Chloe saved your bacon out there, Justice."

The lieutenant departed without further fanfare, leaving Brock and Chloe alone.

"Is that true?" Brock asked. "What she said about you saving me?"

"If you're asking whether I shot Corey, yeah, I did. It's no big deal, though. You'd have done the same for me, I guess."

Brock said nothing for a long moment. He had never wanted to think of Chloe as anything more than his trainee. A temporary impediment to his returning to MCU South and resuming his homicide investigation duties where he was best suited. But Chloe was bright, had great investigative instincts, and she was tough. But above all of that, she had saved his life. Chloe had more than earned his respect. She was exactly what every cop hopes for in a partner.

He forced his head to one side to look at her directly.

"Thanks, partner," he said.

"You're welcome."

Bitter Fall
Detective Justice Book 2

Summer's last breath meets autumn's first kill in Greenville, Maine.

On a moonless stretch of backcountry road, Detective Brock Justice stares down at a crime scene that refuses to play by the rules. A woman lies dead, the apparent victim of a lethal roadside crash—until a stab wound is found hidden beneath her clothing. Two causes of death. Zero easy answers.

Reunited with his partner, Detective Chloe Wright, Justice begins pulling at threads too many people want left alone. The victim had secrets—the kind worth killing for. And each suspect carries enough baggage to sink a body in Moosehead Lake. An ex-boyfriend with a violent past. A married fitness trainer with too much to lose. A combat veteran living off the grid, haunted by ghosts of his own.

As golden leaves turn blood-red against pewter skies, Justice is fighting more than just a killer. The fallout from testifying against a fellow trooper clings to him like a bad debt, and someone inside the department is making sure he pays for it.

Then a game warden's trail camera captures something deep in the woods. But it isn't just a clue—it's a warning.

ACKNOWLEDGMENTS

Crimson Thaw, my ninth published novel and the first in the Detective Justice Mystery Series, is a testament to you, my incredible readers. When I began this literary journey in 2016 with the release of my debut novel, *Among the Shadows*, I could not imagine anything beyond the three novels I was under contract to write. But here we are, looking another novel square in the eye even as I pen the next.

As always, I must give thanks to some amazing folks without whom I might never have gotten this far: Paula Munier and Gina Panettieri at Talcott Notch Literary for continuing to believe in me and my stories; Andrew Watts, Cate Streissguth, Julia Barron, Kate Schomaker, and the rest of the talented team at Severn River Publishing.

My beta readers and fact checkers, Pat Larrabee, Peggy Greenwald, Bill Caron, Mark Holmquist, Darrin Crane, and Chris McDonald of Windham Powersports. Any mistakes were my own.

The countless men and women in the field of criminal justice, true professionals, I was fortunate to have served with, and those who continue to serve (these are their stories).

Lastly, and most importantly, my wife, Karen, for her love, inspiration, and infinite patience. Without you in my life, there would be no story.

ABOUT BRUCE ROBERT COFFIN

Bruce Robert Coffin is the award-winning author of the Detective Byron Mysteries. Former detective sergeant with more than twenty-seven years in law enforcement, he is the winner of Killer Nashville's Silver Falchion Awards for Best Procedural, and Best Investigator, and the Maine Literary Award for Best Crime Fiction Novel. Bruce was also a finalist for the Agatha Award for Best Contemporary Novel. His short fiction appears in a number of anthologies, including Best American Mystery Stories 2016.

Sign up for the reader list at
severnriverbooks.com